ALSO BY

MICHEL BUSSI

After the Crash
Black Water Lilies

TIME IS A KILLER

Michel Bussi

TIME IS A KILLER

Translated from the French
by Shaun Whiteside

Europa
editions

Europa Editions
214 West 29th Street
New York, N.Y. 10001
www.europaeditions.com
info@europaeditions.com

First published in French as *Le temps est assassin* by Presses de la Cité,
a department of Place des Editeurs, Paris
First published in English by Weidenfeld & Nicolson, London

Library of Congress Cataloging in Publication Data is available
ISBN 978-1-60945-442-5

Bussi, Michel
Time Is a Killer

Book design and cover illustration by Emanuele Ragnisco
www.mekkanografici.com

Prepress by Grafica Punto Print – Rome

Printed in the USA

To the friends of our teenage years that we keep all our lives

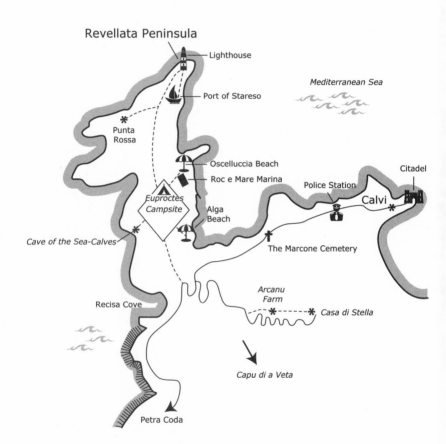

Revellata Peninsula

Lighthouse

Port of Stareso

Mediterranean Sea

Punta Rossa

Oscelluccia Beach

Roc e Mare Marina

Citadel

Police Station

Calvi

Euproctes Campsite

Alga Beach

Cave of the Sea-Calves

The Marcone Cemetery

Recisa Cove

Arcanu Farm

Casa di Stella

Capu di a Veta

Petra Coda

TIME IS A KILLER

1

Arcanu Farm, August 23, 1989

"C lo? Clo?"

Clotilde slowly slipped the headphones from her ears. Irritated. The voice of Manu Chao and the horns of Mano Negra crackled in the silence of the hot stones, barely louder than the crickets thrumming behind the walls of the sheepfold.

"Yeah?"

"We're off . . . "

Clotilde sighed but didn't move from the bench where she was sitting—a tree trunk split in two that grated against her buttocks. She didn't care. She liked the relaxed position, just short of provocative, the stones that cut into her back beneath her cotton dress, the bark and the sharp bits of wood that scratched her thighs every time her leg beat out the rhythm of the horns. With her notebook on her knees, her biro between her fingers. Curled up in a ball. Elsewhere. Free. In total contrast to her father's family—stiff, Corsican, corseted. She turned the volume up.

These musicians were gods! Clotilde closed her eyes, opened her lips, she would give anything to be teleported to the front row of a Mano Negra concert, to be three years older, thirty centimeters taller and three bust sizes larger just for the duration of the lightning visit. To jiggle around good, big breasts beneath a sweat-drenched black T-shirt, under the noses of the spaced-out guitarists.

She opened her eyes. Nicolas was still standing in front of her, looking extremely annoyed.

"Clo, everyone's waiting for you. Papa isn't going to . . . "

Nicolas was eighteen, three years older than she was. In years to come, her brother would become a lawyer. Or a union representative. Or a negotiator in one of the police's special units, the kind of guy who would parley with criminals holed up in a bank, getting the hostages out one by one. Nicolas was like an anvil, absorbing the blows, taking it all on the chin. It must have given him the illusion that he was tougher than everyone else, more sensible, more trustworthy. Which would probably serve him well for the rest of his life.

Clotilde looked away and for a moment studied the twin moons off the Revellata Peninsula, one sunk into the water, the other suspended in the dark sky; they looked like two fugitives pursued by the lighthouse on the peninsula, the first one quivering, the second one startled. She wanted to close her eyes again. It was really so easy to teleport yourself to another planet.

Coordinate your eyelids.

One, two, three . . . then curtain!

But no, she had to keep them open, take advantage of the last few minutes, write everything down in the notebook on her knees before her dream flew away. Etch the words onto the white page. It was a matter of urgency. The utmost urgency.

My dream takes place right near here, but a long way off in the future, on Oscelluccia beach. I recognise the cliffs, the sand, the shape of the bay, they're always the same. But not me, I've turned into an old woman. A grandma!

It took her how long? Only two minutes? The time for Clotilde to write another ten lines or so, and for "Rock Island Line" to play. Mano Negra's songs weren't very long.

Her father took it as a provocation, but it wasn't meant as one. Not this time. He seized her by the arm.

Clotilde felt her headphones sliding off, the right earpiece getting tangled in a tuft of her gelled black hair. Her pen fell to the dusty ground. The notebook would remain on the bench until she had time to grab it, slip it into her bag or at least hide it.

"Papa, you're hurting me, shit . . . "

Her father didn't say anything. He was calm. Cold. Smooth. As usual . . . A fragment of an ice floe lost in the Mediterranean.

"Get a move on, Clotilde. We're going to Prezzuna. Everyone's waiting for you."

Her father's hairy hand gripped her wrist. Tugged it. Her bare thigh stung as it scraped along the wooden bench. Her only hope was that Mamy Lisabetta, her grandmother, would pick up her notebook and put it with the rest of her belongings, which were scattered at random around the farm, without opening it, without reading it. She would give it back to her tomorrow. She could trust Mamy.

Only her . . .

Her father dragged her along for a few meters, then pushed her in front of him, the way you let go of the hand of a baby who's started to walk on its own, always staying a few steps behind, arms outstretched like pincers. In the courtyard of the sheepfold, around the large table, the entire holy family was watching her, faces frozen like wax dummies, the wine bottles now empty, the bouquets of yellow roses fading. Her grandfather Papé Cassanu, Mamy Lisabetta, the whole tribe . . . Like a tableau from the Grévin wax museum. The Corsican pavilion. Napoleon's unknown cousins.

Clotilde had to force herself not to burst out laughing.

Her father would never have raised a hand to her, but there were still five days of holiday left. She couldn't afford to push her luck if she didn't want to see her Walkman, her headphones and her cassettes being chucked off the Revellata

Peninsula into the sea, if she wanted to get her notebook back, if she wanted to see Natale again and maybe bump into Orophin, Idril and their baby dolphins, if she wanted to have the freedom to spy on Nicolas and Maria-Chjara's gang . . .

She got the message. Clotilde trotted over to the Fuego without dragging her feet. So, change of plan, we're off to Prezzuna? OK, she would go along like a good girl and listen to the concert of polyphonic music in that chapel hidden away in the *maquis*, with her father, Maman and Nicolas. She could sacrifice one evening, that was doable. Leaving her self-respect behind, that was a much more bitter pill to swallow.

She could just see Papé Cassanu getting up, staring at Papa and Papa nodding to tell him that everything was all right. Papé's expression frightened her. Well, even more than usual.

The Fuego was parked down below, along the track that led down towards the Revellata. Maman and Nicolas were already sitting in the car. Nicolas shifted over to make room for her on the back seat, giving her a small complicit smile this time. He was also pissed off about this concert in the church out in the middle of the *maquis*, this obsession of their father's.

Even more than she was, in fact; much more than she was. But Nicolas was very good at not letting his feelings show. In years to come, after he'd got his licence as a qualified anvil, he might even become President of the Republic, like Mitterrand, he would learn to put up with everything for seven years without flinching, and hold his nose to be re-elected . . . just for the sheer pleasure of being punched in the face for another seven years.

Papa was driving fast, as he often did since he'd bought his red Fuego. As he often did, when he was annoyed. A silent rage. From time to time Maman rested her hand on his knee, on his fingers when he exceeded the speed limit. He was the only one who wanted to go and listen to this bloody concert. His head must have been buzzing, his ungrateful kids, his wife who always ran to defend them, his roots here on this island that nobody cared about, their culture, their name and the respect that was due to it, his tolerance, his patience; "for once," "just for one evening, is that too much to ask, damm it?"

They sped around the bends. Clotilde put her headphones back on. She was always a little scared on the Corsican roads, even during the daylight, when they encountered a coach or a camper van; the cliff roads on this island were crazy. She thought that at the speed at which her father was driving— whether it was to calm his nerves, or to avoid being late, or because he wanted to sit in the front row—if they came across a goat, or a boar, or any kind of animal roaming about, it would all be over . . .

There was no animal. Or at least Clotilde didn't see one. And no one ever found the slightest trace of one either. Even if that was one of the hypotheses suggested by the police.

It was a tight curve at the end of a long straight section, past Revellata; a bend high above a twenty-meter ravine. A pile of fallen rocks called Petra Coda.

During the day, the view was dizzying.

The Fuego crashed into the wooden barrier at full speed.

The three planks separating the road from the precipice did all they could. They twisted under the impact of the crash; they burst the two headlights of the Fuego; they scraped the bumper.

Before yielding.

They barely slowed the car down at all. It continued in a straight line, like a cartoon, the hero running out into the void, then stopping, looking down at his feet in astonishment . . . then panic as he plummets like a stone

Clotilde felt all those things. The Fuego losing contact with the earth. The real world disappearing beneath her. Like a flaw in logic, something that could not happen, not really, not to them, not to her.

She thought those things for a fraction of a second, before reality exploded, and the Fuego hit the rocks for the first time, before bouncing twice.

Her father's rib cage and head exploded against the steering wheel when the car crashed vertically against the rocks. Her mother's was crushed during the second somersault, by a rock that smashed through the door. With the third, the roof was torn open above them, like a steel jaw.

The final impact.

The Fuego stopped there, balanced uneasily ten meters above the tranquil sea.

Then silence.

Nicolas was still sitting beside her. Back straight. Drenched in blood.

He would never become president; never become even a staff representative in some stupid factory. Nipped in the bud. Not like an anvil; more like an eggshell, the cartilage of a sparrow in the maw of a monster. His puppet body demolished by a roof exploded like a star.

His eyelids shut. Somewhere else, for ever.

One, two, three. Curtain.

Strangely, Clotilde didn't hurt anywhere. The police later explained that the three somersaults had caused three points of impact, one per passenger. Like a killer who had only three bullets in his magazine.

She barely weighed forty kilos. She slipped through the broken glass without even feeling the shards as they lacerated her arms, her legs, her dress. She crawled a few meters away from the Fuego as a reflex, leaving red marks on the slippery stones.

She went no further than that. She just sat down and stared

at the mixture of blood and petrol dripping from the bodies and the metal, the brains spilling from their skulls. It was there that the police, then the firemen, then the dozens of other emergency workers found her about twenty minutes later.

Clotilde had a broken wrist, three cracked ribs, and a scraped knee . . . Nothing.

A miracle.

"There's nothing wrong with you," an elderly doctor confirmed, leaning towards her in the blue halo of the spinning lights.

Nothing.

Exactly!

That was what she was left with now.

Papa, Maman and Nicolas's bodies were wrapped up in large white bin-bags. Men walked around the red rocks, heads lowered, as if they were searching for other bits of them scattered about.

"You have to live," a young policeman had said, settling a silver survival blanket around her shoulders. "You have to live for them. So you don't forget them."

She had looked at him as if he were an idiot, as if he were a priest talking about heaven. But he was right. Even the very worst memories are forgotten in the end, if you pile other ones on top of them, lots of other memories. Even the ones that have been etched on your heart, the ones that have left scars on your brain, even the most private ones. Particularly the most private ones.

Because no one else cares about those.

Twenty-seven years later . . .

I
REVELLATA

August 12, 2016

"This is it."

Clotilde placed her little bunch of wild thyme beside the iron barrier. She had asked Franck to stop a few bends back along the road, so she could pick the mauve flowers from among the gorse that grew between the rocks of Petra Coda.

Enough for three people.

Franck did the same now, without taking his eyes off the road for a minute. The Passat was parked to one side, the hazard lights flashing.

Valentine was the last to stoop down, clearly reluctant, as if bending all one meter seventy of her was an unreasonable demand to make.

They all stood there, facing the twenty-meter drop. The roiling sea hurled itself at the red boulders, filling the fissures in the rocks with brown microalgae, like liver spots on old wrinkled skin.

Clotilde turned towards her daughter. At fifteen, Valentine was already a good fifteen centimeters taller than her. She was wearing a pair of jeans cut off above the knee and a *House of Cards* T-shirt. Not exactly ideal for visiting a mausoleum, leaving a bunch of flowers and respecting a minute's silence.

Clotilde let it go. Her voice softened.

"It was here, Valentine. It was here that your Grandpa and Grandma died. And your Uncle Nicolas as well."

Valentine's gaze was looking off into the distance, at a jet-ski leaping the waves off the Revellata Peninsula. Franck, leaning on the barrier, kept squinting between the ravine and the Passat's hazard lights.

Time stretched, as if lengthened by the heat wave. The sun liquefied the seconds in slow drops. A car passed them in a halo of heat. A driver, naked to the waist, looked out at them with surprised eyes.

Clotilde hadn't been back here since the summer of 1989.

But she had thought of this place thousands of times, had thought of this precise moment. What she would say, what she would think, when faced with this gaping void. The memories that would come rushing back to her. How to present the pilgrimage. As a sign of respect. A way of sharing something.

And here they were, messing the whole thing up for her!

Clotilde had imagined an act of communion, a few delicate questions, an emotion shared with Franck and Valentine. Together, united. But here they stood, pressed against the barrier beneath the blazing sun, as if the Passat had had a flat tire and they were getting bored waiting for the tow truck, lowering their eyes towards their watches or raising them to the sky; looking anywhere at all but those blood-coloured volcanic rocks.

Clotilde urged her daughter on.

"Your grandfather's name was Paul. Your grandmother's name was Palma."

"I know that, Maman . . . "

Thanks, Valentine! That was cool of you.

Her daughter had said the phrase "I know" in the long, drawn out way that was her standard response to her mother's habitual requests.

Tidy your clothes away. Turn off your phone. Move yourself.

Her usual minimal effort at being conciliatory . . .

I know, Maman . . .

OK, Valou, Clotilde thought. OK, it isn't the most fun part of the holiday. OK, I'm doing your head in with an accident that happened almost thirty years ago. But also, fuck it, Valou, I have waited fifteen years to bring you here! I've waited for you to grow up, so that you're old enough to understand, not to ruin your life with it prematurely.

The jet-ski had disappeared. Or been caught by a wave and sunk.

"Shall we go?" Valentine asked.

Without even the minimal effort this time. Not even trying to hide her boredom under an affected mask of melancholy.

"No!"

Clotilde had raised her voice. For the first time Franck took his eyes off the Passat that was winking at him like an obsessive flirt.

No! Clotilde repeated in her head. For fifteen years I've been taking the brunt of it all, for fifteen years I've been defusing the bomb, my girl. For twenty years I've been playing the cool woman, Franckie boy, the one who never complains, the one with the broad grin, the crazy lady, the funny girl, the one who's great in a crisis, the one who puts the bits back together, the one who's reassuring, the one who keeps a steady course, who holds the steering wheel of everyday life, singing to make the journey seem shorter. And what have I asked for in return? Fifteen minutes! Just fifteen minutes of your fortnight's holiday! Fifteen minutes of your fifteen years of life, my girl! Fifteen minutes of our twenty years of love, my darling!

Fifteen minutes, compared with everything else, a quarter of an hour of compassion for my childhood, which was completely destroyed right here, dashed against these rocks which couldn't give a shit, which have forgotten everything and will still be here in a thousand years' time. Fifteen minutes of a life, is that really too much to ask?

They allowed her ten.

* * *

"Can we go, Papa?" Valou pleaded once more.

Franck nodded and the girl walked towards the Passat, her flip-flops clacking against the tarmac, her eyes searching every corner of the road three bends up the hill as if searching for any trace of life amid this rocky desert.

Franck turned towards Clotilde. The voice of reason, as always.

"I know, Clo. I know. But you've got to understand Valou. She didn't know your parents. I didn't either. They died twenty-seven years ago. They had been gone for almost ten years when we met, almost fifteen when Valou was born. As far as she's concerned they're . . . "—he hesitated and wiped his forehead with the back of his hand—"They . . . they aren't part of her life."

Clotilde didn't reply.

In fact, she would have preferred for Franck to keep his trap shut and at least allow her those last five minutes of silence.

Now everything was ruined. Slipping into her head came the mean comparison with Mamy Jeanne and Papa André, Franck's parents, who they visited one weekend out of four, at whose home Valou had spent every Wednesday until she was ten, and where she still sought refuge if her parents refused to indulge one of her whims.

"She's too young to understand, Clo."

Too young . . .

Yet Clotilde nodded to indicate that she agreed.

That she was listening to Franck. As she always did. As she often did. Less and less.

That she was adhering to his ready-made solutions.

Franck lowered his eyes and walked towards the Passat.

Clotilde didn't move. Not yet.

Too young . . .

They had weighed up the pros and cons a hundred times.

Was it better to say nothing, not to involve her daughter in this old business of the accident? Just to keep it to herself? It wouldn't have been a problem; she was used to chewing over her own disappointment.

But on the other hand there were shrink-speak, women's magazines, friends who dished out good advice. A modern mother had to be open with her children, spread out the family secrets on the table, explode all the taboos. Unwrap everything, without questioning it.

You see, Valou, when I was your age, I had a very serious accident. Put yourself in my place for a second. Imagine that all three of us were in a crash, and that Papa and I were killed and you were left on your own.

Just think about that, my girl . . . Maybe that will help you understand who your mother is. Why she has done everything she can to ensure that life slides over her without her ever getting wet.

If that is of any interest to you . . .

Clotilde stared one last time at the Bay of La Revellata, the three little bunches of wild thyme, and then went to join her family.

Franck was already sitting behind the wheel. He had turned off the car radio. Valentine had lowered her window all the way down and was fanning herself with the *Guide du routard*. Clotilde lightly ruffled her daughter's hair, and she groaned. Then she forced herself to laugh brightly and climbed into the car beside her husband.

The seats were scorching.

Clotilde smiled apologetically at Franck; her conciliatory mask, the one she had inherited from Nicolas. It was the only thing she had left of her brother. Along with his anvil heart and that rake he used to gather toghether unsatisfactory love affairs.

They set off. Clotilde rested a hand on Franck's knee. Right by the hem of his shorts.

The Passat rolled along gently between the sea and the mountain, with the sun at its zenith; the colours seemed almost too intense, saturated, like a landscape on an old postcard.

A dream holiday, on a panoramic screen.

Everything had been forgotten already. The wind would blow away the bunches of thyme before the night was over.

Don't turn back, Clotilde thought to herself. Move forward.

Force yourself to love life; force yourself to love life.

She lowered the window, allowing the breeze to blow through her long black hair, the sun to caress her bare legs.

Thinking the way they do in magazines, like her best friends, like people selling happiness in ten easy lessons.

Happiness is simple, you just have to believe in it!

That's what holidays are for, the cloudless sky, the sea, the sun.

To make you believe in it.

To fill the tank with illusions to last the rest of the year.

Clotilde's hand climbed a little higher up Franck's thigh as she leaned her head back, offering her throat to the too-blue sky, like an artificial backdrop. A screen. A curtain put up by a lying God.

Franck shivered and Clotilde closed her eyes. On automatic. Disconnecting her fingers from her thoughts.

Holidays do that too.

Tanned skin, naked bodies, hot nights.

Maintaining the illusion of desire.

Monday, August 7, 1989. The first day of the holidays.
Summer-blue sky.

Hi, I'm Clotilde.
I'm introducing myself just to be polite, even if you can't be polite back because I don't know who you are, whoever it is reading this.

That will be in a few years' time, if I manage to hang on. Everything I write is Top Secret. Totally embargoed. Whoever you are, you've been warned! Besides, o my reader, in spite of all my precautions, I don't know who you might be.

My lover, the one I have chosen for the rest of my life, the one to whom—quivering on the morning after my first time—I will entrust the diary of my teenage years?

Some idiot who has just found it, because, being the total disaster I am, that was bound to happen?

One of the thousands of fans who will rush to get their hands on this masterpiece by the latest literary genius? (i.e. me!!!)

Or me . . . But an older me, in fifteen years' time . . . Or even incredibly old, in thirty years. I've found this old diary at the back of a drawer and I'm reading it as if it were a time machine. Or a mirror that made me young again.

But how will I ever know? So, when in doubt, I write at random, not knowing whose hands this notebook will fall into, or whose eyes will read it.

You have lovely eyes, I hope, beautiful hands, a beautiful heart, my future reader? You won't disappoint me, will you? Promise?

Shall I start with a few words about myself, so you can get to know me? Because we're going to have quite a bit of time to find out about each another.

So, Clotilde. Three points:

Point 1. My age. Already getting on . . . Fifteen. Wow, that makes me feel dizzy!

Point 2. My height. Still small . . . One meter forty-eight, enough to make me feel blue.

Point 3. My look. Death warmed over, according to my mum. The effect I'm going for isn't complicated, I want to look like Lydia Deetz from *Beetlejuice*. If you can't picture her straight away, my reader on the planet Mars, then don't panic: I'm going to bore you to death with Lydia Deetz at least one line out of three in this notebook, given that I'm a total fan of hers. In brief, she's the coolest teenager in the world with her gothic black lace, her spiky hair, her big panda eyes . . . *and* she talks to ghosts! I should add, handsome stranger, that she's played by Winona Ryder, who isn't yet eighteen but is the most beautiful actress in the world. I wanted to take all the posters from my room so I could hang them back up here, in our holiday bungalow, but Maman vetoed me sticking drawing pins in the partition walls.

Yes, OK, fine, dear reader. I know I'm rambling on a bit. So let me get back to the first day of the holidays . . . The big adventure of the Idrissi family of Tourny in Papa's red Renault Fuego. Tourny, just so you know, is in the Vexin region, a beetroot-growing plain stuck between Normandy and Paris with a ridiculous river, the Epte, which, according to local sages, has caused more wars and led to more deaths than the Rhine. We live just north of it, in the middle of some tiny little hills that locals have christened the "Vexin Bossu"—hump-backed Vexin. You couldn't make it up!

Anyway, for a long time I thought about how I was going to write about our grand departure for Corsica: piling up the luggage in the boot in the middle of the night, the endless journey from Normandy, sitting in the back with Nico, who can spend ten hours looking out at the cars, the trees and the road signs without ever seeming to get bored. The tunnel under Mont Blanc and the ritual meal of quiche and salad in Chamonix, the journey down into Italy because, as Papa says, Genoa isn't that much farther than Nice, Toulon or Marseille, but the Italians never go on strike. Yes, I could have described all of that in detail but I'm not going to. It's a narrative choice, dear intergalactic reader of mine. That's just how it is!

Instead I'm going to concentrate on the ferry.

A person who has never taken a ferry to an island can't really know what the first day of the holidays is.

I swear it, on Lydia Deetz!

It's a trial by four elements.

Water, first of all.

The giant yellow and white ferry with the giant Moor's head—the symbol of Corsica—is magnificent at first sight. But when it opens its great mouth it isn't so much fun.

At least, for Papa it isn't. And I can understand that driving for ten hours just to be yelled at when you get there by a gang of over-excited Italians might get on your nerves.

Destra

Sinistra

Italians shouting and waving their arms about as if Papa were taking his first driving lesson.

Avanti Avanti Avanti

Papa manoeuvring the car among dozens of other terrified drivers, with their trailers and their jet-skis on the roof, their convertible sports cars with the surfboards sticking out, their Renault Espaces crammed to the gills with rubber rings and lilos and towels piled so high they can't see anything through the mirror.

Avvicina avvicina

The lorries, the cars, the camper vans, the motorbikes. But everything fits in! Always. To the centimeter. That's the first miracle of the holidays.

Stop stop stop

When they were little, I imagine these Italians on the ferry were experts at things that locked together. So for them, getting three thousand cars onto a boat in less than an hour is just a giant game of Lego.

An Italian smiles and raises his thumb.

Perfetto

Papa's Fuego is one of the three thousand pieces of this game. He opens his door, trying not to scratch the Corsa to his left, and sucks in his stomach to make his way over to us.

Earth, next.

The real change happens between the moment when you take off your things and lie down in your cabin, and when you get up four or five hours later; it's a bit like a snake sloughing off its skin.

Often I'm the first to put on my flip-flops, a pair of shorts, a Van Halen T-shirt, dark sunglasses and emerge out on deck.

Terra! Terra!

Everyone stands by the railings to admire the coast, from the Biguglia lagoon to Cap Corse. The sun is starting to fire its laser beams at anything that moves out of the shadows, and I slip down the corridors of the boat, sniffing unfamiliar smells. I step over a large groggy-looking guy with fair hair who is lying in the corridor on his rucksack. He's so hot! The girl attached to him is still asleep, her back bare, her mane tousled, one hand under the Swedish guy's open shirt.

One day I'll be the bare-backed girl. And I too will have an unshaven backpacker for a mattress, with blond hair on his chest to act as my comfort blanket.

Life, you aren't going to disappoint me, are you?

For now I'll settle for the salty air of the Mediterranean. Leaning against the railings, all one meter forty-eight of me.

Breathing in freedom on the tips of my toes.

Fire, alas.
Ladies and gentlemen, please return to your vehicles.
The fires of hell!

In fact, dear reader on the edge of the galaxy, I think hell must be quite like the hold of a ferry. It's at least a hundred and fifty degrees down there, and yet people jostle each other on the stairs, rushing to get there. As if all the dead people in the world were filing into the innards of a seething volcano. Subway to Hell!

There's a clanking of chains and the screech of metal; the Italians are back and they're the only ones dressed in trousers and jackets, the only ones not sweating when all the holiday-makers wearing skimpy clothes are already dripping wet, mopping our faces.

We stay there, in that oven, for an eternity—perhaps we're all stuck because some clever-clogs parked by the door hasn't woken up yet. The person who turned up last the previous evening. Maybe that blond Swedish guy, annoying us all so much that I already adore him and want someone just like him when I'm older.

The Italians look like demons, all they lack is some whips. It was a trap, we're all going to die here in the carbon monoxide, because some idiot has turned on his engine and everyone else has now done the same even though not a single car is moving.

And then the door of the ferry begins to fall with a loud metallic clang. A drawbridge coming down.

The army of the living dead escapes towards paradise.

Freedom!

Air, at last.
The tradition, in the Idrissi family, is to have breakfast on

the terrace under the palm trees, in the Place Saint-Nicolas opposite the Port of Bastia.

Papa orders us the full continental: croissants, fresh fruit juice, chestnut spread. Suddenly we feel like a family. Even me, looking like a Goth hedgehog. Even Nico, who spun a globe before we left and pointed his finger at random, to find out which language the girl he was going to go out with at the campsite would speak.

Yes, a family, for twenty-one days, three weeks, in paradise.

Maman, Papa, Nicolas.

And me.

I will mostly talk about me in this diary, I'd rather warn you about that right from the beginning!

Will you excuse me? I'm going to put on my swimming costume.

I'll see you again soon, my reader in the stars.

* * *

He gently closed the diary.

Puzzled.

He hadn't opened it in years.

He was worried.

She had come back . . .

Twenty-seven years later.

Why?

It was obvious. She'd come back to stir up the past. To scratch. To dig. To look for what she had left behind. In another life.

He'd prepared for this. For years.

Without ever managing to answer this question. How far down would she want to dig? To which level of the sewers would she want to descend? How far along the foul tunnels of the Idrissi family secrets would she want to venture?

4

August 12, 2016. 10 P.M.

My father didn't turn the wheel."

Clotilde had set down her book and was sitting on the chair, her bare feet and her red toenails digging into the mixture of sand, soil and grass. The lamp hanging from the olive branch above the green plastic furniture made the darkness sway. They had an area of fifteen meters by ten at their disposal, set slightly apart from the others, slightly shaded, to compensate for the absence of nearby washing facilities and the ridiculous size of the rented bungalow, even though it was supposed to be for three adults. We live outside here, Miss Idrissi, the boss of the Euproctes campsite had assured her obsequiously when she had booked the site the previous winter. Clearly Cervone Spinello hadn't changed.

"What?" said Franck.

He was balanced awkwardly and didn't bother turning around. He had spread out a newspaper on the back seat so that he could put his bare feet on it; his left hand was gripping one of the bars on top of the Passat while his right struggled to unscrew a bolt on the roof box.

"My father," Clotilde went on. "When we got to the corner at Petra Coda, he didn't turn the wheel. That's my very clear memory of it. A long straight line, a tight bend, and my father drives straight at the wooden barriers."

Only Franck's neck turned. His hand went on blindly unscrewing the bolt with the wrench.

"What do you mean, Clo? What are you implying?"

Clotilde took a moment to reply. She was studying Franck. The first thing her husband always did on the evening of the first day of the holidays was remove the roof box and the rack from the car. He would justify his eagerness with a whole list of perfectly rational arguments—increased petrol consumption, wind resistance, the feet of the roof rack marking the bodywork. Clotilde saw it as giving them one more bit of clutter to stash away in their holiday patch. And basically it wasn't even that. She didn't give a damn about the roof box that had to be taken down, put away, covered up. She thought the whole thing was genuinely idiotic. Boring yourself half to death taking out all the little screws one by one and putting them in little bags with little numbers corresponding to the little holes.

At such times, Valou wasn't about to play the role of peacemaker. Their teenager had already set off to explore the campsite, assess the average age of the holidaymakers and take an inventory of their nationalities.

"Never mind, Franck. It doesn't mean anything. I don't know."

Clotilde replied in a slightly weary voice. Franck had switched holes and was grumbling about the idiot who had screwed on the bolts too tightly.

That was him, yesterday.

Franck's sense of humour.

Clotilde leaned forward and flicked through the pages of her book, *A Climate of Fear*, the latest Vargas. It occurred to her that *A Nice Cool Climate of Fear* would have been a better title for a summer best-seller.

Clotilde's sense of humour.

"I don't know," she went on. "It's just a strange impression. Looking at the road just now I had a sense that even driving too fast, even at night, my father would have had time to brake, to turn the wheel. And that impression, weirdly, matches the memory that I've been carrying in my head since the accident."

"You were fifteen years old, Clo."

Clotilde set down the book again, without replying.

I know, Franck.

I know that these are only fleeting impressions, that everything happened in the space of two or three seconds . . . But listen, Franck, if you can hear me, down in the depths of your brain. If you can still read in the hollow of my eyes.

There's no question about it. It's an absolute certainty!

Papa didn't turn the wheel. He drove straight towards the precipice. With us inside.

Clotilde stared for a moment at the lamp swinging gently above her head, the swarm of moths frying their brief lives against the bulb.

"There's something else, Franck. As the accident happened, Papa took Maman's hand."

"Before the turn?"

"Yes, just before. Just before we crashed through the barrier, as if he understood that we were going to fly across the void, as if there was nothing he could do to prevent it."

A faint sigh. A third bolt yielded.

"What are you saying, Clo? That your father wanted to kill himself? With all of you in the car?"

Clotilde replied quickly. Perhaps too quickly.

"No, Franck. Of course not! He was angry because we were late. He was taking us to see a concert of polyphonic music. It was also the anniversary of the day my parents first met. We'd been for drinks with the whole family, his parents, his cousins, the neighbours. So no, it wasn't a suicide, of course it wasn't . . . "

Franck shrugged.

"Well, that's sorted then. It was an accident."

He switched to a twelve mm wrench.

Clotilde's voice dropped to a murmur. As if she didn't want

to wake the neighbours. From the next plot came the distant sound of an Italian television series.

"There was Nicolas's expression as well."

Franck stopped what he was doing. Clotilde went on.

"Nicolas didn't look surprised."

"What do you mean?"

"Just before we went through the barrier, a second before, when it was already clear there was nothing we could do, that no one would be able to stop the Fuego, I saw a weird expression in my brother's eyes, as if he knew something I didn't, as if he wasn't all that surprised. As if he understood why we were all going to die."

"You didn't die, Clo."

"I did, a little . . . "

She rocked her plastic chair back and forth. In that moment, she would have liked Franck to step down from the car and take her in his arms. Press her against him, say anything at all. Or even say nothing, but at least give her some reassurance.

Instead, he liberated the fourth bolt, then shifted the empty grey roof box onto his back.

Obelix style, Clotilde thought.

The image made her smile. Always take the drama out of things.

Yes, carrying his plastic menhir on his back, bare-chested with his blue canvas trousers, Franck looked amazingly like Obelix.

Without the paunch.

At forty-four, Franck was still a handsome man, with a broad chest and taut muscles. More than twenty years ago she had been blown away by his open smile, his reassuring confidence, but also his swimmer's physique; it had helped Clotilde to carry on, to love him, to persuade herself that he was the right one. Or at least that there were worse, much worse.

Weirdly, now that year after year, half-kilo after half-kilo, centimeter after centimeter, he had developed the stomach that even the handsomest young men eventually get, she didn't care. It didn't really matter any more, her partner's body, while Franck made a mountain of it, or at least a hill, a pretty, round little hill around his navel.

Obelix delicately set down his menhir.

"You shouldn't let that old story ruin your holiday, Clo."

Translation: *You shouldn't ruin our holiday with your old story, darling.*

Clotilde gave a hint of a smile. After all, Franck was right. They had all been lumbered with her pilgrimage, the whole family.

It was a chore.

Fulfilled, then forgotten.

She allowed herself one final debriefing. Franck had that quality at least: with him you could talk endlessly about the upbringing of children. And hence of Valentine.

"Do you think I shouldn't have talked about it to Valou? Shown her the site of the accident?"

"No, you should have, of course you should. They were her grandparents. It's important for her to . . . "

He came towards Clotilde, wiping his hands on a towel that he had taken from the line.

"You know, Clo, I'm proud of you. For having the courage to do that. After everything you've been through. I do understand where you're coming from. I haven't forgotten. But now . . . "

He wiped his shoulders, his armpits, his chest, then threw the towel aside, leaning towards Clotilde.

Too late, Clotilde thought. Too late, my darling.

Just a few seconds too late, so that her husband's words sounded less like compassion and more like a man suddenly excited by the heat. A civilised male, who still stores away his roof box and protects the bodywork of his car before going to hump his female.

"Now what, Franck?"

Franck put a hand on Clotilde's waist. Neither of them was wearing very many clothes. His hand climbed up towards her blouse.

"Shall we go to bed?"

Clotilde got up and took a step backwards. Gently. Without offending him. But without giving him hope either.

"No, Franck. Not straight away."

She stepped forward and took her towel from the line and picked up her wash bag.

"I need to take a shower."

Just before she reached the path, Clotilde turned towards her husband one last time.

"Franck . . . I don't think we've survived that accident."

He looked at her stupidly, like a lion that had allowed a gazelle to leave the watering hole without even pursuing it.

Without understanding what that phrase had just done to their conversation.

The campsite was barely lit. Having passed the only light on Avenue B, the one where five almost Finnish-looking chalets had been erected six months earlier, Clotilde passed in front of the last pitch reserved for tents. A group of bikers lay there in a circle, beer in hand, arranged around a camping gas stove totem pole, their bikes parked under the trees like a troop of thoroughbreds.

Like absolute freedom.

A perfume shot through with melancholy.

As Clotilde walked across the patch of ground, a dozen heads rose to greet the passage of the beautiful woman, in a weary horizontal Mexican wave. Clotilde's skirt reached halfway down her thigh, and the three open buttons of her blouse revealed the first swell of her breasts.

At forty-two, Clotilde knew she was still attractive.

Petite, yes. And slight. But with curves in the right places, curves where men like to find them. Since the age of fifteen, Clotilde had barely put on four kilos. One in each breast, one in each buttock. Prettier today than yesterday—in her mind at least; in other people's eyes, too. She had never needed to join a gym or go to a swimming pool to keep her figure, it was just the result of everyday training. A healthy mother in a healthy body. Pushing a full shopping trolley, sprinting to school at pickup time, bending and stretching by the dishwasher, the washing machine, the tumble drier . . .

Combining useful with easy on the eyes, isn't that right, Franck?

A few minutes later, Clotilde emerged from the shower wrapped in her towel. She was alone in the block apart from a very brown teenage girl who was busy shaving her legs with an electric razor that sounded like a mosquito zapper. On the other side of the partition, the noisy laughter of a group of boys was accompanied by a relentless techno rhythm.

Clotilde took the time to look at herself in the huge mirror that ran the length of the wall. To smooth her long black hair that fell to below her breasts. This campsite took her back twenty-seven years, to the same body, the same face, in front of the same mirror, when she was fifteen.

To that girlish body that she had dragged around like a ball and chain; to that imagination of hers, which had been her only trump card with the boys, her only weapon. Pathetic. Like a water pistol.

5

Wednesday, August 9, 1989, third day of holidays.
Aquamarine sky.

S orry, my mysterious intergalactic reader, I've abandoned you for two days, and I can't even hide behind the excuse of having had too much to do—I've been lounging around all day. I'll be more conscientious over the next few days, I promise. I need time to get my bearings, check out the location, observe, to find out my position, like a little spy, or an anthropologist on a mission, a traveller from the year 2020 who's been parachuted into 1989.

Incognito.

Hello, my galaxy? Lydia Deetz checking in. Captain's log, live from an unknown planet where it's more than thirty-five degrees during the day and where the locals walk around almost naked.

To tell you the truth, if I've neglected you for a while, it's because I didn't know where to start.

Where to plant my pen.

In the middle of our campsite, like a clothesline, right on the terrace of bungalow C29, the one we've been coming to every year since I was born?

At Papé and Mamy's house, like a Moor's head flag, right in the middle of the yard at Arcanu Farm?

In the middle of Alga beach, like a parasol?

Shazam!

Let's go for Alga beach. I'm going to paint a picture for you, like the kind of postcard you send just to make your friends who are stuck in the high-rises of Vernon salivate.

White sand. Turquoise water. Tanned skin.

Pfff . . . If it makes you happy.

If you had any idea what this dark little rebel was saying to you. She's clever, she has a plan. She's not going to be taken in by anyone. She will find herself a lover to enjoy the rest of her life with. She will have babies that she will fill with constant laughter so that they can hardly bear it. She will have a job that will be a constant fight: a boxer, bear trainer, acrobat, exorcist.

I testify here on Alga beach!

Are you happy now? Next time, I'll tell you about Papa.

But now I must leave you. Maman has squeezed her boobs into her little top and is coming over to MY towel. I don't know whether to be nice or bite her. I don't know yet. I'll improvise.

Bye . . .

* * *

He closed the notebook again.

Yes, without question, Palma was a beautiful woman. A very beautiful woman.

She didn't deserve to die. Certainly not.

But since the worst crime had been committed, since she couldn't be brought back to life, he needed to make sure that no one ever learned the truth.

6

C lotilde had gone to get a baguette, three croissants and a litre of milk that she was holding in a bag in one hand, a litre of orange juice in the other, and had wandered off.

On purpose.

Valou was still asleep. Franck had gone for a run to the Sémaphore de Cavallo.

In the summer of '89, Clotilde remembered, she had been sent off on the breakfast run every morning. She would drag her feet as she went in search of fresh bread at the reception desk; she would zigzag along the avenues of the Euproctes campsite, hoping to bump into someone, but none of the teenagers were awake at that time of day, so she had invented a complicated circuit through the maze of the campsite before coming back. Today, conversely, Clotilde had taken the shortest route possible to get to bungalow C29. The one where she had spent the first fifteen summers of her life.

She recognised only volumes. The size of the bungalow. The area of the site. The trees had grown, big olive trees whose trunks twisted up to form a canopy above the chalet which had extended its reach at ground level: a new electric awning, a terrace, a barbecue, an outdoor seating area. It had all been modernised through the good work of the new director of Euproctes, Cervone Spinello, who, with sharp business sense, had taken over the running of his father Basile's campsite. Every innovation—a tennis court, a water slide, a site marked out for the future swimming pool—confirmed Clotilde's suspicion that barely anything remained of the natural campsite of her childhood, that shady terrain that provided nothing but a bed to sleep in, water for washing with and trees to hide among.

Studying the C29 site in greater detail, Clotilde reflected that she hadn't seen it since the accident. In the days that followed the tragedy, Basile Spinello had brought her possessions to Calvi, to the hospital ward. A large bag containing her clothes, her mini-cassettes, her books. All of her personal items, except the one closest to her heart: her notebook. That notebook in which she had recorded her state of mind during that summer month. The notebook she had left behind on a bench at Arcanu Farm.

She had thought about it often during that time, on the plane that took her straight from Balagne Emergency Medical Centre to Paris, then in Conflans, the home of Jozsef and Sara, her mother's parents, who had looked after her until she was eighteen. Over the years she had eventually forgotten the notebook. Clotilde reflected with amusement that it was probably still waiting for her somewhere, thirty years later, tidied away in a wardrobe drawer, slipped behind a piece of furniture, stuck on a shelf under a pile of yellowing books.

Clotilde walked towards bungalow C29, pushing aside the branches of a smaller olive tree that was planted in front of the terrace. She remembered that there was already such a tree, the same size, outside her window in 1989. Perhaps Cervone had ripped out the old trees to plant new ones?

"Can I help you?"

A man had come out of the bungalow, a New York Giants baseball cap wedged over his greying temples, a cup of coffee in his hand. Smiling. Surprised.

Clotilde liked the simple conviviality of campsites. No barriers, no hedges, no palisades. Not a private home, more of a communal one.

"Oh, don't worry . . . "

A little way off, two little boys were playing football.

"Did you lose your ball under the bungalow?" the Giant asked.

From his smile, Clotilde guessed that he would have loved to see her getting down on all fours in front of the terrace, wiggling her bottom in her tight leggings as she crawled under the bungalow. On reflection, Clotilde also hated that about campsites—the absence of barriers. The blurring of lines. Ordinary lust.

"No. Just memories. I used to come to this bungalow on holiday."

"Really? That must have been quite a while ago. We've been booking this same chalet for eight years now."

"It was twenty-seven years ago."

The Giant's shocked expression implied a mute compliment.

You don't look it.

A woman appeared behind him. A mug of tea gripped between two fingers, curly hair held back by a wooden clip, a colourful sarong draped around her crumpled skin. She was smiling too.

She went and stood beside her husband and spoke to Clotilde.

"Twenty-seven? So this bungalow, C29, used to be yours? I'm sorry, but an idea has just come to me. You wouldn't happen to be Clotilde Idrissi?"

Clotilde didn't reply. Crazy thoughts jostled in her head. They hadn't put up a memorial plaque in the bungalow: *Here lived Paul and Palma Idrissi.* But hadn't the story of her parents' accident been passed down from generation to generation of campers over the decades?

The cursed bungalow.

The woman blew on her cup and slipped a hand under the Giant's T-shirt.

A subliminal but explicit message.

This one's mine.

The universal language of gestures and bodies that live in the open air for the duration of the summer. You expose, you look, you meet, you brush past . . . but you don't touch, even if it's all there within easy reach.

She took a sip of her tea then continued, delighted to be the bearer of a mysterious message.

"I have some post for you, Clotilde. It's been waiting for you for a while!"

Clotilde nearly collapsed on the spot for the second time in less than a minute. She grabbed the topmost branch of the baby olive tree.

"For . . . twenty-seven years?" she stammered.

The Giant's wife burst out laughing.

"Heavens, no! We only got it yesterday. Fred, will you get it for me? It's on the fridge."

The Giant went inside and then came back out holding an envelope. His wife pressed herself against him as she read out the address.

Clotilde Idrissi
Bungalow C29, Euproctes campsite
20260 La Revellata

Clotilde's heart raced for the third time, even faster than before. She almost tore off the olive branch.

"We'll need to see some ID," the Giant said, laughing. "We were going to take it to reception, but since you're here . . . "

Clotilde's damp fingers closed around the letter.

"Thank you."

She swayed along the sandy path. Her ballet flats left twisting curves as she walked, like a skater sliding over a frozen lake. Her eyes were fixed on her surname, her first name, the address on the envelope. She recognised the writing, but it was impossible. She knew it was impossible.

Without planning or even thinking about it, Clotilde went on through the campsite. She needed to be on her own to open this letter and she knew of only one place that would be secret enough for that. Secret and sacred. The Cave of the Sea-Calves. A hole in the cliff that could only be reached by the sea, or directly from the campsite via a small earthen track; a cave where, as a teenager, she had taken refuge a thousand times to read, dream, write and weep. She loved to write when she was young, she was even quite gifted, that was what her teachers and her friends had said. But then the words fled abruptly. Her talent hadn't survived the accident.

She descended to her hiding place without any difficulty. The sand and gravel path had been replaced by a flight of concrete steps. The walls of the grotto had been defaced with lovers' graffiti and obscene messages, and the place now smelt of beer and urine. It didn't matter. The view of the Mediterranean, from inside the cave, remained the same: vertiginous, making the occupier feel like a sea bird ready to plunge on any prey that ventured to the surface of the water with a simple flick of the wing.

Clotilde set down her shopping, went a little way inside the grotto, then sat down on the cool, almost damp rocks and slowly tore open the envelope. Trembling, the way you might open a love letter, even though, as far as she could remember, she had never received such a thing. She had been born a few years too late. Her suitors had flirted with her by text, by email. Digital declarations had been new and wildly exciting in those days but there was nothing left of them today, not a line, not a single note slipped into a book.

Clotilde's thumb and index finger extracted a small white sheet folded in four. She unfolded it. It was a handwritten letter, a careful hand, like the writing of an elderly schoolmistress.

My Clo,

I don't know if you're as stubborn now as you were when you were little, but there's something I'd like to ask of you.

Tomorrow, when you visit Arcanu Farm to see Cassanu and Lisabetta, please go and stand for a few minutes beneath the holm oak, before night falls, so that I can see you.

I will recognise you, I hope.

I would like your daughter to be there too.

I ask nothing else of you. Nothing at all.

Or perhaps just that you raise your eyes to the sky and look at Betelgeuse. If you only knew, my Clo, how many nights I have looked at it and thought of you.

My whole life is a dark room.

Kisses,
P.

Waves splashed against the entrance to the cave, as if God had created it at exactly the right height for it to be showered with sea spray without being flooded. In Clotilde's hand, the paper shook like a sail blown by the wind.

But there was no wind. Just a calm morning, already warm, the sun gently beginning to probe the deepest recesses of the cave.

Kisses.
It was her mother's handwriting.

P.
It was her mother's signature.

Who but her mother could call her "*My Clo*"? Who but her mother could remember those details? The goth-punk outfit that she hadn't worn since the accident.

Who else would have remembered Beetlejuice. *Betelgeuse*, to give it its proper name. Clotilde had hung the poster in her bedroom at the time. It was Maman who had given it to her for her fourteenth birthday, having ordered it directly from Quebec.

Clotilde stepped forward and studied the path leading down to the sea, then above her the clifftop track that led towards the beaches at Alga and Oscelluccia. At the end of the path, a teenage girl was wandering alone, clutching her mobile phone, perhaps searching for the network, or trying to read a message secretively, without her parents peering over her shoulder.

Clotilde looked down at the letter once more.

Who else but her mother would have remembered that phrase that had obsessed Lydia Deetz? That cult phrase from her cult film, that phrase that Clotilde had thrown in her mother's face, during the intimacy and violence of an argument, one evening when they were alone together?

Their secret. Between mother and daughter.

Her mother had wanted to drag her into town the following day to buy more presentable clothes—presentable meaning comfortable, colourful, feminine. Clotilde, before slamming the bedroom door in her mother's face, had hurled at her those desperate words borrowed from Lydia Deetz. The answer like a summary of her teenage life.

My whole life is a dark room. One big. Dark. Room.

7

Friday, August 11, 1989, fifth day of the holidays.
Alfalfa blue sky.

My father, on the other hand, I like.
I'm not sure a lot of people like my father, but I do, three times over.

My friends sometimes tell me he scares them. They think he's handsome, that much is certain, with his black eyes, his raven hair, his short beard on his square chin. But maybe it's exactly that, his confidence, that creates some distance.

You know what I mean?

My father is one of those people who are sure of themselves, who give their opinion with a single definitive word, give their friendship with two and take it back with three, the kind who can mow you down with a look and show no mercy. The scary teacher, the boss that you fear, respecting him and hating him at the same time. My father's a bit like that with everyone. Except me!

I'm his darling little daughter. All his tricks might work with other people—his conductor's baton making them play to his rhythm— but they don't work with me.

Take his job, for example. He says he works in the environment, in agronomy, ecology, that he's helping preserve the green lungs of the planet. In fact what he really does is sell turf! Fifteen per cent of the market goes through him, apparently that represents thousands of jobs in France, and in a dozen other countries, so people keep their mouths shut when he talks about it, when he says it was only twelve per cent of the market when he first started at Fast Green, and that he expects to get to seventeen per cent before the year 2000. Others look impressed when my father says that every minute, an area the size of a football pitch is re-turfed in France, and that whatever you say, at the end of a day, that's the equivalent of the Forest of Fontainebleau. They even look startled when he says he doesn't care about Kentucky Bluegrass or fescues, those stalwarts of the lawns of big suburban houses, given that he's in charge of the whole of the golf-course market in the Île-de-France, and that he only ever sells agrostis stonifera, the blade of grass that tops them all.

It just makes me laugh.

A father who sells turf!

The shame of it. I've told him plenty of times—he could have found something better to fill the dreams of his darling daughter! So I jump onto his lap and tell him I know all his tall tales about turf are only so much nonsense, and that he's really a spy, or a gentleman burglar, or a secret agent.

My name is Grass.

Ray Grass.

Right now, as usual, Papa isn't here. No one is here apart from me.

I'm alone, at Bungalow C29, writing under the olive tree. Nicolas is off with the other teenagers from the campsite, Maman has taken the Fuego to go shopping in Calvi, Papa is at Arcanu Farm, with his parents, his cousins, his local friends.

He's maintaining his Corsitude.

Papa's Corsitude, on the other hand, is no laughing matter. Paul Idrissi.

Lost in Normandy, in the hunchbacked Vexin.

No one laughs about that—except me!

Because to tell you the truth, Papa's Corsitude, from September to June, consists only of a yellow rectangle stuck in the back window of his car. The Cabalistic unifying symbol of

Corsicans lost on the mainland. With the Freemasons it's a triangle. The Jews were made to wear a star.

For the Corsicans exiled in the North, it's a rectangle.

The *Corsica Ferries* sticker.

Just to explain, Papa's Corsitude begins when his yellow
sticker starts peeling off, which means that the days are getting
longer and the holidays are on their way. My Papa is a bit like
those kids who start believing in Father Christmas once
December comes, or old people who start believing in God
when they are told how many months they have left to live.
You know what I mean?

Oh! Wait a minute, reader, just raise your eyes a second,
there's a great procession going on in front of me. There's
Nicolas and Maria-Chjara, heading towards Alga beach with
Cervone and Aurélia hot on their heels, and then the whole
tribe, Candy, Tess, Steph, Hermann, Magnus, Filip, Ludo,
Lars, Estefan . . . I'll introduce you to them, don't worry. All in
good time.

I could go and join them, but no, I'll stay here with you.
That's nice of me, don't you think, choosing to write to you like
someone doing homework on holiday, instead of chasing after
the gang of big kids? Big kids who ignore me, snub me, leave
me behind, abandon me, humiliate me, forget me . . . I could
fill three pages this way, a whole thesaurus, but I'll spare you
the tirade and get back to my chapter about Papa.

His acute Corsitude, his longing for the *maquis* that afflicts
him in June the way other people catch hay fever; I'll describe
it to you in three stages, which will turn into as many family
rows.

The first stage occurs on the motorway just after Paris,
when Papa takes out of God knows where some cassettes of
Corsican music to put on in the Fuego. The second is once
we're on the island, our first meal, local charcuterie, cheese and
fruit from the village, stocking up on produce from the little

shops, buying *coppa*, *lonzu* and *brocciu*, pretending that everything else, everything we put in our shopping trolley for the rest of the year, is just rubbish. The third is the interminable family visits, the grandparents, the cousins, the neighbours, the conversations in a foreign language, and Papa struggling because I can see that these days he speaks better English with the boss of Fast Green than he does Corsican with his friends, but he sticks at it, my Daddy does. It's touching even if, like Nicolas, you don't understand a word, or only bits and pieces. They talk about politics, about the world that is turning around quicker and quicker, and shrinking as if it's losing bits along the way, and their island which doesn't move at all, in the eye of the hurricane, and which looks on in astonishment at the commotion made by humanity. Papa tries his best to follow, like a devotee of a religion who thinks that learning the prayers and reciting them once a year will be enough to get him into paradise. But I watch him all the time, my Ryegrass Papa, and I can tell you that he is no more Corsican than I am, no more Catholic than a Catholic who only hails Mary when he's being christened, married or buried.

Papa is a Corsican in shorts.

He wouldn't be happy with someone who said that to him. Not even me. Even if I'm the only one who would dare.

But I won't do it.

It would only annoy him. And I don't want to do that.

I like my Papa more than Maman. Perhaps because he likes me too. Perhaps because he's never had anything bad to say about my Goth Lydia get-up. Perhaps because he likes my black clothes, perhaps because they remind him of the clothes Corsican women wear.

The comparison stops there.

Black for old Corsican women is the uniform of submission. For me, it's the symbol of rebellion. I wonder which kind of black-clad women my father prefers? Both, Captain?

Submission in public and rebellion in private. A way of owning a treasure that you keep to yourself. A bird that you can put in a cage.

Like all men, I think.

Wanting a mother, a housewife, a cook, but hating you because that's what you've become.

That's the impression I get of how couples live, from the lofty vantage point of my fifteen years.

I'll stop there for today. I think you know enough about Papa now. I'm wondering whether to join the others at the beach or pick up a book. A book's good. It ages you, reading a book, I think.

Anywhere . . . on the beach, on a bench, outside a tent.

It intrigues people.

With only an open book on a towel, you pass from the status of little-idiot-on-her-own-who-has-no-friends-and-is-getting-bored to that of little-rebel-who's-comfortable-in-her-own-bubble-and-couldn't-give-a-stuff-about-anyone-else.

You just have to find the right book.

I need to find a cult book, the way I've done with my two films, *Beetlejuice* and *The Big Blue*. The kind of book you reread a thousand times and recite to the boys you meet to find out if they're the right one, if they have the same taste.

I've packed three novels in my bag.

Three crazy books, apparently.

The Unbearable Lightness of Being
Dangerous Liaisons
The Never-Ending Story

OK, I know what you're going to say, all three have already come out in the cinema. It's true, I admit, I brought them along with me because I liked the films . . . and once I've read them, I'll still be able to tell people I saw the film AFTERWARDS and was INCREDIBLY DISAPPOINTED by the adaptation. Clever girl, eh?

Now, which of the three shall I read first?

Right, I'll go to the beach with *Dangerous Liaisons* under my arm.

Perfect!

Valmont and the Marquise de Merteuil. They're irresistible, John Malkovich behaving badly, and little Keanu Reeves . . .

See you very soon, my reader in the next world.

* * *

With his index finger, he wiped away the tear that had welled up in the corner of his eye, before closing the diary.

Even years on, he still couldn't read that name without being overwhelmed.

That name that lingered around the diary like a ghost.

An inoffensive ghost.

That's what they'd all thought.

8

August 13, 2016, 2:00 P.M.

I t's her handwriting!"
Clotilde waited for a response.
Any response.
Nothing.

Franck's lips were busy sucking on the plastic bottle of Orezza, one litre, about as much liquid as he had just perspired through the pores of his skin. In the end he settled for emptying only three quarters of it, and poured the rest of the mineral water over his bare torso.

Franck had run to the Sémaphore de Cavallo, nine kilometers there and back. Not bad going, especially in thirty-degree heat. He took a moment to hang up his sweat-drenched T-shirt.

"How can you be sure, Clo?"

"I just know, that's all."

Clotilde was leaning against the twisted trunk of the olive tree. She was still holding the envelope, her eyes fastened on her name.

Clotilde Idrissi.

Bungalow C29, Euproctes campsite.

She didn't want to talk to Franck about the childhood postcards sent to her by her mother which she sometimes reread; the folders of signed and annotated correspondence that she had kept since school; the old photographs with words written on the back. Those phantoms that left only scratches. She merely murmured between her teeth:

"My whole life is a dark room. One big . . . dark . . . room . . . "

Franck came and stood in front of her, his chest dripping. The sun shone through his fine fair hair. Everything about Franck was the opposite of night, of darkness, of shadow. Some years ago, that was what she had liked best about him. That he took her towards the light.

He pulled up a plastic chair and sat down facing her, his eyes fixed on hers.

"OK, Clo. OK . . . You've told me, I haven't forgotten. You were a fan of that actress when you were fifteen, you dressed like her, like a gothic hedgehog, you behaved like the worst kind of ungrateful child towards your parents. You made me watch that film, *Beetlejuice*, when we met, do you remember? You paused the film when we came to that part where the teenage girl says, 'My whole life is a dark room,' and you even smiled at me and said that the two of us would repaint it in all the colours of the rainbow."

Franck remembered that?

"I think your Winona Ryder must have stayed like that, a frozen statue on the screen, for almost two hours, watching us make love on the sofa."

So he did remember . . .

"Clo, whoever sent you this letter is playing a terrible joke on you."

A joke? Had Franck really said "a joke?"

Clotilde reread the words that troubled her the most.

Tomorrow, when you visit Arcanu Farm to see Cassanu and Lisabetta, please go and stand for a few minutes beneath the holm oak, before night falls, so that I can see you.
I will recognise you, I hope.
I would like your daughter to be there too.
I ask nothing else of you. Nothing at all.

The visit to her paternal grandparents was scheduled for

the following evening. Franck was still trying to explain something completely unexplainable.

"Yes, Clo. Someone's playing a awful joke on you. I have no idea who it is, or why they're doing it, but . . . "

"But what?"

This time Franck rested a hand on Clotilde's knee before looking into her eyes again. The accomplice had disappeared, and now once again it was the preacher who was talking, the giver of lessons with his rosary of morals and his unanswerable arguments. A patient teacher faced with a pupil of limited intelligence. She couldn't bear his smugness any longer.

"OK, Clo, let me put it another way. On the evening of the accident, August 23, 1989, you are absolutely sure that all four of you were in the car; you, your father, your mother and Nicolas."

"Yes, of course."

"No one could have jumped out before the Fuego plunged off the cliff?"

Clotilde saw before her eyes the images that had been vividly engraved there since the tragedy. The Fuego hurtling like a bomb in a straight line. The tight bend. Her father not turning the wheel.

"No, no one could have, it was impossible."

Franck ploughed on. That was his strength. He believed in two main things: rationality and effectiveness.

"Clo, are you absolutely sure that your father, your mother and your brother died in that accident? All three of them?"

For once, in her head, Clotilde thanked him for his lack of tact.

Yes, she was absolutely sure.

The mangled corpses in the carcass of the Fuego had haunted her for over thirty years. Her parents' bodies, crushed between the steel jaws, the taste of blood mixed with the smell of petrol, the emergency services turning up at the site of the accident and identifying the three corpses, transporting them to the morgue and placing them in drawers so that the devastated family could pay one last visit. The inquiry. The funeral . . . Time making everything decay, nothing ever comes back to life, nothing ever flowers again, ever . . .

"Yes, all three of them died, there's no doubt."

Franck rested a second hand on a second knee and leaned towards her.

"OK, Clo. Then the case is closed. Some joker is playing a sordid trick on you, an old boyfriend or a jealous Corsican, it doesn't matter, but don't let it make you believe anything else."

"What do you mean, anything else?"

Clotilde felt hypocritical, frail, fake, to the point that she was lying to herself.

Sometimes Franck's candour simplified things.

"Don't let it make you think that your mother might still be alive. And that she's the one who has written to you."

Bang!

Clotilde's milky skin, gleaming with sun cream, was flushed.

Of course, Franck.

Of course.

What was she thinking?

"Of course, Franck," she heard herself agreeing. "The thought never crossed my mind."

Fake! Hypocrite! Liar!

Franck didn't press the point. He had won, the voice of reason had spoken, and there was nothing else to add.

"So forget it, Clo. You were the one who wanted to come back to Corsica. I followed you. So now, let's forget it all and enjoy the holiday."

Yes, Franck.

Of course, Franck.

You're right, Franck.

Thank you, Franck.

Franck suggested a drive to Calvi. The town was less than five kilometers away, less than ten minutes' drive if you didn't find yourself stuck behind a herd of donkeys or camper vans.

Franck went off to put on a clean shirt and Valou clapped her hands at the very mention of the word Calvi, which was synonymous with shopping streets crowded with tourists, the marina with its parade of yachts, its beaches crammed with towels. Watching Valou run off into the bungalow to slip into a tight dress, redo her hair in order to reveal her forehead, the back of her neck and her bronzed shoulders, and change into delicate sandals of braided, silvery leather, beaming at the idea of finding civilisation again, and not just any civilisation, but the tanned and wealthy civilisation that fascinated her, Clotilde couldn't help wondering where it had all gone wrong between them.

She and Valentine had been thick as thieves until Valentine turned ten. A dreamy little princess daughter and her crazy mother. Just as she had promised herself they would be.

Silly games, wild laughter, shared secrets.

She had sworn never to become a bitter mother, a mother who extinguished dreams, a mother who saw the world in black and white. And yet everything had become messed up without her even being aware of it. She'd been looking in the wrong direction. Clotilde had been expecting a rebellious teenager, as she had once been; she had prepared for that without losing any of her own values, any of her dreams. By staying the same person she always was.

How wrong could she have been!

So now here she was with a well-behaved, modern adolescent girl who saw her as an outmoded old thing with the ideals of a different age. Now, her crazy mother left her indifferent at best, ashamed at worst.

Valou had found a fringed emerald green handbag that

matched her skirt, and was waiting by the Passat. Franck was already at the wheel.

"Are you ready to go, Maman?"

No answer.

An impatient teenage voice. Used to it, but still impatient.

"Maman! Come on, let's go!"

Clotilde came out of the bungalow.

"Franck, did you pick up my papers?"

"I haven't touched them."

"They're not in the safe."

"I haven't touched them," Franck said again. "Are you sure you haven't put them somewhere else?"

OK, Clotilde thought, I may be the silly brainless fool of the family, but I haven't lost it completely.

"Yes, I'm sure!"

Clotilde very clearly remembered putting her wallet in the little safe built into the cupboard by the front door before taking a shower.

Franck pushed his sunglasses back onto his forehead and tapped nervously on the wheel, clearly inches away from honking the horn.

"If they're not there," he snapped, "you must have . . . "

"I put them in the bloody safe last night and I haven't opened it since then!"

In a fit of irritation, Clotilde went back inside, hoisted her suitcase onto the bed and began to rummage through her things.

Not a sign.

She opened the drawers, ran her hand along the highest shelves, peered under the bed, the chairs and the various pieces of furniture.

Nothing.

Nothing in the roof box, nothing in the glove compartment.

Franck and Valou were silent now.

Clotilde went back to the safe.

"I put them in this stupid impregnable tin can. Someone must have taken them."

"Listen, Clo, there's a key, a code, and there's nobody here but us . . . "

"I know! I know! I KNOW!"

Clotilde didn't like Cervone Spinello's smile. She had never liked it. She remembered hating Cervone when he was a child, an adolescent, always trying to take charge of their gang on the grounds that his father owned the campsite.

Liar. Boastful. Calculating.

A few years later, with the power he had accrued, eighty shaded hectares with a sea view, he became something else:

Obsequious. Pretentious. Lecherous.

Quite the opposite of Basile, his father.

"I'm so sorry, Clotilde," Cervone said defensively. "I haven't had time to come and visit you. We'll have to find a moment to . . . "

She interrupted his suggestion of an aperitif, tearful tributes to his parents and twenty-seven-year-old reminiscences, explaining that her wallet had disappeared, and as far as she was concerned, that could only be explained by a theft.

Cervone frowned with his large black eyebrows.

Annoyed. Already . . .

He picked up a bunch of keys and, leaving the reception, hailed a large man who was busy watering a flower bed.

"Orsu, come with me."

Cervone's order was accompanied by a hand gesture, a finger pointed towards the alley, as if marking his authority over an obedient animal. The gesture of a little Napoleon. The other man didn't hesitate, and went to follow him. Clotilde took a step back when he turned around.

Orsu was over one meter ninety tall. A big unkempt beard and long, thick curly hair covered his face, but not enough to hide the deformity that marked his entire left side: a staring eye, an atrophied, almost hollow cheek, sagging skin from chin to neck, a twisted shoulder, an arm that dangled from his body like an empty sleeve onto which someone had sewn a pink plastic glove, a stiff leg.

For some reason, Clotilde was more troubled than frightened. At first she took her reaction towards this giant to be a form of pity, perhaps an occupational hazard, but something else disturbed her, a feeling she couldn't quite identify. As Orsu walked three meters ahead of them, Cervone whispered in Clotilde's ear:

"I don't think you'll remember him. Orsu was only three months old that terrible August. He's had no luck since then. We've kept him, that's how we do things here, we don't abandon our three-legged goats. He takes care of pretty much everything at the Euproctes, and people call him Hagrid. He's kind, not dangerous."

Everything about Cervone's statement disturbed Clotilde.

The way he addressed her informally, even though he hadn't seen her for twenty-seven years. Talking about Orsu as if he were a rescue dog. Making himself out to be some kind of benevolent pope while Clotilde couldn't rid herself of the image of the little sod who'd persecuted lizards, frogs, and any other poor animal unfortunate enough to fall into the spotty torturer's clutches.

There were four of them, leaning over the tiny safe in the bungalow. Only Valou was sitting to one side on a chair, headphones in, painting her toenails. Cervone had no qualms about staring at her thighs.

Lecherous, obsequious, pretentious, Clotilde corrected herself mentally. She had picked the right three words, but the wrong way round. Orsu, his enormous bulk bent over the steel cube, tried the keys with his one working hand, studied the lock, checked the bolt, the striking plate, the cylinders. Cervone watched over his shoulder.

"Sorry, Clotilde," the manager of the campsite said at last. "There's no sign of it having been forced. Are you really sure that your wallet was inside?"

Clotilde's brain was boiling. Had they colluded? Franck and Cervone, her man and the man who disgusted her more than anyone else in the world. Clotilde merely nodded. Cervone thought for a moment.

"Was there any money in it?"

"A little."

"And your daughter knew the code?"

Cervone was very direct. Compared to him Franck was a diplomat.

"Yes, but . . . "

Clotilde was about to protest, but behind them Valou had risen to her feet.

"If I'd wanted to steal money from my parents, I'd have pinched Papa's wallet."

Cervone burst out laughing.

"Good answer! That more or less gets you off the hook."

More than anything else Clotilde hated the complicit smile that Valou exchanged with the owner of the campsite. Franck, behind them, simply seemed irritated.

"So what are we going to do? Given that my wife tells you her wallet was inside this bloody safe?"

Thank you, Franck!

Cervone shrugged.

"One way or another, if your documents are missing, then you'll have to go to the police station anyway. And while you're there, Clotilde, you can report the matter if you like."

He smiled ambiguously, then added, "But don't expect to

see Cesareu at the station in Calvi. Your old friend retired a few years ago. I don't know who's there now. Officers only spend three years here before heading off to the mainland."

Hagrid was still studying the safe. Checking every part of the mechanism in the lock. He didn't seem to understand. Clotilde inwardly thanked him for not settling for appearances.

She was sure of one thing.

That wallet had been there yesterday, so someone had taken it.

But why?

Who?

Someone who knew the code or had the key to the safe.

9

Saturday, August 12, 1989, sixth day of holiday.
Midnight-blue sky.

Y ou know what?
   At last something is happening in my little corner of
   Corsica. I have something new to say in my diary!
Something new and explosive. I hope you're going to enjoy the
way I tell stories.

So are you ready, my mystery reader?

It all started with a gigantic BOOM. At precisely 2:23 in the
morning. I know, because the explosion woke me up and I
immediately looked at my watch. I took a look outside, towards
the sea, the Revellata Peninsula, Balagne, and its highest peak,
the Capu di a Veta. I couldn't see anything! Then I went back
to sleep.

The next morning there was great excitement in the campsite. The police were questioning tourists, who seemed more
surprised than panicked, pretending not to notice the big grins
on the faces of the local Corsicans.

The hotel complex, the Roc e Mare marina, had been blown
up during the night.

To give you the precise geographical details, the Revellata
is a small peninsula five kilometers long and one kilometer
wide. It is almost entirely wild apart from the lighthouse at the
end of the world, the little port of Stareso, two or three white
villas, the Euproctes campsite tucked right in the middle,
under the olive trees, with direct access along a small path to
two tiny beaches: Alga in the south-east and Oscelluccia in the

north-east. To the west there's nothing but the cliff. You can go down a steep slope to the Cave of the Sea-Calves and Recisa Cove, a pebbly inlet inhabited by windsurfers.

To give you some precise economic details, almost all of this little bit of paradise belongs to one man: my grandfather! Cassanu Idrissi. Despite this, he is happy to live with his entire family at Arcanu Farm in the mountains, an isolated spot with just one steep road to get up there, a large television aerial, some old rocks, a huge holm oak in the middle of the farmyard and all the scents of the *maquis* clinging to the walls. Nothing fussy, no swimming pool, no tennis court. The only luxury is the incredible view of Revellata Bay. Even the campsite belongs to Papé Cassanu. Basile Spinello, the manager, is his friend, and he has one golden rule: no walls, or hardly any, only for the showers and the toilets, bare pitches for tents, a handful of wooden bungalows, just enough to put up the cousins who come over from the mainland each summer, or for friends or a few favoured tourists. Papé Cassanu takes care of his land as if it were a woman he doesn't want to share, who you can admire but not possess; a woman whose skin will never wrinkle, smelling of rockrose and lemons, painted by the indigo of wild orchids, the ones that Mamy Lisabetta loves.

Except that . . .

If you've been paying attention, you will have noticed that I said the word "almost" when I was saying that the whole area belongs to Papé Cassanu. Almost: that means that he still doesn't own a few little bits of cliff overlooking the sea, above Oscelluccia beach, and in particular a few thousand square meters inherited by some sort of distant cousin a few centuries ago. The auction went through the roof and a developer started to construct a hotel complex in the middle of the red rocks. An Italian from Portofino, from what they say. A luxurious affair, in harmony with the colour of the rock, with a terrace overlooking the Mediterranean, a small private harbour, three-star rooms, a Jacuzzi and the rest. They started building in March, except that the Corsican environmental associations put in a complaint, referring to coastal law. I confess that I've never grasped the details, but Papé Cassanu can talk to Papa about it for hours. Apparently the complex could be built because it was to be located more than a hundred meters away from the sea, but the environmentalists then invoked laws concerning the protection of areas of outstanding natural beauty, with relation to the quality of the landscape and its ecological interest, a procedure that involved registering the site, and a pre-emptive intervention by the Coastal Protection Agency . . . In short, it was a total legal mess.

So could the marina be built or not? No one knows. It came down to a battle fought by lawyers, journalists, civil servants and probably to large rolls of banknotes both on and under the table. But in the meantime the bricks of the Roc e Mare complex began to pile up side by side on the concrete foundation poured by some Italian workmen. Very slowly, without waiting for the ruling that might declare the building work illegal, right under the nose of Papé Cassanu. A nose that is rather hairy and ticklish, I can assure you.

Until two in the morning, last night. Then BOOM!

A big hole in the concrete foundations, or what's left of them. In the morning, the workmen found nothing but a large heap of gravel.

It was Aurélia who told me what happened next. Aurélia is the daughter of Cesareu Garcia, an officer at Calvi police station. Between ourselves, I wouldn't say that I liked Aurélia all that much. She's two years older than me and she thinks a great deal of herself, with her big, serious ideas along the lines of "that's the law and that's how it is and if it isn't I'm telling my dad." It's as if she's never been a child, as if she threw a double six in life's game of Ludo and managed to skip the first few squares. I feel sorry for her future husband, if she ever manages to find one. It's hardly a foregone conclusion for Aurélia—the boys look at her even less than they look at me, and that's saying something. Even Nicolas, yet I'm willing to bet the poor thing would give it up for my big brother. It's not that she's ugly exactly, she has big round eyes, black as olives, and big eyebrows that almost meet above her nose, making her look even more severe. It's just that she's boring. The opposite of me, if you like: I act too young and she acts too old. That's why there's a kind of solidarity between the two of us, or no, it's more like a competition, I would say. Two different ways of adapting to the situation. Maybe we'll meet up in a few years and see who's won.

But anyway, on the morning of the big BOOM, Aurélia said to me, in that haughty, pinched voice of hers:

"My father's gone to see your grandfather, Cassanu. Everyone knows he's the one who blew up the marina."

"?????????"

"But no one's going to say anything, of course. *Omertà*. *Omertà*, my dad says. Everyone here has a debt to your frandfather. Basile, the manager of the campsite, first of all, they were at school together. Just think about it, someone plants a bomb, they know it's him but no one says anything."

It amused me to imagine her little father (or rather her big father, because you should see Cesareu, he's the weight of a Corsican bull) climbing into his little police van to go and talk to my Papé, sweating, his knees trembling, like a little mouse going to negotiate over a corner of the barn with the house cat.

I put her in her place.

"There's no proof against my Papé. Your father must have told you that."

"Yes, he did."

I pressed home the point.

"And the people who planted the bomb are right, aren't they? Corsica is much prettier without all that concrete. If we wait for the end of the legal case, with all the scheming and administration, they'll have had more than enough time to ruin La Revellata and the rest of the island, don't you think?"

Aurélia has no opinion on that. Ever.

But this time she did give me an answer.

"Yes. My father said that to me as well, that Cassanu was right to do it. Even if he wasn't acting within the law."

Well, that put me in my place.

I thought about it all day. I even bumped into Papé, who was engrossed in conversation with Basile Spinello at the entrance to the campsite, the two of them looking like conspirators, but not that frightening. There were a few police cars driving around. The explosion was mentioned on the radio. Then everything was settled by the end of the day. No one had seen anything, no one had heard anything. Top secret! Revellata will be returned to the gulls, the goats, the donkeys, the boars. This evening I spent a long time in the Cave of the Sea-Calves, looking out at the sea and watching the sun go down over Revellata Bay.

It was incredibly beautiful in red and gold.

And I was incredibly proud.

As long as my Papé is here, the bay will stay as it is.

Wild, unspoiled, rebellious.

Like me!

For ever, eh, my future reader? For ever, promise me.

* * *

For ever . . .

The little fool!

He closed the notebook.

10

T he bare-chested workmen were suffering from the heat. Motionless, bent over their spades, sitting at the wheel of a stationary bulldozer, or smoking a cigarette in the shade if they were lucky. It seemed as if they were all looking in disbelief at the foundations for the concrete walls set among the rocks, as if this were an insane enterprise, a titanic task. A palace dreamt up by an insane king, impossible to build, or at best to be built in the winter, or at night, not in the midst of this heat wave.

"That's going to be a four-star hotel," Valou said from the back seat of the Passat, clapping her hands like an excited child.

Franck was driving calmly, concentrating on the road, his eyes narrowed. The sun dazzled him every time he rounded a corner. Clotilde turned towards her daughter.

"A what?"

"A four-star hotel. The Roc e Mare Marina. It's an old project that's been resurrected by Cervone Spinello. It's a kind of extension to the Euproctes campsite. There are all these plans in the reception. It's supposed to be finished before next summer. Really top class! It'll have a swimming pool, a spa, a gym, rooms at 300 euros a night with a private balcony and direct access down to the sea."

For a moment Clotilde let her eyes drift over towards the building site. An enormous panel masked off part of the works, emblazoned with the logos of Europe, the Region and the Département. It displayed a picture of an extravagant hotel complex, four or five storeys high. Even tucked away among the rocks, it was the only thing you would see for many kilometers around, from the sea or from the coastal road.

Clotilde was filled with a strange emotion that she couldn't really define. For years she had tried to forget that wild rocky headland, that dangerous road, that deadly drop. But she couldn't. Weirdly, coming back to the site of the tragedy, every turn, every fresh perspective on that divine backdrop took her further away from the accident, to a time before it. Towards all the years, all the summers before the tragedy, even if she had only vague memories, even if all that remained of her child-hood holidays was the certainty that she loved that island, that countryside, those perfumes. That landscape that, neverthe-less, was going to betray her. Corsica was like her, an orphan. Beautiful and lonely. It had been torn from its family twenty million years ago, from the mainland, from the Alps, from Estérel, to be left drifting in the Mediterranean.

Valou went on, craning her neck to point out the founda-tions of the future palace.

"Cervone told me a bit about it when he saw that I was interested. I'll be sixteen next year, so I might even be able to get a job there."

Cervone . . .

Clotilde felt a painful electric shock. Her daughter was already calling that bastard by his first name. That building-developer-gambler-flirt who was twenty-five years older than Valou.

She counter-attacked without even thinking about it.

"I don't understand how they could allow something so horrendous to be built."

Valentine gave in without a word, only allowing her eyes to wander from the billboard to the virgin landscape, as if she were already imagining the hotel sprung fresh from the ground.

The worst teenagers are the ones who refuse confrontation.

Clotilde went on the attack again. Slyly.

"You could always ask Papé Cassanu, your great grandfather, what he thinks about it. We're going to his place for dinner tomorrow evening."

"Why?"

"Just because."

"Is he one of those old Corsican separatists who used to plant bombs? Like that series, *Mafiosa*?"

"You'll see."

"And how old is my great-grandfather?"

"He'll be eighty-nine on the eleventh of November."

"Does he still live in that sheepfold at the ends of the earth? Don't they have retirement homes in Corsica?"

Clotilde closed her eyes.

They were coming to Petra Coda, the precise spot where the Fuego had gone over the edge.

No one spoke. A piece of disco music came on the radio. Franck thought about turning down the volume, but didn't.

By the side of the road there was now no trace of the three bunches of wild thyme.

Calvi community police station, on the way into the city, had a unique view over the Mediterranean and the Revellata Peninsula. You might have expected the policemen's wives to have demanded luxurious apartments with panoramic views, handy for the beach, in return for agreeing to follow their husbands to this dangerous territory.

Clotilde went in on her own, leaving Franck to go on in the car so he could drop Valentine off at Calvi harbour. She would call him to come get her as soon as she was ready. It probably wouldn't take long—she just needed to report the loss of her papers.

The policeman who dealt with her was young, athletic and clean-shaven from the top of his head to his chin. His office was decorated with the pennants and scarves of different rugby clubs.

Auch. Albi. Castres.

None of them Coriscan.

"Captain Cadenat," the officer said, holding out a hand to Clotilde.

After listening to her story, he slid all the relevant identity theft forms towards her, as if apologising for the enormous amount of paperwork that had to be done. He had an open smile that had nothing of the military about it. More like a young man who had been assigned to the police force rather than doing military service and was happy about it.

Clotilde told him about the circumstances of the theft, the locked safe, the wallet that had disappeared nonetheless, the lack of any sign of a break-in. Above the officer's casual smile were two butterfly eyes; blue irises and long eyelashes.

The policeman got up and looked out towards the Revellata lighthouse, which was clearly visible from his window. The police captain had the delicate, slender physique of a three-quarter back.

"Cerone Spinello won't be happy to see us. As a rule, he likes to sort things out at his campsite himself. But if you want me to investigate . . . "

Clotilde nodded.

Yes, she did want him to do that. If only to annoy Cervone.

The three-quarter back straightened the pennant of CA Brive that was hanging on the wall.

"To tell you the truth, miss, I've been in this post for three years now and I'm still having difficulties understanding how things work here. I'm from the south. Name's Cadenat. Jules Cadenat, my great-grandfather, was one of France's greatest rugby players before the war—he was a lock, in the second row. I'm not complaining about being sent to Calvi, and the great thing is that I'm now quadrilingual—French, English, Occitan and Corsican. It's a fantastic island. Great people. It's just that they're really rubbish at rugby!"

He burst out laughing, then began to check the documents that Clotilde had filled in.

Surname: *Baron*

Maiden name*: Idrissi*

First name: *Clotilde*

Profession: *Lawyer. Family law*

"Are you Corsican?" he asked, almost automatically.

"Yes. At heart, I think."

"Are you related to Cassanu Idrissi?"

"I'm his granddaughter."

Cadenat allowed a beat.

"Ah . . . "

The butterfly had settled on a cactus! The three-quarter back froze like a policeman who had just heard the name Vito Corleone. A moment later, he was energetically stamping the administrative documents. As the last stamp hung in the air, the policeman slowly looked up at Clotilde. It was a compassionate look. The butterfly had left the cactus for a rose.

"God, I'm so stupid."

"Sorry?"

The captain stammered, his fingers fidgeting with the stamp.

"You're the . . . "

He tried to find the right word. Clotilde guessed the ones he couldn't bring himself to utter:

The survivor.

The miracle girl.

The orphan.

"You're Paul Idrissi's daughter," he finally managed to say. "Your father died in that accident out on Revellata, along with your mother and your brother."

Clotilde's thoughts ran wild. This Occitan had only been working on the island for three years. The accident had happened twenty-seven years before. Since then, dozens of other accidents, all equally fatal, must have happened on those deadly winding roads. So how come this young man knew all about . . .

The officer interrupted her thoughts.

"Is the sergeant aware that you're here?"

The sergeant?

Cesareu?

Cesareu Garcia?

Clotilde had very clear memories of the policeman who had carried out the investigation into her parents' accident. Cesareu Garcia. His good-natured calm, the delicate modesty of the questions he had asked her as she lay on her hospital bed. His physique, as wide as his voice was gentle. Two chairs to sit on and a whole box of Kleenex to mop his forehead and his neck during the three hours that the conversation had lasted at Balagne Emergency Medical Centre.

She also remembered his daughter, of course, one of the teenagers at the Euproctes campsite: Aurélia Garcia, the tribe's biggest killjoy.

"No," she said at last. "I don't think so. Cervone Spinello told me he'd retired."

"Yes, some years ago. I expect you'd remember him, though. You don't forget a physique like his! He would have made a terrific prop forward if these Corsicans realised that a ball can be oval as well as round. I should warn you, since he retired, he's put on another ten kilos a year."

The three-quarter back came a little closer to Clotilde. The butterfly trembled, as if wary of a pretty but carnivorous plant.

"Miss Idrissi, you should go and see him."

Clotilde stared back at him, uncomprehending.

"He lives in Calenzana. It's important, Miss Idrissi. He talked to me about that accident a lot before he left the force. He went on investigating it for years afterwards. You should go and talk to him. Cesareu is a great guy. A lot more intelligent than people around here think. About the accident, he has . . . how can I put it . . . "

"What?" said Clotilde, raising her voice for the first time.

The butterfly beat its wings one last time before flying off.

"He has a theory."

11

He opened the notebook.
He didn't like what he was about to read.
But he had to do it.
He had to feed his hatred.

* * *

Sunday, August 13, 1989, seventh day of the holiday.
Midnight-blue sky.

There's a dance tonight.

And I should tell you straight away, I'm not queen of the ball!

I'm sitting a little bit away from the others, a bit in the shadows, on the sand with my book on my knees.

When I say a dance, it's really more of an impromptu party at the campsite, with three strings of bunting and the big boom box that Hermann borrowed from his father, resting on a plastic chair. Nicolas has brought all the cassettes with the Top 50 hits he's recorded straight off the radio, so we even get to hear the jingles and the ads between the songs.

And there's one in particular.

THE hit of the summer!

The hit that, if you're lucky, my future reader, you will have never heard of because it's going to disappear from everyone's memories as quickly as it sucked the blood from them this summer.

It's a crazy thing, called the lambada.

It's really more of a dance than a song, and involves the boy sticking his thigh between the girl's thighs. Against her pussy, to be absolutely straight about it.

I kid you not.

Just let anyone try that with me . . .

There's no risk of that happening, by the way. What boy my age would want to do that with a dwarf like me? It wouldn't be his groin he was pressing against my pussy, it would be his knee! So I'm sitting here on my sandy cushion, dressed as a witch, reading *Dangerous Liaisons*.

The campsite version.

Basile Spinello just dropped by to tell us to turn down the music a bit.

"Yes, Papa," Cervone, his twit of a son said.

I agree with Basile.

The music is pollution. Music being wasted like that, I mean, not the kind that goes directly from your ears to your brain along the wires of a Walkman. The music that goes off into the void, flies off into nature, polluting it just the way greasy food wrappers or cigarette butts do, or the gravel of the Roc e Mare marina. It's like a lack of respect for beauty, beauty that should never be disturbed or even shared. It should just be appreciated.

Alone.

Beauty is a secret. To talk about it is to violate it.

That's what Corsica is to me.

It should be loved and left in peace.

Basile has understood that.

And so has my Papé Cassanu.

And my father too, perhaps.

As soon as Basile left, his son turned the volume back up, the beat of the lambada thumping out once more.

There are about fifteen teenagers.

They don't even know La Mano or Nirvana; and what drives me mad is that in a year or two, they'll think those groups are brilliant because everyone will think they're brilliant.

I've got my notebook open, resting on *Dangerous Liaisons*, but no one can see it. I can write in peace. I've told myself that I would introduce you to the tribe today. You're going to have to follow me closely because it's a bit complicated. I'm going to give each member of the gang a letter, to keep things simple.

First of all there's my brother Nicolas, crouching beside the boom box. Let's call him Valmont, because he's handsome enough in his way and he's incredibly successful with the girls, the way he acts all cool and never seems to get angry with anyone. I even have a theory about that. If you like everyone, it means you don't really like anyone. So yes, I see my big brother Nicolas as Valmont, falling in love with all the girls in the world like an unhappy little angel, but unable to love only one.

Nicolas is N.

Beside him, the girl shaking her thing to *Billie Jean* is Maria-Chjara. I'll give you a detailed portrait of her later on, because that little flirt deserves a whole chapter to herself. But for now, just by way of introduction, let's think of her as the Marquise de Merteuil. The manipulative courtesan in the novel. I don't need to spell it out. You'll have guessed that I hate Maria-Chjara, but it would take me a whole sleepless night to line up enough words to tell you just how much.

Maria-Chjara is M.

The one dancing off the beat, alone, as alone as me, except that I don't show it, is Aurélia Garcia. You know her already: the killjoy. The policeman's daughter, oh dear, the music is too loud, oh dear, I'm calling my father, oh dear oh dear, the lambada my God my God, boys, no no no . . . She scratches her eyebrows, smiles stupidly and is probably dreaming of a Prince Charming who would see stars in the reflection of her braces . . . Good luck with that, old thing!

Aurelia is A.

There are other girls—Véro, Candy, Katia, Patricia, Tess, Steph—but I'll skip over them and move on to the boys, at least the ones who make me want to write mean things. The others, Filip, Ludo, Magnus, Lars, Tino, Estefan, are just normal, which is to say that they're handsome, they drink beer, they laugh at rude jokes and they eye up normal girls.

Which means they don't see me.

Estefan, with his fair hair in a ponytail and his southern accent, dreams of being a foreign aid doctor and working in Ethiopia; Magnus wants to shoot the fourth episode of *Star Wars*; Filip to take off from Cape Canaveral on board the *Columbia*; but even describing these hot guys is making me feel depressed, so let's move on.

So, on the boys' side there's Cervone Spinello, who is negotiating with my brother, trying to persuade him to turn up the music even louder. "I promise you, Nico, it doesn't matter, Papa won't say anything." I've already told you a bit about him. The jerk is sure that he's going to be manager of the campsite one day, so he's already behaving a little prince. The heir apparent, the king's oldest son. Generally speaking, the heir apparent is usually incompetent and a pedantic fool. The two things go together when you have power. Cervone is like that. Will be like that.

Cervone is C.

I'll finish with the cyclops. I call him that not because he roasts six at a time (hahaha) but because however long you look at him you will only ever see one of his eyes. So, Hermann the cyclops, always walking around in profile, and only ever looking in one direction. Towards Maria-Chjara.

If you see Maria-Chjara, you won't have to look for too long before spotting Hermann's profile turned in her direction. If Maria-Chjara were the sun, Hermann would only be tanned on one side. Even though Hermann is German, you have to admit that he can jabber away in French and English quite well. He must be a *kolossal* talent back home, the kind who's programmed to swot away and get full marks at school for ten months of the year and then to be a total misfit during the two months of summer.

Hermann is H.

Did you get all that?

I'll sum it up with a diagram of amorous geometry, a kind of dangerous liaisons for idiots. There is a circle, or rather two circles, with N (Nico) and M (Maria-Chjara) at their centre. The normal teens, the ones whose first names I've given you, are arranged in these circles. The girls in the circle N, the boys in the circle M.

A (Aurélia) and C (Cervone) would like to enter the circle. H (Hermann) would like to draw a straight line to M (Maria). But that's not the big question. The big question is: will the circles intersect, join, or be superimposed on one another?

$$N \cap M?$$
$$N \cup M?$$
$$N = M?$$

The answer is coming soon, don't hang up, whatever you do, we've moved from the lambada to a slow dance. Scorpion's guitars are weeping, swearing that they are "still loving you." I listen, I admire, Nico's cassettes are the very model of manipulation. He's programmed this slow dance to come right after "Wake Me Up," the bouncy rock track by Wham! The girls are drenched, their sweat running down their backs to their buttocks and their tops sticking to their nipples. Smart move, my bro!

I move back gently, almost into the darkness, I only need a little light to go on writing.

Couples form.

Steph with Magnus, Véro with Ludo, Candy with Fred, Patricia hesitates between Estefan and Filip, Katia waits for her friend to decide, it's the big summer supermarket. Serve yourself, it's on sale, hurry up, must end by the last day of August.

My buttocks retreat a few more centimeters towards the darkness. If one of these guys asks me to dance I'll tell him to fuck off. And cry about it until the morning.

No danger of that!

Handsome George Michael is back with "Careless Whisper."

In my dark corner I'm enjoying myself, I'm enjoying myself, I'm enjoying myself.

Are you listening to me, my trusted friend? I'm ENJOYING MYSELF! Like a little mouse in its hole.

The first circle has just parted, my Nico has just let go of Tess, a Swedish girl, without so much as glancing at Aurélia, who was holding her arms out to him. Maria-Chjara has just let go of handsome Estefan. The king and queen of the ball are finally about to meet.

Here it comes, the Marquise de Merteuil walks towards Valmont.

One step, two steps, three steps beneath the strings of coloured lights.

There are no circles now, just scattered teenage couples swaying to the weeping notes of a saxophone.

Just two dots coming together.

Maria-Chjara is wearing a white dress that changes colour as she walks with calculated slowness beneath each lightbulb in turn.

Blue yellow red blue yellow red blue yellow red

Nicolas is standing under the last red light, wrapped among the branches of an olive tree.

Blue yellow red blue yellow

She's less than ten meters away from Nicolas now, then suddenly Maria-Chjara stops.

Yellow

Perhaps she has sensed eyes upon her.

Maria-Chjara moves away from the lights, her dress now lit only by moonlight.

White

It's the last thing I expected. Maria-Chjara has turned her back on my brother and is presenting her bare arms, her clammy breasts, her wet waist that a boy's two hands could wrap around . . . to Hermann.

The cyclops can't believe his eyes.

12

August 14, 2016, 6:00 P.M.

T omorrow, *when you visit Arcanu Farm to see Cassanu and Lisabetta, please go and stand for a few minutes beneath the holm oak, before night falls, so that I can see you.*

Those few words, written in a hand so like her mother's, were going round and round Clotilde's head in a loop.

Faster and faster.

Tomorrow . . . so that I can see you . . .

She struggled against two contradictory feelings, impatience and fear, like the feeling a lover gets, both electrifying and petrifying, the night before a first tryst.

Tomorrow . . . the message said.

So in less than two hours now. They were invited that evening to Arcanu Farm, to have dinner with the grandparents. Who would there waiting for them? Who would see them?

Clotilde hesitated by the mirror in the shower block. Should she let her long black hair hang loose over her shoulders, or put it up in a tight chignon? She didn't dare consider the third option, of ruffling it up into a witch-like hedgehog the way she did when she was fifteen. Everything seemed muddled inside her head. She tried to concentrate and remember the details of her grandparents' farm, the dust of the big sunny yard, the giant holm oak that would surely still cast its shade, the sea hidden behind the baked clay buildings on the slope . . . but the next words of the letter were superimposed on these scraps of memory.

I will recognise you, I hope.
I would like your daughter to be there too.

Clotilde had asked Valou to make an effort, to put on a long skirt and a top that wasn't too low cut, to tie up her hair and avoid chewing gum and Ray-Bans. She had agreed grudgingly, without even trying to dispute the reason why she had to drop her tourist outfit to go and visit an eighty-nine-year-old great-grandfather and a great-grandmother of eighty-six.

The shower block was deserted but for Orsu, who was going around it with a mop. He moved slowly, picking up the huge bucket with his good arm each time he went to clean the next shower. Clotilde had noticed that he cleaned each block every three hours, the same rhythm with which he approached the other tasks he was charged with: watering the flowerbeds, sweeping, weeding, lighting. It was slavery!

Clotilde gave him a smile that he did not return. She was putting eye-liner on her eyes to give them a dark oriental depth, slightly gothic, perhaps, even if she refused to admit it, when two teenagers came in behind her.

With mud-encrusted trainers on their feet and cycling helmets in their hands, fluorescent protectors on their knees and elbows, they made straight for the toilets and came out a few moments later. They stared with disgust at the muddy trails they had left across the wet tiles. The taller of the two stopped, as if faced with impassable quicksand, then turned towards Orsu.

"It's filthy!"

The other one stepped forward carefully so as not to slip, avoiding the damp traces of soil and therefore dirtying another part of the floor.

"You're disgusting, Hagrid. Why don't you do the bogs first thing in the morning, or at night, when no one's around?"

The other one backed him up. He was thirteen at most, with a branded pair of underpants peeping out above his tight cycling shorts.

"That's right, Hagrid, that's how it works. At school, at my dad's office, even on the street. Taking the bins out, cleaning up shit, you do that when people are asleep or away."

The smaller one, twelve years old tops and wearing an XXL Waikiki T-shirt that fell past his bottom, added:

"That's how you do the job, Hagrid. It's about service, respecting your customer, having a sense of what the tourist wants. You see, Hagrid, the bogs have to be spanking clean and you've got to be invisible. The shit has to disappear as if by magic. We shouldn't even know you exist."

Orsu opened frightened eyes. Clotilde saw no hatred in them, only fear. Fear of these two little idiots, of what they might say, what they might report back. Perhaps even the fear of disappointing them.

Clotilde hesitated. In her younger days she would have gone in with her head lowered.

She gauged her reaction time at three seconds before turning towards the taller one. Three seconds. Before launching off she reflected that she hadn't really aged that much.

"What's your name?"

"Umm . . . Why?"

"What's your name?"

"Cédric."

"Cédric what?"

"Cédric Fournier."

"And you?"

"Maxime. Maxime Chantrelle."

"OK, well, we'll see about this later."

"You'll see about what, miss?"

"Whether I'm going to put in a complaint."

The two boys looked at each other uncomprehendingly.

Report this guy for not using the mop properly? That was crazy. They didn't want to go that far.

"Whether I'm going to put in a complaint about the harassment of an employee who is going about his duties, insults that constitute," here she rested her eyes on Orsu's stiff arm, "the abuse of authority towards a third party."

"Are you serious, miss?"

"Not miss. You can address me as *Maître. Maître* Baron, lawyer, IENA and Associates, Vernon."

The boys looked at each other again. Aghast.

"Let's get out of here!"

They vanished.

Again Orsu didn't return her smile. Never mind. Clotilde turned back to the mirror, proud of having put the wind up the little fools. She studied the bearded giant out of the corner of her right eye, the one already underlined in black. Orsu stood there for a moment, not moving, then plunged the mop back into his bucket and immediately took out another clean one.

Clotilde's black-lined eye froze, as if trapped; she was seized by a violent feeling of vertigo, and held on to the wall of the shower block with both hands, dropping her eye-liner into the sink.

She tried to steady her breathing, to calm herself, to rewind the scene she had just witnessed, watching Orsu's trivial gesture in slow motion. Throwing a dirty mop in the bucket and taking out a different, clean one.

Impossible, impossible, impossible.

The black drip from the eye-liner slid slowly towards the plughole, like a snake returning to its lair.

A trivial gesture.

Orsu had already turned his back on her and was using a stiff-bristled brush to erase the traces of the young idiots' footsteps.

An unreal gesture . . . from the other side.
She was going mad.

⤸

"You look lovely, Valentine . . . "

Cervone Spinello was standing by reception at the Euproctes campsite, holding his mobile phone, greeting people as they went in and out like a laid-back monitor watching kids coming and going from school. His wife, behind the counter, was talking in perfect English to some Scandinavian tourists who had set rucksacks twice as heavy and bulky as themselves by the counter. Anika was tall, smiling, elegant; refined, attentive and very busy. She was both the heart and the lungs of the Euproctes campsite, its supplementary soul, its patron saint. Cervone was only the priest.

Valentine stopped and turned towards the manager of the campsite.

"Thank you."

She pointed to her hair, which was held back by a modest headscarf, and the long skirt that fell to her ankles, then murmured confidentially:

"I'm on duty. In two hours' time we're having dinner with the grandparents."

"Cassanu and Lisabetta? At Arcanu Farm?"

Valentine nodded with a mocking smile, and brought her hand to her hair to push a rebellious tendril back under the salmon-coloured cloth. She stared at the poster displaying the plans for the Roc e Mare marina.

"According to Maman, we're to avoid talking about your palace in front of Papé."

Behind them, Anika had got up to guide the Swedish girls, bent double under their luggage, around the free sites. Cervone put his phone in his pocket and took Valou by the shoulder, giving her a quarter turn so that she was facing a big map of Corsica. His finger traced across the Mediterranean then stopped in the middle of the big blue.

"You know what the third-largest Spanish airport is, after Madrid and Barcelona?"

Valou shook her head, unsure what Cervone was getting at.

"Palma! Palma de Mallorca. The capital of the Balearics. The Balearics, Valentine, five thousand square kilometers, a million inhabitants and ten million tourists. Half the size of Corsica and four times as many visitors. And let me tell you, the Balearics don't have a quarter of the advantages of our island—two beaches and three caves, a mountain no higher than one thousand five hundred meters." His finger went on running along the blue of the map. "So, Valentine, can you tell me why one island in the Mediterranean attracts people, creating jobs and wealth, and another gets nothing?"

"I . . . I don't know."

"You'll find out this evening. You won't have to ask any questions. You only have to listen to your grandfather."

"My great-grandfather."

"Yes, that's right. You know that Cassanu was one of my father's best friends?"

He turned towards the entrance to the campsite, raised his arms, and pointed his index finger towards the horizon.

"Look. Straight ahead of you."

Valentine examined the Revellata Peninsula, which stretched out into the sea like another huge finger, free of any jewellery.

"What do you see, Valentine?"

She hesitated.

"Nothing."

Cervone rejoiced.

"Exactly, nothing! Corsica is a paradise, one of the most beautiful islands in the world, a gift from heaven, and what have they done with it? Nothing! Look at this magnificent peninsula. What have they done with it? Nothing. Apart from confiscating it the way some old people stuff their treasure under the mattress. They've lost us fifty years. You know what the biggest business is here in Corsica?"

Valentine shook her head.

"Erm . . . No."

The campsite manager excitedly grabbed her arm.

"A supermarket! All the young people bugger off and yet we still have more than 10 per cent unemployment on the island. Because of those self-styled defenders of Corsica. All the exiles go off and work in Marseille or the region around Paris. Economic refugees who spend all year feeling depressed, pining to come back and spend a month in the summer with their family on the island, and crying all the tears of the Mediterranean when they leave again. Is that the way to help Corsica? Is that how they show their love for Corsicans?"

He looked over at the peninsula one last time, before his eyes came back to rest on the poster pinned up in reception.

"The Roc e Mare marina," he explained. "An old, aborted project that has been taken back out of its cardboard box. It took me years to be able to buy that land. It will provide thirty permanent jobs once the work is finished. Three times that in the summer."

Cervone stroked Valentine's cheek.

"This isn't an empty promise, there'll be a job for you. You deserve it, you're an exile too. And not just any old exile. You're the heiress." He came close to her ear, almost whispering. "And I promise, this time your great-grandfather won't say anything about it."

Valentine tried to move away, but he held her back with a slight pressure on her shoulder.

"Everyone here is afraid of Cassanu. Even today. He's the boss."

At last he let her go, then blew on his hands and wiggled his fingers as if scattering magic dust before continuing.

"Everyone here is afraid of Cassanu Idrissi. Everyone but me. Because let me tell you something: I've cast a spell on your Papé. My will is his command."

⁀

The viscous line of eye-liner had almost disappeared down the plughole, leaving only the faintest trace, like the trail left by a slug. Clotilde tried to get a grip on herself. Supporting herself on the rim of the basin she could see Orsu's reflection in the mirror as he worked behind her. After cleaning the toilets further away, he resumed his ritual.

Dropping the dirty mop-head into the foaming water and taking out the one that had been soaking there for several minutes. Squeezing it out with his one good hand and pressing it between his knees. Fixing it onto the mop handle.

Clotilde closed her eyes.

The image hadn't gone away. It was there, very familiar: a bucket, a mop, a wet floor.

Except that it wasn't the shower block of the campsite, it was the kitchen of the house in Tourny, in Normandy, where Clotilde had spent the first fifteen years of her life.

Except that it wasn't Orsu who was leaning on his mop-handle, it was her mother.

Palma had taught them her technique as if it were an old family secret. She'd taught her son Nicolas, her husband, even though he wasn't very concerned with household tasks, and her daughter, Clotilde. Her.

Using two mop-heads to clean, always leaving one to soak while you were making the other one dirty. And then swapping them, to avoid having to squeeze the mop until the black liquid turned pale grey. And old technique inherited from who knows where which had become a family habit, the natural way of doing things, almost a ritual.

Orsu knew that ritual; he practised it. Clotilde opened her eyes and forced herself to think rationally.

Orsu was using this technique like the hundreds of thousands of other men and women in the world who did the housework and also knew the same trick. She had to be careful not to lose her head, not to be sucked in by ludicrous coincidences. She had to control herself, leave as little room as possible for emotion, as she did when she had to conduct an investigation into a case that moved her, securing alimony for a woman who had been left alone with her children, persuading the husband to sell the house that he had built with his own busy little hands in order to divide the sum into two decent households, and then negotiate joint custody.

She had to concentrate.

That evening, over dinner with her grandparents at Arcanu Farm. She had to suppress her emotions and ask the right questions.

Tomorrow, when she met Cesareu Garcia. Clotilde had spoken to the retired policeman on the phone a few hours ago, but he had refused to say anything more. "Tomorrow, Clotilde, tomorrow. Not over the phone. Come here tomorrow, whenever you like. My house is in Calenzna. I'm not going anywhere. I never go anywhere."

Orsu limped out of the shower block with his bucket and mop. Clotilde still couldn't calm herself down, try as she might. Apart from the alarming coincidence of those two mops (the incident would have made all her friends explode with laughter, she told herself in an attempt to play it down), she still felt the insults that the boys had hurled at Orsu as if they were dagger blows. The mere fact that they had called him Hagrid made her see red. Perhaps it was just down to his disability, the fact that Cervone was exploiting him, here in this setting, on this island, among these people that she had once idolised.

Clotilde looked at her watch.

They were expected at the farm in less than an hour.

Someone was waiting there for her. Someone who hoped to recognise her.

Pulling a face in the mirror which she hoped was that of a sulky and slightly rebellious teenager, she ran through the lines of the message in her mind. Like a prayer. Like instructions that you would give to a spy, something she had to learn by heart because it was a matter of life and death.

I ask nothing else of you. Nothing at all.

Or perhaps just that you raise your eyes to the sky and look at Betelgeuse. If you only knew, my Clo, how many nights I have looked at it and thought of you.

The timer switch in the shower block had just gone out, plunging the room into a faint gloom.

My whole life is a dark room.

Franck appeared in the doorway.
"Shall we go, Clo?"

Kisses,
P.

13

Monday, August 14, 1989, eighth day of the holiday.
Pinky-blue sky.

I t's me!
You remember, I dumped you with my teenagers, dancing
to the lambada.

You're not cross with me?

I say my teenagers because I include myself in the tribe,
even if I haven't given myself a letter.

M, N, A, C, H. Maria-Chjara and Nicolas, Aurélia, the
cyclops, Cervone, and all the others. The great business of love
stories. I assure you, you haven't missed a thing, nothing new
has happened, only timid attempts to approach one another.
I'll keep you posted if anything happens.

But perhaps you don't think my bouquet of flirtations is
very serious? Small fantasies that even those concerned will
have forgotten as soon as they become adults.

So I've been thinking about you, and I'm going to tell you
a complicated, unhappy, twisted love story, the kind you like.

A story about adults.

A man and a woman.

My father and my mother.

In fact, they'd been getting on quite well since the start of
the holidays, which isn't to say that things are usually bad
between them, but they aren't all that good either. Let's just say
they're a bit nothing. Papa comes home late, Maman waits for
him, they talk about the things that need to be done in the
house, the next day's shopping, or the fact that the bins need to
be put out; sometimes they go out together, and they probably

make love when that happens. But since the beginning of the holidays things have been going better, as far as I can tell: a little kiss on the neck, a little "You're looking lovely, darling," a little bit of harmless laughter. If I had to choose, I would say that Papa's the one who's making the most effort to recharge the batteries of their libido. And then BAM!

Crash bang wallop. Disaster.

Let me explain. Papa and Maman met in Corsica a lifetime again. Maman was travelling around the island on a motorbike with her friends. Papa lived there with his parents at Arcanu Farm, overlooking the peninsula. I don't know any of the details of their romance, I just know that they met here, on the Revellata, on August 23, 1968, Saint Rose's day.

So every August 23 is the anniversary of the day they first met. That day Papa dutifully goes off and buys a bouquet of flowers—depending on the year, red roses that symbolise passionate love, white roses symbolising pure love, orange roses symbolising desire. But none of them, according to family legend, is as lovely as the bunch he collected for Maman that first summer, a bouquet of eglantine, the free, wild rose that Maman loves so much. *Rosa canina.*

Every year, on August 23, for as long as I can remember, Papa and Maman have given themselves a break and have spent the evening at the Casa di Stella, the best restaurant between Calvi and Porto, with a romantic terrace set under olive trees, a charcoal grill, braised Corsican veal, grilled fillet of grouper, free-flowing Casanova muscat. You can get there on foot via a steep path above Arcanu Farm. They sleep there, in the gîte, I assume they book a double room, with a roughly carved wooden bed, a marble basin on the table, an old-style bath in the middle of the room, and a huge bay window that gives you a view of the Great Bear. At least that's how I imagine it. To tell you the truth, I think I'd love a lover of mine to take me up there, to the Casa di Stella, the house of stars . . . Please let that happen, tell me that will happen to me one day?

End of parenthesis.

My parents' marital bliss on the balcony overlooking the Milky Way, that was before.

This year, KA-BOOM.

It started with the posters that were stuck all over the campsite and along the road. A concert of Corsican polyphonic music. August 23, at 9 P.M. The group is called A Filetta, apparently they're very well known. They tour all over the world, and here they were, performing close by, at the chapel of Santa Lucia, in an almost abandoned village—Prezzuna, above Galéria.

Papa's approach was rather heavy-handed.

Uno: I slow down as we pass the posters.

Deuzio, I tell you they're the best group on the planet, and play their cassettes on a loop.

Tertio: I hint, I outline, I suggest in passing to Mama Palma that we could celebrate our anniversary on a different day, the day before Saint Rose's day, or the day after. Saint Fabrice or Saint Bartholomew's day.

As I said, KA-BOOM.

Mama Palma didn't even say no, she just said, "If you want."

The worst possible answer! Since then you should see her face. She's like the rose in the jar in *The Little Prince*. Straight, proud, annoyed. All thorns sticking out.

My mother is a terribly proud flower.

So ever since that moment, we've been in a state of great suspense. Broadly speaking, I can see two options.

The first is that Mama Palma will make Papa feel guilty enough to give up his concert. Even if I'd never tell him, even under torture, I'm actually on Maman's side on this one. Female solidarity carries its obligations.

The second option, Papa doesn't give in and we find ourselves in a cold war, at least until we get to the ferry, and maybe even after that.

Two options, and as I'm writing this I can also glimpse a third possibility, even worse than the other two, which is that they involve me and Nicolas in their row. Papa getting really annoyed in turn, going on and on about the family, about getting in touch with our roots, about opening ourselves up to Corsican culture and raging against the bubblegum nonsense on the radio, and singing that chorus he likes so much, turning up the sound of a guitar and the voices of A Filetta.

This may seem like a pointless story, almost comical in its obsession.

But do not laugh, my future reader.

We Idrissis are a stubborn bunch.

The fate of our family will be decided on the evening of the twenty-third of August . . . and all for something so stupid.

* * *

Something so stupid, he said again.

Four people dead.

Three men and a woman.

Over something stupid.

14

Franck drove slowly. Not because he was afraid of getting lost, given that there was only one road that climbed through the mountains towards Arcanu Farm, but because with each new bend the chasm gnawing at the side of the tarmac became a little deeper.

Clotilde, sitting in the passenger seat, head against the glass, saw neither asphalt nor barrier, just the void, the car door was like a window onto nothingness, a cabin floating in the sky, connected from one peak to the next by an invisible cable. A cable that could break at any moment.

Arcanu Farm was even further up. It could be reached directly by a path, in less than five hundred meters, but the road twisted and turned for almost three kilometers.

"Keep going," Clotilde whispered to Franck. "You can't miss it, it's the only house."

Franck drove the car straight on, along the narrow asphalt road, passing the only signpost: Casa di Stella, 800 meters. The wooden sign stood in the middle of a small unpaved car park with several hiking paths leading off it. Valentine had lowered the back window: the car was filled with the scent of pine and the changing smells of the *maquis*. Thyme, rosemary, wild mint.

Images flooded into Clotilde's mind, each new bend in the road revealing a new landscape, and yet each one was so familiar: a huge Corsican pine standing almost the height of a man above the other trees, the ruins of an old chestnut mill overlooking a pebbly riverbed, a solitary donkey grazing the grass of an unfenced meadow. Nothing had changed here in thirty years, as if the inhabitants had made a special effort to keep things as they always were. Or had abandoned the place once and for all.

Apart from the Idrissi family.

Three bends further up they saw their first human being. An old woman was walking along the side of the road, on the side of the mountain, bent over and dressed in black, as if she bore the mourning of a whole village that had toppled into the void, leaving her as sole survivor. Franck slowed down and pulled over towards the edge of the chasm. Probably not enough. The woman initially gave them a dark look, as if amazed that any strange car should venture all the way up here. When they had overtaken her, Clotilde looked in the rear-view mirror and saw the old woman pointing at them and muttering insults under her breath. Unless she was delivering some kind of evil incantation. In that moment, Clotilde suddenly felt sure that the witch hadn't mistaken them for lost tourists venturing on to her territory; she knew them, she had recognised them, and her gestures and curses were directed at them.

At her.

The witch disappeared from sight as they rounded the next bend.

A few hundred meters further on, after a slight ledge, a gravel track on the left led to the vast yard of the farm. New images emerged from Clotilde's album of memories and floated in front of her eyes. Arcanu Farm, which everyone referred to only as "the farm," or sometimes "the sheepfold," consisted of three grey stone buildings forming an open U above the slopes of La Balagne: a farmhouse where the Idrissis lived, a barn and a huge shed where the animals slept. All the windows on the north side gave people, goats and sheep a panoramic view over La Revellata and the Mediterranean. In the middle of the farm, the huge stone yard was coloured only by a few wild rose hedges and beds of wild orchids, Mamy's favourite flowers, giving the impression that nothing else could grow in the shade of the three-hundred-year-old oak tree planted at the heart of the property.

Clotilde turned to look towards the barn. The bench was still there. The severed tree trunk where she had listened to music on the evening of August 23, 1989, La Mano Negra wailing in her ears, the notebook open on her knees, before Nicolas had called her.

Clo, everyone's waiting for you. Papa's not going to . . .

Strangely, amongst all the bubbles that rose up from the past it was the memory of her notebook abandoned on that bench that had taken the longest to burst. Who had picked it up? Who had opened it? She hardly remembered the words, the phrases, anything that she had written at the time; she just remembered her intentions, which were often mean, cynical, cruel. Before she met Natale, at least. If anyone had found that notebook, they would have thought she was the most awful bitch! She would have loved to read it again now. Her worst fear, that summer of '89, was that her father or her mother would find it. That they would read it. At least she had escaped that embarrassment. Anyone could have violated her intimacy by diving into the lines of her private notebook, after the accident, after she went back to the mainland—anyone but her parents.

Cassanu and Lisabetta were waiting on the doorstep. Even though Clotilde hadn't seen them for twenty-seven years, they didn't seem much older than they were in her memories. She had always remained in regular contact with them; the odd postcard, a birth notice, some photographs, always accompanied by a few words. Nothing more than that. Her paternal grandparents had long ago stopped setting foot on the mainland, and it had taken Clotilde a long time before she had the courage to return to the site of the accident.

It was Lisabetta who kissed them, hugged them and held them tightly. Not Cassanu, who merely shook hands with Franck, first of all, and then greeted Clotilde and Valou.

It was Lisabetta who invited them in, told them to make themselves at home, who came out with an uninterrupted flood of words, not Cassanu, who already seemed weary of conversation.

It was Lisabetta who showed them around the farmhouse, a succession of rooms with the same dry stone walls and huge exposed beams, not Cassanu, who waited for them, sitting at the table under the pergola in the farmyard.

Other faded images hovered in the fog of Clotilde's memory. The cupboards under the wooden staircase where she had played hide-and-seek with Nicolas every summer; a huge fireplace that she had never seen lit, but where she imagined they could have roasted a whole shark; the view over the sea from each window on every floor, and her mother calling to her not to lean out; the attic as high as a cathedral where they had taken refuge with cousins or local children, furnishing it with blankets, mattresses and sheets attached to the beams with drawing pins. A palace for ghosts, or a place for cuddles.

The real photographs, those framed on the walls, weren't there twenty-seven years ago. Clotilde recognised Cassanu, Lisabetta, Papa, sometimes in close-up. She recognised herself too, and Nicolas—she in her christening dress and her brother as a first communicant. In another photo they were both climbing a Genovese bridge above a waterfall. She had no memory of the place or the year when the photograph was taken, but she didn't care, she just allowed herself to be submerged in the emotions it evoked.

There wasn't a single photograph of her mother.

Not one.

In some photographs, on the other hand, mostly hidden behind Cassanu and Lisabetta, Clotilde recognised the claw-fingered witch, the one they had passed on the road leading up to the farm. A little further down, pinned on to the wall, she spotted some photographs she had sent years ago: her and Franck on the Rialto in Venice; Valentine on a tricycle; all three of them, hats on their heads, posing in front of Mont-Saint-Michel. Clotilde was hypnotised by the pictures, moving from one to the next, inviting the generations to meet inside her head.

It was Lisabetta who urged her to go and sit down because it was getting late. Papé seemed to be dozing in his chair when they came back out into the yard. When they were all seated under the pergola, it was Cassanu who spoke, however, while Lisabetta disappeared into the background, flitting between the kitchen and the terrace, cutting bread and pouring Corsican wine, bringing plates of ham and sausages and jugs of water.

The meal seemed endless. After rushing through their shared memories, the conversation seemed to flag, each subject eked out like a scarce resource. Clotilde couldn't help staring at the sun that was dipping down towards the sea like a huge clock fixed to the end of the table.

Tomorrow, when you visit Arcanu Farm to see Cassanu and Lisabetta, please go and stand for a few minutes beneath the holm oak, before night falls, so that I can see you.

Before nightfall . . .

The sky was turning red, and Clotilde's face was also flushed as she got to her feet. Lisabetta had just served the pudding.

"Excuse me. Excuse me, just for a moment," she stammered.

She took Valou's hand.

"Come with me, don't ask any questions. Come on. We'll only be a few minutes."

⌒

Franck and Cassanu had stayed at the table.

Lisabetta cleared the plates and cutlery with unusual speed, leaving the men with some glasses and a bottle of lemon liqueur, before mysteriously disappearing. Cassanu smiled and looked at his watch.

"Lisabetta will join us again in twenty minutes," the old man explained. "My wife is the perfect hostess, as I'm sure you've noticed. But she is willing to defy three generations of Corsican hospitality in order not to miss an episode of *Plus belle la vie . . .* "

The scene struck Franck as surreal. Hidden away, five hundred meters up, three kilometers away from the nearest house, in the heart of Corsica, watching a soap opera set in Marseille . . .

Life was strange indeed.

Cassanu was an intelligent man, astonishingly quick, and still seemed to be physically active. The kind of man he himself got along with. And the kind of man he would like to remain, despite the passing years. Straight, determined, intransigent if necessary; good, solid hands to lead a family, a square face behind which strong convictions were stored in an orderly fashion, and a hard skull to stop him from changing them.

Franck wet his lips with the lemon-flavoured drink and studied Clotilde, who was standing fifty meters away, with Valou, under the holm oak.

"I don't know what she's up to," he admitted to Cassanu.

His embarrassment sounded like an apology, but Cassanu seemed amused.

"She's going back to her childhood. Perhaps even further than that, to her roots. Clotilde has changed a lot since the last time I saw her."

Franck thought of the surreal photos of his wife as a teenager. Her hedgehog hair. The way she dressed like an undertaker. He imagined the goth rebel probably had some trouble blending in with the local environment back then.

"I suppose."

Cassanu raised his glass. Men together. As if this were some kind of initiation ritual into the Idrissi family.

"What do you do for a living, Franck?"

"I work in Evreux. A small town about an hour from Paris. I coordinate the parks department."

"Did you start out as a gardener?"

"Yes. I slowly climbed my way up, like some kind of wisteria, ivy or mistletoe . . . That's probably how my colleagues see me."

Cassanu looked again at Clotilde and Valou. He seemed pensive, perhaps thinking of his son who had also studied agronomy before ending up selling turf.

"You know why, about fifty years ago, I called this campsite, the first one in the whole north-west of the island, Les Euproctes?" the old Corsican went on.

"I've no idea."

"It might interest you. The euproctus is a small salamander, a species endemic to the island. It lives near water, under rocks, and likes to find quiet places to sleep during the day. It's now a protected species. Its presence is an indicator of the quality of the water, but not only that, it's also a measure of the peacefulness of a place, the absence of noise, of movement, of intrusion, a kind of balance, if you like. There used to be hundreds of euproctus around Arcanu and the campsite, all the way over to Revellata Bay."

"And now?"

"And now they're leaving . . . same as everybody else."

Franck hesitated, drank half his glass and then decided to test the old man a little.

"Surely not everybody? I have a sense that new things are being built around here. The campsite, the Roc e Mare marina."

Cassanu merely smiled. Nothing trembled, not his hands nor his voice.

"In seventy years, Franck, the price of land in this rocky corner overlooking the sea has gone up by eight hundred per cent. Since they announced the construction of the marina it has doubled again. Almost 5,000 euros per square meter. So yes, Franck, everybody's clearing off. And that will go on as long as Corsicans don't have residential status. For every individual who spends a fortune on an apartment in that marina and comes to live here for two months a year, there are thirty local young people who can't find a place to live. It's too expensive! Even if they're being given the option of diving into the water at the palace ten weekends a year."

Cassanu had raised his voice slightly. Franck didn't agree with the patriarch's line of reasoning. Corsica wasn't the only place to undergo property speculation. And the fine houses, the fine cars, the yachts and private jets, were the stuff of fantasy rather than a cause for complaint, even if he could never afford such luxuries himself.

But he didn't reply, he didn't want to have an argument with his wife's grandfather. The most powerful man in the district, from what people said.

He turned towards the holm oak.

"Are you coming back, Clo?"

"Yes, I'll be right with you."

On the horizon, the ball of fire gently fell into the Mediterranean.

Valou groaned.

"What are we doing, Maman?"

"We're waiting, just a bit longer."

"Until when?"

"Until it gets dark."

Ignoring her daughter's sighs, Clotilde slowly scanned the surrounding countryside again. Slightly elevated on the knoll where the oak grew, she had a three-hundred-and-sixty-five-degree view.

Go and stand for a few minutes beneath the holm oak, before night falls, so that I can see you.

Was the author of the message watching her . . . watching them, her and Valou?

Who?

Where?

There were a million places she could be seen from: anywhere at all on the mountain, which formed a huge amphitheatre to the east and the south; by anyone hidden in the *maquis* with a pair of binoculars. Unless the watcher were somewhere close by, behind one of the windows overlooking the yard, in the barn to her right, the shed to her left, or in one of the shepherds' huts scattered around the meadows that sloped gently towards the mountaign range.

It could be anybody.

Anywhere.

"Shall we go, Maman?"

The sun had drowned once and for all. It was hopeless; whoever the watcher was, they weren't going to reveal themselves. They might still be watching if they had a pair of infra-red goggles.

It was pathetic! She was going mad. Cassanu and Lisabetta must have been wondering what she was doing there and

Franck would curse her all evening for having abandoned him at the table with her grandfather.

"Yes, Valou, off you go."

In the mountains, towards the peninsula and along the Bay of Calvi, lights were coming on. Clotilde was just an ant in an apparently infinite field, frightened by the glow worms. A shadow suddenly passed by the entrance to the yard. It stopped and stared at her before disappearing into the darkness of the barn. Clotilde had just enough time to recognise the witch, the old woman who had cursed them on the road and who appeared in the photographs with Cassanu and Lisabetta.

A few stars already shone above the mountains, like shepherds' huts which had been inadequately bound to the earth and flown away.

I ask nothing else of you. Nothing at all.
Or perhaps just that you raise your eyes to the sky and look at Betelgeuse. If you only knew, my Clo, how many nights I have looked at it and thought of you.

Which of those stars was Betelgeuse? She had no idea.

Was someone, somewhere, really trying to contemplate the star at the same time as she was? Were they looking in the same direction in a kind of communion, like Saint-Exupéry looking for the Little Prince's asteroid?

Was it her mother?

It didn't make sense.

Move, Clotilde told herself. Go back and join Franck, apologise, talk a little more, then leave and forget it all.

The dog left the road and came into the yard just as Clotilde was about to descend from the knoll and return to the pergola. In the gloom she couldn't make out the exact colour of its coat, but the animal was as fat as a Labrador. A sheepdog, probably.

Clotilde liked dogs, as she liked animals in general. She wasn't afraid of them; in another life, she would have loved to be a vet. Besides, why be afraid of this dog that was running towards her? Cassanu would call off the great beast before it jumped up at her knees or slobbered over her dress. Her grandfather imposed his authority on every Corsican within a radius of thirty kilometers, so he wasn't about to be disobeyed by a dog.

But Cassanu Idriss didn't say a word, didn't make any kind of gesture.

As the dog approached the hand that Clotilde held out to him, a new shadow broke away from the entrance to the yard. A massive shadow, its arm raised towards the dog, giving precise orders.

Orsu!

A second later, Clotilde heard his voice.

"Stop, Pacha. Wait here, by my foot."

The dog froze and didn't touch her. It was a particularly gentle-looking dog, with humorous eyes that doubtless allowed it to run rings around the goats in its charge. Yet Clotilde's body slowly collapsed against the trunk of the oak, then, centimeter after centimeter, slid down, as though her legs could no longer carry her, until she found herself sitting trembling on the grass.

Pacha watched her in astonishment, hesitating about whether to lick her arm or her cheek, level with its muzzle.

"Pacha, heel," Orsu ordered again.

Pacha.

The name rattled around inside Clotilde's brain, but rather than belonging to a Labrador, it had belonged to a small mongrel of dubious pedigree that her mother had given her for her first Christmas. She had been less than a year old.

Pacha.

HER dog.

For the first seven years of her life, Clotilde had carried the dog in her arms, taken him for walks in her buggy, secretly stuffed him with squares of chocolate and sugar lumps. Pacha had gone everywhere with her, like a living toy that didn't leave her even at naptime or at night; who slept on her bed, who lay tucked up beside her on the back seat of the Fuego. Then one day Pacha had jumped over the fence and he wasn't there when she came back from school with Maman. He had never come back. She had never seen him again. She had never forgotten him either.

Orsu whistled, and at last the dog ran back towards his master.

Surely it was just a coincidence, Clotilde reasoned, trying to calm her crazed thoughts. Another coincidence. There must be thousands of dogs in France called Pacha.

The labrador was no more than ten years old. So it had been born many years after her family had died in the accident. Almost twenty years later. So why would anyone give it the same name as a mongrel from Normandy? A mongrel that had died in 1981? A mongrel that had never set foot in Corsica, since her mother's parents looked after it every year? A mongrel that Cassanu, Lisabetta and Orsu couldn't have known anything about?

Clotilde noticed that Franck was getting up under the pergola. Valou was sitting a little way off on the wooden bench, her fluorescent headphones in her ears.

"Shall we go, Clo?"

Like mother, like daughter, Cassanu and Lisabetta must have thought. At that moment her grandmother came out into the yard and hugged Orsu as if he were her son.

"Yes, let's go," said Clotilde.

It wasn't easy to refuse. It wasn't easy to linger. By standing alone under the oak like that, Clotilde had hardly demonstrated an acute sense of family.

My whole life is a dark room.

In *Beetlejuice*, young Lydia Deetz has the gift of being able to talk to ghosts. Perhaps Clotilde possessed that gift as well?

Before. When she was fifteen.

She had lost it now. She hadn't come into contact with a ghost that evening.

Apart from the ghost of her dog. Her mongrel.

Reincarnated as a Labrador.

15

Monday, August 14, eighth day of the holiday.
Forget-me-not-blue sky.

I admit it. I don't often write to you twice during the same day. I usually pick up my pen in the morning when everyone's still asleep, or in the evening, hidden in the Cave of Sea-Calves, by the light of my torch, being devoured by mosquitoes just for you, my reader in the stars.

This morning, you'll remember, I told you about the concert of polyphonic music instead of the anniversary meal at Casa di Stella. And Maman saying nothing. Nothing at all. Which was worse than anything. Nico and me watching the collateral damage.

Boom! The first bombs went off on the Island of Beauty.

Shall I tell you about it?

The whole of the holy Idrissi family had gathered this afternoon on Rue Clemenceau in Calvi, the big shopping street, for, what shall I call it? A game of poker? I think that life as a couple is pretty much that—a game of poker.

A game of bluffing.

Imagine a narrow street, on a slope, absolutely crammed, worse than Mont-Saint-Michel on an Easter weekend.

That's Calvi. This afternoon.

Maman is dawdling, waits, slows down, speeds up, always a bit ahead, or behind. Lingering just a little bit longer than usual in front of the shop windows. Just a little less chatty. While she's doing this, Papa is frying in the sun at the bottom of the steps that lead up to the citadel, killing time as best he can with Nicolas, taking a few photographs of the harbour below, admiring the yachts, eyeing up the Italian girls. Maman seems magnetised by a shoe shop. At last she regretfully drags herself away but stops again outside Benoa, a shop that sells Corsican clothes. They're really classy and original. Scraps of fabric that look as if they're worth a fortune, on plastic mannequins that don't necessarily have better figures than my mother.

I watch. The Cure is playing through my headphones. I listen to "Boys Don't Cry," "Charlotte Sometimes" and "Lovecats" on a loop. I don't care. My goal is up at the top.

I think it took us an hour to get to the ramparts, and Maman still wasn't saying a word. The first thing she did say was just before we got to the drawbridge at the entrance to the citadel, by the column which claims that Christopher Columbus was born here (sometimes the Corsicans really make me laugh!)

"Have you got the camera?"

Well spotted, Maman. The bag over Papa's shoulder is open. No trace of the Kodak around his neck. My father stammers and stupidly looks down the hill towards the steps at the bottom.

"Shit."

I love my Papa, but he's been asking for it since this morning. Maman shrugs as he runs back down the hill, with one eye on the tourists below to see if anyone is bending down to pick up a black object. Maman doesn't wait for him. She steps under the stone arch and turns to me by the door to the citadel.

"You wanted to go to Tao, Clo. So go!"

She walks on.

Tao it is, then.

At that moment, my puzzled reader, I should furnish you with two short lines of explanatory context: Tao is a restaurant-bar-nightclub at the very top of Calvi's Citadel. It's incred-

ibly famous! Incredibly hip! Incredibly busy! So I'm ahead of
you . . . For what stupid reason did *I* want to go and have a
grenadine or a *menthe à l'eau* in Tao?

Answer A: because the richest and cutest of the young arse-
holes on holiday in Corsica gather there?

Answer B: because it was there that the greatest balladeer
in the world, Jacques Higelin, wrote the most beautiful song in
the world, "La Ballade de chez Tao?"

I'll let you guess.

Onwards to Tao!

So, we're sitting at a circular table on our red mock-leather
seats when Papa comes back, breathless.

"Have you got it?" Maman asks.

She's ordered a piña colada.

"No, not a trace of it."

At that moment, normally, Maman would identify the make
of the camera, the month and the year when it was given to
him, and its emotional value—Maman has a bar code where
her brain should be.

Except that Nico speaks first.

"Are you sure, Papa, that it isn't in your rucksack?"

Then Papa searches through his rucksack, pushes our
glasses aside and empties the haphazard contents on to the
table: keys, pens, a book, a road map, cigarettes, a plastic bag,
until right at the bottom he finds . . . the camera!

"Was it in your bag all the time?"

Maman can't get over it. No danger of her apologising
either.

"I must say, it's such a mess in there."

Papa takes the blow. Maman sorts through the objects scattered on the table, the keys and the rest, until she's surprised
by the presence of a plastic bag, wedged between some sun
cream and a pair of sunglasses.

A Benoa bag.

She opens it, delicately unfolds the package and discovers, to her disbelief, a short dress with a V neck and a bare back; there are dozens of red roses printed on the black fabric. It's the very same dress that she'd stopped to look at! Papa had even slipped a matching ruby-coloured bracelet and a necklace into the package.

"Is this for me?"

Of course it's for you, Maman! And Papa's played an excellent trick on you, pretending to have forgotten his Kodak so he could run back and get it.

In the toilets Maman slips on the dress, and comes back out, the fine black straps disappearing against her bronzed shoulders; her breasts, her hips, her thighs swelling the light fabric (crêpe georgette, apparently—how can such a stuffy name become so exciting when it's worn by a sexy woman?). The barmen at Tao have all turned to look at Maman, even though they must have seen plenty of gorgeous women walking about in mini-mini dresses.

Before sitting down and crossing her bare legs under the table, Maman whispers, "Thank you." Not even a kiss on the cheek. Not even "You're a darling." Not even "You had me there."

God damn it!

She's a confident one, is Mama Palma.

Total mastery of the situation.

If a guy had pulled that on me, I would have cracked straight away and thrown myself at him, even if he'd done the most horrible things beforehand. But she doesn't, she just lets her eyes roam towards the concert posters stuck below the bar, and linger on the one showing the seven singers of the A Filetta group, with their black shirts and their hands on their ears.

Total mastery! Making yourself be desired.

Giving hope. Revealing a little, the bottom of a thigh, the

top of a breast, but keeping everything reined in. Remaining cool-headed. Freezing your feelings. Never giving yourself entirely. Never opening up completely. Forcing the other party to bet, and constantly raising the stakes.

Life as a couple—a game of poker.

Oh, my future reader, I will never be any good at playing it! I'll be trounced by the first handsome guy who comes along. I don't have that confidence the other girls have, that certainty that I'll be the one pulling the strings, working the controls, dangling the guys like puppets.

I'm not like Mama Palma, or Maria-Chjara, because I'm going to have to talk to you about her again, something else has happened.

Anyway, I loved Papa even more after that trick he pulled with the Benoa dress.

But I admired Maman . . . You won't tell anyone, will you? Promise?

I'd be too ashamed if she read that.

So I'll give you my prognosis, right now, for Saint Rose's day, for the evening of 23 August.

Corsican polyphony or a romantic meal at Casa di Stella?

I'm betting everything on Mama Palma!

* * *

He looked up and stared at the stars.

Of course. Of course, everything would have been so different if Palma Idrissi had won.

16

C alvi hadn't changed, that was the first thing Clotilde thought. The same granite citadel overlooking the bay, the same villages clinging to the coast, the same train from the beach to L'Ile Rousse.

Calvi just had more tourists than she remembered. There was a striking contrast between the Euproctes campsite, lost in the *maquis*, Arcanu Farm in the midst of the mountains, and the crowd rammed in along the shore, the families driving round and round in overheated car parks before deciding to go and park somewhere further away and return on foot; that tide of humanity coursing down the little streets like lava, flowing from the citadel and spreading out along the quays, the terraces, the beaches. As if receiving millions of visitors had done nothing to change the island's innate peace, the tranquillity of the areas that had been preserved intact; as if the summer invasion wouldn't trouble Cassanu or the other people who loved the wild Corsica, because the more tourists there were, the more they crammed themselves into the same spots.

Normally Clotilde didn't like crowds, but that afternoon she found them reassuring. Numbers meant anonymity. Noise imposed on silence.

Since last night she had done a lot of talking. About herself. About her family. With Franck, first of all, on the road back to the Euproctes campsite. Clotilde had hated the faint hint of victory in his smile. Admit it, Clo, you might have stood there under that oak tree with Valou for ages, leaving me on my own with your grandfather, but no one came. Your mysterious correspondent stood you up.

Yes, Franck, of course, do go on . . . No flying saucer landed in the yard, no ghost rose up from the ground, there was nothing, nothing but me and my daughter looking out at the empty mountain.

Clotilde hadn't even dared to broach the subject of the new coincidence that obsessed her, and for which she could find no logical explanation.

Pacha.

The name of Orsu's dog.

The name of her own dog. Her childhood dog.

A name which—if she pursued her line of reasoning without someone getting in the way and saying, "But it's impossible, my dear"—had been given to this dog ten years ago by someone who had known Pacha. Who had loved him. Had mourned his death. And since it wasn't her, there could only be one possible explanation.

Only her mother could have named this dog Pacha.

Less than ten years ago. Almost twenty years after the accident, twenty years after she died.

It's impossible, my dear!

Franck had parked the car by the lowered barrier of the campsite and kissed Clotilde on the cheek, holding her in his arms for a moment. There was nothing affectionate in the gesture, she had thought—just a respectful hug between two players after a game of tennis. Was their life as a couple reduced to a competition? One set to Franck.

If Clotilde had hated his condescension, that politeness that a boss uses with an inadequate underling, she had been even less enamoured of Cervone Spinello's smile that morning at reception. When she had approached him, he was putting up a poster advertising an eighties night on Oscelluccia beach.

"Can I get you a coffee, Clotilde?"

No, thanks.

"Your daughter is gorgeous, Clo."

Bastard!

"She reminds me of your mother, she has class, her . . . "

One more word and . . .

Clotilde had calmed herself down. Thanks to her job as a lawyer she had gradually learned to control her impulses, to confront the worst moments of the worst trials, when a client's lack of honesty stretched the limits of the defensible, and yet they still had to be defended. Clotilde had spoken to Cervone with a view to obtaining some precise information. She had no complaints on that score; the manager of the campsite had given her the information she requested, with professional precision. She'd wanted to know more about Orsu.

Orsu was an orphan, apparently. Born to a single mother who had died of exhaustion, loneliness and shame, then brought up by his grandmother, Speranza, the black-clad old witch they had bumped into yesterday on the road and then again at the farm. Speranza had always worked at Arcanu Farm, she took care of the cooking and the housework, feeding the animals and collecting chestnuts. She was almost part of the Idrissi family and Orsu had grown up there, tied to her apron-strings.

Delving as deeply as she could into her childhood memories, Clotilde had managed to remember, on the days spent at the farm with Nicolas, a shadow bringing them dishes, sweeping the floor, picking up their toys. She also remembered a baby, a few months old, who almost always lay motionless in the shade of the oak, surrounded by battered soft toys and dirty, discoloured plastic animals. A silent baby, scrawny and strange.

Orsu?

Had that feeble little thing managed to turn into this giant, this ogre, this bear?

After the boy had turned sixteen, Cervone had hired Orsu to work at the campsite, because no one else wanted him, and certainly not the school. Out of the goodness of his heart. Out of his friendship with Cassanu. Out of pity, yes, if you like, Clo, out of pity, that's exactly it, if you want to call a spade a spade.

Pity.

The bastard!

Clotilde didn't have the strength to vary the insults spat out by her brain. It was saturated with astonishingly precise memories that burst into her mind with each new bend in the road, each encounter, each conversation, colliding with everything she had experienced since the previous day, as if some unmentionable truth were lurking behind everything, a truth that she hadn't been able to grasp back in 1989, when she was fifteen years old.

Twenty-seven years later, she strode impatiently down Rue Clemenceau. The swarming crowd on Calvi's main shopping street calmed her, and she tried to lose herself in the window of the Lunatik shoe shop, lingered over the necklaces in Mariotti, the dresses in Benoa. Other images swam back to the surface, a vague impression of having experienced this same scene before. Then the veil was torn down and she could see the film clearly: the street in Calvi, her mother lingering in front of the shops just as she was doing today, her father giving her the black dress with the red roses and the ruby jewellery that she'd gone crazy about.

The pieces she'd been wearing on the day of the accident.

Only today did Clotilde understand the full extent of her father's gesture, giving his wife the outfit in which she would die, her finery for the afterlife, the most alluring attire for their last loving gaze. Wasn't that the greatest proof of love? Choosing together the outfit for one's death the way you would choose the clothes for your wedding.

Clotilde spent so long outside Benoa that Valou caught up with her. Clotilde didn't often go shopping, even less so with her daughter. But through the miracle of the holidays, she now found herself with her daughter, gazing at the same charcoal dress, like accomplices excluding the man of the family from their game. Franck was waiting ten meters further on, leaning against the wall of the Saint Marie churchyard. This was so unlike them—Papa playing football with the boy, Maman going shopping with the girl. At least that was one advantage of having an only child, Clotilde thought; making that pernicious gender parity impossible.

The stream of tourists continued to struggle up the slope towards the citadel, in search of shade (in spite of the crowds, no one had yet thought of putting in some kind of lift). Once past the drawbridge, Clotilde hesitated for a moment. She thought about suggesting to Franck and Valentine that they could all go and have a drink at Tao, but immediately dismissed the idea as ridiculous: this pilgrimage along the footsteps of her youth had its limits, and Valou had probably never even heard a song by Jacques Higelin. Instead, Clotilde preferred to lose herself in the labyrinth of the streets in the citadel. She also lost Franck.

He joined them nineteen minutes and seven texts later, on the terrace of A Candella, a little square shaded by olive trees with a panoramic view over the harbour. When Clotilde saw Franck appearing along the ramparts, in front of the Tour de Sel, his hand behind his back clumsily concealing his Benoa bag, she forgot for a moment the sequence of mysteries dancing the devil's salsa all around her. Franck had turned back to go to the clothes shop. Running back down two hundred meters. Just as her father had done.

As a girl, she remembered not being able to resolve her conflicting emotions: pride at her father's attentiveness, admiration for her mother's elegant charm, and jealousy like a large hat, casting its shadow over everything. Back then she had dreamed, she now realised, of playing the same game. Of being the consenting victim to a husband's playfulness. She hadn't done badly, in the end. Franck could still surprise her, some-times.

Knowing how to surprise your partner, Clotilde thought, was the number one key to a lasting relationship. Even though Franck had done it less discreetly than Papa, with less theatre, less imagination, supplying no explanation for his hurried departure, and holding the Benoa bag clumsily behind his back.

Don't be too picky—the second key to a lasting relation-ship.

Franck pushed the glasses of grenadine aside and set the bag down on the table.

"For you, my darling."

His darling, the one to whom Franck presented the bag, was Valou.

"I'm sure it will look gorgeous on you, my lovely girl."

Total eclipse. A storm could have fallen on the citadel, a tsunami could have carried away all the yachts moored in the harbour, a gust of wind could have ripped away all the parasols and flags . . .

The bastard! The total and utter bastard!

Clotilde was still raging in silence when Valou came back from the toilet, the charcoal dress hastily slipped over her swimming costume. It was sexy, figure-hugging, perfect.

"Thank you, Papa. I love you."

Valou kissed her Papa with conviction. Clotilde took the blow. They should have had two children, an only child was nonsense, a trap for any couple. Yes, two kids, one each.

Having your own daughter steal away your man was rock bottom.

What a shitty life! She felt murderous.

Valou had got up and was standing by the parapet, holding her camera, the teeming Bay of Calvi behind her. A selfie to make her friends envious! A present from my darling little Papa.

It was surreal. What a shitty life shitty life shitty life.

And that fool Franck still smiling as he gazed at their daughter, putting his hand under the table as if stealthily giving his balls a good scratch.

And then, who took out another Benoa bag!

"For you too, my darling."

The bastard. The adorable bastard!

Of course Franck wasn't a match for her own father, back then, that trick with the camera, but his double bluff was still pretty good.

Clotilde felt heartbroken. Why did she have to be so vulnerable?

Don't be picky.

Make yourself voluptuous, moist, sensual.

Kiss your man without restraint.

Don't be picky . . .

Silence that little voice that was telling her, over and over again, that everything was happening exactly as it had twenty-seven years ago. The same place, same story, same family scene. That dress her husband had just given her, just as her father had given one to her mother all those years ago . . . perhaps it would be the one she would die in.

A few hours later, back at the campsite, alone in the shower block without even Orsu mopping up or some teenagers to yell at, Clotilde slipped on the dress and looked at herself in the mirror. It was quite obvious. Even if she had to wear that dress on the last day of her life, she would never make as sexy a corpse as her mother had.

The stretchy fabric sagged where her breasts failed to fill it out, it floated around her undistinguished hips, covering her short thighs all the way to the knee.

She definitely wasn't a match for her mother.

And Franck wasn't a match for her father.

They had died too soon to bring her up. Bring her up in the purest sense, up to their level.

Why?

Why had they died?

Perhaps she would find out tomorrow.

Cesareu Garcia, the retired policeman who hadn't wanted to tell her anything over the phone, wanted to see her the following morning. "You've been waiting for the truth for twenty-seven years, Clotilde," he had said before hanging up. "You can wait a few more hours."

Tuesday, August 15, 1989, ninth day of the holiday.
Sky beached jellyfish blue.

Hello, hello? Alga beach here, live.

Each to their own towel.

Mine is black and flame-red with rows of pretty little white crosses, and I can tell you that finding a Metallica *Master of Puppets* beach towel is no mean feat! Nico's is a bright red towel with the yellow Ferrari logo, about as tacky as Maria-Chjara's, which is a bright orange sunset with the shadow of a palm tree and a naked couple embracing. Hermann's, placed between Nico and Maria-Chjara's, is black and white with a giant B and an unpronounceable name running across it. *Borussia Mönchengladbach*—as glamorous as it gets! But you have to give the cyclops his due, he's swift and responsive, because he wasn't the only one who wanted to put his towel down next to the beautiful Italian girl's. Towels on the beach are like desks in a classroom. You elbow your way through until you've found the right one, next to the right person.

I don't care. As usual I sit apart from the others, a bit further along the beach, on the edge of the shade cast by the pine trees, my knees and buttocks tucked under my big T-shirt. From my position I can see the whole of the beach, I can make out all the different shades of blue in the water, which becomes ridiculously transparent when you dive into it; the incredible flashes of turquoise among the deep blue of the clumps of posidonia. Not to mention the whole ecosystem of human beings to observe.

If I look towards the Revellata headland, I can still see the ruins of the Roc e Mare marina that was blown up three days ago. Still no news of the investigation into the explosion. I even tried grilling Aurélia, the policeman's daughter, but to no avail! Besides, she still annoys me, wandering about the beach looking so superior, fully dressed just like me. I hate the fact that people might think we look like each other. That I have anything in common with this girl who stalks the sand as if she were on duty, as if the whole beach belonged to her, as if there were a time limit on the towels and she was in charge, checking the little kids filled in the holes made by their sandcastles before they left the beach, spying on everyone with her falcon eyes. Before reporting everything to her father.

I'm not like her, please tell me I'm not! I'm the opposite of Aurélia, you agree, don't you?

I don't judge people.

I don't condemn.

I just analyse, I learn. I document the pleasures that are still forbidden to me.

I store them up, in theory at least. For later on. When I'm grown-up.

Opposite me, Maria-Chjara has turned over her caramel-coloured skin on her orange towel and is blindly stretching a hand out towards Hermann, as if she didn't know who was lying next to her on the beach, and didn't care. In her hand there is a tube of sun cream. Not one word, not a look. Only a gesture, an explicit gesture of undoing the zip on the back of her bathing costume and pressing her big breasts against the towel, hiding her nipples in the cloth. Just like Maman, who's a little way off with her friends from the campsite. Parents on one side, teenagers on the other; that's the law of the beach.

Mama Palma always brings her big bag, her bottle of water,

her big book that she never leaves without; she must have got to page twelve, I checked, and the bookmark hasn't moved in a week.

Papa isn't here. He hates the beach. He's probably hanging out at Arcanu, with his father, his cousins, his friends, all the Corsicans together . . . In previous years, Papa did make an effort to put his feet in the sand—he would kick a ball about with Nico, build a castle with me (OK, that was a long time ago), dive into the water and sleep for an hour holding Maman's hand.

But not this summer! Maman and Papa are still sulking over the concert on Saint Rose's day; it's as if he's cross with Maman, or Maman hasn't got over it yet. If I ever have a lover one day, I hope I don't end up like them.

I turn my head. The beach is a theatre, a ten-thousand-square-meter stage with hundreds of actors, of all ages and every colour.

My eyes come to rest on a young couple. One towel for the two of them.

I want to be like them!

The couple look like dozens of others. So happiness isn't that hard to achieve. You just have to be twenty years old, which happens to everyone. You just have to look beautiful with your clothes off, which almost everyone is when they're twenty, particularly when they have a suntan. A boy and a girl, gazing into one another's eyes and holding hands, and caressing one another, and admiring each other's bums when they get up to go for a swim, and smiling at each other, and even laughing, paying attention to one another. They must be vaguely aware that you shouldn't spoil those moments because they're the best in your life and you won't get them back. So you savour them, you fall in love, you love each other, it's as simple as that.

My eye wanders back up the beach the way you wander back in time.

I find what I'm looking for. A couple in their thirties.

He's not bad looking, athletic, on all fours, almost buried in the huge sand pit that he's digging with his creamed and hatted children, aged about two and four. He looks as if he's loving it, even more than the children. She is reading distractedly, and every now and again she looks up and observes them. Happily. She adjusts the hat of the fair-haired little boy, holds out a cool bottle with a nipple on it, swats away a fly.

She's on guard.

Each of her gestures is sexy. You sense that she's where she's always wanted to be. She's achieved what she wanted to achieve. The apogee. The peak.

She's keeping watch.

Because all that she owns—her devoted husband, her well-behaved children, her fine body—she wants to keep.

As if it could all last forever.

You're dreaming, my dear!

My eyes slip away again, I'm spoiled for choice, and I settle a few meters further along.

They are forty. Maybe fifty.

She's reading, really reading. Concentrating. The last few pages of a giant doorstop. Beside her, he's getting bored. He's not bad—tall, greying, something powerful in his expression. But he's looking elsewhere. On a beach there's no shortage of pretty things to look at.

Or I take another couple. The same, same age, but the other way around. He's lying on his side, back to the sun, in the shade of a parasol, his slightly paunchy belly sliding under him like a deflated balloon. Beside him, still gorgeous, she's getting bored. Slender, elegant; wearing make-up, nicely turned out. She looks elsewhere. Her eyes come to rest on some children playing in the distance. Hers must be too old; or not old enough to have given her grandchildren. She's bored, resigned to waiting like this for the rest of her life.

It's a long downhill slope, my darling . . .

Time passes. My eyes wander. I search for a long time before I find the rare specimens I'm looking for.

They're about seventy, maybe eighty. I can't hear what they're saying, but they're talking to each other, that much is certain. He must be asking if she's not too hot, she must be asking if he wants his book, his glasses, his cap. And then all of a sudden they get up.

I don't like their naked bodies. If my skin was as wrinkled as that, with the bones looking as though they're piercing it, the heavy flesh sagging at the chin, the neck, the belly, the buttocks, I'd go into hiding.

My hands twist in my T-shirt.

I'm fascinated by those two old people, holding hands as they wade into the water, not even pausing before they go in, not even shivering at the waves' cold bite, pressing their lips against each other for a moment, and then setting off towards the sailing-boats doing an impeccable and coordinated crawl.

"You're watching old people now?"

I look up.

It's Cervone. Cervone Spinello. Bermuda shorts, Hawaiian shirt, trainers. I've never seen him in a swimming costume before. I've got the whole beach to myself all year round, I heard him saying once. In summer I leave it for the tourists.

How long has he been there? How long has he been looking at me? Me, my mother, the other mothers, the other teens? As if caught off guard, my eyes go back up the beach as if I could rewind everything I've seen and get back to the start.

Three hideous towels.

Nicolas's bum is still on the rearing horse of his Ferrari, sunglasses on his eyes, no cream and no hat, as if he couldn't give a damn what happened to his beautiful muscular skin. Maria-Chjara is still arching under the gelatinous caresses of Hermann, eyes fixed on the bare-chested teenagers playing volleyball a little further off: Estefan with his dreams of becoming a doctor, Magnus and his Oscar-winning ambition, Filip and his reveries about the stars. The young German rubs and rubs the cream over the back of the beautiful Italian girl, he starts the fifth layer, hesitating to venture elsewhere, to slide his fingers over the edge of those gilded curves towards the taut elastic of the swimming costume, towards the beginnings of her breasts at the sides of her unzipped costume.

Poor little cyclops . . .

It's time to have a real conversation with you. To tell you who Maria-Chjara really is.

I think you're going to like this!

* * *

He closed the notebook and let a handful of sand from Alga beach slip through his fingers. After all, it was logical enough to read this diary at the scene of the crime. Because this was where it all began, that day.

Undeniably, Clotilde had a great talent for describing feelings. For a fifteen-year-old it was nothing less than astonishing. You would have thought the story hadn't been written by her; or by her, but years later, with hindsight and maturity. Or that her story had been rewritten, like a retouched photograph, even if it contained no flaws, even if the ink, like everything else, had long since dried.

18

1 9, Rue de la Confrérie," Cesareu Garcia had said on the phone. "Behind Calenzana Church. You can't miss it."

Strange. At 19, Rue de la Confrérie there was a building with a dilapidated façade, the yellow plaster coming away, revealing holes left by grey bricks that hadn't been sealed properly, ancient window frames barely concealed by nailed-up and gaping shutters.

"Don't knock before coming in," the retired policeman had added, "I won't hear you. Just push the door then walk through the house. Don't pay too much attention to the mess, I'm an old man. I'll be waiting for you in the back garden. In my swimming pool."

A swimming pool . . .

Clotilde had imagined a magnificent villa, above the village, with a veranda, a sun terrace, parasol and lounger. Like the one on the posters hung all along the road, announcing an eighties night the following evening at the Tropi-Kalliste discotheque on Oscelluccia beach.

Clotilde focused once more and pushed open the door, passed through two rooms that were as tiny as they were cluttered, a musty kitchen that smelled of grilled figatelli sausage and a sitting room that was occupied almost entirely by a convertible bed so battered that it looked as if it couldn't be folded back into a sofa. Torn curtains floated over the door to the garden at the end of the room. Clotilde parted them tentatively, the way you might touch a cobweb spun on a condemned piece of furniture.

"Come on in, Clotilde."

Clotilde lowered her eyes towards a voice that seemed to be emerging from a manhole.

The garden, even smaller than the room she had just left, was reduced to not much more than a stretch of concrete, surrounded on three sides by a fence, and reached by three steps. Cut into the cement was a hole around a meter in diameter, the size of a well. And soaking in that well was Cesareu. All that could be seen of him was his bull-like shoulders, his thick neck and his head in a swimming cap bearing the words *Tour de Corse 97*.

His swimming pool?

More like a hippopotamus stuck in a dried-up swamp hole.

"Come on over. Pull up a chair, Clotilde. I'm not coming out of my water hole before that bloody sun has gone down behind the garden walls."

She sat down on a plastic chair.

"I'm like a big whale," the policeman continued. "A beached whale. As soon as the temperature gets above twenty-five degrees, I need to be in the water. And to move as little as possible, or else I'll die!"

Clotilde looked at him in disbelief. Cesareu ran his finger around the concrete rim.

"Made to measure, my love . . . Dug as a precise match for my waist size. Oh yes, pretty one, Sergeant Garcia has put on some weight since the last time you saw him."

She merely smiled. Yes, she remembered. Of course, everyone around here had always called Cesareu Garcia "Sergeant," no one had ever called him by his real rank. Was it captain? Lieutenant? Deputy?

"I'm glad you came."

"I don't know . . . "

"Nor do I, I suppose."

Good start. Cesareu went quiet; he seemed to be gently going to sleep in his bath. Unless it was an old sea-elephant's trick. Letting her come to him so that he didn't have to break through the ice.

If that was what he was waiting for . . .

"How is your daughter, Cesareu? It would be strange to see her again. In my mind, Aurélia is still seventeen, but she must be over forty now. She's two years older than me."

"She's fine, Clotilde. Fine. She's married, you know. Has been for years.

"Married?"

Who would have agreed to share their life with such a killjoy? And for years? Poor man!

"Any children?"

The beached whale poured water over his red face.

"No."

"I'm sorry."

"You can be sorry if you like. I really don't mind not being a grandfather."

Cesareu rose up a little bit more above the water. Clotilde imagined that he must be sitting on a sort of stepladder, and had brought his buttocks up a step.

"So, Cesareu. What's this big secret of yours?"

For a long time Cesareu looked around the pocket garden, the fence, the open door to the house and the floating curtains, as if his home were being bugged by the intelligence services.

"You know, my lovely, because you are incredibly lovely, Clotilde, I think I'm not the first person to tell you that since you came back to the island. You were lovely then too, by the way, but you didn't know it. A girl's charm is like happiness, miracles, talismans, all that nonsense—you just have to believe in it for it to work. Really believe, believe in it stupidly, like those fakirs who can walk on fire without burning themselves."

Clotilde didn't even try to conceal her irritation. She waved her hand around as if swatting an invisible fly, then rose to her feet and walked around the hole, taking a position behind the sergeant's back.

"Why did you ask me to come here, Cesareu?"

Wedged in his tub, the former policeman could only hear Clotilde now. He tried to twist himself round, then gave up.

"You remember, Clotilde, I was in charge of the investigation at the time. Just me. There was an incredible amount of pressure, believe me. Three people killed at the height of summer. Even though the Corsicans drive like lunatics, that's rare. Not to mention the fact that your father wasn't just anyone. The son of Cassanu Idrissi. At the time, Cassanu owned half of the district, and you know what they say about Corsican districts, they're bigger than some of the regions on the mainland, they extend from the line of the mountain ridge to the horizon, you can go alpine skiing in winter and water-skiing in the summer."

Clotilde interrupted him.

"It was an accident, wasn't it?"

"Yes, an accident, of course. An accident, and everyone's happy."

All of a sudden the sergeant got to his feet. His obese body splashed water over the concrete as he climbed up the stepladder. In the well, the water level fell abruptly, leaving it almost dry. A tiny pair of red trunks disappeared beneath the folds of his belly as if he were wearing a thong backwards, with the pouch over his buttocks and a G-string to cover everything else. Without even drying himself, he went into the house and grumbled as he moved furniture around, "Where has Aurélia put that damned file this time?", and then came back out a few seconds later wearing a dressing gown around his shoulders and with a cardboard folder in his hand. He picked up a plastic chair and pulled it towards the shade of the fence, holding the dossier out to Clotilde.

"Open it."

Clotilde sat down, put the folder on her knees, opened it and found the first page.

A name. A registration. A date of birth.

Renault Fuego. Model GTS. 1233 CD 27. First on the road 03/11/1984.

Photographs of the corpse of a car.

In colour.

An eviscerated roof. Charred tyres. Close-ups of broken glass. Clotilde almost retched.

"Go on, Clotilde. Go on before I explain."

A few more pages.

Red rocks. Three bodies lying on the rocks. Blood. Blood everywhere.

Another page.

A name, Paul Idrissi, born October 17, 1945, died August 23, 1989.

A dozen photographs, details taken from the earlier pictures, enlargements, a swollen face, an arm twisted into a right angle, an asymmetrical torso, a heart crushed in a vice.

Another page. Nicolas Idrissi, born April 8, 1971, died August 23 . . .

Clotilde couldn't read any further. She swallowed the bile rising in her throat, tried to look back at the file again, then dashed towards the circular swimming pool, knelt down and vomited her guts up.

Cesareu held out a tissue.

"I'm sorry," she said. She remained kneeling on the ground.

"I'll bet you are. They say it's going to be thirty-seven degrees today. And the person who does the maintenance for my pool is on holiday until the twenty-first of August."

Clotilde's eyes rested on the net used for fishing out leaves that was leaning against the fence. The sergeant held her back by the shoulder.

"Leave it, Clotilde. I'm teasing you. I don't care. It's my fault, but I wanted you to go all the way through . . . All the way to . . . "

"To the photographs of my mother?"

Cesareu nodded.

"My mother isn't dead. Is that it?"

She had guessed. It was obvious. All the clues were so obvious, convergent. That explicit letter about the dark room, Orsu's mop, the Labrador called Pacha. So many mysteries that could only be explained by the presence of her mother, here, alive on the island. Cesareu Garcia knew the key to the solution of the impossible problem: how had Palma Idrissi survived the accident?

"My mother isn't dead?" she repeated.

Cesareu looked at her as if she had blasphemed.

"What on earth are you talking about, Clotilde?" He seemed genuinely devastated. "Don't go getting an idea like that into your head, you poor thing. There's no doubt about it. Your mother died in the ravine at Petra Coda, along with your father and your brother. You saw them die in front of your very eyes. I saw their bodies too, it was the worst experience of my life. There were dozens of other witnesses. So no, I didn't bring you here to tell you that your mother has come back from the dead."

Clotilde pressed her lips together to stop herself crying.

"S . . . so what is it?"

"Look at the following page. After the photographs."

Clotilde took the folder again, skipped the page about Nicolas but summoned the strength to look at the one about her mother—six pictures of her shredded body, six enlargements of the photograph of her corpse, which looked as if it had been torn apart—before turning to the next page.

Crumpled metal replaced battered flesh. She found photographs of the Fuego. The whole thing, first of all, then pictures that probed the intimacy of the carcass, the engine, the passenger compartment. Clotilde studied close-ups of a fan belt, a cam shaft, a steering column, the double wishbone suspension, a brake cable. At least that's what she imagined them to be. She'd only ever had to open a car bonnet once in her life, in the middle of winter, to clean some dirty spark plugs, and that day she had shocked herself by navigating the huge steel puzzle almost instinctively.

She set down the file and turned towards the policeman, her eyes level with his belly. Clotilde had a sense that the sergeant's body was almost melting in the sun, that he'd told her the truth, and that if he stayed out of his water hole for too long he would indeed turn into a puddle of viscous, gelatinous flesh.

A huge wave of disgust bubbled up in her stomach again. She nearly screamed.

"What are you getting at then?"

"That last page, Clotilde, those photographs, they aren't official. If you check the date you'll see that they were taken a few weeks after the accident, when the investigation had officially closed. I waited until everything had calmed down before asking one of my mates to examine the remains of the Fuego. Discreetly. Ibrahim has a garage in Calenzana. We've known each other since we were children. He keeps his hands clean, even if the judges have never actually sworn to it."

"Why wait so long?"

He smiled.

"I told you, we were under incredible pressure, Clotilde. The son, the grandson, the daughter-in-law of Cassanu Idrissi, I don't know if you have any idea of what it was like. The case had gone all the way up to Deputy Pasquini and President Rocca Serra. So they just passed the whole business on to some poor guy who was given the task of botching the investigation. Me. Sergeant Garcia. An investigation whose solution had already been determined. AN ACCIDENT."

Clotilde tried to clear her mind of the images of the Fuego crashing through the barrier, plunging into the void, bouncing three times, killing three times.

It was an accident, of course it was. What was this fat policeman trying to say?

"Look at the third photograph, Clotilde. That's the rack and pinion steering system. And at either end you've got the tie rods and the ball joints."

All she could see was an iron rod, a piece of conical metal and a big bolt.

"It was one of these ball joints that went. All of a sudden. Just as your father tried to turn, just before the Petra Coda ravine."

Her father hadn't turned.

She saw the Fuego flying off the road like a football. It wasn't suicide. The steering had failed. Her voice softened.

"So it really was an accident?"

"Yes, as I told you, that's what the official report said, just before the word END. A steering joint failed. The only guilty party is the car. Except that according to my friend Ibrahim . . . "

Thick droplets pearled on his belly.

"According to my mate," he said again, "the failure of the ball joint was not, how can I put this . . . it didn't seem normal."

"Normal?"

He leaned towards her, his belly resting on his knees like an apron.

"Let me be more precise, Clotilde. I've thought about it hundreds of times since then, I've talked to Ibrahim, I've examined the photographs and the evidence. And in the end I've reached my own conclusion."

"Just tell me, for goodness' sake!"

"The steering was sabotaged, Clotilde. A bolt on the ball

joint was unscrewed, just enough so that the vibrations would knock it out after a few bends, the rod would give all of a sudden and the driver would find himself with a steering wheel turning in the void and an uncontrollable vehicle."

Clotilde said nothing. She clasped her arms around her knees, in a huddle. Prostrate.

The shadow of the pachyderm fell across Clotilde, stealing the sun. He had got to his feet.

"I had to tell you, Clotilde."

She felt cold. She was shivering. She was drawn by the well. As long as it was bottomless. Then she could fall for all eternity.

"Thank you, Cesareu."

A long silence passed before she said another word.

"Who . . . who else knows about this?"

"Only one person, the only one who had to know. Your grandfather, Clotilde. I gave a copy of the entire file to Cassanu Idrissi."

She bit her lips until they bled.

"What did he say?"

"Nothing, Clotilde. Nothing at all. He didn't react. It was as if he'd known all along. That was what I thought at the time. That he'd known all along."

The sergeant didn't add anything else. He took an infinity to do up his dressing gown, observed the filthy surface of his pool, then slowly made his way over to the net resting against the fence. He turned to Clotilde one last time.

"Do call in and see Aurélia, she'd be delighted."

Go and see that bitch? The very idea!

"She isn't far away. You'll remember the way. She lives at Punta Rossa, below the Revellata lighthouse."

The words became a blur, caught in a whirlwind.

That bitch Aurélia.

Punta Rossa.

Revellata lighthouse.

Cesareu took off his cap and stared intently into Clotilde's eyes.

"I thought you'd be surprised, my lovely one. I was too. If they'd told me that twenty-seven years ago, I wouldn't have believed it either. But yes, that's where Aurélia lives, it's where she's been living all this time. You know what that means, my pretty, I don't need to put it in writing." He gave Clotilde a moment to sort out the tangle of her memories. "Aurélia lives with Natale."

Clotilde swayed above the concrete pool. She had fallen into that bottomless well for the second time in less than a few minutes. And that second time left her even more breathless than the first.

Was more painful.

Oh, so much more painful.

19

Wednesday, August 16, 1989, tenth day of the holiday.
Fairy-blue sky.

O nce upon a time . . .
   Once upon a time there was a little Calabrian
   princess.
Maria-Chjara Giordano.

This story starts like a fairy tale because Maria-Chjara is a
real princess. She was born three years before me, the same
year as my brother, in 1971, in the little village of Pianopoli,
near Catanzano in Italy.

Her father runs the biggest broccoli business in Calabria,
apparently that's the speciality down there, very green broccoli. He's already sixty years old, with sixty million lire in the
bank when she was born; her father is handsome, a handsome
old thing, as they say, which is to say that the only handsome
things about him now are his brown eyes and his curly silver
hair. Her mother is nineteen years younger than her husband
and nineteen centimeters taller in heels; she's a model for
Ungaro and has acted in B movies made at Cinecittà, none of
which have ever been shown in France. I've been keeping an
eye out, believe me.

Better watered than my Papa's cauliflowers, Maria-Chjara
grew quickly.

Quicker than me, anyway. When she turned fifteen, she was
already over one meter seventy. She slowed down a bit over the
years that followed, ending up at one meter seventy-five, but
those extra centimeters that hadn't made her thighs, her back
or her ankles any longer had spread elsewhere, swelling her

bosom, curving her hips, plumping out her bottom. A small miracle of harmony, the figure of the heroine from an Italian graphic novel, the ones Papa hides in the library between Tintin and Asterix. A girl created by Manara.

That kind of girl.

Papa Giordano, probably in order to forget the smell of broccoli and enjoy the extra nineteen centimeters or so of his starlet, bought a villa on the slopes of Revellata and comes back here every summer. The little Calabrian princess, his sole heir, grew bored on her own in her stone palace, and every now and again, then more and more often, for longer and longer spells, her dad's Suzuki 4x4 would drop her off between Alga beach and the Euproctes campsite so that she could enjoy herself with girls her own age. Girls, and boys.

In the summer of 1989, Papa and Mamma Giordano had set off to sail around Sardinia in their yacht, which was moored all year round in Calvi Bay, and Princess Chjara, having just reached the age of majority, had told them that there was no way she was going to spend the next month getting bored to death with them in a floating prison that measured thirty meters by ten.

She would manage on her own. Her father had dropped the keys of the villa in the palm of her hand.

Chjara didn't barter.

And she did manage very well on her own.

Dancing the lambada better than Kaoma. Singing "Una storia importante" better than Eros Ramazzotti. Delivering lines from *Cinema Paradiso* better than Agnese Nano, kisses included.

She was all set to be a star.

To shine in the galaxy before all the other stars went out.

To seduce or to perish!

Maria-Chjara. The story of a princess.

I'm still here in the shadows, on my bit of beach, on the

edge of the pine trees with the needles digging into my bottom, *Dangerous Liaisons* lying open on my knees. All of a sudden Maria-Chjara got up from her towel, and Hermann the cyclops was left with his sticky hands in the air, stroking the void.

Not fast enough, Hermann . . . Ha ha ha!

Maria-Chjara got up just like that, without putting the top of her costume back on. She went and ordered a Coke at the other end of the beach, and the whole beach turned to look at her. I swear, from my slightly elevated observation point the spectacle was very striking, like a field of sunflowers following the course of the sun, but speeded up a thousand times. With poppies, pansies and ears of corn twisting on their stems as well.

I deliberately look down at my book.

I was wrong, in fact.

Valmont isn't my brother! Valmont is Maria-Chjara.

The libertine seducer, in the 18th-century novel, couldn't be a woman, times were different. But nowadays, of course she could! The girls you respect, the girls you admire, are the ones who take things for granted, who are confident, who do what they want with their bodies and their hearts, who do what they want with guys.

I'm a long way off being like that!

Maria-Chjara is a virgin. That's the rumour doing the rounds. In tents, on the beach, in the girls' showers and the boys' toilets. It's almost as if she'd shouted it through a loud-hailer, or pinned it up on the campsite notice board.

I'm a virgin . . . and I don't plan on staying one.

Maria-Chjara has taken a vow of non-chastity.

She's practically announced it, like a bowls competition, a ping-pong tournament or bingo night. She's going to get her-self a man. For the first time. Just one! Before the end of the summer.

Ever since then, Maria-Chjara has been strolling about in a thong, her breasts in the air, going to get her scoop of pistachio ice cream, her sandwich, her copy of *Jeune et Jolie*. Valerie Kaprisky in *Year of the Jellyfish*, if that gives you some idea.

And now here she is, coming back with her Coke.

Three steps forward, slowing down, head thrown back, a sip, forward again, curves to the fore, a twist of the waist, a sway of the hips, casually letting a few drops spill, wiping her sugary skin with the back of her hand.

Walking on.

All the men lying at her feet, the papas' spades freezing above their sandcastles, bottles of ice-cold beer pressed against swimming trunks, volleyballs rolling about with no one running after them. Estefan, Magnus, Filip, all thunderstruck!

It's filthy.

But I can't help admiring her . . .

Being jealous of her . . .

Hating her.

Hating the way men's eyes stare at her chest, which defies the laws of gravity.

I'm screwed, even though I have a theory about that whole thing. You want to know what it is? Anyway, I'm not asking your opinion, I'm just letting off steam by telling you this. Going out with a girl who has small breasts, a girl you want to spend the rest of your life with, I mean, a girl like me, for example, is a long-term investment. A thirty-year guarantee. A choice you aren't going to regret after decades as a couple. Big breasts, on the other hand, will inevitably disappoint, they will sag. It's obvious, isn't it? It's a mathematical, physical law! Consequently, even if that little hand grenade Maria-Chjara is ahead of me at the moment, I'll catch up with her eventually, at my own rhythm, a quiet trot.

You just have to be patient.

Up with small hearts, small bottoms, small breasts!

Shall we talk about it again one day, Chjara?

A long time from now, a very long time, because at the moment you're the one who's making the auction rise. And the stakes are already high, very high.

The beautiful Italian has returned to her towel after walking around it three times like a suspicious cat. Cervone, who is also hiding among the pines, hasn't missed a shred of this display, his hand stuck to the resin of the tree trunk. The cyclops has frozen Egyptian-style, facing his goddess (Bastet, the cat goddess, my ignorant reader!), and even my Nico, my indifferent, handsome brother with his Ray-Bans, has moved his neck almost imperceptibly.

He's lost, too.

Once upon a time . . .
Once upon a time there was a little Calabrian princess
With a hot little treasure
You know where.

* * *

He looked at the poster, and thought about tearing it down.

What would be the point, there were so many others, dozens along the road.

Tonight. 10 P.M. Oscelluccia beach. Tropi-Kalliste Discotheque.

He would be there.

Not to hear Maria-Chjara sing.

To shut her up.

20

T he posters had been taped up everywhere, even on the doors of the shower blocks, the barriers at the car park and the local dump. Valentine stopped by the one opposite their pitch. She had wrapped a sarong around her waist, and her flip-flops were clacking against the soles of her feet as if they were stilettoes on the parquet floor of a ballroom; the baguette under her arm made her look like a majorette. Clotilde stood beside her daughter, anxious to move on; she was carrying the rest of the shopping, and the melons, grapefruits, oranges and the half-watermelon weighed a ton in the plastic bags she was holding in each hand.

Valentine looked up and read.

Eighties Night
10:00 P.M. Tropi-Kalliste discotheque
Oscelluccia beach

On the poster, multicoloured foam spilled from a huge plastic swimming pool that had been placed on the beach. A girl in a bikini leapt from it under a shower of gold sequins.

"Apparently it's a great tradition at this campsite," Valou insisted, staring at the girl. "Nobody's talking about anything else. She used to spend her holidays here, and since then she's become a star in Italy."

Amazed, Clotilde took her eyes off Valou's sparkling expression and concentrated on the poster. The siren's face was unrecognisable beneath the heavy make-up, her perfect body was like the thousands of others that would appear if you tapped "starlet" or "bikini" into the Internet, but her stage name provoked another explosion of childhood memories.

Maria-Chjara.

The plastic handles of the shopping bags cut their way into Clotilde's fingers.

"Cervone even told me you knew her, Maman! He said you spent five or six years together and that Uncle Nico knew her well, too."

Uncle Nico. So she'd suddenly remembered she had a family.

Clotilde had heard vague news about Maria-Chjara since August 1989. She had spotted her once, almost twenty years ago, in an Italian film on TF3; a cameo role, a girl riding a bicycle, skirt flying in the air, along the streets of Lucca. She had also seen her name and recognised her face when she had stayed in Venice with Franck, sixteen years ago, before Valou was born. An old four-euro CD in a bargain bin: flashy colours, songs she'd never heard of. So Maria-Chjara's fame was probably relative, even in Italy.

"You know, Valou, she was eighteen back then. She might be a bit . . . old-fashioned these days."

But Valentine didn't care. It was the pretext that mattered.

"Don't you want to see her again?"

Oscelluccia beach was just down the hill from the Euproctes campsite, and could be reached directly by a steep path bordering the sea. Clotilde studied the poster, the foam, the pool, the bikini with as much enthusiasm as if it were an advertisement for a bullfight.

"Are you joking?"

"I could go with you, Maman? I'd just go for the party but then you could see your friend."

Sly little thing that she was.

Clotilde was going to say, "I'll think about it, darling, we'll see, first of all I need to get rid of these bags of fruit because they're pulling both of my arms out of their sockets," when Franck suddenly appeared behind her. He took the shopping bags from Clotilde without a word, with no obvious effort, apparently without even thinking about it.

Gallant. Virile. The perfect man. What are you complaining about, you old thing?

"What's up, my lovely girls?"

Valentine explained about the party on the beach, the star of the Revellata Peninsula, Maman's childhood friend.

"Would you want to go?" Franck asked, turning towards Clotilde. "Would it be fun to see that girl again?"

Why not? Why not, in the end?

Franck rested his hands on his daughter's shoulders.

"There's no way that you're going to that beach party on your own. But if your mother goes with you . . . "

"Thank you, Papa."

The ungrateful hussy threw her arms around her father, the hero, without a word of thanks to the mother who was going to have to endure the eighties night, from the start of the evening to the demons of midnight. It had been an eternity since she had set foot in any nightclub.

Clotilde didn't think about it for the rest of the day. From beach to bungalow, from deck chair to towel, her head immersed in the Mediterranean or under the shower, three questions ran through her mind in a loop. She gave herself until the evening to find three definitive answers.

Yes or no.

To go and see her grandfather, first of all, Cassanu Idrissi, and call a family meeting with Mamy Lisabetta, perhaps even with that witch Speranza and her grandson Orsu? And the dog Pacha as well. Install all those lovely people under the holm oak in the yard at Arcanu, then place on the table the revelation that was eating away at her: that her parents hadn't been the victims of an accident. That the steering system of the Fuego had been sabotaged.

Answer: YES, even if it wasn't yet clear what form this meeting would take.

And then secondly, should she talk to Franck? Talk about the policeman's revelations. Show him the photographs of the bolt and the blasted steering rod, ask his opinion, his advice, he could identify anything under a car bonnet.

Answer: NO! Under no condition did she want to face his sarcasm once more, his appalled pity, his simplistic binary solutions—to put in a complaint or let the matter drop.

And last of all, whether she should take a trip to Punta Rossa, via the customs path along the Revellata, just something casual, a stroll up to the lighthouse, enjoying the panoramic view, like dozens of other tourists, and why not bump into Natale, who might be busy mending a net, smoking a cigarette on his terrace, watching the world go by.

Answer: NO. Definitely NO!

The speakers spat out a crackly version of "Life is Life", which didn't stop the crowd from responding in chorus, with no need for rehearsal.

Clotilde and Valou walked among the dancers crowded onto the little beach of Oscelluccia. Slotted in between two tongues of rock, the little inlet was another of those small pieces of paradise that had been confiscated by Cervone Spinello. The closer you got to the sea, the more the stones and pebbles on the path seemed to have been crushed by thousands of tourists' feet, in a hurry to reach the water, the stones reduced, summer after summer, to coarse sand whose quality, according to certain tourists, depended on the number of people visiting the beach.

While the half-built walls of the future Roc e Mare marina were barely visible from that point, you couldn't miss the Tropi-Kalliste, the straw hut facing due north, with a terrace, bar and bamboo ceiling, all of it no doubt easy to dismantle at speed if there was a storm warning or an impending visit from a zealous new police chief. The name, which had Cervone's hallmark stamped all over it, evoked both the tropical heat of the night and the ancient name of Corsica, *Kalliste*, the most beautiful. The disco was nothing more than this straw hut, fitted with spotlights and lasers that lit up the sky all the way to the moon, large speakers placed right on the sand, a floating platform on which less than a quarter of the crowd was dancing, and—especially for this evening—a raised stage, two meters high, thin and long like a catwalk or a large diving board. Below the dais a big inflatable swimming pool had been set up, lit by blue fluorescent lighting and guarded by three motionless black bodyguards who didn't appear to be appreciating the chorus to Opus's song "Life is Life."

For once Cervone had brought his prices down, but even at seven euros a ticket, nine euros for a mojito and fifteen euros for a pitcher of Pietra, he still must have been raking in the money.

Frankie Goes to Hollywood was now ordering the enthusiastic audience to relax. Clotilde estimated the crowd to be between two and three hundred people. Of all ages. Teenagers who seemed to have known these cheesy songs by heart since they were in nappies; hysterical adolescents, some of whom already seemed to be drunk; couples, too, and a few groups of older people.

Old in comparison to most of the audience.

Old in terms of their age.

"I'm off, Maman!"

Clotilde stared at her daughter uncomprehendingly.

"Clara, Justin, Nils and Tahir are here. Just over there. I've got my phone. Text me when you want to go."

Valou disappeared into the crowd.

If anything happened to her, if he found out about this, Franck would kill her. Not his daughter—his wife.

But Clotilde didn't care.

Let Valou enjoy herself. My God, let the girl enjoy herself! What could happen to her here?

She moved away slightly from the dancers and walked towards the sea, avoiding a few bodies lying around as if they'd been washed in by the tide. A boat floated a few meters out from the beach, moored to an iron ring that had been drilled into the rocks. Clotilde pointed the torch of her phone at the flaking bow of the fishing boat.

The *Aryon*.

It was almost impossible to make out the A, the Y and the N; she was probably the only person capable of still deciphering the name. The hull looked rotten, the mooring rope worn, the keel split. No oars, no sail, no engine. The boat looked like an escaped animal that had had a noose looped around its neck and then been forgotten about. At least that was Clotilde's impression, as she held back the tears that came to her at the sight of this new wreck abandoned on the road of her journey into nostalgia.

The music suddenly stopped. For a moment, the beach was plunged into darkness, before a green laser machine-gunned the crowd and the strobe turned them into epileptic zombies.

Maria-Chjara appeared on the catwalk wearing a long sequined sheath dress, quite decent, apart from the revealing cleavage.

A synthesiser provided the rhythm for her first few dance moves, before her lips approached the microphone to sing the first few notes of "Future Brain," the global hit by Den Harrow, the king of eighties Italian disco . . . a song completely forgotten ever since.

Or at least that's what Clotilde thought.

The crowd immediately joined in, chanting the words.

Some hits last forever.

Since returning to Corsica, Clotilde hadn't been back to Oscelluccia beach. Too many questions haunted her now. Why, since this bit of paradise had always belonged to Cassanu Idrissi, had her grandfather allowed Cervone to put up this squalid nightclub here? Why was this boat still floating here, abandoned and rusty? Why was anyone tolerating this noise that sounded like a bad drug, this mesmerised crowd, these hypnotic lights? Why hadn't silence won? If it didn't win here, on Oscelluccia beach, where could it win?

Why hadn't a big bad wolf come over to this straw house on the beach, a local wolf who was friends with her grandfather, no need even for a balaclava or a bomb, a jerry-can or a lighter, all you'd have to do was blow it down. All it would have taken was a bit more wind; this wind which, rather than sweeping away the straw hut, was carrying the decibels all the way to Calvi.

Maria-Chjara continued. Under the spotlights, with all the shadows and the lights, with all that make-up, it would have been impossible to guess her age.

Forty-five. Precisely. Clotilde knew.

Maria-Chjara was extremely confident. The songs flew by one after another. Italian, English, French, Spanish.

Valou appeared and disappeared again.

Clotilde was getting bored.

After a "Tarzan Boy" continued the endless call and response of the sandy choir, waking up every mammal from the Pelagos animal sanctuary to Monaco, the lights suddenly became less garish, the synths faded away and Maria-Chjara murmured into the mike with a strong Italian accent.

"I'm going to sing you a song that is sung without any accompaniment at all. No instruments. Just my voice. It's a song I'm sure you know, "Forever Young", but this time I would ask you not to sing along with me. Except those who can (she gave the crowd a smile like a kiss). I'm going to sing it in Corsican. Just for you. 'Sempre giovanu.'"

A white spotlight settled on Maria-Chjara. The Italian chanteuse closed her eyes, letting her unadorned voice defy the waves and climb ever higher, making even the moon weep.

And, carried by a soprano voice purer than anyone could have imagined, the tune became a hymn, the crowd shivering in the darkness, not even one nervous laugh, like a small miracle, as if everyone had understood that the singer was only agreeing to perform in this circus on the grounds that she was allowed these four minutes, that she was left in peace for the duration of her prayer, her a cappella credo.

A parenthesis, that had to close again.

The sound of the drum machine exploded even before Maria-Chjara had opened her eyes again, even before the last octave was whispered by her parted lips, followed by an insipid synth note which all the beachgoers seemed to recognise from the first chord.

Maria-Chjara's dress had just fallen to the stage. As if by magic she appeared in her bikini.

White. Immaculate. Clinging.

The crowd began to shout the chorus of "Boys Boys Boys" even before the backing tape started up.

Maria-Chjara stopped, swayed, smiled, stepped forward, stepped back and then took a swift run.

The crowd continued to chant, repeating the words again and again.

She dived.

And re-emerged from the pool below the stage, under a

shower of sequins, her hair sticking to her head, her make-up washed away, her foundation furrowed, but it didn't matter, the important aspect was elsewhere: the top of her wet bikini was shining, intoxicating, transparent, just as the legend said it was, almost like a trademark.

Maria-Chjara now took up the refrain, repeating it ad infinitum. She had been brought a different microphone, a big rainbow-coloured plastic ball, and cannons spewed forth foam. The singer held out her hand as if blowing a kiss, and beckoned to the crowd.

As if expertly choreographed, the three bodyguards parted at last and clothes rained down on the beach. Soon there were a hundred people in the tiny pool, singing the words to "Boys Boys Boys" for the thousandth time.

The more daring of the girls took off their bikini tops.

But not Maria-Chjara.

As if she were too old for that.

Because only the hits never get older.

⌒

"I'm a friend of Maria-Chjara's. I knew her when we were children."

The bodyguard didn't seem convinced.

The crowd was still dancing at the other end of the beach, to techno beats that no longer had much to do with the eighties.

Are we staying on here for a bit, Maman?

Yes, but not for long, Clotilde had replied to her daughter's anxious text after Maria-Chjara's last song. That was twenty minutes ago. Since then she had been waiting by the caravan parked on the unpaved car park that served as the backstage area. It wasn't as if she was stuck in a queue of groupies. Clotilde was alone, but the door was closed and the bouncer wouldn't hear a word about it.

"At least knock on the door. Tell her there's a fan who wants to talk to her, she'll like that."

The bouncer smiled faintly, or felt sorry for her. At last he knocked on the partition.

"Miss Giordano. It's for you . . . "

Maria-Chjara poked her head out a few seconds later. She had wrapped a dressing gown around her shoulders and a towel on her hair. Not a trace of make-up, foundation or lip gloss. She turned towards Clotilde, only half-opening the door.

"Yes?"

She was still beautiful. Clotilde hadn't expected that. She'd probably had face-lifts, liposuction, scalpels and silicon, but she still looked good. Like a customised car, Clotilde thought, a bit vulgar, but proud to be different, proud to attract people's attention. Whether it was admiration or criticism, she didn't care. Monster or icon, what did it matter?

"Have you got a ciggie for me?"

The muscle-bound bodyguard, who must have been twenty-five years younger than her, nervously took out a cigarette and, like a trembling John Wayne, brought it to Maria-Chjara's lips, not knowing where to look.

A shy little boy with his teacher.

"So," Maria-Chjara said, addressing Clotilde at last, "you're my last fan? And you think I'm going to open my door to you? Don't count on it, lovey, I'm not like all those cocksuckers who suddenly turn into muff-divers when the men start turning their backs."

She exploded with laughter.

There was something feline about her gestures, her claws, her almond eyes. Even though Clotilde hated the word "cougar," it seemed an apt term.

Or tigress.

"I'm Clotilde. Nicolas's sister. Nicolas Idrissi, do you remember?"

Maria-Chjara narrowed her eyes, seeming to scour the depths of her memory. Yet Clotilde could have sworn that the woman had recognised her as soon as she saw her. A slight pressure of her fingers on the door of the caravan, a tightening of thumb and index finger on the blistered metal.

Maria-Chjara shook her head.

"No idea. An ex of mine?"

She seemed sincere. Clotilde was sorry not to have thought of bringing some pictures of Nicolas.

"The summer of '89. And the five years before that."

Maria-Chjara blew smoke in the bouncer's face, pushed a damp lock of hair beneath her towel, let the dressing gown slip slightly, revealing a tattooed rose, the prisoner of black briars climbing up to her shoulder and onto her arm.

"The summer of '89!" the starlet said, astonished. "Well, darling, that doesn't make us any younger. I was a dish back than, a gourmet dish, and the boys were a bit like the liquorice in a bag of Haribo, that brother of yours was just one among many."

The year you lost your virginity, oh pussy my love! Don't give me that, you don't forget something like that!

"He was tall and fair. A nice guy. It was the summer of the lambada. He didn't dance as well as you."

Maria-Chjara spat out the cigarette butt. Her red thumbnail picked nervously at the paint of her metal lodging.

"I'm sorry, darling. I have five thousand fans on *Copains d'avant*.[1] And I'm talking about the ones who got me into bed, not the little virgins who just felt me up."

She was lying. Clotilde had no choice. She took a deep breath, filling her lungs with air, before blowing the house down.

---

[1] French equivalent of Friends Reunited.

"I'm talking about the boy who died, Maria. The one who died on the Revellata road. The evening when you and my brother Nicolas were supposed to do it for the first time."

The red nail broke. Cleanly.

No smile from Maria-Chjara. Cold.

The prize for best actress goes to . . . Hats off.

"I'm sorry. I don't remember. I'm exhausted. Come back later. Bye."

21

Thursday, August 17, 1989, eleventh day of the holiday.
Big Blue sky.

The port of Stareso consists of a concrete jetty and three houses. For a long time, apparently, this pocket-sized harbour below the Revellata lighthouse was basically forbidden to the public because it was home to a small scientific base researching the marine life of the Mediterranean. But this summer they've opened the site to allow a few visitors, some divers, fishermen and also, once a week, about fifteen street vendors who come and sell their local products on the quay.

Maman couldn't miss that. Maman loooooooves markets.

She loves looking pretty in her hat, wandering about, showing an interest in things, being enthusiastic, chatting, disagreeing, going away, changing her mind, coming back, negotiating, bargaining, buying, changing her mind again. During that week in Marrakech when I was twelve, I thought I would die of shame in the souk and not come out of our *riad* for a week. And this morning at breakfast, fatal mistake, I agreed to go with Maman to the market. There goes the morning! When I got fed up of being jostled by holidaymakers, and having my feet run over by buggies, I went and sat on the only bench. Blazing sun. Camouflage gear. Headphones and Manu Chao in my ears and, for a change, a newspaper on my knees, the *Corse-Matin*, whose banner headline had grabbed my attention.

FALLEN FROM HIS BOAT?

Someone called Drago Bianchi, a businessman from Nice, had been reported missing according to the few lines I read on the front page. They'd found his yacht but not him, just his fishing rod, which was found floating in the water with nothing on it. The guy had made his fortune in building and public works, the kind of man who could turn concrete into gold. Perhaps he'd got the formula wrong this time; perhaps all the gold in his pockets had turned back into concrete and made him fall to the bottom. The other brief news items from the island got on my nerves, so instead I chose to admire the landscape in front of me.

Shall I describe it to you? Let me try and find the words.

So in front of me there's a fishing boat, blue and white, which looks more like a large rowboat than a trawler. No sails, just an engine, iron chains piled up everywhere, and nets, sea-green, forming a huge cocoon on the jetty, with a giant caterpillar of yellow buoys imprisoned inside it. Perhaps, when the net is cast, the biggest butterfly in the world will come fluttering out of it.

I'm sure this fisherman would be quite capable of that.

I've been staring at him for almost an hour from behind my Lolita glasses.

Shall I describe him to you? Have I talked to you about *The Big Blue*? Can you picture Jean-Marc Barr, the dolphin man with every shade of blue imprinted on his eyes, starry chasms, like two marbles containing the entire universe? Well, his spitting image is right in front of me. A fisherman who's just as magnetic: baby-round head shaved with an electric razor three days ago, from skull to chin, the same poetry in his eyes. He's the same, I'm telling you! Just as dreamy, except that he clearly doesn't spend his days free-diving under water; he's more likely to spend them above the waves. He works with his hands, he toils away, unknotting his wretched nets with great concentration whilst being fried by the sun.

I wait.

How old? Ten years older than me, max?

I wait like a little flirt, I wait until the sun has grilled him medium rare, I imagine his tanned arms pulling his wet T-shirt over his head, his damp muscles twisting the fabric, his hands . . .

"Come on over."

He's spoken to me. Damn it. Caught red-handed!

"Come here," he says again. "I need some advice. Come and take a look."

What would you have done in my place?

Don't try to be clever, my future reader. The same as me, obviously! So I set down my newspaper and my Walkman, I pushed my sunglasses back on to my forehead and stepped towards his boat.

"I need your advice. Look, what do you think?"

And even if you don't believe me, I don't care, the dolphin-man really was a dolphin man, as if I'd read something in his face and he'd picked up on that. Like some kind of telepathy, the same way cetaceans can communicate with each other, by sonar, brain to brain. OK, so it was less than five meters from my bench to his boat, but we were just starting out. My dolphin-man and I can train ourselves, we'll get better, and in the end we'll be able to communicate from one ocean to another.

"So, are you looking?"

He shows me a little blue poster painted on plywood, showing three dark outlines on a sparkling sea.

Sea Safari—swim with dolphins
Every day until the end of August.
L'Aryon
Port of Stareso
04 95 15 65 42

"What do you think?"

"It's good."

To tell you the truth, his poster is a complete rip-off of *The*

Big Blue, he hasn't exactly over-exerted himself. Bresson could sue, I think.

Then I add:

"Except that it's nonsense."

I like to provoke. The dolphin-man pauses and stares at the death's-head sphinx on my T-shirt. He pulls the face of a wandering poet who's walked into a glass door.

"Is that what you thought when you read it?"

"Yep."

He brings his two hands to his face, clamping it like a vice as if to flatten it, except that it stays as perfect as ever, the curves of an appetising round fruit. I love it when his face splits into a smile

"Shit. That's why I asked you. It's little mermaids like you that I'm trying to attract." (Two lychees twinkle above his watermelon smile.) "Mermaids who dream of swimming with dolphins. In the open sea."

I stare in disbelief at my mermaid-fisherman. The hook's pretty big!

"Are you joking?"

He nods and bursts out laughing. I'd guessed a moment in advance, thanks to our telepathy.

"It's not rubbish at all, though. There are thousands of dolphins in the Mediterranean. And hundreds off the coast of Corsica. The boat-trip guys in Porto, Cargèse and Girolata promise to take you out along the coast of the Scandola nature reserve, but given the number of bathtubs floating around out there, you don't have even a one in a hundred chance of seeing so much as a fin. Dolphins prefer fishing boats, they like to bite through your nets and steal the fish."

"Have you ever seen them?"

He nods as if it were obvious.

"Like all the fishermen in the Mediterranean. But as a general rule dolphins and fishermen aren't exactly the best of friends."

I roll my eyes the way Maman does when she's haggling in the market.

"But you are. And now you're going to tell me you've even managed to train them."

"It isn't hard. They're intelligent animals that can recognise the sound of a boat, the voice of a human being."

"And you've gained their trust?"

"Yes."

"I don't believe you!"

He smiles at me again. I think he likes the way I stand up to him. I also think he's telling the truth. I think my fisherman is a little child who's spent his life dreaming about dolphins, all by himself in his room, and who's ended up finding them, approaching them, loving them, I think that . . .

"You're right, Clotilde. You should never trust people straight away. Nobody."

Wow, he knows my first name!

"Your Papé must have taught you that. It takes time to tame someone."

"My Papé?"

"You're Cassanu's granddaughter, aren't you? The Idrissi are well-known around here, as you know. And you don't exactly go unnoticed, with your disguise."

My disguise? Since he didn't have hair or a beard, I'd happily pull his eye-lashes out. If he didn't have such beautiful eyes.

My disguise indeed!

This peasant has clearly never seen *Beetlejuice*. He's never set foot in a cinema, he's never opened a book, nothing matters more to him than his fish, his passion. My God, do men like that really exist?

I go on the attack.

"What about my disguise?"

"Nothing really. But I'm not sure you can approach dolphins with a skull on your T-shirt."

"What would you prefer? A day-glo T-shirt? A pink cloud? Gilded angels?"

"Because you've got all that under your T-shirt? Are you really hiding all those colours?"

The bastard! He's unmasked me with just a few words. Like a little girl who says she hasn't had a snack, but still has Nutella on her lips.

I'm preparing my answer when the boat starts rocking.

"She isn't annoying you?"

I don't believe it!

It's my mother. Without any embarrassment at all, she's boarded the boat and forced her way into the conversation.

And from that moment everything changes.

He changes first.

It's as if there were nobody on the boat but my mother, Mama Palma, with her frightened-fawn eyes resting on a life-raft, getting her heels caught in the net, crushing her dress against a lobster pot, squeaking like a terrified mouse.

As if he has forgotten me already.

Or even worse than that.

As if he only invited me on board in order to lure my mother onto his little boat. I saw the great big hook he dangled in front of me, but I hadn't understood a thing. I'm not the fish, I'm only the bait!

A worm!

A worm to attract my mother.

"Now don't go telling her fairy tales about your dolphins," Mama Palma simpers, looking down at the *Big Blue* poster. Her rebellious air conceals a marshmallow heart.

A marshmallow! That's all my mother has to stick on her own hook.

I hate her!

"I'm not joking, Madame Idrissi," the dreamy fisherman

replies. "As strange as it might seem, dolphins are my real business. A pair and their calves have settled off the coast of La Revellata. They trust me. I really can take your daughter to see them if she'd like."

My mother has sat down. Bare legs, squeezed tight together. I can see that she's trying to cross swords with the laser eyes of this stargazer.

"You'd have to ask her."

She crosses her legs.

I fold my arms, sulkily. Idiot. Jerk.

There's a moment of silence.

"Another time, perhaps!" she says, getting to her feet. "Shall we go, darling?"

And we go.

He doesn't say anything, but he doesn't need to.

He holds his hand out to my mother to help her back on to the jetty. He rests his other hand on Maman's waist, and she leans against the bare, tanned shoulder of her brave knight. To finish the dance, Maman leaps across the gap between the boat and the jetty, her skirt flying, her legs doing the splits. Like an improvised move that they had secretly practised.

"If Clotilde changes her mind, can I get in touch with you?"

"Of course, Madame Idrissi."

"Palma. Call me Palma. Spoken hereabouts, Madame Idrissi sounds like the queen mother."

"A princess, I'd have said."

The princess clucks like a turkey. But you have to admit, she has a smart comeback.

"Princesses hardly ever turn into queens," she says. "But in French at least, *dauphins* might turn into kings . . . isn't that right, Monsieur . . . Monsieur?"

"Angeli. Natale Angeli."

On the way home I ruminate on my certainty.

It's like a revelation.

Yes, my mother *is* capable of cheating on my father.

Cheating on him with that man.

Natale. Natale Angeli. A fisher-king of mermaids, princesses and dolphins.

While I . . . I'm having a lot of trouble writing these last few words.

But I couldn't care less!

No one is going to read them. I know, my future reader, that you don't exist.

While *I'm* the one he loves. I'm the one who loves him.

I knew it at first glance.

Don't make fun of me, I beg you. Don't make fun of me, it's serious, serious enough to make me weep all the tears in the world over this notebook.

I love Natale.

I love, for the first time.

And no other man will ever be able to change that.

* * *

He closed the warped pages of the notebook and sat there for a moment.

Echoes of techno music rose up from Oscelluccia beach.

He stepped into the path to hear it more clearly.

22

August 17, 2016, 2:30 A.M.

Franck looked at his watch.

What on earth were they up to?

The breeze from the sea carried the sounds of electronic music but all he could hear was the dull, percussive notes of the bass, repetitive, obsessive, as if a drum-skin had been stretched out by the sea and every wave were striking it. An endless rhythm.

Boom boom boom boom . . .

In the campsite, however, everyone else was asleep. Franck had to admit that with the doors and windows closed, the noise was almost inaudible inside the bungalows, the mobile homes and the Finnish chalets. Too bad for those actually camping! The disco was perhaps another way of getting rid of them and replacing the sites with fixed dwellings that multiplied the profitability of each plot ten times over.

What were they up to? Surely Clotilde wouldn't want to be dancing all night to this techno soup?

Franck continued waiting for another half hour, wandering around the campsite, coming across only a few shadows, other insomniacs, dog walkers, pensioners who were allergic to David Guetta, concerned parents.

The torch of Clo's mobile phone lit up the end of the path at 3:04 precisely. Franck could have sworn as much to a policeman; he was checking the time on his mobile almost constantly. He recognised her as soon as she passed beneath the light at the entrance to their pitch.

"Where's Valou?" Franck immediately reproached himself for not asking any other question, even for form's sake: How was your evening? How was that Italian girl? How was the seaside disco?

But Clo was on her own.

She looked exhausted. Her eyes were drawn, her gait weary. As if she were ready to collapse without saying a word, without explaining anything. Tomorrow, tomorrow, I'm shattered. Franck didn't like this attitude, this carelessness, bordering on contempt. He hated feeling as if he were being left out and yet still had to justify himself.

"Where's Valou?" he said again.

Clotilde slumped onto a chair. He was annoying her, he could tell.

His wife's words came out slowly, dragging their feet.

"She stayed on. With friends. Some girls from the campsite. They'll come back up together."

"Are you fucking serious?"

His words came out just like that, unplanned, at a sprint. And there was a whole team just behind them.

"She's fifteen, damn it! Are you oblivious to that, or what?"

A team of executioners.

He machine-gunned her with his eyes.

"I'll go. I'll go and find her."

Clotilde didn't react and Franck plunged off into the darkness.

⁓

When Franck came back, Clotilde was asleep.

At least she was lying under the blankets, wearing her *Charlie and the Chocolate Factory* T-shirt.

Eyes closed.

She had left the window open, and Franck didn't dare close

it. He undressed quickly, in the semi-darkness, and pressed his body against his wife's.

"It's fine, Valou has gone to bed."

Lips pressed tight together.

Franck rested his head on Clo's shoulder, slipped a hand underneath her and gripped her left breast.

Heart closed.

He felt her breath against his palm, the echo of techno through the open window gaving him the illusion that he could hear its beat, amplified a million times.

"I'm sorry, Clo. I'm sorry for speaking to you like that. I was just concerned about Valentine. There are drunk guys down there. Weed. The beach, the sea, the rocks."

The heart calmed down slowly as the music speeded up.

Lips parted, at last.

"What did she say?"

"Valou? Nothing. She was surprised to have been allowed to stay up so late, I think."

Boom boom boom boom.

Outside.

Eyes wide open now.

Clotilde turned over gently and gazed into his eyes.

"You were just worried, it's fine. Let's leave it at that. You're . . . you're an amazing father."

Franck's hands ventured under the T-shirt again, and the more daring of the two touched her other breast.

"And a useless husband?"

She let him stroke her, gently fill her heart with desire, her mouth with sighs, her belly with pleasure, before the seams burst one by one and she murmured, "Shut up, you silly fool!"

They made love in silence. So as not to be heard. By anyone outside, by Valou, as if they were a pair of teenagers.

Too quick.

Clotilde closed up again almost immediately.
Back turned. Sheet crumpled. Body bent.

Franck lost his erection.
Clotilde was slipping away from him.
Had it all been written since the outset?
He thought again of their first meeting, almost twenty years
before; a fancy-dress party at a mutual friend's house, both of
them recently separated, she dressed as Morticia Addams and
he as Dracula. Without that morbid similarity, Clotilde probably wouldn't even have noticed him. What does a life hinge
upon? A mask that you wear or don't wear? Until the evening
before the party he'd been looking for a Peter Pan costume, in
which he could have returned home . . .
Franck's cock was now nothing but a soft, damp, ugly thing
that he would have liked to tear off. People meet each other
through coincidences, he thought. A throw of the dice. If couples survived after chance had brought them together, it's
because things could have worked just as well with another girl
if fate had decreed it that way. So no one love story was better
than another, a thousand other lives could have been possible,
perhaps better, perhaps worse. Basically, Franck thought, staring out of the window at the square of starless sky, the only true
love stories were the ones in which one party cheated at the
outset, played with chance, disguised themselves, put on the
right costume, wore the right mask, waited for years before
taking it off. Long enough for the other person to be used to
it, conditioned, trapped.
"And the beautiful Italian girl?" Franck asked her back
gently.
"Beautiful. Still beautiful . . . "
He felt like he was going mad. Clo was just worried.
Perturbed. They would get over this as a couple. He would have
to maintain his bearings. He ran his finger up his wife's spine.

"Beautiful," she went on. "But weird. She doesn't remember Nicolas."

His finger zigzagged a little.

"Twenty-seven years later? You think that's weird? What about you? Do you remember your friends? The people you knew here when you were fifteen?"

She hesitated.

"No, you're right."

Franck halted the track of his finger just before he reached Clotilde's neck, disappointed.

He knew she was lying.

23

Saturday, August 19, 1989, thirteenth day of the holiday.
Sky the inky blue of your eye.

Dear future reader,
I'm writing you a postcard from Corsica, a short post-card, because to tell you the truth I've got better things to do these days than write to you.

I'm too busy.

To do anything but dream.

So I'm forcing myself, after abandoning you for a few days, I'm giving you some news, a bit like the only time I went to a holiday camp, in the Vercors, and my mother gave me stamped, addressed envelopes for the entire family, with instructions to write to all my uncles, aunties and cousins.

So then, if it's compulsory . . .

Dear all,
I'm still in Corsica.
Everything's fine, I am enjoying myself, I have lots of friends.
And I'm in love. Since the day before yesterday.
With a dolphin fisherman. I think of him all the time.
He doesn't know. He will never know. He will never love me.
Perhaps he will love my mother instead.
My life is nothing but one big misunderstanding.
Otherwise everything is fine.
Love and kisses.
Clo.

*

Yes, I know, it's short. Apologies!

For two days now, ever since I met Natale, ever since my heart has rocked to the rhythm of his boat, I've distanced myself slightly from the tribe of teenagers and all their tribulations. I see Maria-Chjara walking by in the distance, it's weird, she's painted her buttocks blue, the colour of denim, just down to where her thighs start, with pockets, a fly, fringes, it's incredibly realistic, you'd think it was real fabric, except that isn't possible, because I don't see how she could have got her pretty little bottom into such tiny, tiny shorts, as tight as a second skin . . . All the guys are following her about like stray dogs, like they can't help themselves, sniffing around after her . . . Maria-Chjara keeps an eye on them in her little rear-view mirror, and plays at being Thumbelina, scattering bras and knickers around the big forest, like a tracking game for her army of suitors, her dozen or so starving little ogres.

Maria-Chjara still hasn't lost her virginity, but she's told everyone she's getting back on the plane to Bari on August 25, and has confirmed that she will lose her cherry before she reaches the runway. That's in six days' time. What a way of cranking up the temperature in the heads of those little males being driven crazy by their hormones.

You want my opinion? My favourite, the one who's a whole length ahead of everyone, is the one who's running the slowest. Who's letting the others tire themselves out. My brother Nicolas! I'm taking bets. He's the one that Maria-Chjara is going to choose. When the time comes. She knows. He knows. It's making my brother a bit too proud. Borderline arrogant. Borderline jerk.

But I'm not objective.

I'm in love.

I want to see Natale again. I want him to take me on board. I want him to notice me.

I didn't know something like this could exist, looking at a

man for a quarter of an hour, swapping a few words and then not being able to think of anything but him, day and night.

Is this love, can you tell me?

Suffering unbearably for a man who has nothing to do with me, who's probably forgotten me already, who only spoke to me as a way of getting close to my mother.

Tell me?

Besides, Maman is now a length ahead of Papa. They talked yesterday about the evening of the twenty-third, there was some hard bargaining, and Papa finally gave in. We're all going for drinks at my grandparents' place, Arcanu Farm, before my parents go on up to Casa di Stella to celebrate their anniversary.

All the cousins are going to the A Filetta concert. Everyone except us.

Maman has won. She deserves her bunch of wild flowers on Saint Rose's day. That's making her a bit conceited too. But at least it means we don't have to go and listen to the polyphonic music, that's certain now.

I'll tell you about it, but first I have to tell you about August 19.

About what happened on August 19, 1989, i.e. today.

Far away, very far from here.

But close, very close to Maman's heart.

A crazy thing.

* * *

August 19, 1989 . . . he thought again.

After that day, nowhere in the world, nothing would ever be as it was before, even if no one had really measured the scope of what happened on that day. The biggest revolutions, the ones that overwhelm mankind, wear a mask.

August 19, 1989. The dawn of a new world.

No one cared, however, everyone was on holiday.

No one cared that day, no one except Palma.

24

I've been waiting for you, Clotilde. I even thought you would come before now. I thought I'd be the first person you would come and see."

Clotilde gazed at the sea through the enormous bay window of the Punta Rossa villa. The view was still as dizzying as ever. The house felt as if it was hooked onto the cliff, and you'd only have to open the French windows to plunge straight into the Mediterranean. Turning on your heels and looking through the opposite window, you could see the entire Balagne mountain range, Notre Dame de la Serra at the front, then Capu di a Veta, Monte Cinto behind that.

A timeless wonder.

Only Natale had aged.

He'd aged a great deal.

She stepped towards the viewing platform above the rocks of Punta Rossa, taking care not to be spotted by the few tourists standing by the lighthouse. She had told Franck she was going to see the police in Calvi, to ask Captain Cadenat if he had any news about her wallet. And it was only half a lie, after all, since a policeman's daughter lived here, at least when she wasn't reporting for duty at the Balagne Medical Emergency Unit. Aurélia Garcia had become a nurse at the Unit's hospital complex in Calvi, she started early and wouldn't be home before midday.

Natale had offered her a coffee. Clotilde had accepted.

Natale was taking his time.

It would take some time to break the ice.

Clotilde let the wind ruffle her hair. She was fine out here, on the terrace. She had no desire to go back inside the villa. Normally, she thought, houses are a bit ordinary on the outside, boxes on standardised plots, almost identical, even in the most affluent areas. But hidden behind the boring façades were naked intimacies, rooms in which every trinket on every surface, every frame hung on every wall, every book on every shelf revealed an identity. A person with a particular taste, a soul.

The very opposite of Punta Rossa.

The strange chalet set down on the red rocks, constructed entirely of wood and glass, had been built by Natale, plank by plank, window after window, when he was been barely twenty years old; it could only have been inhabited by some exceptional individual, at least in the eyes of the hikers who spotted the building at the top of the customs path. Every detail had been conceived with the greatest originality, from the shells built into the pillars to the dolphins sculpted in the beams. The Punta Rossa villa had been photographed, googled and facebooked thousands of times, as Clotilde had discovered through all those years of tapping its name into a search engine and dreaming, fantasising about the architectural marvel . . . and the person who built it. And yet, which hiker could have imagined that the house contained the most banal, the most kitschy interior decoration? Above IKEA cubes arranged in a wide variety of shapes—bookcases, television table, side table, stools, coffee table—a few posters attempted to bring some colour to the lacquered whiteness of the furniture: Klimt kisses, Renoir piano lessons, Monet water lilies.

"Your coffee, Clotilde."

Natale had told her he was in a bit of a hurry. He started

work at eleven o'clock. He was in charge of the fish counter at the Super U supermarket in Lumio.

"Don't look at me like that, Clotilde."

"Like what?"

"As if I've disappointed you. With all this. With the person I am."

"Why? Why would I be disappointed?"

"Don't make it worse."

He went off and came back a few seconds later with a glass in one hand, a thimble-sized goblet, filled to the brim with pink liquid.

A liqueur or medicine?

Clotilde knew Natale must be just over fifty now, but she still thought he was handsome. Even more handsome than he had been at twenty-five. But disillusioned. Melancholy. Almost cynical. She left the terrace to join him in the villa. A photograph of Aurélia hung above a sideboard with a sliding glass door that revealed a collection of eggcups, rolled-up napkins and tea caddies. Clotilde stared at the photograph. Aurélia was smiling. A designer dress. Tanned skin. Plucked eyebrows.

"I'm not disappointed, Natale, it's just I would never have believed it."

"Neither would I."

He turned round. His thimble was already empty, and full again. Clotilde had spotted the bottle this time, and it wasn't on the shelf of the medicine cabinet.

Myrtle liqueur, 40°, Damiani Cellars.

Clotilde couldn't leave it there. Not after all these years.

"Natale . . . "

Too late to retreat. She looked away from the picture of Aurélia.

"Natale, I can tell you now, it's all in the past, as they say. But you know, all those years, even if we never wrote, phoned, or contacted one another, you were still always there with me.

I'm not talking about the summer of '89 when I was fifteen, our boat trips, Revellata Bay. I'm talking about afterwards. My life afterwards. You were the proof that everything is possible, Natale. A kind of compass, with a fifth cardinal point, somewhere among the stars."

His answer cut through the air.

"You shouldn't have thought that, Clotilde. I didn't deserve it. That's what life is about, seeing your teenage idols ageing in front of your eyes. Seeing them disappoint you. Seeing them die in front of you."

At the point I'm at, Clotilde thought, I might as well empty the old toy box right down to the bottom.

"It doesn't matter, I was still in love with you."

Another thimble emptied.

"I know . . . but you were fifteen years old."

"Yes. And I collected skulls. I dressed like a zombie. I loved ghosts."

Natale merely nodded, so Clotilde went on.

"You were in love with my mother. It drove me mad. If only because of my father."

Natale walked over to Clotilde. He seemed to hesitate before resting a hand on her shoulder.

"You hated your mother too much. And you loved your father too much. Logically, it should have been the other way around, but at fifteen you didn't understand."

Clotilde recoiled. The implication behind Natale's words had taken her by surprise.

You didn't understand.

"What do you mean?"

"Nothing, Clotilde. Nothing. There's no point shedding light on old shadows. Let your parents rest in peace."

Natale turned his eyes away from the Mediterranean to look towards the mountains, losing himself in Capu di a Veta.

"I didn't hate my mother," Clotilde continued. "I was jealous, that's all. It was so ridiculous, when you think about it. So ridiculous when you know what happened next."

For a moment Natale's eyes lit up, and Clotilde felt as if she was fifteen again. Natale answered, looking away from her.

"You were stupid, most of all! I liked you, with those black clothes of yours, your rebellious teenager look, your notebook and the novels that you wedged under your arm. You were a dissident, like me. But another kind, another colour."

Other words collided in Clotilde's head, words uttered by Natale in another life, on Oscelluccia beach, words she had never forgotten.

We're the same, you and me, Clotilde. Fishers of dreams against the rest of the world.

Natale filled another thimble, then sat down on an awful aubergine velvet armchair.

"I've seen *Beetlejuice* since then. I've also watched *Edward Scissorhands* again. And each time I thought of you. That crazy girl Lydia Deetz who talked to ghosts. Are you still as wild about Winona Ryder?"

You'd better believe it, sweetheart!

"Definitely. I saw her again in *Black Swan* with my daughter Valentine. Five years ago. She didn't like the film or the actresses. But I loved it."

Another thimble. He'd already had quite a lot, even if the level of the bottle from Damiani Cellars hadn't dropped that much. Clotilde went on: scraps of complicity coming back.

"You know that Winona Ryder wasn't even eighteen when she fell in love with Johnny Depp, who was nearly thirty. They were together for four years. They got engaged. Johnny Depp was so madly in love that he had *Winona Forever* tattooed on his arm, can you believe it?"

Natale didn't say anything. That in itself was a kind of answer, particularly when you knew what happened next, the break-up of Winona and Johnny. Johnny altering his tattoo when he couldn't get rid of it, changing it to *Wino Forever* . . .

The myths of adolescence.

Believing, being disappointed, fading away.

Myths drowned in myrtle liqueur.

Natale had nothing more to say.

But Clotilde did. She wasn't going to give up quite so easily. She looked at Natale sitting in the armchair that was too low for him; there was no guarantee he'd be able to get up to go and sell whelks and codfish from his frozen fish section.

"I saw Maria-Chjara last night. She was singing on Oscelluccia beach."

"I know. Hard to miss the posters."

"She didn't sing too badly, either. I saw the *Aryon* too."

"I'm sure, she's still moored there. Still clinging on."

Natale was clutching his empty glass, as if he no longer had the strength to fill it again.

"I've also seen Cervone. To tell you the truth, I see him every day. I'm staying at the Euproctes campsite. Orsu, too, although I didn't recognize him. Papé Cassanu, obviously, and Mamy Lisabetta. I didn't remember Speranza, but . . . "

"What are you searching for, Clo?"

I'm trying to provoke you. To get a reaction out of you. To make you smash that bottle of myrtle liqueur against the wall and hurl yourself into the Mediterranean to sober up. I'm trying to talk to you about all the mysteries that are twisting my guts, I'm asking you to help me, you, the only person I can trust.

"The truth. Is that OK, Natale? I'm searching for the truth! I can unwrap it for you, if you like—everything that's gone wrong since I came back to La Revellata. Sergeant Garcia, your father-in-law, told me that the steering mechanism of my parents' Fuego was sabotaged. My papers were stolen too, from the safe in our bungalow. With no signs of a burglary. It's impossible, but that's what happened. And that seems almost normal compared to everything else. The letters. You're going to think I've gone mad, but too bad! I've had messages from the beyond. Messages from Palma."

Natale was shaking. He set the thimble down on the table closest to him. As if it were burning his hand.

"Can you say that again."

"A letter, it was waiting for me at bungalow C29. Somebody delivered it there a week ago. A letter to me that only my mother could have written." She forced herself to laugh. "It's the kind of thing that would make you believe in ghosts, don't you think, Natale? If only I still had Lydia's gift."

Natale got up. He came towards her with great determination, as if he had suddenly sobered up.

"They do exist, Lydia."

"Lydia?"

"Clotilde, I mean. They do exist."

"Who?"

"Ghosts."

Clearly he hadn't sobered up after all.

"I'm going to let you in on a secret, Clotilde. It's something I've never dared tell anyone, let alone Aurélia or her father. If I'm living in this house as if it's a prison, if I'm living with Aurélia, if I've abandoned all my dreams one by one, it's because of ghosts. Because of one ghost in particular. You were right, Clotilde. Ghosts do exist, and they ruin our lives. I know you're going to think I've lost my mind, but I don't care. You've got to go now. Aurélia will be back at midday and I don't think she'd like to find you here."

Out of the question. Natale was messing her about.

"What are you doing with her anyway? And don't talk to me about ghosts."

He looked out through the bay window, staring at the cross on the top of Capu di a Veta.

"It's funny, Clotilde. You've aged more than I have, in the end. Now you're the one who doesn't believe in the strange or the irrational. In spite of all the signs. But since you don't want to hear me talk about this ghost of mine, I'll simply tell you that I had my reasons for giving in to Aurélia's advances. Good reasons, compelling reasons."

The spark that had appeared in his eyes had gone out once and for all.

"You know," he went on, "rational couples, the ones who start out without attraction, without illusions, are the ones that last the longest. For one simple reason, Clotilde. One implacable reason. Because you can't be disappointed! Because things can turn out better than you expected. Who can say that about a love story? Who can say that about passion? That it's better at the end than it was at the beginning?"

A voice screamed inside Clotilde's head. Not you, Natale, not you! Anybody can come out with this stuff, any old bastard, but not you!

For years, when things were going badly, she had thought of him. Of Natale Angeli, fisher of mermaids, dolphin-trainer, a man who believed in the stars, in his dreams, as big as the ocean. Who could communicate that faith to a young girl. Who could make her believe that life wasn't messed up in advance.

Natale Angeli.

Who set down the thimble in which he had drowned his illusions, ready to go off to his shift at Super U. That same fearful gaze, from one window to another, like a euproctus salamander in a vivarium, caught between *mare* and *monti*, as if he didn't know from which direction the ghosts might appear to spirit him away.

"And what about you, Clotilde, are you part of a happy couple?"

And bang! What did she think?

Pontificating at him like that, being a bit arrogant, border-line stupid.

The rebellious girl, the skulls, the raven-black hair.

What did she think?

That Natale wasn't disappointed in her, too?

25

Saturday, August 19, 1989, thirteenth day of the holiday.
Prussian blue sky.

It's funny.

It's the afternoon and people are watching television. Well, some of them are.

Glued to the screens as if something serious has happened. As I walk along the diagonal path, I try to peer in to one of the mobile homes owned by some Italians—the ones who put up a huge screen, built a concrete flight of steps in front of their door, a tiled garden path and a little wall around their site planted with pansies and geraniums. Apparently they live here nine months a year.

I don't see anything on the screen.

Or I do, but they're ordinary images, not the kind of scenes you'd expect from an attempted assassination or a declaration of war. Honestly, you won't believe it—all I can see are people picnicking, with little picnic blankets, in a field, surrounded by small bumpy hills.

That's what these people are watching? Other people eating?

At last a journalist starts talking but I can't hear what he's saying, I can only read the words that appear beneath him.

"Live from Sopron."

Sopron?

Obviously that isn't going to make you jump, but I did. Sopron is the name of a little town in Hungary, with sixty thousand inhabitants, near the Austrian border. Don't imagine that I'm a total geography swot, it's just that Sopron, if you remember, is the town my family comes from, on my mother's side.

Crazy, right? I warned you.

For what stupid reason have all the cameras on the planet gone to Sopron?

I sprint, believe me, I sprint to C29, our bungalow.

Everyone is at number 25, where the Germans are staying, Jakob and Anke Schreiber, Hermann's parents.

Everyone is at number 25 because they have a television. We don't.

"What's happening, Ma . . . "

Mama Palma raises a finger to hush me. No one turns around, they are all sitting on their plastic chairs, staring at the screen, and it's still showing nothing but these families in tracksuits eating chicken legs and drinking beer. What is this madness? What is happening in Hungary?

The resurrection of Sissi?

The end of the world?

A flying saucer landed on one of the picnic blankets with ant-sized mini-aliens inside?

It takes me a few minutes to work out why the whole world is focused on these yokels having their lunch. The yokels are Germans on holiday in Hungary. East Germans, to be precise. And the hills are Austrian.

Have you got it?

Not completely? OK, let me give you the background.

Today, on August 19, 1989, the Hungarian authorities decided to open the borders. The ones belonging to the Iron Curtain. For the Hungarians this had been possible for a few weeks, and generally speaking they'd go home after taking a little tour of the west. But this time they'd got rid of the border for everyone, with no regard for nationality. Operation open gate! Lasting exactly three hours, from three till six, long enough for people to organise an enormous picnic, a Pan-European Picnic, as they call it. The army sat back, folding their arms.

Then the rumour went around, and the East Germans didn't need to be asked twice.

More than six hundred of them, who happened to be on holiday in this corner of Hungary, crossed the border before the gates closed again. And according to the journalists, they're in no hurry to go back.

The journalists are insisting that this is a historic moment, it's the first breach in the wall between West and East, even if it's just a test to see how the Russians will react.

That's a foregone conclusion.

No reaction.

Gorbachev doesn't care.

The only people it's really bugging, judging from the TV, are the East German rulers. They are pictures of the big boss of the GDR, Erich Honecker, looking absolutely furious. In front of all the cameras, live from East Berlin, he goes on bawling, hand on heart, finger on the hem of his jacket, the visor of his cap between his thumb and his forefinger, a Stasi army nodding behind him:

The Berlin Wall will stand for another hundred years!

Die Mauer bleibt noch 100 Jahre!

He repeats those words.

Die Mauer bleibt noch 100 Jahre!

As if it's a historical truth.

Something to remember, to recite, to carve in stone.

Die Mauer bleibt noch 100 Jahre!

In gold letters stamped in the great book of history's mistakes.

* * *

He recited it again in his head, almost amused.

Die Mauer bleibt noch 100 Jahre.

26

August 19, 2016, 9:00 A.M.

The heat in the bungalows was already almost stifling, from the moment the rays passed over the branches of the olive trees, warming the metal cube like a tin can abandoned in the blazing sun. Clotilde liked to cook like that, like cannelloni in a bain-marie. She liked lying in bed on her own, feeling the temperature rise until it became unbearable, until her body was dripping with sweat. All she needed was a shower or, even better, a swimming pool to throw herself into as soon as she got up.

Franck had gone running. Valou was still asleep, and her attentive father had let her have the room that was in shade until midday. His little darling.

Except that it was Clotilde who felt like an excited teenager. Her fingers slipped again over the keypad of her mobile phone. She reread the three lines of the message that had arrived during the night. At 4:05 A.M..

> *Happy to have seen you again.*
> *You've become very beautiful, Clotilde, even if I preferred you as Lydia Deetz.*
> *Probably because since then, I've learned to live with ghosts.*
> *Natale.*

She read and reread those three lines, weighing each word of her response.

Happy to have seen you again.
You're still as handsome as ever, Natale, even if I preferred
you as a dolphin-chaser.
Since then I've learned to live without ghosts.
Clo.

She was lulled by a delicious feeling of euphoria. This Natale bore little relation to the man whose memory she had guarded so jealously, but strangely, the feeling of disappointment had faded, evaporated. As if one of her teenage idols, some singer with a perfect body displayed on a shiny poster, had come down from his billboard, and each of his imperfections made him even more charming. More human. More lovable.

Clotilde remembered a Natale who drove her crazy. An inaccessible fantasy for her fifteen-year-old self. Today, she had discovered a fragile man. All of his dreams shattered. Misunderstood. Misloved. Mismarried.

But still free, all in all.

Still free! From the depths of her bed, Clotilde found the expression paradoxical. Natale was still free because a woman had stolen his freedom. She laughed gently to herself. Basically, all lovers steal freedom. They dream of finding Prince Charming, only to lock him up in a basement.

She placed the phone on the bedside table and fell back into a doze, rolling herself up in the warm, damp blankets.

How much time had passed when Franck's voice made her jump?

"Thanks for breakfast."

More than half an hour.

Clotilde woke up with a start and accepted Franck's kiss on her forehead. Sweat against sweat, Franck's from his efforts to jog up to Notre Dame de la Serra, and Clotilde's from lounging in her oven.

She struggled to imagine the reason for this rare kiss.

Thanks for breakfast

She got to her feet in surprise.

The table was laid.

Fresh bread, croissants, coffee, tea, honey. Fruit juice and jams.

Franck? Had Franck laid the table to impress her? Was his "thanks for breakfast" an ironic formula to make her get up? Her husband, the bold athlete, shaking the lazy slugabed?

Clotilde's eyes fell on the mobile phone beside the bed and she felt a tremor of guilt.

Don't spoil everything.

She kissed Franck's neck.

"Thank you."

Franck looked surprised.

"For what?"

"This perfect breakfast. The only thing missing is a rose in a single-stem vase."

Franck was totally flummoxed.

"It wasn't you?"

"No, I was asleep."

"And I've only just got here."

Their baffled eyes moved simultaneously to the door of their daughter's room.

Valou?

That she should have performed this gesture for her parents seemed harder to imagine than a discreet intervention by house elves. Franck received confirmation of this in the form of a grunt from beyond the grave as soon as he pulled open the curtain in the girl's bedroom.

Not Valou, not Franck, not her . . .

Who then?

Clotilde put on a shirt and studied the table, troubled by details that she hadn't noticed at first. There weren't three bowls, three sets of cutlery and napkins on the little camping table, there were four. But the number was unimportant compared to the other coincidences.

Franck came out of Valentine's room, and Clotilde pointed to a glass of pink juice and the white bowl placed beside it.

"Nicolas always sat there, at the end of the table. He always had a grapefruit juice and a bowl of milk for breakfast."

Franck didn't reply, so Clotilde went on, indicating a cup and a coffeepot that were both still steaming hot.

"Papa sat opposite him, there. He had a black coffee."

A teapot, two teabags.

"Maman and I had tea. She had bought some jam at the market in the port af Stasero, fig and arbutus."

She gently turned the pot of jam beside the pointy baguette. Fig and arbutus.

Clotilde put her hand on the table, feeling dizzy.

"It's all there, Franck. It's all there. Just like . . . "

Franck raised his eyes to the ceiling.

"Like it was twenty-seven years ago, Clo? How can you remember the flavor of the jam you had for breakfast twenty-seven years ago? The brand of tea? The . . . "

Clotilde stared at him almost spitefully.

"What? Those were the last moments I spent with my family! The last meals we ate together. They have haunted my nights ever since then, thousands of nights, and thousands of days, the ghosts of Maman, Papa and Nico sitting beside me, at my breakfast table, every mornings when I was alone, when you were away, when you were at work. So yes, Franck, I do remember. Every little detail."

Franck quickly beat a retreat. A ruse, the better to change his angle of attack.

"OK, Clo, OK. But it could just be a coincidence, admit it. Tea, coffee, fruit juice, local jam. Nine out of ten families would scoff that lot for breakfast."

"And the table? Who set the table?"

"I have no idea. Perhaps Valou is playing a trick on us. Or on you. Or me? Or it's just a bad joke. A thoughtful gesture from your friend Cervone, or his devoted servant Hagrid. After all, he seems to worship you."

Clotilde gave a start at the mention of Orsu's nickname. She resisted the desire to deliver a kick to the four aluminium legs, to send everything flying in a spray of coffee and melted butter.

Franck's calm attitude made it even more unbearable.

"It's someone who's trying to make you think about the past, Clo. Don't play their game. Don't even try to find out who . . . "

Clotilde wasn't even listening to her husband's arguments. She had noticed a newspaper folded in two on one of the chairs.

Le Monde. Today's paper.

She looked at it as if it were about to catch fire.

"And . . . the paper?"

"The same thing," Franck went on. "It's all staged. I imagine your parents read that paper every morning, like everyone always does on holiday."

"No, never!"

"Then, you see. Our mysterious waiter has made a mistake. Which proves that . . . "

"Never," Clotilde cut in. "My parents never read the paper on holiday. Except once. Just once. Papa went out to get a copy of *Le Monde* from the newsagent in Calvi, and brought it back before Maman even woke up. He slipped it onto her chair. It was the first breakfast we'd had together. The last meal with the four of us at the table. The next day, Papa went off sailing for three days with some cousins to the Îles Sanguinaires, and he didn't come back until the twenty-third, the day of the accident."

Franck studied the paper on the armchair.

"On August 19, 1989, the Hungarians opened up the Iron Curtain for the first time. At Sopron, on the Austrian border, my mother's birthplace. For the first time in my life, Maman read the newspaper at breakfast, the newspaper my father had bought for her. The paper dated the nineteenth of August, Franck, the nineteenth, the same day as today. It can't be a coincidence! And yet . . . "

"And yet what?"

For a moment Clotilde had a sense that Franck was playing a trick on her, that he must know everything, that no one but him could have laid this table without waking her up. She chased the idea from her mind and went on.

"And yet no one else could have known. No one but Nicolas, Maman, Papa and me. It was a family thing, a meaningless anecdote. Papa bought the paper without planning to, Maman read the article in five minutes, half a page, and then she put the paper on the barbecue and we burned it at lunchtime. No one could have known that detail. No one apart from the four of us. Do you understand, Franck? Whoever put that newspaper on my mother's chair has to be one of us four. One of the four, and still alive."

"That isn't your mother's chair, Clo."

Yes it is, Clotilde was about to reply. Yes, she was going to scream.

Valou got in before her.

"Are you done yelling at each other?"

She was standing there, wrapped in a Betty Boop dressing gown, her hair tousled and her expression drawn. She sat down at the table, on the seat belonging to Nicolas's ghost. She reached out one arm to pick up the paper, another to bring the coffee to her lips, then pulled a face.

"Ugh, it's cold!"

Clotilde watched her, annoyed.

"They'll have to take fingerprints, Franck."

He sighed. He gazed lovingly at his daughter, and then looked at his wife as if she were mad. As if one had definitely taken the place of the other—her youth, her beauty, her *joie de vivre*, her reasoning.

His daughter opened the pot of jam with an energetic twist of her hand, bit into the bread with gusto, living life to the full, preparing to devour the day with a hearty appetite, after a lie-in and a sunny breakfast. A gilded holiday. A dream life. And yet Clotilde couldn't shake this idea: that Valou was desecrating every object she touched. Destroying, with each movement, a secret, sacred order.

Franck was right; she was going mad.

⌒

"Isn't your husband here?"

"No, he went diving in the Gulf of Galéria."

Captain Cadenat had taken over three hours to get there. Franck had given up waiting after less than an hour. The policeman had said on the phone that he didn't understand the business about the breakfast table, but that he would come anyway, not least so that he could sort out the story of the stolen wallet once and for all. He had made vague inquiries, but not found anything. No clues, not the smallest hint of a trail.

He had been pacing around the bungalow for less than two minutes.

"What about your daughter?"

"She must have left, she's supposed to be going canyoning."

Cervone Spinello was standing close by and he nodded. Half the kids from the campsite had gone off in a minibus to spend an afternoon in the gorges of Zoïcu.

"I don't see what else I can do, Madame Baron."

Take fingerprints, you idiot! Then compare them to the prints of all the tourists in this campsite, because one of them must have played this trick on me. Question witnesses, anyone who happened to be passing by my bungalow this morning. And above all, stop treating me as if I've got some kind of learning difficulty.

The rugby three-quarter back exiled on the Isle of Beauty stared at her, his arms dangling by his sides. Cervone had briefed him about the whole story. The accident twenty-seven years ago, the memories returning, the survivor losing her marbles just a little.

Cervone rested a hand on the policeman's shoulder. A gesture from one man to another. The post-match complicity between the thirsty sportsman and the guy who's paying for the next round. "Can I get you a glass of something before you head off?"

The policeman didn't say no.

As she watched them leave, Clotilde understood that she would never be able to rely on the help of the police, or anyone else. That she would have to get by on her own. Alone, even if that meant she had to plan a long series of emergency meetings, interview witnesses, question them and get to talk.

That bitch Maria-Chjara, who had slammed the door in her face, as if she had seen a ghost.

Her grandfather Cassanu, who had known about the sabotage of her parents' car from the beginning.

Natale. Natale, who also had a ghost of his own to show her.

The more the mysteries deepened, the more convinced Clotilde became that the solution lay somewhere in her memories, her memories of the summer of 1989, of which she retained only fragments, fleeting impressions, flashes filtered through her nightmares. How could she trust those? She needed more concrete memories, tangible facts, reliable witnesses. She would have given anything to have her diary, the one in which she had recorded every detail that summer. The one she had never got back.

Why?

She needed a starting point, the end of a thread so she could unravel the rest of the tangled knot, the start of a film that was real, so that the rest of the images would follow. She knew where to look.

Clotilde stared at the breakfast table again. A little further down the path, Orsu, with his rake and spade, was watching her as if waiting to clear the table. As if he knew. As if he knew everything, but couldn't say a word.

That could wait. It wasn't Orsu who was hiding the evidence. Nor Maria-Chjara. Nor Cassanu.

They could wait too.

Clotilde was furious not to have thought of it before now. Just a short walk away from her, three alleys and three mobile homes away, was the archive of memories for the Euproctes campsite. Every deed and every gesture. All the faces. All the looks.

Fifty years of history.

She would just have to persuade the keeper of the museum to open up his book of magic spells.

27

Saturday, August 19, 1989, thirteenth day of the holiday.
Fever-blue sky.

Gripping my pencil, o invisible confidant, I'm writing to you for the third time this day. The flurry of excitement over Sopron seems to have subsided, the rattling iron curtain has closed again—all the better for the people who stayed on the right side of it—Mama Palma went off to sun herself on the beach as soon as they stopped showing pictures of the Austro-Hungarian hills on the TV (replacing them with a panel of global political experts), and I've gone down to the Cave of the Sea-Calves to wait for the sun to set. I haven't told you this yet, but sea-calves are really just a type of seal but they feel the cold and they like the water to be twenty-five degrees and to tan themselves on the rocks. They were all killed years ago, so I'm squatting in their home. You just have to climb over a few rocks to find this cave, which smells slightly of piss, ashes and salty seaweed, and where the sea comes and licks your feet. From here you can see everything without being seen, apart from the fishermen who come and catch crayfish, lobsters or sea urchins.

I'm a bit like them.

A kind of sea urchin.

I just want to throw words down like that, higgledy-piggledy. Don't even have the energy to make phrases anymore. I'll leave that to others, the people who have something to say, *Le Monde* journalists talking about a curtain being torn at the other end of the world; the ones from *Corse-Matin* who are forever going on about the businessman from Nice, Drago

Bianchi, whose body has now been found, at least a body in what was left of his clothes. He was supposed to have gone under a ferry in Ajaccio harbour.

"Is something wrong, Clotilde?"

The first thing I see is the end of a fishing rod, then, at the end of that, I find Basile Spinello. The owner of the campsite. Papé's friend.

I'd be happy enough to talk to him. And tell you about it afterwards. Happy enough.

"What's wrong, Clotilde?"

"Mmm."

"It's not like you to be so melancholy, Clotilde. At least you don't normally let it show."

He must have said a magic word. I don't know why, but I start telling him my life story.

"I'm in love."

"It's your age, my dear."

"That's exactly it. I'm not in love with some idiot my own age."

"Are you thinking of anyone in particular when you mention an idiot your own age?"

"What?"

"My son? Cervone?"

"No, not him!"

Basile bursts out laughing. I like his big mammoth laugh; it almost brings down the stalactites in my grotto.

"You know, my dear," he says with a wink, "the Corsicans have only one shortcoming: they love their families. It's sacrosanct."

He stops there, but I can see what he doesn't dare say.

The Corsicans love their families, it's sacrosant. But when you've got a twit for a son, you've got a twit for a son!

Basile changes the subject.

"So who are you in love with?"

It comes out almost against my will.

"Natale Angeli."

"Aha!!!"

"Do you know him?"

"Yes. You could do worse. Natale's not too lazy, not too stupid, not too ugly. He comes from a good family too. His father, Pancrace, was in charge of the clinic in Calvi for a long time, before he got divorced and went off to open another one on the Riviera. They say that Antoni Idrissi, your great-grandfather, gave him a thousand square meters on the Punta Rossa, in exchange for a coronary bypass that added five years to his life. Natale was angry with his father when his parents divorced, but here family is family, and before leaving for Italy, Pancrace left Punta Rossa to his son. People around here think of Natale as a gentle, enlightened type with his villa built below the lighthouse and all that stuff he does with dolphins. They see him as a charming idealist. But if you want my opinion, I think Natale is hiding his game—he looks like a dreamer so he doesn't scare anyone. His plan to create a dolphin sanctuary, with boat trips to see the creatures close up, might work. Natale is sincere, people sense that, and they're willing to pay through the nose for it. Sincerity. Authenticity. Yes, my love, your Natale is a bit of a gold digger who's hit pay dirt, and he'll go on whistling as if nothing's happening, so that everyone doesn't catch on. But Natale is also an old bachelor, much too old for you, my Clo."

Basile says it in a considerate, incredibly gentle way.

"I know . . . I know. But a guy like that is exactly what I want."

"You'll find him. If you're patient. If you know how to wait. Without revising your ambitions too much."

"He's suggested we go and see the dolphins tomorrow morning, off La Revellata."

"Well, say yes, then. Dive in! He might even need you."

"Me? Why?"

"Have a good think. You're not stupid. Why would he need you? And your mother too, I'd have thought."

Is Basile already aware that Natale and my mother are flirting. Am I that stupid? Is it all right under my nose, does everyone know and I can't see a thing?

"Think about it, Clotilde. Natale has a grand project. A dolphin sanctuary, with a sort of aquarium, and a museum, so that people can study, conserve, and look after them. An eco-building to fit in with the seaside environment. Have a think, what does your mother do for a living?"

"She's an architect."

"And who does the land for his sanctuary belong to?"

"My grandfather."

"Exactly, to my friend Cassanu. I know him very well, the old lunatic. Natale Angeli's project could work, but Cassanu is suspicious, and he's cautious. He won't be an easy man to convince, he doesn't like change."

So if I'm following him correctly, Natale is using me and Maman to soften up Papé?

Or perhaps Basile is talking nonsense.

"Papé is right to be suspicious, don't you agree with me, Basile? Even though I only come here once a year, I'm crazy about this part of the world, the Euproctes, Oscelluccia beach, the Revellata peninsula. I'd like everything to stay the way it is, I don't want anyone to be allowed to touch it during the eleven months of the year that I'm not here. Like in *Sleeping Beauty*, a magic wand to make everyone go to sleep when I leave in September, and I don't wake them up again until July."

"But everything changes, Clotilde. You will too, you'll see. You'll change. More quickly than the landscape."

"It doesn't have to happen. You haven't changed, for example."

Basile was amused.

"No, that's true! But that's a shortcoming rather than a virtue. The great shortcoming of the Corsicans, perhaps—not being able to change. I'm like your Papé in that regard. Honour, tradition, respect. But everything will move on anyway, despite us. Because we're not going to live for ever, he and I. After I'm gone, everything will change completely. (His eye swept across the landscape, all the way to the tents at the campsite, whose flagpole was just visible.) And to tell you the truth, I'd rather not be around to see that."

Except that he was still here.

And he could see it already.

A procession of teenagers was coming down the path that started above the cave and led down to the sea, in a hurry to get there before sunset. Maria-Chjara walked at its head, all dressed in white lace. Hermann followed after in his cyclopean way, with a radio on his shoulder wailing out "You're My Heart, You're My Soul" by Modern Talking; the radio continually changed shoulders as Maria slalomed down the path. Behind him, Cervone and Estefan were pulling a small trolley loaded with packs of beer. Nicolas dawdled a little way behind the others. And Aurélia appeared a few meters behind my brother. Then came Tess, Steph, Lars, Filip, Candy, Ludo . . .

The herd was on the move. Going to Alga beach, I assumed.

* * *

He closed the notebook and rested the palm of his hand on the cold stone of the cave.

Basile had been right to let his cancer of the colon take him away.

Since then, paradise had been conquered by fools.

28

E*verything's fine*
Valou

Attached to the text was a photograph of Valentine with a helmet on, strapped into a harness, perched with a group of teenagers above a spectacular waterfall. There was no reason to worry, there were trained instructors in charge of the canyoning activity, and Valentine was a sporty type. Yet Clotilde couldn't quite rid herself of the feeling of unease. She put it down to the mysteries that seemed to be piling up around her; the strange, sly pressure they exerted. Franck, who had gone off diving in Galéria for the day, was right on one point at least. She mustn't brood. She needed to move on.

She walked along the pink gravel path that led to mobile home A31, reputedly the best looked-after in the campsite. The owner had even installed solar panels on the roof, a water-butt and a small wind generator perched on top of a pole, right next to the German flag.

Jakob Schreiber was the oldest resident of the Euproctes campsite. He had first come here with his wife in the early 1960s, a rucksack each and a motorbike between them. Then he had come back in the seventies, with an Audi 100 and a Canadian tent for three. Their son Hermann had been less than three months old. Then they came back every year, renting mobile home A31 for the first time in 1977 and buying it in 1981. Those were the best years, the ones during which

Jakob personalised his plot, cultivated his garden, set up a veranda. From the nineties onwards, history began to go backwards. First of all Jakob and Anke spent their holidays on their own again, when Hermann turned nineteen and chose to stay on in their flat in Germany, working for a chemical company over the summer months. Then from 2009, when Anke closed her eyes for the last time, Jakob continued to come back to the Euproctes alone, for more than three months a year.

Just as villages always have a knowledgeable old man who preserves their history, and companies have a document-keeper who looks after the archives, in the campsite there was an old tourist who conserved all the pictures.

More than fifty summers, since 1961.

Jakob had given the most beautiful pictures to the camp managers; they were hung on the walls of the reception, in the bar, under the pergola; pictures in black and white, photographs of women in bikinis from the old days, people dancing on the beach in flares, Franco-German football matches from 1962 until 2014, smiling children, giant barbecues . . . Jakob Schreiber was a passionate photographer. Inclining towards manic and obsessive. Over time, he had become an almost mute witness.

Jakob Schreiber invited Clotilde in with a slightly old-fashioned courtesy. Most of the walls of his mobile home were covered in large picture-boards displaying hundreds of photographs in no apparent order. Clotilde's first impulse was to look around at random for the years that interested her, but she refrained out of politeness.

"Monsieur Schreiber, there are some photographs I'd like to see. Anything from the summer of 1989."

"The year your parents and your brother died in that accident?"

Jackob spoke with a strong German accent. He talked loudly to drown out the radio, a German station that didn't broadcast music, just the monotonous voice of a presenter.

"I understand, I understand."

While they were still talking, he hurriedly took out his mobile phone and started tapping on the keys. He did this for more than thirty seconds, and Clotilde thought about returning his rudeness and getting up to look for the pictures she wanted to see.

"Sorry, Mademoiselle Idrissi," Jakob said just as she was about to do so. "I'm only an old man with a little boy's hobbies. Do you know the programme 'Who wants to win a million in their own sitting room?'"

Clotilde shook her head.

"It's the same as on television, but adapted to the radio. You have to subscribe with your phone and download an app. When the presenter asks questions, you have to reply in less than three seconds, so there's not enough time for you to look up the answer on the Internet. You tap A, B, C or D. If you've got it right, you progress. It's only the last three questions that aren't multiple choice."

"And you really win a million if you get all the questions right?"

"Yes, apparently. It's all paid for by advertising. The programme is a huge hit in Germany, there are hundreds of thousands of subscribers. But like the vast majority of Germans I've never got beyond the tenth question."

"And now?"

"I'm on the ninth, you reach the second level on the twelfth. But I've got time, the next question won't come up for another fifteen minutes. It's all the advertising, as I said. So, the summer of '89, is that the one?"

Jakob got to his feet. The seventy-year-old still seemed quite alert. He went into another room of his mobile home.

"Hermann's room," he explained. "I turned it into a dark-room in the late nineties."

Dozens of filing boxes, all labelled and numbered, were lined up neatly on the shelves.

Summer '61.

Summer '62.

And so on up to 2015. The most recent years were archived in several files.

"I take a few hundred photographs a year," Jakob explained. "Particularly since it all went digital. But even before that, I used up dozens of films each summer. So here we go, '89."

He climbed onto a stool, took down the box and came back to Clotilde.

"If your parents didn't die in an accident, but were murdered, there is every chance that the murderer's face will appear in one of these shots."

She thought at first that he was serious, but then the old German smiled at her.

"And I'll be the witness they need to get rid of. But I suspect you're only here out of nostalgia. That happens sometimes, former visitors asking me about old photographs, for a wedding or an anniversary."

He looked at his mobile phone again—it was almost a tic, because the radio was still broadcasting a series of jingles in German—then he opened the box.

For a second, Clotilde thought that Jakob was going to have a heart attack right there on the spot.

Valentine waited until it was her turn before throwing herself into the void. It didn't look too difficult. First of all you had to abseil down seven meters, hang above the little platform half-way down the waterfall, then take a deep breath, hold your nose and jump. The basin below, the largest of the natural pools in the Zoïcu gorges, was three meters deep, according to the instructors.

Nils and Clara had already gone down. There was only Tahir ahead of her.

Valentine couldn't have known. Perhaps it was better that way.

Valentine couldn't have known that the carabiner holding the harness, the one that supported her weight, was about to break. That at the slightest sudden movement her safety harness would fail, and the clasp would give.

Valentine looked at the void with an excitement that left no room for fear. From the platform, Tahir had just leapt into the waterfall. His almost animal cry had changed into a an explosion of laughter as soon as he surfaced.

Pure happiness. Valentine buzzed with adrenaline.

She couldn't have known that the equipment she had been given a few minutes before leaving had been sabotaged.

It was her turn.

Jérôme, the canyoning instructor, put his hand on her wrist and guided her towards the void, passing the rope around her waist.

⌒

There was nothing in the box.

Summer '89.

An empty file.

Not a single photograph, not a single negative.

"I . . . I don't understand," Jakob stammered.

He put his hand inside the box as if to check that it didn't have a false bottom. It was almost comical. He climbed back on the stool and pulled out the boxes on either side to check that nothing had fallen out, but didn't find anything.

He went on opening the nearby boxes, grunting *scheisse* and *verdammt*. For him, finnding that box empty was like watching a whole well-ordered life be turned upside down; as if the contents of the rest of his files were going to fly away in turn, like a game of dominoes, toppling one another. Clotilde was about to tell Jakob to forget it. That it wasn't his filing system that was at fault, that he hadn't made a mistake. That a ghost had passed through this place.

As with her wallet in the safe; as with her mother's letter, as with the breakfast table.

"I don't understand," Jakob kept saying, over and over again.

A jingle on the radio seemed to pull him out of his obsessive cul-de-sac: "Who wants to make a million?" was about to start again.

The tenth question.

Jakob suddenly froze. The presenter asked something incomprehensible, in a slightly surreal voice, and then, even faster, listed the four options:

A, Goethe, B, Mann, C, Kafka, D, Musil.

Ein, zwei, drei . . .

A ding burst from Jakob's phone.

"*Ja, Antwort B*, only Thomas Mann stayed at Davos sanatorium, there's no doubt about it!"

He was in a state of euphoria for a few more moments, before the box at his feet brought him back to sad reality.

"Maybe I'm losing my marbles, Mademoiselle Idrissi. I spend my days organising these damned files, and the one day someone asks to see one of them . . . "

"It doesn't matter, Monsieur Schreiber. As you said, it's just nostalgia."

"I must be going mad. But as you have seen, Fräulein, I do still have that *verdammte* memory of mine."

On the radio, the presenter confirmed, *Antwort B,* Thomas Mann, followed by another endless tunnel of advertising.

Clotilde got up. She'd hit another dead end. She still needed to question Maria-Chjara and Cassanu. Go back and question Sergeant Cesareu Garcia as well or, even better, have a conversation with Aurélia, his daughter.

Ding.

This time the message came from Clotilde's phone.

Natale.

She felt herself blushing and, like a young girl caught talking to her lover, she turned off her phone. She would read his message later. Perhaps in the Cave of the Sea-Calves.

"Let me say it again, it doesn't matter, Monsieur Schrieber."

The German scratched what few grey hairs he had left on his head.

"If you aren't in too much of a hurry, I could find everything you're looking for in the cloud."

"The what?"

"The cloud. It's a kind of backup space on the Internet. It's taken me years but I've scanned all the photographs since 1961 and stored them in that virtual bunker. Can you imagine what would happen if my *Landhaus* caught fire, or was carried off by a storm? In the cloud, the files are archived for all eternity, like a plot paid for in perpetuity in a graveyard. I just need a good Wi-Fi connection, a USB drive, and I should be able to find it all for you."

Clotilde didn't know much about computers, but it seemed hard to imagine that the invisible ghost could climb into the clouds and steal files guarded by angels.

Her hope returned.

"I'll have to take my laptop to reception," Jakob explained, "that's where they've got the best connection. I'll ask Cervone Spinello to reserve me some space this evening. I've got a printer here to print them out. If everything goes according to plan, you'll have your photographs tomorrow morning. Does that work for you?"

Clotilde almost threw her arms around him.

The radio went on wailing its silly jingles. She found herself wishing that the presenter would ask another question so that she would have an excuse to leave.

To rush away. To turn her mobile phone back on and read the message in her cave.

For the first time a song came on the radio.

"Can I offer you some tea, Mademoiselle Idrissi?"

Jérôme was looking after Valentine's descent. He had wrapped the abseiling rope around her waist, and was letting it out in little bursts, ten centimeters at a time.

She was a pretty girl, with a sparkle in her eyes.

He checked her descent. Another five meters and she would reach the platform where she could let go of the rope and throw herself into the waterfall, as they had taught her, stiff and straight as a rod, so that she entered the water feet first without breaking her back or her neck on impact.

Little Valentine really was pretty.

Jérôme lost his concentration for a brief moment. If it had been longer, it wouldn't have changed anything.

First he felt the rope slacken, as if it wasn't supporting any weight. Then, in the same second, he saw it hanging in the void like a runaway snake.

Valentine's body was falling.

Not like a rod, but rolled up in a ball, head first, dropping like a stone.

29

Saturday, August 19, 1989, thirteenth day of the holiday.
Mischievous-Smurf blue sky.

T*ime*: exactly midnight
   Place: Euproctes campsite, Alga beach, far away from
   my parents.
Agenda: The August 23, 1989, Plot
Present: everyone invited by the plotter-in-chief.

Pay attention, my invisible confidant, this is the plan, it's a secret plan, so I'll tell you everything because I trust you, but no one else must know!

Cross your heart and hope to die?

OK, in all likelihood you're going to be reading this after August 23, 1989, but you never know, perhaps you'll be reading it after the year 2000, but they'll have invented some kind of time machine that will let you go back to 1989, a few days before the plot, and intervene.

I assure you, there is nothing lethal about this plot.

The head of the gang is Nicolas. Yes, my brother. Little Nico, playing his cards close to his chest. As nice as pie in front of our parents, in front of the grown-ups, in front of the girls. But he's the one who's up to all kinds of schemes. He's the provocateur, the ideas guy, the mastermind.

To sum it all up, Nicolas has devised a plan for the evening of Saint Rose's day.

It's very clever. Perfect. He's plotted the timing as if he were rehearsing the robbery of the biggest casino in Las Vegas.

From 7 P.M.: Drinks with Papé Cassanu and Mamy Lisabetta at the Arcanu Farm, with parents, cousins and neighbours.

Between 8 and 9 P.M.: My parents will go to have dinner at Casa di Stella. They will spend the night there. They won't wake up until late the following morning, in love with each other.

From 9 P.M.: Almost all the Corsicans who live in Revellata Bay, and in particular the ones who drink and eat at the Farm, will desert the place to go the concert of polyphonic music at Santa Lucia church, in the middle of the *maquis*. And given the size of the chapel, they won't want to be late if they want to get a seat.

After 9 P.M., in summary:
Freedom!
Freiheit!
Libertad!
Libertà!

It's the only window in the whole holiday when our parents won't be around, Nico said, assuming the voice of a Mafioso. We can't miss this chance. As soon as the adults have turned their backs, Nico has suggested that we go to the biggest nightclub in the area, the Camargue, on the road towards the pine forest just past Calvi. So Nico is busy hatching, imagining, anticipating, planning. All he has to do is assemble his commando unit, like in *Mission Impossible*, and choose the other teenagers who are going to pile into the Fuego.

The poor, feeble-minded idiots.

They don't understand that, as in any decent heist movie, the whole aim of the leader of the pack is to set them up—there's always a secret plan behind the secret plan. Nicolas's objective isn't to take four spotty teenagers to wiggle around on the dance floor at the Camargue. Nico doesn't give a hoot about the nightclub, the foam night or the lambada. The only treasure he wants to steal, the only diamond he wants to get hold of that evening is the one hidden inside Maria-Chjara's thong.

August 23: the big night out, the night when he goes into action, the night of the grand lottery prize.

He knows it.

She knows.

They know.

That's their secret plan.

The secret of Saint Rose's day. Nicolas has always liked doing things the way Papa does.

And me?

Thank you, my future reader, for being concerned about me. You're the only one who is.

So what about me? And me and me and me?

As usual.

I settle for the role of silent witness. The one who keeps her mouth shut, who merely ruminates all night when tomorrow she's getting up at dawn to follow a smooth-talking fisherman who's made her believe she's going to swim with dolphins. The witness who knows everything but says nothing, you know, the one in the film whose curiosity gets the better of them, and who eventually gets bumped off.

At the age of fifteen.

I'm too young to go with them, I know. Nicolas told me that without even having to labour the point.

I'm pissed off with him . . .

I wouldn't mind if they got caught just before the evening of the twenty-third.

* * *

He shut the notebook and stood up.

He mustn't lose his concentration. Little by little, Clotilde was getting closer to the truth.

He couldn't go on simply observing. He had to act.

Do something.

There was someone he had to silence.

30

For the fifth time, Clotilde tried to get an answer from the hospital.

"Pick up the phone, please! Pick it up!"

She was leaning against an olive tree, tears in her eyes, her back scratched to bits, her heart ready to explode. It took more than ten minutes of cursing at an automatic answering service, tapping 1, then 2, then #, then *, getting put through to the wrong person, insulting a nurse who hadn't done anything, who didn't know anything, who was going to try to put her back through to reception.

Beep beep beep . . .

"Put me through to my daughter, damn it!"

An operator had put her on hold when she saw she had an incoming call.

Franck. At last.

"Franck? Where are you?"

The tone of her husband's reply sounded more contemptuous than a top surgeon being consulted about a pimple.

"At Calvi hospital. With Valentine."

"How is she?"

Just answer, damn it, answer me!

"I'm with Cervone Spinello. He was the one who drove Valou here in the campsite's 4x4 Touareg. Cervone has been trying to get through to you for almost an hour, but each time he called he got your voicemail. Shit, Clo, why was your phone turned off? You're irresponsible! I left Valentine with you. Where were you?"

She had spent an hour talking to Jakob Schreiber, forgetting that she had turned off her telephone. It was impossible to get away from the old German, who'd gone on and on about himself and his son Hermann, and how successful he was. The cyclops had become an engineer working for the medical branch of a chemical company, was married to an opera singer, and had fathered three children who were as fair as every generation of Schreiber offspring since William II. Clotilde had even left with the son's mobile phone number in her pocket. Hermann was another witness to the summer of '89.

"Where were you?" Franck said again.

Concentrate. Don't crack. After all, Franck had been out of contact too. No one knew where he was, it was Cervone who had to look after Valou. Clotilde asked again, without raising her voice:

"How is Valentine?"

Franck didn't seem to hear her question, but it was if he could read her mind.

"Luckily Cervone managed to inform me. In the end he got through to someone on the diving club switchboard, and they contacted the instructor on the boat. They got me back on board and took everyone to Galéria straight away, all fifteen people who had paid for the trip. I got back as quickly as I could. I was ten meters under the water when Valentine fell, Clo. You were at the campsite, and yet I was the one who . . . "

He had an answer to everything, except the one question she had asked. This time Clotilde exploded.

"Shit, Franck, how is Valou!?"

"So you're worried about her now, all of a sudden?"

The sarcasm in Franck's voice was like a drop of sulphuric acid on her heart.

You bastard! Just tell me how my daughter is!

"Please, Franck," Clotilde begged.

You've got what you wanted! You've heard the sob in my voice. So fine, just tell me.

"She's all right," Franck conceded at last. "She has a few bruises, on her elbows and on the soles of her feet. Jérôme, the canyoning instructor, has nothing but praise for her. She assumed the rod position without panicking, in less than a few seconds. It was a ten-meter drop and she came out with barely a scratch. She's clever. There aren't many girls who would have come out of it the way she did, and not many boys either. You have an extraordinary daughter, you know. Exceptional. Beautiful. Brave. A good head on her shoulders."

OK, Franck, I've got the message. Your little darling is perfect and her mother should give you a break.

"When will you be back?"

"Not straight away. The doctors still want her to rest here for a while. There's a ton of papers to fill out too. It could have been serious, Clo, very serious, a tragedy . . . You have no idea!"

Oh, but I do, you bastard!

Clotilde saw the Passat parked in front of the bungalow as she was returning from the showers. It was almost eight P.M. She quickened her step while Valentine slowed hers. Without thinking, Clotilde took her daughter in her arms. Her face just about reached Valou's neck, great tall thing that she was, but that didn't prevent Clotile repeating over and over again: "My poor little daughter, my poor little girl, thank God you're all right."

Valentine seemed slightly embarrassed.

"You're all wet, Maman."

Clotilde pulled away from her daughter at last. The towel wrapped around her had soaked Valou's Adidas T-shirt. Nothing serious.

"I'll go in and change."

Less than two minutes later Valentine had changed her T-shirt for a neon green top, her jogging bottoms for a skirt that came halfway down her thigh, she had done her hair up into a skilfully shapeless chignon, and put make up on her lips and eyes.

"I'm going to see the others."

She had brushed shoulders with death, and clearly she couldn't care less. For her, death was probably just an old lady you had to say hello to politely when you bumped into her; but an old lady she would never see again. At fifteen, you're immortal.

"Who are the others?"

"Tahir, Nils, Justin. Do you want to see their IDs?"

Clotilde didn't reply. Once again, she struggled to suppress the feeling, the sense of danger lurking around them.

Franck had poured himself a Pietra. He seemed marked by the hours he had spent in the hospital. But Clotilde couldn't feel genuine compassion for him. She still hadn't digested the veiled inferences he was making on the phone. After all, he didn't have a monopoly on anxiety, and her stomach had plummeted just as much as Franck's when she'd heard about Valou's accident. She too had worried herself sick and was still struggling to calm herself down. What did he think?

Franck was playing Candy Crush, lining up the green, red and blue sweets, as he answered Clotilde's questions in an off-hand voice, as if he'd just come home from an exhausting day at work.

Yes, the carabiner had failed, no, he didn't know why, apparently the equipment was worn, but nobody had noticed when they were checking, no, the instructor wasn't under any suspicion, quite the contrary, his reaction had been outstanding, yes, they were all really sorry, but these things happen sometimes, no, he didn't want to cause a fuss, to report them or take things further, yes, everything would be fine in the end, why didn't they all get a good night's sleep and move on.

The words still rattled around in Clotilde's head.

Irresponsible. You have no idea. Where were you?

This time, after throwing his knives, Franck had left them there; once the surge of emotion had passed, he hadn't uttered a word of apology. She had held back her tears. She remembered the phrase she had read somewhere: *A woman who weeps in front of her lover gets everything she wants from him; a woman who weeps in front of a man who no longer loves her is lost.*

She hesitated, then launched in.

"Are they sure it was an accident?"

Franck suddenly sent his sweets, which were supposed to be lined up in threes, flying in a shower of confetti. His whole attitude, from the tone of his voice to the expression on his face, changed from weariness to aggression in the blink of an eye.

"What exactly are you trying to say?"

"Nothing . . . It's just all these coincidences, they keep coming. Valou falling, a clip giving way. My papers being stolen six days ago. The breakfast table this morning . . . "

"Stop!"

He banged his mobile phone down on the camping table, making the plastic legs shake and raising a fine cloud of dust.

"Stop! Your daughter nearly died, Clo, so come down to earth and stop spouting all these old stories of yours, old letters, friends you lost and found again. Good God, Clotilde, stop all this nonsense or I'll explode!"

The plastic chair went flying as he got to his feet.

Franck's nerves were fraying, which was unusual for him. Probably because he was at the end of his tether, because thinking his daughter was dead, or paralysed for life, was unusual too.

Because she should have been as messed up as he was?

An unworthy mother?

Franck picked up his phone, slipped it into his pocket and turned to leave.

"One more thing. When you go to take a shower, don't leave your phone on the bed."

Shit!

Clotilde immediately thought of Natale's texts. She had exchanged a few messages with him before going for her shower, after reassuring herself that her daughter was OK. Clotilde would be seeing Natale again tomorrow; he had invited a ghost to tea, those were his terms, a ghost who would talk only to Lydia Deetz. There was really nothing compromising about their exchanges, but Franck wasn't stupid, and each phrase was underpinned by a hint of something else.

Clotilde was capable of losing it too. Or biting, if she had to.

"My phone that I left on the bed? Did you look inside, did you rummage through it?"

"Why, do you have something to hide?"

Had he dared to do that?

Franck took three steps into the darkness.

"There's a game of poker at the bar. A few regulars. Cervone invited me. I think I'll go."

Before disappearing into the night once and for all, he turned again and said, "For the last time, Clotilde, I beg you, forget it! Pay attention to your daughter. Pay some attention to your husband. Pay attention to what's happening today. And forget the rest!"

31

Sunday, August 20, 1989, fourteenth day of the holiday.
Abyss-blue sky.

He's a charmer. All men are charmers.
A fraud, a scam, not worth a damn.
Designed to trap me.

And the *Aryon*, still rocking on the waves, Natale still chatting, tirelessly going on about dolphins, belugas, narwhals, porpoises, all the cetaceans of the Mediterranean, their natural environment, their intelligence which isn't just a legend, their ability to learn. He explains how to find them, using a word I've never come across before: *upwelling*! It means discovering a bit of the sea which is very deep and has a strong current which, if I understood correctly, pushes the deep water to the surface very quickly, bringing nutrients with it. Even if the currents move all the time, dolphins are clever and know how to spot them. Natale does too! And in particular the most important one, the Liguro-Provencal current, which, by a stroke of luck, passes less than ten kilometers off the coast of La Revellata.

Who'd fall for that one?

Not me, at any rate. He'll find plenty of little girls who will, who'll think they're really going to dive into the middle of a crowd of dolphins, girls dressed in Hello Kitty, with Barbie bikinis and Minnie Mouse headphones. But despite the fact that he looks like a pirate, has the body of an adventurer and a shipwrecked smile, he won't have me. He even tried telling me to change my outfit, so as I wouldn't frighten off his tamed cetaceans, well, he's seen that I'm not the kind to alter my uniform. I put on a pair of black jeans, a *Jaws* T-shirt and a *Shark* cap. More suited to flirting with sharks than dolphins.

We reached the heart of his sanctuary. I felt nothing but a bit more wind on my cheeks, perhaps a little more rocking. Behind us, the Revellata lighthouse looked like a toothpick stuck in an *île flottante*. Natale turned off the engine of the *Aryon* and started praying, or as good as.

It was a prayer I knew.

And you float there, in the silence. And you stay there,
And you decide that you'll die for them
Only then do they start coming out.
They come, and they greet you, and they judge the love you
have for them.

I continued the quote. Natale looked impressed.

If it's sincere
If it's pure
They'll be with you

I let him finish.

And take you away forever.

It was crazy, really, I don't know if you can imagine it, reciting the words from *The Big Blue* in the middle of nowhere with the sea all around.

Natale had lit a cigarette. Without offering me one. Like one more sign that, in his eyes, I was just a kid.

"We won't wait for long," he said between two puffs. "You know the story of the Little Prince? When he tames the fox? Do you remember the most important thing?"

"Hmm."

"To come at the same time every day, so that the fox's heart is ready to greet him. You'll see, my princess, dolphins are like foxes—they get their hearts ready too, and they always come at the same time each day. Hang on . . . "

And gently, he points his finger to his left.

I can't see anything. It's just charm. He's trying to charm me again when he takes my hand and guides it in the right direction.

"There . . . Don't move . . . "

And then there they are, my God . . . I've seen them!

Yes, as I've told you, just as I can see this pen and this page right now, I've SEEEEEN them!

Four dolphins, two large ones and two smaller ones. I didn't just see their fins, I saw them swimming and leaping, diving, coming back up, diving again.

And I wept.

I swear, I burst into tears like an idiot, while Natale talked to them, throwing them fish. I rubbed my eyes, trying to hide the tears, and noticed the charcoal smears from my wet mascara on my fingertips

"Are you hungry, my Orophin? Leave some for your sweetheart! For your little ones! Go on, Idril, catch it. Galdor and Tatië, move over a little."

I swear to you, the four dolphins were less than three meters away, making those little noises they make. We weren't in Marineland or some dumb theme park, we were in their home, just the two of us, and they were there, demanding another bucket of frozen fish.

"Do you want to join them?"

I looked at him with my wet-charcoal eyes, dumber than ever.

"Can I?"

"Of course, if you can swim."

Can I swim?!

I slipped out of the black jeans I was boiling in, the T-shirt with the big teeth, and Natale couldn't help smiling at the sight of me in a bikini. Not a lascivious smile, more that of a father discovering that his little daughter still has her princess costume on under her pyjamas.

I didn't give him time to study the indigo tones of my costume, the sapphire sequins and the little flowers decorated with pearls.

I dived straight in.

I even touched them. Especially the babies, Galdor and Tatië.

You don't believe me? I don't care, I was there! I put my hand on their fins, my palm on their sleek skin, trying to feel its slight flakiness, I looked under the water when, with a flick of the tail, they slipped ten meters below the surface, I saw them come up again with two waves of their bodies, I brushed against them when they jumped and splashed. It isn't even a dream, my future reader, it's beyond that . . . It's beyond anything you can experience.

I have swum with dolphins!

"Come on," Natale said to me, starting the engine again. "There's something I've got to show you."

* * *

The sun had just set behind the bungalows of Alley C.

He closed the notebook and looked at the photograph of the summer of '61 hung above the bar. It was time to finish it. To silence the past once and for all; to put all trace of it on the bonfire, burn it and scatter its ashes.

As if it had never existed.

32

August 19, 2016, 8 P.M.

Your beer, Herr Schreiber."

Marco, the young waiter at the bar in the Euproctes, had checked that the bottle was cold before serving Jakob his Bitburger. The boss ordered eight packs every summer, for the sole use of the oldest customer on the campsite, a kind of imperial privilege dating back to the days of Bismarck.

"Danke."

The German hadn't even looked up from his computer. Schreiber was the exactly the kind of customer Marco couldn't stand. The customer who thinks he's interesting. Who smiles at you with a slight look of contempt, who explains all the whys and wherefores of every single thing, going on about how things were better before, the waiters in the old days, the espressos in the old days, the motorbikes in the old days, the Mediterranean in the old days . . . There was only one thing he couldn't reproach Jakob Schreiber for: at over seventy, he still had the energy and curiosity of a young man, demonstrating for you the superiority of carbon pétanque balls over stainless steel, the superiority of analogue over digital photography, of craft beer over industrially produced.

His days at the campsite were organized as rigorously as a Mannschaft 4-4-2. A game of pétanque in the morning, between ten and twenty photographs in the afternoon, and thirty-three centilitres of beer in the evening. An unchanging way of life.

And to think that he still had a good twenty years to bore them senseless . . .

He wouldn't be the kind to join in with the poker game in the next room.

But in front of his computer, that evening, Jakob was getting bored. At his age, the unexpected was not recommended. *67 per cent of files copied*, said the grey bar that was slowly turning green. Files flashed across his computer screen at great speed, the way they do on those new police dramas where as many different images slide past during the opening titles as there are in a whole episode of *Derrick*. The download still wasn't going fast enough for Jakob's liking. He had calculated that he would have to download about eight hundred photographs from the cloud, all the pictures from the summer of '89, stored at 300 dpi. His old laptop was struggling, either that or the Wi-Fi connection in the Euproctes bar left something to be desired.

Download complete in 11 minutes, it said on the screen, but it looked like one of those dishonest signs telling you the estimated wait in a queue, or an unmoving traffic jam. The second hand of Jakob's watch, on the other hand, kept circling the face.

9:12 P.M.

The next question on "Who wants to make a million?", the last of the day, would be asked in less than half an hour.

73% of files copied.

He waited there, irritated, staring at the five posters that decorated the walls of the bar, five photographs that he had given to Cervone Spinello, and formerly to his father Basile, without claiming any privilege in return other to be served beer, pretzels and Knackwurst imported directly from the Rhine.

The summers of 1961, '71, '81, '91 and 2001.

Jakob gazed at his photographs with pride, those five pictures which gave a synoptic vision of the passing of time, from the first Canadian tents to pop-up igloos, from sleeping bags on the beach to self-inflating mattresses, from wood fires to self-lighting barbecues. Just when he was least expecting it, the download suddenly speeded up, going from 76% to 100% before he had time to finish his Bitburger.

Scheisse!

He downed the beer in one, grabbed a handful of pretzels and tucked his computer under his arm, and with his other hand grabbed his case of boules, because he refused ever to be separated from his Prestige Carbone 125 Demi-dure which, according to the German, were worth their weight in gold. Malicious gossips claimed that Herr Schreiber slept with his pétanque balls under his mattress, like the princess and the pea.

Night was falling. Crickets hidden in the olive trees announced the end of the day like a thousand muezzins perched in as many trees. Amidst their din, in the gloom, Jakob Schreiber paid no attention to the sound of footsteps behind him. He walked quickly and with great determination.

With his feet comfortably protected by his socks, and his socks solidly strapped into his leather sandals, they could have found their own way to the bungalow. They had already done that before in fact, on the day when Jakob had emptied the entire eight packs of Bitburger with tourists of every nationality, on July 8, 1990—the evening when Germany won the World Cup. Hermann and Anke had still been with him in those days. He had spent the rest of the summer drinking Pietra on draught, and had sworn that he would never allow himself to be as generous again. Two years ago he had been alone in his mobile home when he had witnessed his country gaining another victory. This time he hadn't even opened a bottle to celebrate Mario Götze's goal in extra time.

Hermann and Anke weren't there any more.

As soon as Jakob opened the door of his mobile home, he set down his pétanque balls and turned on his transistor radio. He had time to prepare himself, the radio was still broadcasting advertisements, the twelfth question wouldn't be asked for another nine minutes. He sat down at the sitting-room table and turned on his laptop. He clicked distractedly on the file *Summer '89*, thinking about questions 9, 10 and 11, which he had answered with an ease that even he had found disconcerting. In the seven years he had been listening to this programme, he had never got past the tenth . . . Might little Clotilde Idrissi have brought him some luck? With the tenth question, he had won a twenty-four-volume Brockhaus encyclopedia, of which he now had three copies, or seventy-two sizeable volumes to store at his house, and he had seriously considered bringing one of the sets here, to his cramped second home.

The twelfth question corresponded to the third level, the level reached by less than one player in a million according to the statistics provided by the website. You didn't get any money, but you did get a VIP entrance pass to the Pinakothek, the monumental assembly of museums in Munich, with a visit to corridors normally forbidden to the public, access to restoration studios. Above all, before you left, a bust of you would be created by a sculptor which was then exhibited in a special room. So far only seventeen Germans, their heads crammed with facts, had entered into posterity like that.

Jakob was just one question away from becoming the eighteenth.

Distractedly, he flicked through the photographs of the summer of '89. His memory of the faces remained amazingly precise. He easily recognised little Clotilde, Nicolas Idrissi, Maria-Chjara Giordano, Aurélia Garcia, Cervone Spinello; slightly less the ones who had spent only that summer here, but some names came back to him—Estefan, Magnus, Filip. He sped through photographs of landscapes, adults and scenes of everyday life, concentrating solely on the teenagers.

He was worried about why his pictures had been stolen,

because they *had* been stolen, there was no doubt about that. There was clearly some connection to Clotilde Idrissi coming back to the island, even if he couldn't tell what it was. One thing at a time, he told himself, just now he had to concentrate on the competition. He would examine the photographs properly after that.

Concentrating harder than ever.

Concentrating too hard to hear the crunch of gravel outside his mobile home.

The radio presenter announced that he would he asking the famous twelfth question in less than a minute. Jakob's right hand gripped his mobile phone, his left hand trembling slightly. To calm the tremors, he clenched the mouse and clicked on the slide show to keep it going.

The summer of '89 flowed in front of him. Alga beach at sunset, the Cave of the Sea-Calves in the early morning, a game of pétanque, the teenagers dancing, the reception area at the campsite, the car park.

Noch 30 Sekunden, the radio announced.

Jakob frowned; something in the photograph intrigued him.

He didn't hear the door of the bungalow slowly opening.

Noch 15 Sekunden.

Jakob, as if hypnotised, studied the few cars parked there, including, recognisable among all the others, the Idrissi family's red Fuego. The one that would crash less than twenty-four hours later on the rocks of Petra Coda. *23 August, 1989*, said the caption on the photograph, but what intrigued the old German wasn't the car, it was the teenager who was staring at it, with the look of someone who . . .

Noch 5 Sekunden

. . . the look of someone who knew in advance what was going to happen.

Noch eine Sekunde

Jakob closed his eyes, his thumb raised slightly, now concentrating entirely on the question that the presenter delivered at high speed, like the engine of an MG 08. Three seconds to answer.

Answer A) Mönchengladbach, B) Kaiserslautern, C) Hamburg, D) Cologne.

Ein

Jakob knew the answer!

Zwei

He had no doubt, even though he was cautious by nature. As if in a dream he saw his finger resting on the screen, entering the right answer, the journalists contacting him, his name making the headlines of his local newspaper.

In the big corridor of the Neue Pinakothek, in bronze, his skull on display.

Three

It was the second-to-last image his brain ever registered.

Jakob would never reach the third level.

His thumb stopped a few millimeters from the touch screen, just at the moment when the case of Prestige Carbone 125 Demi-dure smashed into his right temple. Jakob collapsed to the ground, taking with him the table, the laptop, the telephone.

In the narrow sitting room of bungalow A31, drenched in blood, his skull shattered.

The German's eyes, before they closed, drowned by the

scarlet spring spurting from his forehead, fixed on one last image on the computer lying on the floor next to him, a few centimeters away from his face.

Still the same photograph, the one of the Fuego in the car park and the teenager staring at the vehicle as if he knew that the steering was going to fail that evening. The teenager that he knew, who he had bumped into that evening, whose hand he had shaken, who had even asked him why he wanted a Wi-Fi connection at such a late hour.

Cervone Spinello.

He waited for several minutes, far too long.

Getting rid of the photographs would be child's play, he just had to delete them, go outside with the laptop and throw it into the nearest rubbish container, leaving not one trace, no proof. Getting rid of the pétanque balls wouldn't be complicated either. They would never find the murder weapon.

But how to get rid of the old German's body?

Take advantage of the darkness? Take advantage of the silence?

It was already too late.

Outside, in Alley A, a noisy group was approaching, probably players from one of the poker tables that had finished their game and were talking about bluffing, beginner's luck and going all in. Others would follow, as each table emptied.

He'd have to think of something else. Now that it was all over, he needed some peace and quiet.

33

He wiped the blood from his hands, from the pétanque balls, the scarlet stains from the floor of the mobile home, then he walked, walked away and waited until he had found a street-light isolated enough that he could start reading the diary again.

Red, everything was red.

Apart from that notebook, and its deep blue words.

* * *

Sunday, August 20, 1989, fourteenth day of the holiday.
Delphinidine sky.

Delphinidine, my future reader, is the scientific name for the blue pigment in flowers. Incredible, isn't it? It's the pigment that roses don't have. That's why no true rose will ever be blue!

I'm not a rose.

I'm letting myself dry on the rocks of Oscelluccia beach. I haven't put on my T-shirt. This time Natale can peer at my innocent water-nymph bathing costume for as long as he likes; no skulls, no skeleton, not even a single drop of black, nothing but every shade of blue.

The *Aryon* is moored alongside us, attached to a ring hammered into the rocks. Oscelluccia beach isn't really a secret inlet that can only be reached by sea, there's a little path that leads almost directly from here to the Euproctes campsite—it's a steep slope, too steep to go down wearing flip-flops and carrying a parasol, but it's a lot less busy than Alga beach.

For the moment we're on our own.

Natale Angeli goes on talking, sweet-talking. Except this time I'm actually listening to him.

"You see, Clotilde, this would be the ideal spot for my sanctuary. At first you'd just have to put up a pontoon, some moorings, maybe a ticket desk and a little bar. I'd model it on the Baie des Tamarins on Mauritius, maybe you've heard of it?"

I shake my head and close my eyes. He can say anything he likes . . .

"It's a bay where dozens of dolphins have settled. Outings are organised every morning, it works like a dream, they've even had to limit the number of boats. It's turning into an industry, but that's not what we'd do here. We'd limit the number of trips. We'd raise the bidding, it would be a privilege, we'd create thousands of disappointed punters and just a few of the lucky elect. And then, if that works, if the money comes in, we could start thinking big. A real building, a sea-water pool, a wellness centre, a small research team . . . "

Then I sense him turning towards me, approaching, his shadow falling over me, making me feel cold.

"Would you talk to your grandfather about it? Would you do that for me?"

I open my eyes. Or rather it's Natale who opens them for me.

There he is, in his swimming shorts, as handsome as a pirate, unattainable, with his tanned skin, the bandana on his shaved head and his bare feet leaving footprints in the sand. Christ, this guy who's asking me to do him a favour knows how to talk to dolphins! He's come straight out of a novel, or a film, he's taken my hand and now he's pulled me into it.

"Of course I will. Why would Papé say no?"

"Because he doesn't give a damn about cetaceans, tourists or me. But if his dolphin-loving granddaughter were to beg him . . . "

I know I should start bargaining, negotiating, setting out my conditions, but I can't do it, so I simply clap my hands.

"Whatever you like! Where do you imagine you'll put this museum of yours?"

Natale becomes unstoppable and starts using words I don't understand—environmental standards ISO something, composite materials, recycling systems—he's even started talking about budgets, it's all very technical, and I switch off until he slips a word that makes me jump into the middle of his costs totalling thousands of francs. *Maman*.

I think I use the familiar *tu* for the first time.

"So you've talked to Maman about it?"

"Of course. Your mother is an architect specialising in eco-buildings. She has a real sense of the practicalities. According to her, you can achieve energy self-sufficiency with just a few solar panels here and there."

He points his finger towards the flatter rocks.

"Have you brought her here?"

He does a brilliant imitation of a grouper, or whatever you call that fish with the big round eyes.

"Yes. Your mother is very skilled, brilliant even. If my project goes ahead, I'm sure she'd be the best person to design it."

I cut him off.

"If she's so fantastic, why don't you ask Maman to talk to Papé?"

He sits down beside me like Robinson Crusoe. I love that cool way he has of hunching himself up. I see a mixture of strength and childishness, a man who is sure of himself and still a little boy in each of his gestures.

There's only one person like him on this planet and I've found him. Except that I was born ten years too late.

"Let's just say that your mother, well . . . as a daughter-in-law she isn't exactly loved. How can I put it? The fact that she isn't Corsican is already a handicap. A surmountable one, I grant you. But to make things worse, she's the one who dragged your father over to the mainland, and not to Aix or Marseille, but to the far north, way above Paris. In the eyes of the Idrissis who stayed here, she stole your dad."

"I live north of Paris too."

"Yes, but you have Corsican blood. You're an Idrissi, a direct descendant. You might inherit all this one day, the eighty hectares. Perhaps that will be enough to persuade your Papé . . . "

To tell you the truth, if you haven't worked it out already, I was truly falling in love. Experiencing that feeling of wanting to give everything to a man, to sacrifice everything, all your values, all your honour, all those promises you've made yourself—sworn them, spat them out—to be a free woman. My understanding of this was all over the place, and yet like some female Darwinian reflex, I hardened; as if the women who had survived over the millennia were the most cautious, and all the impulsive, naïve and spontaneous ones had been liquidated. As if, at the end of the evolutionary chain, caution had become almost second nature, a means of survival.

"Why would I help you, Natale? You adore my mother. I'm sure you've done the whole dolphin thing with her, you've gone sailing with her, let her dive far from the shore, brought her back to this beach. Why would I help you when you prefer her and you don't give a damn about me?"

Natale gave me a look that I registered, without knowing how to decode it; but I already knew that that was the way I would like men to look at me for the rest of my life. An astonished look, a look of intrigue, both uneasy and fascinated. The look of a poker player wondering what his opponent has in his hand, one who keeps on betting just to see . . .

At last he replied.

"Clotilde, cards on the table, you're fifteen. OK, you're more mature than other girls your age, you're original, you're rebellious, imaginative, you're just the kind of girl I admire; but you're fifteen. So my suggestion is that I take you on as an associate. Are you OK with that? With us becoming collaborators? Sharing the same dream, nothing but that. Saving the dolphins, saving the planet, saving the universe; I can tell you, there aren't many girls I've made that suggestion to."

He holds up his hand like a summer camp monitor who's just scored against some nine-year-olds, and we high-five.

When I'm dreaming about him leaving his hand in mine.

Putting his lips to mine.

Pressing his skin against mine.

"We're the same, you and me, Clotilde. Fishers of dreams against the rest of the world."

He's brought Maman here.

Perhaps he's kissed her.

Perhaps he's undressed her, perhaps they've made love.

Perhaps he desires Maman's body, what man could fail to desire her, but perhaps it's me he was thinking of when he caressed her, when he murmured in her ear that he loved her, when he entered her.

Perhaps it was me that he loved, even if his morals forbid it.

"I want a contract, Natale. A contract that commits you to thirty years. I want thirty per cent of the profits from your business, a boat with my name one day, an office all in glass with a view of the sea, a pair of dolphins all to myself, and I want to be able to dress the way I like. If you can grant me all

that, then I will go and jump on Papé Cassanu's knee and discuss your crazy idea."

He burst out laughing.

"And will that be all?"

"Yes . . . Plus a kiss on the cheek."

34

The sea carried away empty bottles, wet confetti and broken streamers like so many dreams abandoned at the end of the night by exhausted dancers, party-goers on the brink of despair; the waves returning them the following morning, bleached and faded.

It was still early.

The *Aryon* floated among all the detritus. Natale, lost in thought, seemed oblivious, as if he had long since abandoned hope that the sea would spew up the bottle he had thrown into it many years before.

Clotilde was late. But she stopped for a minute, just before going on down to Oscelluccia beach. A few seconds to go back in time. It was the same sand as twenty-seven years ago, the same pebbles, the same foam, the same spray mixed with the pungent, peppery smell of the flowers nestling in the hollows of the rocks. Nothing had changed if you didn't look towards the Tropi-Kalliste beach hut or the building site of the Roc e Mare marina. Something keeled over in her heart, rocking it like a boat unsettled by the swell.

My God but Natale was handsome.

He just had to be there, he had to be sitting there scanning the horizon with his lagoon-blue eyes, his eyes that could detonate all the coral reefs in the world, allowing the triggerfish and clownfish to escape so they could add colour and make the oceans laugh.

Natale was wearing a salmon-coloured sweatshirt with a

hood. A pair of jeans that were slightly too big for him. Leather sandals. Clotilde imagined that he might often pose like this, like a statue; that he had retained from his abandoned dreams the magical power to transform reality, for a few fleeting seconds, into something more beautiful inside his head. That he had learned to settle for that. To turn the fish counter at the Super-U in Lumio into an inviolate marine sanctuary. The Cour Napoléon road in Ajaccio, car pressed against car, into a one-man transatlantic crossing. A hasty clinch in darkness with the woman who falls asleep by his side every evening into a starry night of love with one of the passers-by he bumped into earlier that day. One of the passengers who had boarded the *Aryon* in the old days.

Handsome. Solid. Fragile.

"Natale?"

She had slipped on a lilac dress that floated against her thighs. She had slipped off her sandals to walk on the sand that was still cold, almost damp.

He turned around, his eyes fixed on hers.

Handsome. Solid. Fragile.

Dangerous.

Nothing could be more dangerous than men with lagoon-blue eyes, Clotilde thought to herself. Blowing up the reef also meant letting in all the sea monsters, which might enter the protected space where families paddled in safety.

They advanced towards one another, without crossing the final meter that separated them.

"You're playing with fire, asking to meet me here," Natale said. "I had promised never to set foot on this beach again."

"There were a lot of other things you promised too."

He didn't reply. His eye slipped to the *Aryon*, still moored to the rocks.

"You were lucky. I'm free today. I'm not due back at work until tomorrow morning."

Clotilde pinched her lips.

"I'm not. My husband has gone for a run, half an hour or an hour at the most, to Notre Dame de la Serra. I need to be back at the site when he returns. It's . . . it's complicated . . . I told him I lost an earring here. A big silver hoop. It's not just an excuse, by the way, I really did lose it the other night, during the concert."

All the tiny wrinkles on Natale's face began to move in harmony, as if, for all those years, they had been rehearsing a dance designed solely to make his smile irresistible.

"Can I help you look?"

He took her hand. The gesture felt entirely natural. They walked slowly, their eyes lowered.

"You remember?" Clotilde asked.

"Of course. Do you think I often took girls to my sanctuary?"

Oh yes, my handsome mermaid-fisherman, you shouldn't have deprived yourself, in those days!

She stared at the sea.

"Are there still dolphins?"

Natale's eyes didn't move from the sand. He didn't reply. Clotilde went on. Afterwards, she would shut up, she promised herself. She would let him explain. She would just listen, as she had before.

"Galdor and Tatië should still be alive," she said. "Orophin and Idril too, they say that dolphins can live to be over fifty. And that they have the memory of an elephant! Even better than the pachyderms, in fact. The longest amorous memory of all the mammals. I read somewhere that they're capable of recognising a partner just by the sound of their voice, twenty years after they were separated. Do you know a single man who would be capable of that?"

Eyes in the sand. Still.

Why had she mentioned that stupid earring?

She studied the closed Tropi-Kalliste beach bar in front of them, the overflowing dustbins, the chained grey caravan. According to the posters, Maria-Chjara was continuing her tour in the west of the island, Sartène the previous night, Propriano tonight, but she was coming back to Calvi in two days' time.

Clotilde gripped Natale's hand even tighter, as if to warn him about what she was going to say.

"What is this madness? This squalid nightclub, these filthy sheds? Your pontoon, your nature reserve, your museum should have been built here. Explain it to me, Natale. Explain to me why Cervone Spinello won. Why he won out over your project."

Disembowelled plastic bags were flapping through the air, beer cans rolled about, it would take hours for a clean-up unit to tidy all this, and then it would all start again the day after tomorrow. How could her grandfather Cassanu have accepted this sacrilege, how could he have allowed this dump of a beach bar to thrive, rather than Natale Angeli's dolphin sanctuary?

"It's an old story, Clotilde. It's all in the past. Please."

OK, don't push him.

"You brought my mother here too."

You're crazy! Clotilde regretted her words instantly. You call that not pushing him?

This time Natale did react. His feet burrowed into the sand, as if he really did hope to recover the earring.

"Yes . . . And you were ready to get your claws out, your pointed teeth and your spines, a little hedgehog rigid with jealousy over your mother."

"I had reason to feel like that, didn't I?"

"No!"

They stopped walking, turned on their heels and found themselves facing the *Aryon*.

"I was fifteen, Natale but I wasn't a complete idiot. When

you looked at my mother your eyes . . . how can I put it it . . . your eyes seemed to undress her! And she looked at you with the same desire. I never saw her look like that at any man . . . not even Papa."

Gently Natale's thumb stroked the palm of her hand. Like the way the wing-beats of a butterfly can supposedly trigger a tsunami on the other side of the world, those tiny rubs on her skin provoked sensations deep in her belly.

"Right, Clotilde," Natale said, suddenly raising his voice. "Let's take off those masks. They're about as battered and old as our faces are wrinkled. Back in the summer of '89 I was twenty-five and your mother was forty. We were attracted to one another, I grant you. Physically attracted, I should say. But your mother was faithful, and nothing happened between us, believe me, even if she was tempted."

"Like good little angels," Clotilde said sarcastically.

Natale went on as if he hadn't heard her.

"If your mother was tempted to deceive your father, it's not because she fell in love with me, let alone because she'd stopped loving your Papa." He smiled sadly. "It was quite the opposite, in fact."

"Quite the opposite? I don't understand, Natale."

"Your mother approached me, your mother flirted with me, she came on to me, she walked around in public with me so that people could see us, so that people would start talking . . . but it was your father that she loved. Do you understand that now?"

"I still don't. I'm sorry . . . "

"Your mother wanted to make your father jealous. It's as simple as that, Clotilde. She wasn't interested in my sanctuary, the dolphins and my hands that smelled of fish. She just wanted to get a reaction out of your father."

Clotilde let go of Natale's hand. The wind brushed at her face, caressed her legs, more gently than any man.

"Things were also a bit complicated, Clotilde, between your father and your mother."

She didn't want to hear any more. Not here. Not now.

"It's the oldest story in the world, Clotilde. *Dangerous Liaisons*, you remember, the book you were reading on your bench, in the Port de Stareso, opposite the *Aryon*? Your mother was playing with me, she used me because she loved someone else . . . and like a total fool I didn't realise what was happening, I fell for it completely. Palma was very charming, she had class, she was interested in my project, she was an architect, she had concrete ideas. I almost believed that we would be able to make it happen together. I felt that there was some kind of bond forming between us. When in fact . . . "

It was Clotilde's turn to scour the beach. No buried jewel, only cigarette butts, beer bottles and perhaps some condoms if you dug the sand a little deeper.

"When in fact," Natale went on, "that bond was really between you and me . . . not with Palma, with you. I think that mattered too."

Clotilde reached out for Natale's hand, grabbed it in mid-air and pulled him towards her so that he span round until he was facing her. After all, if the carnival was over, if they were throwing their masks into the sea . . .

"Fantasising about the mother while letting the daughter fantasise about you was a slightly twisted plan, don't you think?"

"No, Clotilde. Of course not. You were a stunning fifteen-year-old, even if you looked barely thirteen. But there was no ambiguity there. Absolutely none. It's just that I'd guessed."

"Guessed what?"

His foot rummaged in the sand, embarrassed. Adorably embarrassed.

"I'd guessed what you would become, over time. A girl steeped in imagination, a lively and intelligent girl, effervescent, a wonderful girl who would devour life. A girl who, even when she was older, would look at it through the same glasses as I did."

A far-away voice echoed in Clotilde's head. *"We're the same, you and me, Clotilde. Fishers of dreams against the rest of the world."*

"But I was ten years too old, Clotilde, that's no small thing, ten years . . . for us, it meant two curves that were already crossing, yours rising towards the peak of your seductive charm, and my own that was already beginning to tumble."

"Stop!"

He bent over suddenly, as if to escape her arms.

"Stop it, Natale. Stop blackening everything. Stop destroying yourself. You know very well that . . . "

He stood back up without letting her finish. Between his thumb and his index finger he was holding a silver ring.

"Is it yours?"

Incredible!

Magic. Pure magic.

"Thank you."

You should never fight against magic, Clotilde thought. It brings bad luck. Her thoughts suddenly fell into place, like the enchanted wrinkles on Natale's face.

It was so obvious. Kiss him.

Just one kiss. To honour a twenty-seven-year-old contract.

Just one kiss to put to rest a twenty-seven year-old ghost.

Just one kiss, then that's it.

So as not to die in ignorance, not to regret it for all those years to come, when her own body would begin to decline.

Just to feel on her mouth the taste . . . .

Gently, Clotilde placed her lips on Natale's.

For a moment, just a moment.

Then their lips parted, as if it had been agreed, as if it was agreeable.

For a moment, just a moment.

Before their fingers intermingled around the silver circle, before Clotilde's hand gripped the back of Natale's neck, and Natale's hand the small of her back, before their mouths melted into one and their tongues brought back lost time, and their bodies pressed against each other as if they had always been designed to fit each other.

As if, from now on, they alone could exist.

They stayed like that for a long time, kissing, she pressing her breasts against his torso. No longer knowing what to do to hold back time. Her head resting on Natale's shoulder, Clotilde stared at the *Aryon*, attached to its mooring. The fisherman's fingers ran over her back, hasty, tireless, clumsy, like quintuplets learning to walk.

"Let's get her back on the water again, Natale. Let's get on board, and come back with the dolphins, let's shoot the sequel to the film, there were at least five *Jaws* movies, surely we can come up with a *Big Blue 2*."

He smiled sadly.

"It's impossible, Clotilde."

"Why?"

She kissed him again, until she was breathless. She felt so alive.

"Impossible, impossible to tell you."

"Why? Why did you chain up the *Aryon*, Natale? Why did you marry Aurélia? Why are you the one, today, who is scared of ghosts?"

Because I've seen them, it's as simple as that, Clotilde."

"Damn it, Natale, ghosts don't exist. Even at fifteen, even disguised as Lydia, I didn't believe in them. It was all a game Ghosts are the opposite of vampires. One kiss and they vanish."

She kissed him again.

"I've seen her, Clotilde."

"Who, who have you seen?"

She brought her lips close to his again, but he turned away, merely resting a hand on the small of her back to press her in towards him.

"You're going to think I'm crazy."

"Find something else, I think that already."

"I'm not joking. I've never told anyone, not even Aurélia. But it has haunted me ever since."

"Since when?"

"Since the twenty-third of August, 1989."

She clung to his shoulder.

"Tell me, Natale. Tell me."

"I was at Punta Rossa. At home, alone. I was drinking. Less than I do today but I was already drinking. At least I was that evening. I knew I wouldn't see Palma that day. You know why, of course, it was the anniversary of your parents' first meeting. St Rose's day. Their sacred day. So I was drowning my pathetic jealousy in myrtle liqueur, my eyes turned towards the peak of Capu di a Veta. The ghost appeared at 9:02 P.M. at the top of the hill, I have no doubt about the time, Clotilde, the television was on, that programme *Thalassa* had just started and the screen was showing the exact time. 9:02 P.M.. The ghost was standing about a hundred meters away from the house, on the customs path."

9:02 . . . August 23, 1989.

Clotilde shivered, and huddled against Natale's burning body; she buried her cheek in the hood of his sweatshirt.

The Fuego had plunged into the void at exactly 9:02 P.M., all the police and fire service reports were absolutely positive about that.

"I know it's impossible to believe, Clotilde, I know you're going to think I'm crazy, but the same second when your parents' car crashed onto the rocks of Petra Coda, the second when your brother, your father and your mother lost their lives,

I saw her appear here through my window, I saw your mother, as clearly as I can see you now. She stared at me as though she wanted to see me one last time before she flew away. She stayed there for a long time, not daring to cross the last few meters that separated her from me. When I understood that she wasn't going to move, I decided to go out and join her. And in the time that it took me to set down my glass, open the door, and run towards her, she had disappeared."

His quintuplet fingers firmly gripped Clotilde's back.

"I didn't hear about your parents' accident until a few hours later," Natale went on. "That was when I understood. It couldn't have been your mother. At the moment when she appeared to me, she was four kilometers away, dying. So it could only have been her ghost . . . And who would believe that?"

"Me."

I do, I do believe you! Clotilde hammered away at her brain to admit it. Of course I believe you. Because that ghost has written to me. Because that ghost has looked at me while I stood under the oak tree at Arcanu. Because that ghost has had her breakfast here, has read her paper, because that ghost adopted a dog so she wouldn't grow bored.

Clotilde planted a long kiss on Natale's neck. Then, gently, they pulled away from each other.

Regretfully.

"I've got to go. Franck will be back soon. Everything . . . everything will be so complicated. Seeing each other again. Really seeing each other."

She forced herself to smile before going on.

"That must be rule number one in all the 'Infidelity for Dummies' books—never take a lover when on a family holiday with your husband and daughter."

"I'm working tomorrow morning," Natale said with a confidence that worried her. "But I'm free this afternoon. You can come and join me."

"It's impossible, Natale." She waved the silver ring in front of his eyes. "I won't be able to find any credible excuse. Franck is already suspicious and he . . . "

"The Marcone Belvedere," the fisherman cut in. "One o'clock. Your husband will let you go there on your own."

The Marcone Belvedere.

Natale was right.

Franck would never suspect her of going there to meet her lover.

The Marcone Belvedere was famous for its cemetery. For its mausoleums belonging to the wealthiest Corsican dynasties in La Balagne, and the most monumental among them—the one belonging to the Idrissis.

Her parents' grave.

35

Monday, August 21, 1989, fifteenth day of the holiday.
Smoke-without-fire-blue sky.

I'm not going to write to you this morning. I'm just going to copy something out!
Honest truth.

It was in today's *Corse-Matin*. More about that company boss from Nice who went straight to the bottom with his pockets full of concrete, or his gold, can't remember. A story that's come at precisely the right time, according to the journalists. That's why I'd rather copy it out, because I don't know what to think. There's a whole file on the acquisitions made by the Coastal and Lakeside Conservation Association, about the endless procedures around zoning maps, about the precise perimeter of protected areas. After reading this morning's *Corse-Matin* I don't know whether I should love my Papé even more, or be a bit afraid of him. I'll let you make up your own mind.

Extract from *Corse-Matin* August 21, 1989
The Shepherd's lucky star. Who is Cassanu Idrissi?
Interview by Alexandre Palazzo

"Cassanu" is the oldest word for an oak tree, from the Celtic, from Occitan, from Old Corsican. In 1926 the late Pancrace Idrissi gave this Christian name to his only son, in tribute to the three-hundred-year-old oak that grows in the middle of Arcanu Farm, so that his son could draw on its strength, its longevity, its roots.

Sixty-three years later, the old patriarch's wishes have come to pass, probably beyond everything he had dreamed. Cassanu Idrissi has become one of the emblematic figures of the Balagne region, one of the most influential, even though he remains an unclassifiable and atypical character. The Shepherd of Arcanu is not the mayor of any village, there is no regional councillor in his family, no deputy, no chair of an association. Cassanu presents himself as a simple shepherd, a shepherd who rules over eighty hectares of desert, at the gates of Calvi, inhabited only by a campsite and three villas. Cassanu Idrissi is a loner.

The pensioner, calm and athletically-built, welcomes you to Arcanu Farm with the most considerate hospitality. Whilst his discreet wife Lisabetta prepares a hearty snack for you, he takes you off on a guided tour, telling you that as far as the eye can see, or almost, everything belongs to him. And a second later, he tells you that it all amounts to nothing—that none of it really belongs to him, any more than the desert belongs to the Tuaregs or the steppe to the Mongols; that he is only its guardian. He didn't inherit this land, because inheriting it would mean that he owned it, that he could divide it, sell it, chop it into pieces; no, Cassanu Idrissi explains to you, pointing out the peak of Capu di a Vita with his stick, this land has been entrusted to him, he simply holds responsibility for it. Then, while Lisabetta brings you a chestnut tea and fiadone *and* canistrelli *with almonds and raisins, Cassanu unfolds some old maps on the table, and deeds of ownership, some dating back to the days of Pascal Paoli, Sampiero Corso or Napoleon Bonaparte, and announces that they barely matter. According to him, the recent planning documents, which the administration enjoys accumulating, have no greater legitimacy. In the end, they only represent boundaries drawn by human beings, lines usually drawn on large sheets of paper, as if men passing through this earth could possess a single grain of sand, drop of water or blade of grass and take it with them to the beyond. As if, in the event that by the greatest of miracles paradise did exist, you could get into it with all your suitcases. As if the earth wasn't going to go on existing after us. Because if water and fire, the roots of the trees and the winds are capable of bringing down even the greatest walls, of cracking Genoese towers and eating away at the stone bridges over rushing torrents, then what can they do to these lines drawn in pen on a piece of paper? Nature doesn't care about the heritage we claim to protect in its name.*

So, the shepherd continues, growing heated and waving his arms around, while his wife protects the glasses and cups, you can draw zones, perimeters and boundaries as much as you like, divide up the oceans and the ice floes, the heavens and the stars, the mountains and the rivers, decide who each pebble belongs to, each olive stone and each columbine petal if that's what takes your fancy, what makes you feel important and gives meaning to your life, but you won't change this truth one whit: the land is only entrusted to us. My land is entrusted to me. And no human law will ever make me give up my duty to return it in the condition I found it in.

Corse-Matin: *Precisely, Monsieur Idrissi, since you have mentioned human laws. The newspapers have talked a great deal lately about the murder of Drago Bianchi, the businessman from Nice who planned to build a luxury hotel on the top of the Revellata Peninsula, and who boasted in the pages of this very newspaper less than a month ago that he had obtained the support of the local authority prefect, the region and the regional tourist board. What does this murder mean to you?*

—Nothing more than it does to most Corsicans around here. I didn't weep at the news of his death, I didn't send a wreath to his funeral, but I don't remember his friends the prefect, the regional president, or the chairman of the regional tourist board

having been moved to do any of those things either. You have to be careful about what you read in the newspapers and the protection you think you might have. That's my answer, but perhaps your question contained some kind of innuendo? If that is the case, I'm sorry, it was put in the wrong way. And is pointless. (He smiles.) You can't possibly imagine that I would confess, over tea and while enjoying canistrelli *prepared by my wife, that I was the one who murdered him?*

Corse-Matin*: Of course not. Of course, Monsieur Idrissi. Let us forget about that affair and stick to principles and values. How far would you go to protect your land? Would you go so far as, and I'm going to be a little bit brutal here, as far as killing someone?*

—Why would I find that brutal? You're asking the same question as before, aren't you? (Another smile.) And without wishing to vex you, it is equally badly put. Obviously I do not wish anyone dead. How could I wish for someone to be crushed at sea by the five hundred tons of a ferry, or to be shot on a café terrace in front of his fiancée, or for a bomb to explode under his car straight after he's dropped off his children at school? Who could wish, approve or order such misfortune. Certainly not an old man who wishes only to live in peace. Do not seek evil on my part. Seek it in men who are pursuing a different agenda, a strange need for power, for money, for women. Here in Corsica, power, money and women often depend upon the goods that you possess, real estate, land and stone. So if those men, rather than contenting themselves with what life has entrusted to them, prefer to covet or seize or speculate, what can I do about it? What can I do if they only find their lives interesting when they're in danger, like those lunatics who enjoy high-risk sports? As if they could defy the natural order of things. Do we accuse the wave of killing the foolhardy surfer? The crumbling rock of betraying the

incautious climber? The hairpin bend of killing the impatient driver?

Corse-Matin: *Thank you, Monsieur Idrissi, I think I can read between the lines of what you're saying. Given such covetousness, are you not concerned—since you own, I'm sorry, since you have been* entrusted *with, so much property—that someone might wish to dispossess you of it? Put more prosaically, that they might want to kill you?*

—No, Monsieur Palazzo. No. (A brief silence.) I might legitimately be worried if I possessed something that I might lose. But since I am only a guardian, if I should fall, then another man would take my place, and another after that, or a woman for that matter, a friend, a relative, any man or any woman who shared the same values, the same code of honour as myself. Members of my family, and in my family I include people who are not of my own blood, who would know what to do should some misfortune one day befall me. (A long silence this time.) Just as I would should misfortune one day befall them.

Corse-Matin: *Vendettas. Do you agree with them? Can I sum up your reply using that word?*

—A vendetta? My God, who've you been talking to? (He sighs.) Who still talks about vendettas apart from journalists? The murders publicised in your pages have been committed by bandits, thugs, and Mafiosi, for a few banknotes, a few grams of drugs, a few stolen cars. What would I have to do with all of that? What would an isolated pensioner living on his farm have to do with that, a man who couldn't even recognize a piece of cannabis, a Yugoslavian prostitute or a box of Minitel terminals fallen off the back of a lorry in Ajaccio harbour? A vendetta, my God, that's for tourists who have read Mérimée's Colomba. *(The*

smile returns.) Everything is much simpler than that. Don't touch my land. Don't touch my family. And then I will be the most peaceful, the most harmless shepherd in the world.

Corse-Matin*: And otherwise? If someone does touch your land or your family?*

—Otherwise? Otherwise what? Your question is badly expressed once more, Monsieur Palazzo. (He laughs.) It's like asking an army general if, in the case of an attack, he would press the red button that sets off the nuclear bomb and destroys the planet. He won't answer you, because it won't happen. You must understand, I don't think that anyone wants to touch my land, even less touch my family, and if your newspaper can be of any use at all, it's in reminding your readers of that. Here, have some more canistrelli, *my wife made them especially for you.*

Corse-Matin *(with mouth full): Many thanksh, Monshieur Idrishi.*

The ending, the final reply, and the line before that, were added on by me. It would have been funny, would it not, if the journalist had actually dared to write that? But I think that, once he had asked his last question, the journalist was keen to get out of there as quickly as his legs would carry him, rather than enjoy one of Mamy's cakes.

* * *

He closed the notebook.
A harmless pensioner . . .
How funny was that?

36

August 20, 2016, 11 A.M.

F ranck hadn't said a word since Clotilde had returned to the bungalow. Hard to guess how long he had been there—he had already had his shower, cast aside his jogging shorts, and had a coffee.

"I found it," was all Clotilde said, showing him the silver hoop. His ironic smile was also hard to interpret.

Clotilde only did what every wife in the world does when her husband creeps into his shell, refusing to communicate, when he gets stuck like a weary vacuum cleaner that needs to be given a short rest: she filled the silence, she talked about everything, about nothing, as if everything were normal, as if everything were fine, she talked about Valentine, she even talked about cooking.

"A marinade? Does that sound good? I'll pop to the market and make that at lunchtime. It'll make a change from chips."

It was all Franck was waiting for, in fact. For everything to return to normal. For her to be a normal wife again. For them to lead a normal life. For today, for today at least, she could play the part.

"Are you coming with me? Valou? Franck?"

No reply. She was off to get the shopping on her own.

Mission accomplished. A normal life.

⌒

Even though her shopping bag weighed a ton, Clotilde was particularly proud of what she had found: peppers and olive oil for a piperade, marinated ribs of beef *stifatu* style, mangoes and pineapple to make a fruit salad. She would ask Franck to light the barbecue, so that everyone could play their part to the hilt in this sunny stage-play—the Baron family holiday. Waiting at the till of the Intermarché supermarket in Calvi, which must have made 80 per cent of its takings during the two summer months, thus justifying the interminable queue, she had scribbled a list of questions on the back of her shopping list. With no answers.

Who had written her that letter signed P.?

Who had stolen her wallet?

Who had named the Arcanu dog Pacha?

Who had laid the breakfast table yesterday?

Who had taught Orsu the way to use the mop?

Who had sabotaged the steering of her parents' Fuego?

Who had sabotaged the clasp on Valentine's harness?

Who was the ghost that Natale had seen, at 9:02 P.M. on August 23, 1989, at Punta Rossa?

It couldn't be the same person. It couldn't be her mother.

It couldn't *not* be her mother, for at least half of the answers to her questions.

Franck was probably right, if you wanted to be happy you were better off making a shopping list than a list of questions, concentrating on insignificant ingredients rather than the blank page on the other side.

Only reading the recto of life.

And maybe slipping a lover into your trolley.

While weighing up the consequences of her resolutions, she couldn't resist tweaking reason a little; a detour of less than thirty meters on the way back, taking Alley A rather than C, and passing by mobile home A31, just to see if Jakob Schreiber was there, if he'd had time to recover the photographs from that cloud of his.

Not to look at them: just to ask him.

Nobody there.

"Jakob?"

Perhaps the old German was deaf? Perhaps he was listen-ing to his tedious radio programme? Question seventy-two, win a trip to the moon.

"Jakob?"

It wasn't like the German to leave his house open like this. And yet it was hard to imagine that he might be hiding some-where in the twenty-eight square meters of this cabin resting on breeze blocks. Strange . . . Clotilde reflected that if Herr Schreiber came back with his pétanque boules in his hand or his camera around his neck, she risked spoiling everything. The old German wasn't the kind who'd be too happy about someone entering his place without permission; particularly if he'd spent part of the evening before looking for old photo-graphs on your behalf.

Silly little fool, get out of here, go and peel your peppers, come back this afternoon, or tomorrow . . .

Clotilde was about to leave when her eye fell on one of the photographs stuck to the wall.

Her brother, Nicolas.

Clotilde walked over. In fact, among the hundreds of pho-tographs taped to the walls of the mobile home, it wasn't hard to spot the ones that covered the years he had spent there, from 1976 until 1989. Neither the tanned bodies nor the setting changed, the sea, the sand, the waves, Calvi citadel in the foreground, Cap Corse at the back; but the clothes, often nothing more than swimming costumes, clearly identi-fied the decade in which each photograph was taken. The length of a pair of shorts, the brand of a swimming cap, the amount of breast or bottom covered by patterned fabric. It really was quite startling, in fact, so much change in the details of clothing, while apparently nothing else altered from one year to the next. Clotilde had always felt as if she got out the same clothes every June—the ones she'd put away the previous September.

Get out of here now, you silly fool.

She set down her shopping bag. She heard campers passing by outside.

In this particular picture, Nicolas was less than five years old. The photograph took her breath away. She saw herself too, in her mother's arms; she was less than one, with cheeks as red as apples, a terrible little navy-blue hat with an elastic strap under her chin that looked as if it was annoying her, and chubby little feet that seemed only to have one desire, to walk in the hot sand or the cold water. No Papa in the photograph, she looked for him. She found him in another one: Nicolas was eleven and she was eight, it was the 15th of August, there were fireworks, and everyone at the campsite was standing on Oscelluccia beach. There was as yet no beach bar but among the sea of faces, Clotilde recognised an eighteen-year-old Natale, incredibly handsome, holding the hand of an amazing blonde with hair down to her bottom, a girl she had never seen before; she also recognised Basile Spinello, Sergeant Cesareu Garcia, Lisabetta and Speranza standing side by side.

She heard footsteps outside, very close by. On a campsite, you get used to that sense that your neighbours are inhabiting the same space as you. Her eyes continued to scan the wall of photographs. She had spotted others from the summer of '89, she was sure. She recognised her mother's black dress from Benoa, the one with the red roses that Papa had bought her in Calvi. The photograph must have been taken a few days before the accident.

"Your mother was beautiful."

Clotilde turned around with a start.

An icy hand settled on her bare shoulder.

"Gently, now, Clotilde, gently. Really, don't you think your mother was beautiful?"

The snake had slithered its way in, silently. What the hell was he doing here? Even worse, why wasn't he asking her what she was up to? He should have been surprised to find her here. Instead, he seemed to be interested in everything apart from her, was anxiously studying every corner of the mobile home.

"Is Jakob here?" was all he asked.

Clotilde shook her head.

"Damn it," Cervone swore. "What's that Prussian up to? Serge, Christian and Maurice are waiting for him at the pétanque court. He's never been late in thirty years."

He shrugged and lowered his eyes to the floor.

"He's past the age when you might follow a female tourist into the *maquis*, but we should still wait a bit longer before calling out the cavalry."

Cervone examined the wall of photographs.

"Maybe he just got fed up with always taking pictures of the same spot, and has gone off somewhere with his camera."

Clotilde still didn't reply, so Cervone carried on.

"Because while the old Kraut might be the most annoying client on the campsite, you have to admit he's good at portraits. He can bring memories back to the surface better than if he'd filmed them. Look . . . "

Cervone pointed at another series of snaps.

A group of teenagers was standing around a campfire. Clotilde remembered that the photograph had been taken the day before the accident, late in the evening, on Alga beach. Nicolas was trying to play the guitar, with Maria-Chjara's head resting on his shoulder; the whole tribe could be seen around the flames, Estefan with a djembe between his thighs, Hermann holding a violin, Aurélia gazing hungrily at the musicians with her olive eyes, and at Nicolas in particular.

"Those were our years!"

Cervone seemed as happy as a little boy all of a sudden, but when he looked at Clotilde's tight expression, he froze.

"I'm sorry, Clotilde. I'm a total idiot sometimes."

Sometimes . . .

"Our years. I was thinking about my own teenage years, about the girls, the parties, but of course you . . . "

"Forget it, Cervone. If I didn't want to hear about it, I would never have come back to the Euproctes."

"Except that you want to know the truth."

This time Clotilde stared at him intensely.

"What do you know about the truth?"

Cervone nudged the door of the mobile home closed with his toe. In his hand he held a case of three rusting pétanque balls. If that was a weapon, Clotilde thought, she would be no match for it with her string bag and three peppers. She was forcing herself to be facetious, but she was worried. What was the boss of the campsite doing here? Had he followed her? If he tried to do anything to her in this construction of planks and sheet metal, she could always scream, and people would hear her. The first face that came into her mind was Franck's, not Natale's. Because Franck was closer. Stupidly, that was what she thought.

"Look."

In the gloomy mobile home, Cervone pointed at a photograph. In front of the cars parked in the Euproctes car park, some men were playing pétanque. Clotilde didn't recognise them, but there it was, behind them. Unharmed. She trembled with the shock. The red Fuego.

"Did you go and see Sergeant Garcia? I imagine he told you about his theory."

Was Cervone aware? Did he know about the sabotaged steering system? Yet Cesareu Garcia had assured her that his investigation had remained confidential, that he had only informed Cassanu Idrissi. No one else. Not even his daughter. So what was Cervone Spinello's part in this whole business?

Play for time.

"What theory?" Clotilde asked, trying to feign innocence.

The campsite manager smiled, without taking his eyes off the Fuego.

"That the steering column of your father's car failed. All of a sudden. And that it wasn't just an unfortunate stroke of luck."

And bang!

"Except that the old sergeant doesn't know everything," Cervone added.

Spinello's finger ran across the photograph. His index finger stopped on a man with his back to the camera.

"Take a good look at your father. And look behind him, you can hardly see but . . . "

He was right. It was her father, picking up his pétanque balls. And a little way further back, between the players, it was impossible to miss him even if his whole body was almost entirely concealed from view.

Nicolas.

Her brother was not interested in the game. But he was in the parked car.

Cervone was delighted.

"These pictures are unbelievable, don't you think? If you take the time to study them, the foreground, the background, the expressions, the attitudes, they all tell a story. Almost all of them reveal a secret."

"What are you getting at, Cervone?"

His hand rested once more on her bare shoulder, as if he were about to lower the strap of her dress. As if he wanted to negotiate, but of course it was probably all just her imagination.

"Nothing, Clotilde. Nothing. I know you aren't particularly fond of me, that you hate me as much as you loved my father. That in your eyes I represent more or less everything you missed in life, as if I were the incarnation of your lost dreams, the promises of youth which are extinguished one by one, the idiots who get all the power in a shitty world. But I'm not going to apologise for that, Clotilde. I'm not going to apologise for having made my own accommodation with life. Because I have no disappointments, Clotilde, I have no regrets." He stared at the picture of the campfire, before coming back to the game of pétanque in the car park. "I'm happier today than I ever was back then. The passing of time has made me more confident, more powerful, richer, even more handsome. So I'm not going to apologise, because I've sweated blood to get where I am. That's why, if you don't like me, it's not reciprocal. I have no hatred, no bitterness, only sympathy for other people, the sympathy of someone who's made a success of their life. Sympathy for you too."

He set down the pétanque balls. Another palm was about to settle on another bare shoulder. Each of Cervone's hands seemed to want to take a slightly greater risk in order to shock the other. She took a step backwards. Perhaps hitting him in the face with those peppers wouldn't be such a bad idea after all.

"It's fine, Cervone. Spare me your little homily. What do you know?"

"Don't take this the wrong way, Clotilde. Believe me. And it's up to you to answer a question, just one question. Do you really want to know the truth?"

"Do you know it?"

"You're not in court, Clotilde. So take off the costume, remove the mask and just answer my question. Do you want to know the truth?"

"About . . . about my parents' accident? That bloody bolt? To know who tampered with it?"

"Yes."

"Do you know?"

"Yes, but you're not going to like the answer. You're not going to like the truth at all."

"In all these years, I've never really liked the lies either."

He smiled and looked at the photographs one last time.

"Sit down, Clotilde. Sit down. I'm going to tell you."

II
SAINT ROSE'S DAY

37

Monday, August 21, 1989, fifteenth day of the holiday.
Mum's-the-word-lotus-blue sky.

It must have been almost noon. I was calmly sitting in my Sea-Calves grotto, in the cool, secretly reading *The Never-Ending Story*, with *Dangerous Liaisons* plonked under my bottom, when Nicolas came to get me. When he entered my grotto he was like a big bear blocking out the sunlight. To make me panic, for starters. And then to stop me reading. I was still able to take advantage of the darkness to quickly swap Bastien and his pudding-bowl hair for Valmont and the Marquise. As soon as Nico moved, his black silhouette parted from the sun that hung behind his back, like in a film, when the police inspector points the light straight into the eyes of the accused.

"I need to talk to you, Clo."

Well, go ahead then.

He assumes his serious face, which generally conceals some kind of monstrously idiotic plan.

"I know you like snooping about, spying, playing the little mouse and writing everything down in your notebook, but this time you've got to stay out of it. I'm not saying you have to shut up, but you've got to stop trying to know."

"Trying to know what?"

I love driving my big brother mad.

"Clo, I'm serious."

He bends a little, as if weighed down by the revelation he's about to make, or just trying not to bump his head on the roof of my grotto. The result is the same, the sun full in my face, and here my Chief Inspector adds:

"I'm in love!"

Well, well, well . . .

"Who with? Chjara?"

He didn't like me calling her that, he only calls her Maria, or Mary, or MC, pronounced the English way, emcee.

And he didn't like the way I looked at him, he didn't like that one bit. As if he'd told our parents that he wanted to give up school to become a professional footballer. But I carried right on, waving my book in front of his nose.

"You shouldn't get the two things confused, brother dear, it isn't love, it's just excitement. Excitement among the boys because of the competition. Who's going to be the first to touch her boobs."

I love being vulgar with my big brother.

"The guys definitely aren't going to be in a hurry to touch a pair of fried eggs."

The scum. I've copied that out because that's exactly what he said. I hope you're touched by my honesty, o reader on the other side of the galaxy.

So we moved on. I love making up with my big brother.

"OK, then, Casanova, what do you want from me?"

"Nothing . . . Nothing, just stay out from under my feet, keep your distance, don't draw Maman and Papa's attention to me. Or, if necessary, keep them away from me, tell them fibs when I'm not there, say we're playing guitar on Oscelluccia beach or building a shack in the Belloni woods with Filip and Estefan, I don't care, I'm just asking you to cover for me for two days, until the evening of the twenty-third."

"St Rose's day? What's happening then? Are you going to go and pick a bunch of *rosa canina*, like Papa did? The winner's bouquet? The big prize on the tombola? After the lambada, are you going to play put-it-there? Put it there in the Chjara-pussy?"

I really love being vulgar with my brother. He can't say a thing, he's the one who taught me.

"That night I'm going to slip away, little sister of mine, and you are not going to discover my true destination. Maybe in a year or two we'll let you have the black box."

"When you're married to your Chjara, with a string of brats? Is that it?"

Nico changes position, masking the sun from me once more and switching to negative mode.

Just a shadow.

"That's right. We'll invite you."

I don't want to push it.

"Mm, right . . . Are you absolutely sure?"

"Of what?"

"Of being the first to pluck that little orchid? There's some pretty fierce competition, isn't there?"

"Yes, I'm sure!"

"And your rivals?"

"It's like a game of chess, sweetie, you have to have a strategy, to be thinking a few moves ahead."

"Can you explain it to me? Your strategy?"

The shadow bends down and sits beside me, wraps me up in its protection. Nicolas has taught me everything, he's opening up a path through the *maquis* of my life.

"I use cunning, oh, sister of mine. You know, like in that book you're pretending to read, *Dangerous Liaisons*. I plot, I come up with a plan, I have a diagram in my head, a simple diagram. It's a circle, with the first names of the entire gang, one guy one girl, one guy one girl, one guy one girl, and arrows linking them up, like in that game where everyone has to kill someone while being killed by someone else. It's crazy how easy it is, you just have to whisper to a girl that another guy is after her, or to a guy that a girl has noticed him, and bang, you've made your move. I've hooked up Aurélia, who would have liked to go out with me, with Hermann the cyclops, who would rather have gone out with Maria. And as Maria quite liked Cervone, even if I don't get what she sees in Spinello junior, I've hooked up that daddy's boy with a daddy's girl, who's fresher than you think: Aurélia. And there you have it, full circle."

Aurélia! With her holier-than-thou attitude and those big eyebrows of hers, she's ready to bang anything that moves? While with her fuck-me-now look, Maria-Chjara won't sleep with anyone but my Nicolas? Isn't he just putting on a film in his head, my campsite Valmont? In my opinion, his fairy fingers aren't anywhere near plucking her string.

Even if he thinks they are.

"So you promise? You'll help me? You'll cover for me?"

"If it was the other way round, if I had a boyfriend, would you do that for me?"

"I will do. As soon as you grow a pair of breasts."

The total bastard!

I love throwing myself at him and pretending to punch him. Usually in my bedroom, I throw all my soft toys in his face, but here I haven't got anything. So I have no choice but to jump on him for a play-fight.

OK, big brother. I'll grant you your two days of freedom, until the twenty-third of August. Normally I would have promised all kinds of things and spied on you anyway, but this time I don't care. I don't care about your teenage circle in which everyone wants to go out with everyone else. And that's the right word, by the way. Go out. It doesn't really matter who goes out with who. What matters is getting right out of that circle. So I'll leave you guys to sit playing postman's knock.

One o'clock, the postman hasn't been . . . Two o'clock, three o'clock . . .

I've got better things to do. I have a contract!

A kiss on the cheek.

From a man who isn't about to go into any circle, who will never be locked away, who will teach me the meaning of true freedom.

I have a contract. I have a mission. Natale Angeli gave it to me.

To persuade my Papé Cassanu. And believe me, if you don't know me yet, I'll do it!

* * *

He closed the notebook and hid it under his jacket.

A killer, a game of death, according to Nicolas Idrissi, the master of the game.

That was the purest truth.

38

C lotilde waited. Cervone Spinello had taken five minutes to emerge from the toilet. Perhaps he was freshening his make-up, or perhaps it was just a manoeuvre to keep her waiting. A few more minutes added to twenty-seven years. One last, mean act of revenge.

She turned toward Cervone as soon as he stepped into the corridor of the mobile home, making no attempt to hide her impatience. The campsite manager merely froze with a look of concern, pointing at the old German's photographs.

"Are you still sure you really want to know what happened?"

He didn't wait for her answer, he didn't look at Clotilde, but simply continued to stare at the pictures.

"You remember, Clotilde, the night of the twenty-third of August, your brother Nicolas had suggested going to a nightclub, the Camargue, just past Calvi, while your parents spent the night at Casa di Stella. They were supposed to climb up there, leaving the Fuego parked on the road by Arcanu Farm. Nicolas had planned to borrow your parents' car, in secret, and take everyone who could pile into it for a spin. You will also remember that his plan involved a Phase B, to leave all the others on the dance floor, while he reserved a sofa for himself and Maria-Chjara. With the help of mojitos and a few joints, he hoped to take his beautiful Italian to a place that might have been less comfortable, but was a lot more discreet. You remember all that, Clotilde?"

So far, yes.

"Yes."

"And what happened next. How can I tell you? Nicolas didn't go boasting about it. Certainly not in front of his beloved little sister. Because in fact Maria-Chjara was dragging her feet. Not about the sofa, the weed, the rum cocktails and what they wanted—both of them—to do afterwards. As far as that was concerned, Maria-Chjara was quite willing."

His finger stopped again on the photograph of the camp-fire, Alga beach, Maria-Chjara with her head resting on Nicolas's shoulder while he played the guitar. Cervone's finger caressed the Italian girl's long, loose black hair, then her short, low-cut white blouse, her skin bronzed by the day's sun and the midnight fire.

"No, Clotilde," he went on. "Maria-Chjara was dragging her feet for one reason only: the car. Nicolas didn't have a licence. Only about ten hours of driving lessons and a few hundred outings in the car with his dad. It was as simple as that. Maria-Chjara was thinking about the narrow roads, the bends, the ravines, the stray wild animals; in short she was scared of getting herself killed."

"So they didn't go."

"No, not on the evening of the twenty-third of August, you already know that, and you know why. What no one knows is what happened before that. To persuade Maria-Chjara, Nicolas suggested proving to her that it wasn't dangerous."

Slowly, Clotilde's body froze; an army of invisible insects immobilising her feet.

"A few hours before going up to Arcanu, your parents were very busy. Your mother was getting ready for her romantic evening, and your father, just back from a boat trip, was going through a file that he wanted to discuss with Cassanu later. So it was the dream opportunity, the only opportunity, in fact. Your brother took the keys of the Fuego and asked Maria-

Chjara to come with him for a little spin, just a few kilometers, down to Galéria, a few sharp bends, to show his sweetheart that he was in charge, that he didn't need a bit of paper to be able to hold a steering wheel, that he was careful."

The cannibal insects climbed up along Clotilde's thighs. Others had managed to work their way into her lungs, and were spreading out in seething swarms to block her breathing.

"They returned ten minutes later. Nicolas parked the Fuego in exactly the same spot. They both got out. I was in charge of reception at that moment, and I was the only one who saw."

The insects, gathering at the top of her trachea, allowed her only a ridiculously thin whimper.

"Saw what?"

"I saw and I heard them. Nicolas bent down to look under the car before assuring Maria-Chjara: 'There's nothing, nothing at all.' When he brought his hands, black with grease and oil, close to her lacy white dress, Maria recoiled as if he had the plague, and let him have it with both barrels. I was listening. I worked out what had happened."

Clotilde gulped. Thousands of little feet were crowding into her throat, climbing along her temples, piercing her eardrums with their stings in a deafening buzz. But not deafening enough. Not enough to cover the words she would never have wanted to hear.

"Nicolas had crashed. After less than three bends he had carried straight on and scraped the undercarriage of the Fuego against the rocks of the Capo Cavallo belvedere. Nicolas had had to stop and reverse, without knowing what the car was rubbing against, what was twisting, what was tearing beneath the bonnet, beneath the wheels, with an unbearable noise of crunching metal that was lost among the mountains."

Spit. Vomit. Dissolve the insects in a great magma of gastric acid.

"I only made the connection a few days later, when some local guys started talking about a disconnected steering rod, a twisted bolt, a sheared-off nut."

Clotilde threw up in front of him, over the old linoleum tiles of the mobile home, over her bags, the peppers and the marinaded beef, over her shoes. Cervone didn't look away.

Don't believe it.

Don't imagine for one second that it might be true.

That Nicolas might have chosen to say nothing, not realised the danger, preferring instead to put the car keys back in secret and not be yelled at.

"You wanted the truth, Clotilde. You asked me for it. I'm sorry."

The image of Nicolas appeared in front of her eyes, his face, a few moments before impact, just before the Fuego hung weightlessly in the void. That stubborn impression that had pursued her all these years: that Nicolas knew. That Nicolas had been aware of something she didn't know. Nicolas hadn't looked surprised when the car hadn't turned, as if he'd known why they were going to die.

Of course, that explained everything.

He was the one who had killed them all.

⁓

"Aren't you having anything?"

There was a hint of irony in Franck's question.

Clotilde had thrown everything away, peppers, *stufatu* ribs, exotic fruits. The promised wifely feast had turned into a jumble of cubes of ham, sliced tomatoes and tinned sweetcorn.

Franck had given Valou 20 euros to go to reception and get a tray of chips, a coffee Magnum, a strawberry Cornetto and Clo, what would she like?

"Thanks. Nothing for me."

Clotilde had decided not to speak. Not straight away. Not now. Not like this.

There was only one thing she wanted to do.

Melt into strong arms. Beat her fists against a manly chest, weep a torrent of tears into the hollow of a shoulder, curse life while screaming into the ear of someone who would, in return, murmur calming words of love. Abandon herself completely to a man who would understand, who would say nothing and simply love her.

Franck wasn't that man.

She got to her feet, stacked the plates, cleared the table, picked up a sponge, a basin and a cloth.

"I'm going to my parents' grave. After doing the washing up. The Marcone Belvedere. I won't be long."

The Corsicans believe in ghosts. Their graves are proof of this. Why else would they build such monumental crypts? Family mausoleums sometimes even more imposing than the houses they once lived in? Why else would they reserve the most splendid settings for these sumptuous second homes, where seven generations of skeletons live squeezed together? Why would they reserve the most beautiful panoramas for their graveyards if not so that the dead could enjoy the mist rolling in above the crashing waves, the bell towers silhouetted against the hillside. The sunsets over Calvi citadel. At least the ones who can afford it, not the ones relegated to the rear of the graveyard, resting amid stones in the full glare of the sun, in the rows prone to flooding and rockfalls, where each storm threatens to cover the graves with a fresh layer of mud, or carry the coffins away.

The crypt of the Idrissi family could resist the weather for an eternity. It rose proudly above the wall of the Marcone cemetery, with its azure-blue dome, its Corinthian columns, so that no one passing along the coastal road could forget that name and its glorious ancestry. Among the oldest Idrissi forbears were an admiral (1760-1823), a member of parliament (1812-1887), a mayor (1876-1917), Clotilde's great-grandfather, Pancrace (1898-1979).

And three ordinary people:
Paul Idrissi (1945-1989)
Palma Idrissi (1947-1989)
Nicolas Idrissi (1971-1989)

Natale was waiting just inside the cemetery, invisible from the road, in the shadow of the limestone and plaster wall. Clotilde fell into his arms, kissed him, wept wept wept, and finally collapsed beneath the nearest tree, a yew whose trunk was twisted by the wind from the sea, heedless of the flat needles pricking the bare flesh of her thighs. The cemetery was deserted, apart from an old woman bent over the furthest graves, struggling with the watering can that she had just filled from the fountain.

Only then did Clotilde speak. Natale sat next to her, holding her hand. Their bodies didn't touch, only their fingers remained connected. Clotilde let everything come spilling out. Cesareu Garcia's revelations about her parents' car, her life which was nothing but a big dark room, the unravelling of her love for Franck, the daughter who was escaping her, who would never be like her, so much so that she found herself wondering whether she really did love her, and then the past as well, that past that was like a cannonball, the mother of whom she was so jealous, the father whom she worshipped, the guy who talked to dolphins, whom she had never forgotten (just after saying this she kissed him), and her big brother Nicolas, her big brother who had opened up a path through life for her, sweeping away the dust in front of her, carrying her on his back when the hill was too steep, teaching her shortcuts, her brother who had abandoned her there, at La Revellata, who had asked her to keep a secret, who hadn't dared to speak, who had silently got into a car that was a death trap, without being conscious of it. A lack of awareness, that was what it was, a lack of consciousness.

Clotilde poured out all her fears, all her resentments, as if they weighed a ton and it was only by expelling them that she could become light again, a balloon. And Natale's hand held her the way you would hold a helium balloon, a little too tightly, the way you might hold a creature that was worryingly frail.

The Idrissi family plot was covered with flowers. A bunch of wild roses, lilies, orchids, most of them freshly cut. It was the most colourful site in the whole cemetery. Cassanu and Lisabetta were not the kind to let the Idrissi ghosts, from that distant admiral to their only son, catch the scent of faded flowers in brackish water. In front of them, in the blazing sun, the old woman with the watering can was approaching.

Clotilde kept wondering, as she twisted Natale's fingers, her balloon body seeming to want to regain its freedom, why Nicolas hadn't said anything. Sensible, well-behaved Nicolas, Nicolas the anvil who bore the blows of everyone and everything, Nicolas the model, Nicolas straight as an I and round as an O, Nicolas the handsome, the kind, Nicolas who had everything going for him. Why had Nicolas stolen the keys of the Fuego? Driven the car without a licence? Conceived that crazy plan to visit a nightclub?

The answer was simple, cruel, pitiful, contemptible, dirty.

For a tart. To impress a girl he didn't even love. To hold a pair of breasts in his hands. To stuff his penis into a vagina that was being withheld from others but perhaps not from him. Because Nicolas, brainy Nicolas, was just a little animal, like all other men, and all of his principles, the whole of his education, all his reading and all his knowledge, meant nothing when faced with those tanned curves, those two panther eyes gazing into his, those lips imparting mute promises. Yes, it was as ridiculous as that. Nicolas had killed her father and her mother, he had killed himself, he had doomed Clotilde to a life sentence, all in order to possess a girl for the first time, a girl who didn't deserve him, and not even a girl, just her body, an object, a doll at best.

She saw again the frightened expression on Maria-Chjara's face as she stood in the door of her dressing room, the evening when Clotilde had said Nicolas's name and mentioned the accident. Her silence. Her denial. Her flight. She understood, she understood now how great a burden that secret must have been for Maria-Chjara. She, who hadn't asked for any of it; yet who had provoked it all. She, who had done nothing but throw aside the stub of her cigarette. What fault of hers was it if the sun shone, if the wind blew on the dry grass, and the dead wood?

Arsonist and innocent, all at the same time.

You can't condemn an object, not even a doll.

"Promise me, Natale. Promise me that not all men are like that. Promise me that . . . "

Their lips stopped a few centimeters apart.

"Excuse me."

The old woman's watering can left behind her a trail of droplets that disappeared as if by magic a few seconds later into the ochre clay path. It was then that Clotilde recognised her face, framed by a black veil the same colour as her dress.

Speranza. The witch from Arcanu. Orsu's grandmother. Lisabetta and Cassanu's daily helper.

Without deigning to glance at them. Speranza emptied the water from one of the five vases placed on the grave, delicately removed the flowers one by one, filled the vase with fresh water, then rearranged the flowers, pulling off a few leaves and cutting withered stems with a pair of secateurs that she took from the depths of her pocket. She then moved slowly on to the second bouquet.

Suddenly, as if her precise, mechanical gestures had masked an intense hesitation, she turned around.

Her words rattled the silence.

"You shouldn't be here!"

Clotilde shivered.

Speranza was looking solely at her, as if Natale didn't exist. She put down the watering can, and slowly ran her fingers over the letters carved on the mausoleum.

Palma Idrissi (1947-1989).

"Nor should she."

Those first words seemed to have been the hardest for Speranza to spit out, like bubbles building up behind a cork. The ones that followed came like an explosion.

"She shouldn't be here. Her name doesn't belong here, engraved with the rest of the Idrissi family. I'm not the one who is the *streia*, the witch of the mountain, that's your mother! You know nothing, you weren't even born," she crossed herself quickly, "but your mother cast a spell on him."

Speranza's eyes stared at the name of Paul Idrissi inscribed on the tomb.

"Believe me, women are capable of that. Your mother cast a spell on your father, and once she had him in her power, she stole him from us. She took him away, caught in her net, far away from all those who loved him."

Far away, Clotilde thought, meant the Vexin, whether hunchbacked or not, north of Paris, where he went to sell hectares of lawn. She hadn't guessed to what extent her father's choice might have been difficult for his family to accept.

Natale gripped her hand, careful and reassuring, without intervening. Speranza furiously emptied the water from the second vase; faded petals settled like confetti on her black dress.

"If your father hadn't met her," Speranza continued, brandishing her secateurs, "he would have married here. He would have had children here. He would have started a family here. If your mother hadn't emerged from hell to steal him away, then return here with him . . . "

Her hand decapitated three roses, two orange lilies and a wild orchid. Her voice grew calmer for the first time.

"It's not your fault, Clotilde. You're a stranger here. You don't know anything about Corsica. You're not like your mother. Your daughter is. Your tall daughter is like her, and she will become a witch too. But you have your father's eyes, his way of looking at things, of believing in things that other people don't believe in. I'm not angry with you."

For the first time, Speranza's eyes settled on Natale. Her wrinkled hand nervously clenched the secateurs, which opened and closed in mid-air as if to cut off the oxygen that they were breathing. Then, suddenly, she aimed the blade at the marble of the tomb, and slid it screeching across the stone, trying to erase the name of Palma Idrissi. The steel of the secateurs left a white scar on the grey stone, splintering some of the letters: the A, and the M.

The old woman's eyes rose to the name carved above it.
Paul Idrissi.
Once again Speranza crossed herself.

"Paul should have lived here, if your mother hadn't killed him. He should have lived here, do you hear me? Lived here. Not come back here to die."

⁓

Natale walked Clotilde to the car. Old Speranza was still cursing Palma's memory as they left the cemetery, as if they were being chased away by a deranged spirit.

They kissed for a long time by the open door of the Passat.

The concrete parapet that lined the road made it look like a station platform, it was almost as if a whistle was about to blow, signalling the departure of a train. Clotilde summoned the strength to joke about it.

"My mother doesn't seem to have been very well liked here. Not while she was alive, or during her life as a ghost. You were the only Corsican who loved her, from the sound of it."

"Not the only one. Your father loved her too."

Touché!

"I've got to go."

One last kiss on the platform.

"I understand. I'll call you."

She risked one last question. After all, she was the one driving the train.

"The hatred of the Corsicans, Natale, the hatred of the Corsicans towards my mother when you and she were, let's say, close. Your abandoned boat. Your marriage to a policeman's daughter, does that have anything to do with this story? With this burden, this pressure, with the curses that all the old women of Corsica have threatened to put on you?"

He merely smiled.

"Off you go, my princess, go back to the castle where you are imprisoned. Escape while your brave knight holds the witches at bay."

Clotilde drove, her eyes misted with tears, distorting the cliffs that slipped by as if diluted by the sea. At each bend in the road the Revellata Peninsula appeared, drowned in a fog that existed only in her eyes. The damp landscape was washed out, the wet electricity poles twisted, but Clotilde drove slowly, at less than thirty kilometers an hour, so that she could see the face of Maria-Chjara on the posters on every other pole.

Eighties Concert, Tropi-Kalliste, August 22, Oscelluccia beach.

The day after tomorrow. The same formula as four days ago. Cervone had no reason to change a successful recipe, particularly for holidaymakers who rarely remained in the same place for a long time.

But Clotilde couldn't let such an opportunity go by. She had to go back and see the Italian singer once more. She had to find a way to talk to her, to get rid of the bodyguard outside her door, to make her admit what had happened with her brother Nicolas on August 23, 1989. Leaving the road, the damaged steering rod, their tacit silence. Only Maria-Chjara could confirm Cervone's version of events. But how to make her do that? For the Italian, to confess was to acknowledge her own complicity, her direct responsibility for the deaths of three people, years after it had happened. She was bound to deny it. Even if by some miracle Clotilde managed to get close to her, she would deny it.

She would never know the truth for certain.

The tears were still flowing freely, and now she was driving at less than twenty kilometers per hour. A giant motor home with an NL registration was getting impatient behind her, tailgating her, apparently determined to push her towards the precipice if she slowed down any more. In a stupid reflex, as if to wipe away the watery landscape, she turned on her windscreen wipers.

It was only then that Clotilde noticed the envelope wedged between the windscreen and the wiper. A flyer perhaps? The bit of paper, clinging to the windscreen only by one corner, flew off after it had gone back and forth once more.

Clotilde braked hard.

The motor home blasted its horn even louder than the ferry coming in to the port of Bastia, a redhead in the passenger seat insulted her in Dutch and all the children in the back seat pressed their noses to the door and studied her as if she were a curious animal.

Clotilde didn't care. She parked the Passat randomly in the gravel, with two wheels on the tarmac. Leaving the door open, she ran after the envelope, which was flitting from rock to rock. Eventually it caught on a bramble bush and she picked it up, scratching her forearms and cursing her insanity. Franck was right, she was losing all sense of perspective. Her emotions were becoming uncontrollable. She had almost killed herself over an advertisement, the special opening of a supermarket next Sunday, or a car-boot sale, a concert, perhaps even Maria-Chjara's concert.

All for a piece of paper.

Her hands were trembling.

The envelope was white, apart from two words:

For Clo.

It was a woman's handwriting. Handwriting that she would have recognised anywhere.

Her mother's.

39

Monday, August 21, 1989, fifteenth day of the holiday.
Broken-crystal blue sky.

I took your advice, Basile, I went to see the dolphins with Natale."

And I lay it on thick, believe me. The Euproctes bar is full to bursting, it's drinks time, the Casanis and the Pietra are flowing and there are so many olives in bowls that all the trees on the east of the island must have been stripped bare.

There are probably about twenty clients here. All men. So I tell them about my cruise on the *Aryon*, about Orophin, Idril and their little ones, Galdor and Tatië. I confirm that Natale speaks to them, he must be a bit of a magician, and I add on a bit from *The Big Blue* which none of them has seen, apart from the youngest ones, perhaps, and they probably only remember Rosanna Arquette's ski-jump nose and the freckles on her bottom.

Go. Go and see, my love!

I'm cunning, I've prepared my story. I think I've startled them a bit, this army of hairy brutes, all bearded and paunchy, with the T-shirt that I've chosen deliberately—black and white, WWF in blood red and underneath it a decapitated panda.

"The most complicated part," I simper, overplaying an innocence at odds with my bloody clothing, "will not be to persuade the dolphins, it will be building the sanctuary."

The campers don't care, they don't believe in dolphin safaris any more than they believe in the resurrection of sea-calves.

"I'm Corsican too, just like Natale Angeli, so concrete is out of the question. We need something else, different building materials, wood, glass, stone, it has to be beautiful! There's no question of spoiling the site, the land belongs to Papé."

I love that. Calling my grandfather "Papé" in front of all these men who are putting the world to rights, Corsica and the *maquis*, amid the scents of aniseed, myrtle and tobacco. I have the impression that for them Cassanu Idrissi is some kind of major general whose name cannot be uttered without them being changed into stone. Then along I come, turning up on their island looking like a zombie, and calling their supreme emperor Papé!

And just wait—I haven't produced my secret weapon.

"Luckily," I continue, "we'll be working as a family. Papé can supply the land and my mother, who is an architect, will be able to build the house for the dolphins."

I hesitate to go any further. I'm worried that I'll overdo it. But no, men who are quenching themselves like a herd of zebus around a watering hole are rarely the most wily of animals.

"I think my mother and Natale get on well. Is there a toilet here?"

And down I go, perky as anything. The toilets at the bar are about three hundred steps down, at the end of an endless tunnel, almost as if they'd been built on the mainland. Except that I only go down ten steps and wait for the light to go out before going back up seven. Fine, I admit it, it's a rubbish plan, it's mean and borderline unhealthy. So in my defence, I want to confess everything.

Yes, I am jealous! Yes, thinking about my mother totally makes me want to kill someone. Yes, I want to know if my mother is sleeping with Natale. Yes, I'd prefer Maman to belong completely to Papa and Natale to belong only to me.

So, I wait, in the darkness, like a curious, slightly anxious little mouse.

I don't have to wait long. Men drinking in a herd tend to chat. In this regard the only difference between men and women is perhaps the amount of alcohol. And as soon as the subject of sex rears its head . . .

A first voice launches in. A voice that's slightly too high-pitched for a man from the *maquis*, with the intonation of a wailing baby, a bit like Elmer Fudd, Tex Avery's stupid hunter.

"Natale's got a brass neck. Having a go at Cassanu's daughter-in-law . . . "

I hear collective laughter. A man with the nasal voice of a duck chimes in.

"I have to say, Paul's wife, she'd make me want to turn into a tree-hugger."

Slightly anxious silence around the bowls of pitted olives.

"Those tree-huggers have been trying to reintroduce wolves back into the woods for over twenty years," Daffy Duck explains. "I wouldn't mind getting my hands on her little wolf."

There's more laughter, I'm not making it up. I recognise the voice of Basile, who tries to impose some kind of order.

"Maybe he really does need an architect," the campsite boss suggests. "And even if Palma is getting a bit too close to that handsome Natale, she might have her reasons."

A mini-hunter who must be around my age and whose voice hasn't yet broken dares to intervene in the grown-ups' scrum. He has the voice of Tweety Pie. But I thank him for it. He asks the question as if I had prompted him.

"Why would she have her reasons?"

Daffy Duck clearly has another good line up his sleeve. He guffaws even before delivering his response, which seems to be one of his favourites.

"Petiot, in this corner of the world there's a proverb that

says: In La Revellata the shepherds bring in their animals in the winter, and their wives in the summer, the moment Paul Idrissi steps off the ferry."

The laughter explodes in my face like a bomb.

Elmer throws another grenade before I can bury my head, my face, my ears in my arms.

"You've got to understand. Paul gets bored up there with all those Parisiennes hiding out in the Métro. We've got wild game all year round, here on the Island of Beauty."

"Well he's certainly landed himself some of the most beautiful trophies, even though he only hunts for two months a year."

"He could let his friends have a look in, some scraps for the hounds."

Carpet bombing. The walls are collapsing around me. A siren sounds, but I can't move, can't escape, can't take refuge in a shelter. An airtight box. Nothing but silence.

Basile's voice emerges through the fog.

"But Palma is pretty . . . "

"Yeah," Daffy is off again. "He showed her his dolphins, and she showed him her whales, the ones in the top of her swimsuit."

Loud laughter. Laughter raining down on my shredded body.

"Still," Elmer chips in, "Natale could have found someone younger. And more importantly, less married."

A sudden silence.

"Shush," a voice murmurs.

For a moment I think they've spotted me. But no, a second later I hear the cries of a baby. The only newborn baby I know of is the little disabled one that his grandmother, who does the housekeeping at Papé and Mamy's house, pushes around the place in a pram.

It's over.

No more noise.

I go on down, stumbling on each step of the black staircase. I plunge into the endless tunnel, an eternity, I tiptoe through all that remains of my childhood, and by the time I reach the toilets a whole lifetime has almost passed by. I lock myself in, as if I've crossed to the other side of the Mediterranean, of humanity, of the Milky Way. I sit down on the toilet seat without turning the light on, relying only on the faint light that trickles in; I take out my notebook and transcribe all the words that have just exploded out there, in black, I draw letters with feet, as if they were alive and swarming.

I copy them out.

Lines and lines. To punish myself. To expiate the guilt of my family.

Write them out. Write them out for me a million times.

My father is cheating on my mother.
My father is cheating on my mother.
My father is cheating on my mother.
My father is cheating on my mother.
My father is cheating on my mother.

* * *

There were three pages like that.

He flicked through them, amused.

If this diary was published one day, how much of that would the publisher dare to keep?

40

August 20, 2016, 3 P.M.

Cars passed, sounding their horns as they swerved towards the precipice, insulting the oblivious owner of the Passat that was parked halfway across the winding coastal road. Clotilde didn't hear them. She held the envelope in her hand, thunderstruck. Gently, she opened it.

She read it slowly, like a child in its first year at primary school reading the words of a retired teacher.

> *My Clo,*
>
> *Thank you, thank you for agreeing to do that. Thank you for standing under the oak tree. Otherwise I don't know if I would have recognised you. You have grown into a very pretty woman. Your daughter too, perhaps even more beautiful. She looks like me, I think. At least she looks like the woman I once was.*
>
> *I would so like to talk to you.*
>
> *This evening. It's possible this evening, if you can do it.*
>
> *Around midnight, go and stand at the bottom of the path that leads to the Casa di Stella.*
>
> *Wait there. He will come and guide you.*
>
> *Wrap yourself up, it's bound to be a bit cold.*
>
> *He will lead you to my dark room. I won't be able to open the door. But perhaps the walls will be thin enough for me to be able to hear your voice.*
>
> *Until midnight. By the light of Betelgeuse.*
>
> *Kisses,*
>
> *P.*

For the rest of the day, Clotilde forced herself to be cheerful.

Franck hadn't said anything about her silence over lunch, about her sudden desire to visit her parents' grave, about her mood swings, her mobile phone and the messages he could have read there. The afternoon passed like a day's leave in wartime, slowly, without any real enjoyment. Staying at the beach until she grew bored, coming back on foot, hanging up the wet towels, sweeping the sand from the terrace, peeling fruit to make a fruit salad and finding this time almost pleasant, losing herself in the everyday tasks that usually riled her.

Clotilde even went and rested a hand on Franck's shoulder. She found the sight of him almost touching, as he knelt down to fight the colonies of ants that were opening up new routes to the breakfast shelves; Franck putting everything in order, blocking up holes, the sugar, coffee, the biscuits, checking the impenetrability of all the packets and retying the knots on all the bags. A little boy almost helpless in the face of the cunning and perseverance of insects.

Clotilde left her hand on his bare shoulder. In her gesture there was some guilt, some fear and a great deal of strategy. Not with regard to Natale, not at that moment; but with regard to her midnight assignation.

All of this was in her voice as well.

"You just need to give me some time, Franck. I'll explain it all to you, soon. I've received some information. Some new information."

She hesitated a little, too long perhaps; Franck turned his back to her, still crouching down, talking to the ants.

"No ghost stories this time, Franck, I can assure you. Nothing but the truth. Some old photographs, evidence, and the cruel truth."

She paused, then bent down and kissed him on the back of the neck. At that moment, strangely, the gesture felt sincere. More so than before; than before she had a lover. Franck turned around and stared at her for a long time, as if he were trying to decipher her thoughts, to observe the colonies of ants running through the brain of this mad woman he had married; as if he were thinking to himself that she might be protected from her delirious ideas, too, if they could be stored in hermetically sealed sachets.

"As you wish, Clo. As you wish."

⁀

Was it a trap?

Clotilde was lost in her thoughts.

"Will you pass me the mayonnaise, Maman?"

Around midnight, go and stand at the bottom of the path that leads to the Casa di Stella.

Wait there. He will come and guide you.

"Girls, are you still up for sailing tomorrow?"

I would so like to talk to you.

This evening. It's possible this evening, if you can do it.

Was this some horrible new trap she was about to tumble into? A sequence of questions circled in her head, questions that someone had deliberately provoked, in an ordered way and with premeditation: that first envelope in bungalow C29, her stolen papers, that dog bearing the same name as the one she had owned in a different life, that table laid out for breakfast, the letter on her windscreen.

"Clo, Valou, did you hear me? I reserved the 470 for the day. You'll love it. The wind, the silence, the freedom . . . "

Cervone's revelations didn't answer any of these questions, even if they continued to crush her heart, even if she was haunted by the last expression she saw on Nicolas's face, the expression that she was now able to comprehend: he had understood that he was a murderer and, in the same second, that he was going to die, that he would be executed. Might there be an explanation that connected those two insanities; Nicolas's plan to seduce Maria-Chjara and the letters from beyond?

Only one, Clotilde thought. More insane than anything.

Her mother was still alive.

⁓

11 P.M.

Franck, after spending the evening checking his compass, his marine charts, his perfect little sailor's manual, had gone to bed. They were getting up early the following day. Almost six months ago, he had booked the 470 for the twenty-first of August. Franck had left nothing to chance, he had obtained the papers he needed, done some training and, for a large chunk of the previous day, he had revised. Clotilde sat counting the lines of her novel, like watching the grains fall through an hourglass, letting her thoughts wander as she studied her husband. When you knew them well, adventurers must be quite boring people. Meticulous characters who left no room for chance, for the unknown, the unforeseen, whether they were climbers, surfers or skippers.

She watched her husband fold his napkin in four, put away the dustpan and brush, delicately put on his cap.

The reverse wasn't true.

Not all meticulous types were adventurers.

"Shall we go to bed?"

Franck had just finished ticking off his checklist for being a sailor for a day.

"Coming, I'll follow you. I just want to read for a bit longer."

"We have to get up early tomorrow, Clo."

A barely veiled reproach. Clotilde took it with a smile. She was startled by her own confidence. By the ease with which she lied, or at least didn't tell the whole truth.

"I know. Tomorrow, you're going to give me a day sunbathing naked on the deck of your boat, with an attentive man serving me frozen mojitos. That is the deal we made when you booked this last winter, isn't it? You haven't forgotten, my darling?"

11:45 P.M.

Clotilde set her book down on the table, leaving behind the cup of tea that she had barely tasted, as if to suggest that she wasn't far away. Franck was already snoring.

Gently, silently, she disappeared into the darkness.

⤍

As she left the Euproctes campsite and followed the deserted path beneath the olive trees, the silence of the campsite quickly made way for the sounds of the night. All the shy and ugly things frightened by the sun were waking up. Fearful wood mice, keen-eyed owls, lascivious toads. Clotilde walked for ten minutes, using the torch on her iPhone, until she reached the beginning of the path that led to the Casa di Stella, marked by a large wooden panel that stood in the small beaten earth car park.

She stopped.

Wait there. He will come and guide you.

Wrap yourself up, it's bound to be a bit cold.

She had put on a fawn cotton pullover, like an obedient little girl, as if it really was the ghost of her mother issuing this advice.

Ridiculous.

There was still time to run away, to get undressed, to press herself against Franck and show him the letter, tell him what had happened.

Ridiculous . . .

Six months ago he had circled the date of August 21 in his diary. Nothing could have stopped her husband from going sailing with his family, not even this letter. Not even if she confessed that she had a lover.

Far off in the forest, a toad croaked. A plaintive cry of love, or of encroaching death.

A lover, Clotilde thought again. Wouldn't the best solution be to send a text to Natale? To explain, to ask him to drop everything and come and join her, to go with her, to protect her?

Ridiculous.

At that time of night, her brave knight was fast asleep in the arms of a policeman's daughter who went to bed early because she got up at dawn to clock in at Calvi hospital while he took delivery of boxes of frozen fish.

Ridiculous.

Her whole life was nothing but a charade. In novels that dared to invent stories as surreal as her own, you would gradually realise, as you turned the pages, that the heroine was mad, that she suffered from schizophrenia, or multiple personality disorder, and that she had made up all those letters, that she had written them herself.

Clotilde heard no sound, she noticed no shadow. It was just that the darkness in front of her suddenly seemed darker, deeper, more intense, even though she couldn't say why.

The lights of Calvi Bay and the lighthouse of La Revellata suddenly disappeared.

Then they reappeared all of a sudden, while the stars marked by yachts on the Mediterranean went out.

The black night was moving.

As she staggered forward, she could hear it now.

The huge mass that had concealed the light was standing in front of her. Clotilde only recognised who it was when she pointed her torch at its dead hand, its neck, its face.

Hagrid . . . Hagrid was the name that came to her, despite herself, even though she hated herself for it.

"Orsu?" she murmured.

The giant didn't reply. He merely held out his good arm and stared at her with the frightened look of an elephant waving its trunk at a mouse. Then he pointed out the way.

He turned on a torch whose beam reached ten meters further than Clotilde's phone, and set off ahead of her, at surprising speed in spite of his stiff leg, using it almost like a jointed cane. After a few minutes they left the path signposted to Casa di Stella, and plunged into the *maquis*. The soft branches of the broom and the arbutus caressed her in the darkness. The climb seemed endless. Not once did Orsu utter a single word. Clotilde had been hesitant about asking him any questions at the bottom of the hill.

Where are we going? Who's waiting for us? Do you know my mother?

She had said nothing, probably because she knew that Orsu wouldn't reply, or perhaps in order not to disturb the solemnity of the moment, as if their walk had to be done in silence if they were fully to appreciate its meaning, its deep significance. So that an intimate certainty would be imposed.

That the person waiting for her was her mother.

He will lead you to my dark room.

Who else could have used those words?

They passed by a small stream, then advanced up a steep hillside that was bare except for a few scrubby trees. Orsu frequently turned round, as if to check that there was no one behind them. Instinctively, Clotilde did the same. Surely it was impossible for someone to be following them? They were climb-ing about a hundred meters above the path, using a torch, and it would have been impossible to steer through the pitch dark-ness without a light. Any light but their own, however far away, would have been as immediately visible as the evening star.

One thing was certain, Clotilde thought. They were alone.

Another certainty: that she was being reckless.

Of her own accord, she was plunging into the *maquis*, answering a call from beyond the grave, in the company of a lame and silent ogre in whom she had placed her trust from the outset. This pilgrimage towards a place, a ritual, a God she knew nothing about, would last another hour.

They progressed up the hillside, amidst low-lying under-growth. Opposite them, in the distance, brightly lit, the citadel of Calvi looked like a fortified island linked to the land solely by the neon strip of bars in the harbour. They walked on for a long time, turning their backs to the sea, and after plunging into the forest once more they reached a small clearing. Orsu lit a path through a carpet of cistus flowers, climbed some steps cut into the slope, then stopped. He directed his torch ahead of him.

Clotilde thought her heart was about to explode.

The beam picked out a little shepherd's cabin, right in the middle of nowhere, or that was how it seemed to her. Perhaps Orsu had led her round in a large circle to bring her back to somewhere very close to the starting point. The cabin seemed to be well looked-after, and Orsu aimed his spotlight as if to display its state of repair, the perfectly cut dry stones, the tiled roof, the closed shutters, the rough wooden door. Clotilde managed not to rush towards the cabin, grabbing the torch from his hands; or, even better, throwing it onto the ground so that it broke and she could check that there was indeed a thin thread of light filtering out beneath the door and through the grooves in the shutters.

Because someone lived here.

Because there was someone inside waiting for her.

Her.

Palma.

Maman.

She was very close, Clotilde could sense it.

Orsu was her ally.

He will lead you to my dark room. I won't be able to open the door. But perhaps the walls will be thin enough for me to be able to hear your voice.

Outside the cabin door, the land was flat and clear. Orsu, as if reading her thoughts, took a step back and turned off the torch. Clotilde walked on, keeping her eyes on the ray of light, waiting for the door to open.

What would her mother look like?

She hadn't calculated how old she would be today. Her hair would be grey, of course, but would her face be wrinkled, her back bent? Unless her ghost hadn't aged, unless she was still the gorgeous woman that Clotilde remembered, the one she was jealous of, the one Natale was in love with.

You have grown into a very pretty woman.

Your daughter too, perhaps even more beautiful.

She looks like me, I think

Yes, only her mother, only her ghost, eternally young, could have written such hurtful words to her daughter. But the door was going to open, and they would throw themselves into each other's arms. Clotilde stepped forward.

But the light wasn't coming from the cabin in front of her; or from Orsu's torch behind her. It came at her from the side, aiming straight at her temple, then settled right between her eyes, like the sight of a sniper.

Footsteps.

Quick. Manic. Breathless.

The stamping, the breathing, the excitement, everything about the arriving shadow betrayed its anger, breaking branches as it passed, crunching gravel beneath its feet.

Worse than anger: hatred.

A beast was charging towards her, a raging beast.

It was a trap. Orsu had disappeared. He had led her to this place in exchange for a few banknotes.

It was only thirty meters away, but Clotilde knew she would never reach the shepherd's cabin. Suddenly the beast was right in front of her.

Clotilde recognised it.

She hadn't been wrong, not about the anger or the hatred.

But the creature couldn't have followed them into the *maquis*; it had been waiting here for them.

How had it known?

It didn't matter now. She was lost.

41

My father is cheating on my mother.

He skimmed through the words, the lines, the pages, recto verso, endlessly repeating this simple phrase, then carefully examined the black drawings on the notebook, the spiders, the cobwebs, as if the dry ink might sting him, even after all these years.

Then the writing begin to calm down, like anger gently subsiding.

Not his.

* * *

Monday, August 21, 1989, fifteenth day of the holiday.
Binbag-blue sky.

I cheat
You cheat
He or she cheats

I'm on the beach, turning the pages.

Maman is sunbathing and Papa's asleep.

Papa insisted on taking us to the beach at Port'Agro, an almost secret inlet hidden beyond the rocks of Petra Coda. To get there, you have to follow a donkey and goat track through the middle of the *maquis*, climb a bit, then walk in single file among the needles of the junipers that sting you worse than a regiment of mosquitoes, past a ruined Genoese tower, then another kilometer in the sun without a drop of shade, then twist your ankles on a steep dusty path that leads straight down to the sea, plunge into a sand dune and there, just behind the last of the dunes, you suddenly spy the beach, a paradise that not even ten hikers will have been bold enough to reach during the course of one day.

Almost inaccessible, you are thinking . . .

One last effort before we get to play at Robinson Crusoe in paradise.

And then it's true, I swear—there are at least a hundred tourists on the beach. And right in front of us, blocking the horizon, sailing boats, yachts, Zodiacs, dozens of them, anchored beyond the row of buoys that marks the edge of the swimming area. The hulls and white sails of the boats dirty this landscape, like scraps of paper torn up and thrown in the gutter. Robinson Crusoe? You must be joking! Or maybe this is the Corsican version, in the summer. A Robinson Crusoe who's sent out thousands of messages in a bottle, and guess what, they've all been found!

We cheat
You cheat
They cheat

Mama Palma has spread out her towel facing the biggest yachts. We've all done the same. The *Blu Castello*, whose varnished wooden deck I've been staring at for three hours—Madame with her Chihuahua, Monsieur with his panama, Gino with his sailor's jersey and captain's hat, fat Teresa with the towels and the feather duster, a teenager my age who hasn't budged from her deck chair—leaves me with one observation, which is beyond dispute.

Yachts are boring!

It's true, when you think about it; the smallest plot in the shittiest campsite is bigger than the largest sailing boat. Even on a thirty-meter yacht, you can do the full circuit of it pretty quickly. A bit like being shut up in a bungalow all summer. There's nowhere you can go to be on your own, no porthole that you can sneak out of, flirt through or slam the door of to lock yourself in; there's water all around, nothing but water, kilometers of water. The more I look at the *Blu Castello* moored off the island, the more I understand this crazy and obvious fact: the people with the most money in this word lock themselves up in prisons, prisons they've bought themselves, prisons that cost millions, just because, when you've got millions to chuck around, you don't want to walk down to the beach, sleep on a campsite beside a family that lets its baby cry, share the smell of barbecued sausages. And since they're bothered by all this, they leave the island, they go into exile. So basically I think it's cool to reject those water-bound toffs, they spoil the horizon a bit.

The teenage girl on the *Blu Castello* has got up from her deck chair, taken three steps, exchanged three words with her parents who are lying crammed together on the deck, she's switcheds sides, port-starboard, three or four times, then gone back to sit in the same place.

I wouldn't swap with her. Even if her parents love each other. Perhaps money helps with that at least.

I have cheated
You are cheating
He or she will cheat
Maman is asleep and Papa is looking around.
How can you cheat?
Cheat on the person you live with. And still go on living?
Do you cheat on someone because you've cheated yourself?
Cheated on your wife, cheated on life, cheated on your dreams?
Will I cheat on life as well?
Will I cheat on someone too, one day?

42

Y
ou?"
"Were you expecting someone else?"

Clotilde didn't know whether to answer, or yell her fury into the night.

They defied one another in the shadows, face to face in front of the shepherd's cabin, like boxers puffing out their chests.

Dog and wolf.

Prey and predator.

Robber and cop.

Wife and husband.

She and Franck.

Once she'd got over her astonishment, Clotilde tried to collect the thoughts that were scattering around her head like sparrows after a rifle shot, trying to line up the questions that jostled against one another. After the "who?" she concentrated on the "how?"

How could Franck have known that she would be here? That he would find her here, since it would have been impossible to follow her without being spotted in this barren scrubland? So her husband had been waiting for them in front of this cabin lost in the *maquis*; he knew about their meeting-place. She pictured him sleeping, snoring, when she had tiptoed away from the Euproctes only an hour before. He'd been play-acting. He had organised this whole thing.

Franck landed the first blow.

"Your tea's going to get cold. You left it on the table before you went off."

"What are you doing here?"

He burst out laughing.

"No, Clotilde. Not this time. We're not going to reverse the roles."

"What are you doing here?" Clotilde said again.

"Stop that, Clo . . . When the thief is caught red-handed, you don't ask the police why they were in the right place at the right time."

"But I'm not married to a policeman. So tell me, how did you know?"

"I followed you."

"That's impossible, try something else."

Franck looked startled for a moment, as if reluctant to backtrack without saying anything else. He held back.

"Please, Clotilde."

"Please what?"

"OK, you want us to dot the i's? So let's do it. My lovely wife receives texts all day, and answers them; my lovely wife comes up with a thousand excuses, including a visit to her parents' grave, to go and meet her lover; and since they still don't have enough time, my lovely wife waits for me to fall asleep so she can go and spend the night with him."

Clotilde exploded.

"Were you trying to trap me? Is that it? The letter I found wedged under my windscreen wiper, did you write that? Modelling it on the first one?"

Franck sighed.

"Of course, Clotilde, if that's what you want to think, imagine that it's been me, right from the beginning, that I've been assuming all the identities—your husband, the father of your daughter, your mother suddenly brought back to life. Your lover. I suppose I was even the one who wrote the texts from that guy Natale Angeli on your phone?"

Franck had read the messages on her mobile. He'd admitted it. Even worse, he assumed that it was OK.

"I know I've disappointed you, Clo. You're forcing me to do things I'm not proud of. That I would never have believed myself capable of. So yes, I did go through your phone, to read what that Angeli guy was saying, at least before you started keeping the phone on you at all times."

He would pay for that, Clotilde promised herself. Franck would pay for that later. While he was talking, Franck had grabbed Clotilde's arm and was forcing her to walk back down the hill with him. Clotilde resisted as best she could, keeping an eye on the shepherd's cabin, which was now nothing more than a silhouette in the darkness. Orsu had melted into the mountain.

Her husband owed her an explanation.

"You couldn't have followed me this evening, Franck. No one could have followed me without a light, a light that I would inevitably have seen. You knew where I was going. So please, Franck, tell me. I need to know if you were the one who sent me that letter and brought me here. If it was you who . . . "

She was at the end of her tether. Someone was trying to drive her mad. And someone was succeeding.

"Oh, shit! I just want to know whether it was you or my mother who wrote that letter!"

Franck stared at her, alarmed, almost frightened. Shadows played across their respective faces, like two actors in a badly lit black-and-white film.

"Fuck it, Clotilde! React! I'm trying to make you understand that I'm going to leave you, because you kiss another guy the moment my back is turned, because you make love with that bastard as soon as I've gone to bed. Valou is sleeping in our house, not suspecting a thing, while you're busy throwing it all away. Or we're throwing it all away, if you prefer, and the only thing you're interested in is your mother. Worse than that, your mother's ghost! Christ . . . " He tried to laugh. "I know that some men leave their wives because of their mother-in-law, but not a mother-in-law who died twenty-seven years ago."

He stepped back again, pulling his wife's arm; the cabin had disappeared into the darkness.

"Do you have nothing else to say to me, Clo? Bury the dead, damn it! Even if you want to destroy us as a couple, you still have a daughter. Surely you must care about her?"

A veil lifted in Clotilde's mind.

The man talking to her, barking at her, was a complete stranger. This was the man who had come on to her at that fancy-dress party, dressed, as if by chance, as Dracula. He was the one who had wanted to marry her. He was the one who had wanted to stay. All she had done was accept his presence, for all those years.

Accept, smile, say nothing.

"I do care, Franck, but I'm out of my depth. Do you understand? So where I'm at right now is that I could just tell you everything: yes, I think my mother is alive. And yet I know it's impossible. I didn't dare talk to you about it. I know who killed my parents, who messed up the steering of the Fuego, who . . . "

"I don't care, Clotilde!"

Franck had raised his voice.

"I don't care about that accident, I don't care about your parents who died twenty-seven years ago, I don't care about the brother I've never met. I don't care about any of it! All that matters, the only thing that is driving me insane, is that you kissed someone who wasn't me, someone who felt you up, and who you wanted to meet up with and fuck this very night. I can't accept that, Clo. I can't. You've spoiled everything by coming back here, Clo. You spoil everything!"

During the whole of their long descent they didn't say another word.

Franck sat hunched over his coffee, his face drawn. Valou sat with a bowl of chocolate milk covered with a mountain of cornflakes, two fried eggs, and an orange juice, as fresh as a rose.

Behind them, Clotilde was going into action. Franck took a sip of his coffee before speaking.

"You want some good news, Valou? That boat, the 470 that I've hired for the day? We can keep it for longer, two days, three days, maybe even a week. I did some bargaining, and it's all arranged."

Valou broke the two yolks on her plate.

"So the three of us are going to spend a week on a sailing boat?"

"The two of us, Valou. Maman isn't coming with us. We'll make a few stops. Ajaccio, Porticcio, Propriano . . . Not to mention the inlets that can only be reached from the sea."

Valou mopped up the fried egg with some fresh bread, without asking anything further, then took out her mobile phone like a managing director who needed to cancel her meetings for the next few days.

Behind them, Clotilde came and went, filling Valou's bag with warm clothes, medicine, toothbrushes, sun cream, her favourite biscuits, Franck's favourite biscuits, enough for the two of them. Might she be able to help repair the past by playing the part of the perfect wife, thoughtful and attentive?

How stupid could she be.

Why see it as a role now, when these were the same tasks she had been carrying out for years?

Franck got up.

"Leave it," Clotilde said. "I'll clear up."

8:57. The campsite minibus was waiting for them. Clotilde and Franck walked towards the car park, weighed down by heavy bags. Valentine came after them, eyes fixed on her mobile phone as if she had downloaded a GPS app that would prevent them getting lost in the campsite.

Franck was running away.

He was scampering off, going underground, sailing away on a sloop while the boat was sinking. Was this line of thought, Clotilde wondered, a way of denying that she was the one who had cheated on him? That she was the one who had provoked all this? But still she couldn't feel guilty. Everything that was happening seemed to have been planned years ago; she was nothing put a toy. She couldn't help thinking that Franck had spied on her, that he had hidden part of the truth from her; that he was basically the best placed to have organised everything, from the theft of the papers from their safe to the laying of that staged breakfast table. That he was trying to drive her mad. That he had prevented her from seeing her mother the day before. That today he was stealing her daughter. That he was angry with her for having run off for a few hours to see Natale, while here he was, disappearing for several days, and she didn't even know where he was headed.

It was Franck who had imposed this break, to give himself time to take stock. To protect Valou, he had claimed. Clotilde hadn't said no. After all, it was what she wanted too. Some time to investigate.

Marco the driver was standing in front of the minibus.

"We've got to go . . . "

Clotilde kissed Valentine, then stood in front of her husband like an idiot.

"Will you call me? Promise you'll call me?"

"If we have any coverage in the Bermuda triangle," Valou said without putting away her phone.

The minibus disappeared off down the road. Franck had arranged with Cervone Spinello for them to be driven to Calvi harbour, where they would pick up the 470, leaving the Passat for Clotilde. The only words he had addressed to his wife that morning concerned the car—the papers in the glove compartment, the oil level, the tyre pressure, the key to the petrol tank; she had only half-listened, apparently already familiar with the workings of an engine. Franck was playing a part too, that of the husband whose pride had been wounded but who was making it a point of honour to remain attentive.

His male alter ego.

As stupid as she was. And perhaps more cynical. As he made his recommendations, he hadn't been able to stop himself from showing her how to work the reclining seats.

Other single-seaters, other motor homes, other cars, other families were passing along the road to Calvi. Clotilde felt a huge weight in her stomach. But it wasn't the first time they'd left her. Franck took Valou to basketball every Saturday. For a few hours, not a few days. A few hours Clotilde could take advantage of in order to escape; lying down with a novel, not a lover.

Clotilde had already lost sight of the minibus, but she didn't move. She couldn't help thinking about her father, who had also gone off on a sailing trip, just a few days before the accident at Petra Coda. At least that was what she had been told. He hadn't come back until Saint Rose's day, the twenty-third of August.

The day after tomorrow.

A hand brushed her arm and she turned round. Cervone Spinello was standing behind her.

"You shouldn't complain, Clotilde. Your husband is going off with your daughter. Most guys would leave you holding the baby."

"Drop it, Cervone."

Spinello didn't take it to heart. And he didn't take his fingers off her arm either. Clotilde bit her lip. No way was she going to burst into tears in front of this bastard! No way was he going to be the one who handed her a handkerchief. Looking for a way out of the conversation, she remembered that she hadn't seen Orsu at the campsite that morning. Where had he gone after their midnight walk to the shepherd's cabin? Of course, she could have asked Cervone, but she had no desire to take the campsite manager into her confidence. Instead she headed towards a different question.

"Still no news of Jakob Schreiber?"

"Nothing," Cervone replied. "If I haven't seen any sign of him by this evening I'll call the police."

Clotilde wondered why he hadn't done that already. Cervone seemed to be good friends with Captain Cadenat. She was about to ask him, when Spinello cut in ahead of her.

"I have a message for you, Clotilde. From Mamy Lisabetta. She phoned reception. She sounded as if she was in a complete panic. Your Papé Cassanu wants to see you, as soon as possible."

"At Arcanu?"

"No."

He left her in suspense for a few seconds before continuing.

"Up there."

He stared at the clouds that clung to the mountain, over towards Capu di a Veta. Clotilde followed the line of the crest as well, until her eyes came to rest on a tiny black cross outlined against the sky.

Memories came flooding back, pure and light, only to be spoiled by a single phrase from Cervone.

"Unless he's had himself set down there by helicopter, the old lunatic will die by the time he gets to the foot of that cross."

43

Tuesday, August 22, 1989, sixteenth day of the holiday.
Earth seen from the stars-blue sky.

H ey there, are you awake, my confidant?
Is everything fine? Can I tell you my dreams and
nightmares from this morning? From very early this
morning? If I tell you what time it is you'll go nuts.

You remember my mission, my contract, Natale's kiss on
the cheek on condition that I persuade my grandfather
Cassanu? I didn't back out, I arranged a meeting, a business
meeting and Papé accepted. At Arcanu, that didn't surprise
me, but at five in the morning!

When my parents never usually see me out of bed before
midday.

Five in the morning? Well, Papé, I went there, not knowing
what to expect.

I must tell you, my discreet and patient reader, that I have
experienced some extraordinary feelings during this holiday, as
if everything were oscillating each day between the worst, these
pages I've blackened with spiders' webs woven from the lies of
grown-ups, and the best, like swimming with dolphins, and
what I'm experiencing today, feeling free and light, so free and
light that I could catch the clouds and pull the tails of the
golden eagles.

Shall I tell you everything?

So, at five in the morning, long before dawn, Papé was waiting for me in the yard at Arcanu, by the foot of the oak tree,
walking stick in hand, binoculars around his neck, which he
then placed around mine.

"Look."

He made me look along the line of the crest, towards the south, in the direction of Asco, above Notre Dame de la Serra, and higher again.

A cross. Or what remained of it.

"We're going to sit and talk beneath that cross, Clotilde. Are you ready?"

And he looked with amusement at my Guns N' Roses sweat-shirt and my trainers.

I pretended to sprint off.

"Shall I wait for you up there?"

It didn't take me long to slow down.

Seven hundred and three meters! And you might say that we were starting at sea level.

A four-hour climb, gentle at first, then steeper and steeper and, right at the end, a sheer slope for the last two hundred meters, with me ending up on all fours like a mountain goat. Papé barely said a word the whole way up. Just a pause for a snack, some goat's cheese and coppa, halfway up, just as the sun rose behind Cap Corse. It looked like a set from one of Tolkien's books. A big iron ring rising above a long limestone finger.

While I'm writing to you, I've calmed down. My heart has returned to a normal rhythm, my thighs are starting to obey me again, my feet aren't trembling any more and my head isn't spinning.

So, I'm finally sitting beneath the cross. Papé explained to me once we got there that it's called the Austrian Cross because it was some mountain climbers from Vienna who opened up the path to the peak about fifty years ago. The cross dates back to 1969, and it's been allowed to get into a terrible state over the last twenty years. I feel like a gust of wind might blow it away.

The Austrian Cross—it makes Papé laugh. He told me that

the local Corsicans hadn't waited for the Viennese to climb up Capu di a Veta, that he'd reached the summit for the first time when he was less than eight years old, with Pancrace, my great-grandfather.

I understand why.

It isn't easy to explain in words, but when you're at the top, on that little dome of stones where the two of us sat together, you have a sense that you rule the whole world. The wind thunders in your ears, inviting you to keep turning your head and enjoy the incredible three hundred and sixty-degree view. Like a giant. Or children, perhaps, children who have built a plasticine island.

It's a feeling of floating. A feeling of being alone in the world with my Papé, who didn't seem to be out of breath, who waited for me every twenty meters during the climb. The feeling of being able to tell him anything.

Now, you who know me so well, you will be expecting that I held nothing back.

"There's one thing that amazes me, Papé. I have this sense that everyone here is afraid of you. But I think you're nice."

Operation Beluga. I must not forget. It was as if I was hoping to soften him up.

"Nasty. Nice. Those words don't mean anything, my girl. You can cause disasters with niceness, you can mess up your life with niceness, you can even kill with niceness."

Kill with niceness?

OK, Papé, I'll write it down in my notebook. I'll take another look when I'm in my final year, studying philosophy.

I turned my head to admire the landscape, like the Geode at the Cité des Sciences (THE school trip of the year!).

"Papé, how far does the land that belongs to you reach?"

"The land that belongs to *us*, Clotilde. Nothing ever really belongs to only one person. What would they do with it? Just imagine, the richest man in the history of the world—who would that be? The one who had got rid of all the others? Living alone on the planet, with all the weatlth that had ever been produced? He would be the richest man who had ever walked the earth, but the poorest as well, because no one on earth would own less than he did. To talk about wealth, there needs to be at least two of you, like the settlers in westerns, a couple who set up home in the desert in the middle of nowhere, who build themselves a shelter to live in, to have a child there. Wealth grows with a family, with other children, grandchildren, so that the land, the house, the memories, can be passed on. And so, in an absolute sense, wealth should belong to the tribe, to all those people who have helped each other. It belongs to an island, to a country, to the whole country, if humanity were capable of the same solidarity that unites a couple, a family or a tribe." And here Papé looks me straight in the eye. "But it isn't so. It will never be so, we have to defend what belongs to us. We have to be the guardians of the balance between the selfishness of the individual and the madness of the world. So to answer your question, my dear girl, this is what belongs to us."

He points along the Revellata Peninsula all the way to the Lighthouse, to the Euproctes campsite, to Alga beach. His fingers stops at the edge of Calvi in the north, and by the rocks of Petra Coda in the south, and then he explains that hundreds of square meters belong to the Coastal Conservation department, or the scientists in the Port de Stareso. Strangely, he does not mention the area of Punta Rossa left by his father to Natale's, nor the heights above Oscelluccia beach on which the Roc e Mare marina was blown up.

My Geode-head turns again.

A hundred and ninety degrees. A full view of the Monte Cinto range, the highest in Corsica. 2706 meters. Apparently if you add on the hundreds of meters of the marine trench under the Mediterranean, the one from which the favoured food of the dolphins rises, it's a total of over 3500 meters, as high as the peaks of the Alps!

I turn towards my grandfather.

"I love you, Papé, When you talk like that, it sounds as if you've stepped straight out of a film. You know, those films about godfathers defending their clan."

"I love you too, Clotilde. You'll do something with your life, something good. You have ambition, you have convictions. But . . . "

"But what?"

"But, you won't get annoyed, will you? You won't leave me here and run all the way back down?"

"What is it, Papé?"

"You're not Corsican. You're not a real Corsican, I mean. Here, the women wearing black don't have skulls on their dresses. Here, women are discreet, they say nothing, here women rule over the household, but nothing else. I know what I'm saying will make you jump, my little rebel, but what do you expect, I'm used to things being as they are. I'm used to loving women like that. Everything you represent goes over my head, Clotilde, even though I too place freedom above everything else. If I'd been born forty years later, perhaps I'd have married a woman like you."

"That's what Papa did!"

"No, my dear. No. Palma isn't like you." He remained silent for a long time. "So, come on, what did you want to ask me?"

Forty-five degrees. A bird's eye view of the Balagne. The panorama of the garden of Corsica runs from Calvi to L'Ile Rousse. With a little imagination you can even make out the desert of Agriates and the port of St-Florent at the foot of Cap Corse. I stare at the sea, as if taking a deep breath before diving, and then explain everything. The dolphins, Orophin, Idril and their babies, Natale who talks to them, the *Aryon*, a jetty to moor it to, then a bigger jetty to moor a bigger boat off, the off-shore sanctuary and, on the shore, a terrace, a bar . . . And I stop there. I don't immediately mention the dolphin house, and certainly not the female architect that Natale has been speaking to.

Papé listens to me without saying a word.

Three hundred and twenty degrees. A direct view of La Revellata. From here the peninsula looks like a sleeping crocodile! The grey-green skin, with the Oscelluccia headland and Punta Ross forming its big feet, and its mouth floating in the water at the end of the peninsula. A thousand white rocks lined up like teeth, and the lighthouse that looks like a pimple on its nose.

And then at last my Papé speaks. With a little smile curling the corners of his mouth.

"What's so extraordinary about a dolphin?"

That's the last thing I was expecting.

So I try to explain what I felt on the *Aryon*, when I dived, when I swam with the cetaceans. He must be able to hear the emotion in my voice, my arms are trembling, I'm welling up just thinking about it. So I seize the moment, because I'm sincere and it's obvious.

"Please say yes, Papé, say yes. Say yes, just for the happiness of all those people who will be able to dive like I did. Natale just wants to share this treasure."

And there we go, I should never have put the words "share" and "treasure" in the same sentence. Papé talks to me again like an old, white-bearded sage, as if he wants to take the secret notebook in which I keep my words and turn it into a book of spells.

"You see, my dear, there are only three possible attitudes you can have towards a treasure, this has always been true, whether that treasure is a woman, a diamond, a piece of land, or a magic spell: you can covet it, own it or protect it. Just as there are only three types of men: the jealous, the selfish and the conservative. No one shares a treasure, Clotilde, no one . . . "

At first I liked Papé's speeches, but now I'm starting to get annoyed. And I don't want to annoy him, but I don't really see the difference between the selfish ones who possess and the conservative ones who protect without sharing. I don't say anything. I have another, more cunning way to make him react.

"If you like, Papé, if you say so. But most of all I think that basically the real reason is that, like all Corsicans, you don't love the sea. You don't like dolphins. You don't like the Mediterranean. You don't like turning in that direction, towards the horizon. If the Corsicans really loved the sea they wouldn't leave it to the Italians in their yachts."

He laughs.

That last phrase was too much, now he's going to make fun of me rather than getting angry.

"I like your image of the Italians, but you're wrong, Clotilde. About the Corsicans and the Mediterranean. You know, I haven't always been a shepherd. I spent five years in the merchant navy, I've been around the world three times."

You are amazing, my Clo, it worked!

Two hundred and fifty degrees. I have a sense, following the coast towards the south, that I can see all the way to the nature reserve at Scandola and Girolata, where the rocks turn red and the buzzards build crazy nests that look like watchtowers on top of the volcanic peaks.

"Look, Clotilde, straight ahead, towards Arcanu. If you continue towards the sea in a straight line you reach the rocks of Petra Coda. Thirty meters, the highest of them. When I was your age, all the young Corsicans, the ones who in your view are afraid of the water, used to dive into the sea there. And, I must admit, your grandfather was the most daring of them all. My record was twenty-four meters. As the years passed, I began to jump from lower and lower heights.

Fifteen meters . . . ten meters . . . But I still swim as often as I can, from Petra Coda to the Cave of the Sea-Calves, sometimes as far as Punta Rossa. Giving up the sea is giving up on one's youth, nothing less."

"Then say yes, Papé, say yes for the dolphins, say yes for my youth, say yes just for me."

He smiles.

"You never let go, do you, my dear girl? You would make a good lawyer. I'll think about it, I promise. Just give me some time." He laughs. "Everything is going too quickly. Women are changing, and doing the talking." He laughs again. "Dolphins are changing, and talking to fishermen. I don't want my Corsica to change as quickly as that . . . "

"Then it's yes?"

"Not yet. There's one more question, a question that you haven't mentioned, my darling."

The shadow of the cross stretches over us.

"I don't know if this Natale Angeli is trustworthy."

* * *

He murmured between gritted teeth.

You had it, Papé.

You had your answer.

And it wasn't the one you expected.

44

M *idday.*
"You missed the sunrise, Clo. You were more of an early riser when you were fifteen."

Cassanu sat leaning against the wooden cross, in the shadow of the seven-meter monument pitched at the top of Capu di a Veta. He looked like a pilgrim who had carried his cross to the roof of the world in order to plant it there, dig his hole in front of it and bury himself.

Clotilde didn't rise to her grandfather's comment. She had just climbed for four hours and was getting her breath back, startled that this old man, at almost ninety years of age, had been able to climb all this way, while she was completely exhausted.

Exhausted, and on edge. Throughout her solitary ascent, in spite of the breathtaking beauty of the landscape, she hadn't been able to empty her mind, to enjoy the moment, the wind, the scents of mastic trees, citron or wild fig. On the contrary, various questions had been tumbling around her head, and were all summed up by a single one: was it her mother who had been waiting for her last night in the shepherd's cabin? She regretted not having dared to knock on the door after Franck appeared. She was cross with him for that as well, for breaking the spell. She had hardly slept that night, had been constantly thinking, delving into her memories in the hope of finding an answer to the idea that obsessed her.

How could her mother be alive?

She replayed the film of August 23, 1989, in her head, and there were only three possibilities.

Her mother wasn't in the Fuego.

Except that her mother had been sitting in the passenger seat, with Nicolas sitting behind her, and Papa at the wheel. Clotilde had seen her, before getting into the car, after they had set off, on the journey. They had smiled and talked to each other. There was no doubt about it, all four of them had set off from Arcanu.

Her mother had got out of the Fuego before the accident.

Except that the Fuego hadn't stopped, it had barely slowed down on the descent from the farm, and Clotilde was sure she hadn't dozed off on the journey before Petra Coda. In any case they had only driven a few kilometers, and her mother was still in the car when the Fuego had left the road. Papa had taken her hand.

Her mother had survived the accident.

This was the only believable hypothesis, even if the Fuego had performed three somersaults, killing each time, even if she had seen the three bodies, shattered, exposed, then wrapped in plastic bags before being taken away . . . But she had been in a state of shock. Perhaps her mother was still alive? Perhaps the emergency services had performed a miracle? But then why announce her death? How could they justify resuscitating a patient, saving her, and then not telling anybody? Not even her daughter. Why make her an orphan? To protect her mother? Because she was the one someone had wanted to kill? She was losing her mind. She didn't know who to trust. Was Cervone telling the truth about her brother Nicolas and her parents' accident? Was Franck, her husband, playing some unlikely double game? Had Natale really seen her mother's ghost? What did grandfather Cassanu know? Who was the one pulling the strings right from the beginning?

Like a reluctant teenager being dragged along on a hike by

her parents, she had spent a good part of the climb on her phone, trying to get through to three people.

To Franck and Valou, first of all. To no avail. No reply, just a silent voicemail service that endured her insults without complaint.

Then she had managed to get through to Natale, at the beginning of the climb, and demanded that he join her, that he go with her with to the top of Capu di a Veta, but the fisher of dreams had declined her invitation. It's impossible, Clo, I can't get away before this evening, I'm working all day at the shop, but Aurélia is on duty at the clinic tonight, so, yes, Clotilde, tonight if you can, if you want to.

OK, until this evening, my brave knight.

More than anything, Clotilde had had the impression that, even after all these years, he didn't want to see Cassanu. Her pirate wasn't much of a mountaineer, and perhaps he was also a bit of a chicken.

It wasn't important anyway. Papé Cassanu seemed harmless enough. Leaning against the vast wooden cross, he looked as if he would never be able to get back on his feet after that insane climb. They were both panting from the exertion and could barely speak.

Towards the middle of the climb, Clotilde had made her final call, the most unexpected of the three, and this time the person at the other end had answered after two rings, in almost impeccable French, with a German accent barely any stronger than his father's.

"Clotilde Idrissi? *Mein Gott*, how strange to speak to you after all this time."

Clotilde was amazed—Hermann Schreiber didn't sound at all surprised to receive her call.

"My father phoned me yesterday," he explained. "After your visit. We talked a bit about the summer of '89."

He addressed her formally. His voice had a slightly dis-agreeable authoritarian tone. Clotilde wondered if Hermann remembered his nickname, the cyclops. She dismissed the idea of throwing that sobriquet at him.

"You remember that summer?" she asked instead.

"Yes, all the names, even the faces. It was quite a traumatic summer, though, wasn't it? For all of us."

Especially for me, you great plank.

She decided to forge ahead and tell Hermann the reason for her call, summing up in a few words what Cervone Spinello had revealed to her: her brother Nicolas, crashing the car a few hours before the accident, damaging the steering column and the bolts without realising it. Hermann sounded surprised, as if he couldn't believe it. Then, after a moment's reflection, his voice became almost solemn.

"Then we are the ones who should have died. All five of us. Nicolas, Maria-Chjara, Aurélia, Cervone and me. We were all supposed to get into your parents' car at midnight and go to that nightclub, with your brother at the wheel." He seemed to reflect for a long time before continuing. "Yes, that changes a lot of things. It feels quite strange, after all this time. A bit like missing a plane that then crashed." Another pause. "It was us, all five of us, who should have ended up in that ravine. If I'm alive, it's entirely down to one question, Clotilde, one question to which only you can have the answer: why did your father change his mind that evening? Why did he decide to take the car and his family and go to that concert after all?"

"I . . . I don't know."

"These things don't just happen by chance. If examine your memories, you are bound to find an explanation."

Hermann's tone had become abrasive again. It was the voice of someone who was used to being obeyed. Clotilde guessed that for the last twenty-seven years his sole concern had probably been to make others undergo the humiliations he had suffered during his adolescence. But he was right too, the most important thing was that key question: why had her father changed his plan on the evening of August 23? She had no explanation. The well of her memory seemed desperately dry. Perhaps the solution was written somewhere in her diary from the summer of '89, that notebook she had been scribbling in right until those final moments on the bench at Arcanu? Perhaps she had protected her memories by hiding them in that journal? Or perhaps it contained nothing, only mere invention, the imaginings of a lying, jealous, frustrated teenager. The person she had been.

"There shouldn't be any shortage of clues to follow," Hermann Schreiber went on. "Corsica is complicated, land and family, life and death, money and power. But above all, Clotilde, are you sure you can trust Cervone Spinello? Have you found any other witnesses? What about the rest of the five? They must still be alive?"

Apart from Nicolas, Clotilde thought. The cyclops was still the emperor of tact.

"I've seen Maria-Chjara," she replied.

Hermann laughed heartily.

"Ah, Maria-Chjara! I was crazy about her. In those days I thought quoting Goethe and playing Liszt on the violin would be enough to seduce a girl. Basically I should thank her—it was to impress girls like her that I worked so hard." A few more bursts of laughter. "Girls as beautiful as her, I mean. My wife is like her, only blonde. Except that she's a soprano with the Cologne Opera, not a singer on TV reality shows."

Clotilde suddenly wanted to cut short the conversation. Was it a kind of curse, always needing to put down everything you'd loved during your teenage years?

"Never mind, Hermann. And you can't think of anything else?"

"Well, I can, in fact. Go back and see my father. He didn't

just collect photographs, he always talked to everyone on the campsite. I think he came up with some kind of theory. Something that bothered him after your parents' accident, something that didn't add up, but he only talked about it to my mother, Anke, not me."

Clotilde didn't dare to admit that she'd heard nothing from Jakob Schreiber for a couple of days. She felt even more cowardly as Hermann went on.

"To tell you the truth, I'm getting a bit worried about my father. He has an open invitation to stay with us, with his son and his grandchildren, in our villa on the island of Pag in Croatia, it even has a swimming pool, yet the stubborn old mule prefers to spend his holidays in Corsica, all alone, in his mobile home."

The cyclops's haughty self-assurance irritated Clotilde again. Who, amongst his entourage, could imagine the shy and intimidated teenager he had once been? Hermann had started from scratch; like everyone does, he had rewritten the story of his life. Clotilde fought the urge to call him by his nickname, just to bring him face to face with his past. The German got in first.

"Go back and see my father," he said again. "He spent his whole life pinning down the past with that camera of his, the way other people pin butterflies. He was like a spy, with his zoom lens pointed at anything that seemed unusual, his single eye, even though I know it was me that you lot called the cyclops!"

⌒

"Take a seat, Clotilde."

Cassanu's words dragged her from her thoughts. Later. She would think again later about the questions raised by Hermann Schreiber. Her grandfather seemed to be breathing more regularly now. He pointed at the rock nearest to him, inviting her to sit down. Below them, to the north, the citadel of Calvi seemed ridiculously small compared to the town that now sprawled its way on to the slopes of the Balagne. It hadn't looked that way to Clotilde twenty-seven years ago.

Papé's voice didn't quiver. He turned his neck and looked up at the huge wooden beam he was leaning against.

"You remember, my dear girl, in 1989, the cross that was here before? The wood was rotten, the nails were rusty, it threatened to come crashing down on us. Since then they put up a new one, which didn't last very long, and then another, this one, less than three years ago. At least the Austrians are consistent."

"Why did you want to meet here?"

"For that."

Her eye took in the sweeping view. She recognised the sleeping crocodile. The coast, from L'Ile Rousse to Calvi, from the Revellata Peninsula to Galéria, looked like a rim of white thread, a fine piece of lace, a pure line drawn by a sure hand. She knew, however, that it was merely an illusion, a question of scale. The coast was jagged, and the white rocks threw themselves into the sea, pointed like a thousand sharpened knives.

"For that?" Clotilde repeated.

"For that. For this view. This landscape. For the privilege of looking at it one last time. With you. You can call our little family meeting whatever you like, a blessing, a handover. You are our sole heir, Clotilde, the only direct descendant. All of this," he drew a large circle with his hand, "will be yours one day."

Clotilde didn't reply. Such a legacy seemed so unreal, so remote, so alien to what she was going through, to the urgent questions at stake. She didn't want to provoke her grandfather straight away, to ask him about the sabotaged steering column of the Fuego; she preferred to stick to her plan.

Check first, then accuse. Like any good lawyer. Check if Cervone Spinello was telling the truth. Only then accuse her brother Nicolas. And for that she needed Cassanu. She adopted the tone of an angry nurse, assessing the seven hundred meters of altitude.

"Do you think it's clever, engaging in this kind of feat at your age?"

"You call this a feat! I read about a Japanese man who climbed Everest at eighty, and his father had skied down Mont-Blanc at ninety-nine. So climbing to the top of this goat path . . . "

His voice had got louder. Cassanu seemed to be in outstanding shape, but it had probably been more of a test than he was letting on. He coughed for while, then continued.

"The first time I came up here was in 1935, and then from 1939 onwards I climbed up here several times a day to help the partisans, bringing them food, guns and ammunition. We were the first to get rid of the Nazis, here in Corsica, well before the Normandy landings, and without any help from the Americans! The first French *département* to be liberated, but the history books have forgotten that. The first time you climbed up here, my dear girl, you were fifteen. You remember? Of course you do, it was just before . . . "

Papé couldn't finish his phrase. Of course Clotilde remembered. The binoculars around her neck, the snack of goat's cheese and coppa, the rising sun, the peregrine falcons wheeling through the sky. Cassanu had seemed old to her even then. But he was indestructible, more indestructible than the cross.

She studied the varnished wood, which was already cracking. The iron nails, already rusty.

Her grandfather would survive this one too.

Perhaps.

"Lisabetta must be dying of worry," she said.

"She's been dying of worry for sixty years."

She smiled.

"I have some questions to ask you."

"I'm sure you do."

Clotilde's gaze wandered seven hundred meters below. The coast was merely a sequence of peninsulas, like grey tentacles covered with moss that a god seemed to have allowed to proliferate to increase the number of secret inlets, watering holes, paths. A corrupt god who would have understood the profit to be drawn from them one day.

Before she began, Clotilde's eyes turned due east, towards the sea. From here you could make out the bungalows of the Euproctes campsite, the foundations of the Roc e Mare marina, the shadow of the Tropi-Kalliste beach hut on Oscelluccia beach.

"The last time we both sat here, there was nothing, Cassanu, nothing but olive trees to pitch your tent under, a track to take you down to the beach, a fisherman's boat moored in the sea and, in Revellata Bay, some dolphins. How is that you've allowed Cervone Spinello to develop his business? All his ambition, his concrete. He's telling everyone that he has the all-powerful Idrissi eating out of his hand."

Cassanu didn't take offence.

"It's complicated, little one. Everything changed years ago, a great deal. But I suppose you can sum it all up in one word. Five letters. Money, Clotilde, money."

"I don't believe you! You don't care about money. So tell me something else. Find some other way of explaining to me why Cervone's shack hasn't burned down. Why the foundations of his hotel haven't been blown up."

Plainly Cassanu couldn't find anything.

He seemed to be having trouble breathing.

Clotilde checked that her phone was working all the way up here, that she had no more messages, and most importantly that she could dial 15 if she had to. It would take a helicopter less than five minutes to get here from Calvi. Saving hikers lost in the mountains was a daily occurrence for the Corsican emergency services. Reassured, she continued to interrogate her grandfather, as if twenty-seven seconds had passed rather than the twenty-seven years since they'd first had this same conversation. On this very spot.

"Cassanu, why did you choose that pig Cervone's projects over Natale Angeli's dolphin sanctuary? You virtually promised me. You almost said yes. What made you change your mind? Because Natale was in love with my mother? Because by getting close to your son's wife he was violating the family's honour?"

"Honour, Clotilde, is what remains when you've lost everything."

Clotilde looked out over the vast terrain in front of them, the eighty hectares of land that belonged to the Idrissi family.

"Lost everything? I think there's some left over, isn't there? But you haven't answered me, Cassanu. In the Idrissi family a woman doesn't cheat on her husband, is that it? While a man . . . "

She waited for Cassanu to react.

Not a word. He was waiting.

OK, Papé, if you really want me to deliver a good kick to our family secrets . . .

"I'm not a little girl any more, Cassanu. I know my father cheated on my mother. Everyone knew about it, the locals all made jokes about it. So why be angry with Natale and Palma?"

At last the old man reacted.

"The problem lies elsewhere, Clotilde. It started long before all that, long before you were born. The problem is that your father never should have married your mother."

And there we were. Twenty-seven years later, there we were.

"Because she wasn't Corsican?"

"No, because your father was already promised to another girl. Before he met your mother, before he fell in love with her, before he gave up everything for her."

"A Corsican girl, I suppose?"

"Her name was Salomé. She was part of our clan, almost part of our family. She was faithful to him, and would have remained faithful. And Paul would have remained faithful to his island. Your mother wasn't the kind of woman he needed. There it is, Clotilde, there's the fatal flaw. Your mother wasn't the woman you thought she was."

The words floated in the silence, the wind seemed to have carried them there so that they clung to this isolated mountain peak. Speranza's words in the Marcone cemetery:

Believe me, women are capable of that. Your mother cast a spell on your father. She took him away, caught in her net, far away from all those who loved him . . .

They mixed with the laughter of the men at the Euproctes bar, when she was fifteen and learned of her father's infidelity.

Paul should have lived here, if your mother hadn't killed him. He should have lived here, do you hear me? Lived here. Not come back here to die.

Cassanu coughed, noisily, like cannon shots scattering the voices of the past.

"It's as simple as that, dear girl, your father shouldn't have married your mother. He regretted it. We all knew he would. But by then it was too late."

"Too late for what?"

He stared regretfully at Clotilde.

"You were born. You and Nicolas."

"And?"

He closed his eyes for several seconds, as if hesitating to say any more, then he seemed to make up his mind.

"And . . . Palma had joined the scene, like a worm in an apple. After that no one could avert the tragedy."

The tragedy?"

Was Papé talking about the accident?

First of all they had accused her brother, now it was her mother's turn?

"Don't try to find out any more," Cassanu added. "I'm sorry, Clotilde, despite our shared blood, despite the land that you will inherit, you will never be part of our clan. For that, you have to live here. There are things you can't understand, things you can't learn."

Clotilde was about to protest, but Cassanu raised his hand and continued.

"You see, my dear girl, right now you're looking at me with that pitying look, as if you think I'm about to die here at the foot of this cross. No one here, no one in our clan, looks at me with pity. No one has ever called me Papé."

She was aware that she wouldn't get anything more out of her grandfather; no statement, no confession. It didn't matter, she had expected that, and it wasn't what she had come searching for.

"Nor do I, if you've noticed, I don't call you Papé any more. The little girl who called you Papé died, Cassanu, on August 23, 1989, on the rocks of Petra Coda. Her family died. Her childhood died. Everything died that day. We have at least one point in common, Cassanu—we both lost our hopes and dreams that evening. So if I came up here to see you, it wasn't to make you break the *omertà*, nor was it out of pity." She stressed that last word. "I need you. I need you to do me a favour."

The old man's dark eyes lit up again.

"What is it?"

"A favour that only someone who isn't afraid of the police could do. Someone who isn't afraid of making his own laws."

"What makes you think that's me?"

"I may not be part of your clan, but it still seems obvious to me that you aren't too keen on official justice, and that you don't put too much trust in the local prefect, in the notaries, in the police . . . "

This made him smile.

"I've tried as best I can, throughout my life, to correct injustices."

She rested a finger on his lips.

"Shh. You remember the words you said to me here, twenty-seven years ago? A throwaway phrase: "You never let go, do you, my dear girl? You would make a good lawyer." And I did, in the end, perhaps thanks to your advice. So do let me know when you need my professional services, but in the meantime I don't want to know anything about businessmen who sank to the bottom of the sea, or villas that went up in smoke, about the unidentified body that was found in Crovani Bay this morning, according to the radio, about the trucks that exploded with their cargo on the Algajola road . . . Even though I think it's a shame that Cervone Spinello wasn't on that list."

That drew another smile. He was getting his strength back; perhaps Papé wouldn't need to be taken home by helicopter. She went on confidently.

"This has nothing to do with any of that. I need you to help me stage an intervention. An intervention that isn't entirely within the law. It's potentially dangerous. I need you to get hold of a handful of determined men. Armed."

He was staring at her now, astonished. Perhaps he was even revising his judgement. That perhaps a little of his blood did flow through the veins of his granddaughter. That she might even be able to dip a toe into the bosom of his clan.

"Armed? I'm an old man, I have no influence any more. Who do you want me to . . . "

"Ta-dah," Clotilde held out her mobile to him. "I'm sure you only need to make a few calls. I'm sure your Corsicans will be lining up for a mission like this."

"That depends on the mission."

"To neutralise a bodyguard. Maybe two. A muscular body-guard, but definitely not armed."

He closed his eyes and visualised the scene.

"Where would this happen?"

"It'll bring back memories." She gazed at the shadows on the beach seven hundred meters below. "The Tropi-Kalliste, Oscelluccia beach. I'm not sure you'll have paid any attention to the posters, but I want to get close to Maria-Chjara Giordano."

"That whore?"

Yes, he clearly had paid attention to the posters.

"Why do you need to talk to her?"

She replied crisply, as if wielding a cleaver.

"I want to find out the truth. The truth about the death of your son. My father. My mother and my brother. She's the only one who knows. A truth that even you don't know."

This time the shock hit Cassanu head-on. He seemed to suffer from a sudden fit of dizziness, his eyes were closed, he wheezed and coughed then slowly slid down the cross, his limbs spread, as if he wanted to die here, his arms in a cross in challenge to the one erected by the Austrians.

Clotilde took his hand and spoke to him: "Are you all right, Papé? Are you OK?" She thought about calling the emergency services, and gave him some water. "Gently now, Papé, gently." She calmed his quivering legs, she calmed his thumping heart. "It's fine, Papé, you're OK." She gripped his ten fingers in her ten as if his life were a bird ready to fly away, hidden in the hollow of his hand. It took a few minutes before Cassanu was fully conscious again, as if he had analysed all the data in his badly ventilated brain; then slowly his breathing returned to normal, and he was able to get up and grab his cane.

"Help me up, Clotilde. It'll take us at least an hour to descend. Give me your telephone so I can use it on the way. Armed men in balaclavas, yes, I should be able to get hold of some of those."

45

Tuesday, August 22, 1989, sixteenth day of the holiday.
Porcelain-blue sky.

Like everyone else, I am part of the movement, I sing holding on to my neighbour's hand while swaying gently to "We Are the World," standing, around the fire on Alga beach, for the big communion of big sentiments. Nicolas stands in the middle, probably hoping that the light of the flames will help him pick out the guitar chords he doesn't know. He keeps to the rhythm as best he can, my brother-in-arms—if he played like Mark Knopfler, we'd all know about it. Estefan thinks he's Manu Katché and is accompanying Nicolas on the djembe.

It's almost midnight below Betelgeuse and her friends. Tonight is the good little boys and girls' party. We're grilling marshmallows, singing Bob Marley, Maxim Le Forestier and theme tunes from the TV. This evening's festivities are meant to reassure the parents; a way of masking tomorrow's trip to the Camargue organised by Nico, the party for the older kids and the ones over eighteen, with laser balls replacing the stars, techno replacing the guitar, and joints instead of Haribo.

That's Nico's plan; to move from childhood to adulthood within the space of twenty-four hours.

It's a bit quick, don't you think, my trusted reader?

As if they don't know how it will all end. It's like they're in a hurry to hit on each other and sleep with each other, left, right and centre, then to sleep with the same person all the time, then to set up home together, get married, sleep with each other less often, once a month, once a year, on the anniversary of the first time, to remember it, to dream about it, then sleep with someone else, someone who's already set up home elsewhere. As if they're in a rush to follow the same path as their parents. My parents. As if they're in a rush to start pretending.

Maria-Chjara thinks she's Cyndi Lauper and howls over the chorus of "We Are the World." She's got a lovely voice, you have to give her that. The only one sulking is Hermann. He wanted them to sing "99 Luftballons," but apart from Tess and Magnus, the Dutch kids, he's the only one who understands Nena's song in German. Which leaves him sitting there like an idiot. He even brought his violin along, but got nothing but boos when he suggested playing it to accompany us. We still prefer Nicolas's rubbish guitar, and I'm not just saying that because he's my brother! Now Hermann is holding hands with his neighbour Aurélia, and Aurélia is holding hands with Cervone, who is holding hands with Candy. And so it goes, a pocketful of posies, all fall down.

We move on to a sequence of songs—"Loin des yeux, loin du coeur;" "Petite fille de casbah;" "Le monde est bleu comme toi;" "Au Macumba, Macumba;" "Moi aussi, j'irai là-bas"— until silence finally falls. Until Hermann takes advantage of the break, gets out his violin, and strikes up with his bow before anyone has time to stop him, wresting from it notes of sorrow and passion.

He plays well, you have to admit. Even if we don't immediately recognize the tune. It's Maria-Chjara who works it out first. She sings the words to "Forever Young" and, this time, everyone falls silent. It sounds as if he and Chjara have spent the whole summer rehearsing.

Chjara's voice and Hermann's violin rise softly towards heaven. No one speaks. There are times when words fail even the most gifted of writers. I just wish you could have been there, listening to Hermann's violin weeping and Maria-Chjara's voice consoling it.

It's ridiculous, but when songs, even stupid songs about love, are sung well, they make you shiver, even if you're wearing a *Back in Black* T-shirt.

Nicolas, a good musician, has let his guitar drop to the sand. Aurélia lacks his class; she stares at the German and the Italian with the eyes of a jealous little police cadet who dearly wishes that she could lock them up for disturbing the peace, exceeding the permitted number of heartbeats per minute, and the lack of a seatbelt in their rocket to the Milky Way. She darts loving glances at Nicolas, but there's no danger of my clumsy brother catching any of them.

There they go, the last notes on the violin disappear into infinity, and then it's over.

Everyone applauds.

Forever young.

They know that's over too.

Hermann is sensitive enough to stop there, and go back to the circle, taking the hand of Aurélia, who takes the hand of Cervone and so on. Nicolas makes big eyes at me and I know why, I've been given a Cinderella pass and I've already disobeyed it. I have to add that I wasn't granted a visit from my fairy godmother before the ball, just a threat from Mama Palma:

Bed, midnight!

I reluctantly head back towards the campsite, leaving the little men and the little women three years older than me to their utopia. The last image I have as I leave the beach is that of the circle scattering like confetti, usually in pairs. Aurélia's hand in Hermann's. Maria-Chjara's head resting on Nicolas's shoulder. Cervone surrounded by Tess and Candy.

I reach the bungalow, dragging my feet in the gravel, making noise on purpose—slamming the door of the fridge after I've poured myself some water, my skull belt clanging against the cupboard door, my rings spinning like tops on the bedside table. I say "fine" when Palma asks me how it went, and I kick the door of my doll-sized bedroom, keep my T-shirt on, and open the window because it is crazily hot. I go to bed but I can't get to sleep. I try, I swear, I go for hours like that, I think, but sleep is locked up in the marital bedroom next door, so I get up again and this time I don't make as much noise as I did before. Being forty kilos, thin as a boobless, bumless Barbie, is handy when it comes to sliding out of the window of a doll's bedroom.

It's four in the morning. I know, I know, I promised Nicolas not to do the little mouse thing, not to spy on him, at least not until Saint Rose's day. I said yes, definitely yes, I had better things to do, persuading Papé about the dolphins and so on.

Except I've already done that! He said yes this morning, Papé did. Natale's going to be so impressed.

So, you understand me, I'm not about to sit around here getting bored!

The beach is deserted, almost all the teenagers have gone, the fire is nearly out. There's just Nicolas, sitting by the embers, strumming away on his own in the darkness, the sound like a shy cicada practicing before the sun rises.

Where are the others? Have they all gone to bed?

Where's that other one?

A voice answers me, she's rising from the water, like a nymph or a mermaid or a naiad (I've never really known the difference between all those creatures with women's bodies that end up in sailor's nets).

"Are you coming?"

Maria-Chjara emerges, and with what remains of the light from the embers and the moon in the sky I see a shape first of all, then her silhouette, and then the shadows on her silhouette. She's still in the water, up to her waist.

"Are you coming, Nico?"

"You're crazy, it must be icy cold in there."

I observe them, hidden in the darkness, subjugated. I'm learning. I'm learning things that your mother doesn't teach you.

"Come and catch it!"

Before I even have time to notice her arms moving, the top of Maria-Chjara's bikini is dangling from a finger.

"Come on, then, catch it."

She's dancing, and each one of her movements seems calculated to make the shadows play over her curves, to caress her, hiding her bosom before suddenly revealing it, concealing a pair of nipples before illuminating them, like two black-gloved hands settling on each of her breasts, pressing them, lifting them, crushing them. Playing with them to make the night aroused.

Nicolas gets up.

So is that how it works? Seduction. A whirlwind, dizziness, a pompom waving in the air? Is it the same after the first spin on the merry-go-round?

"Too late," the Italian girl's voice simpers.

The lacy bikini top goes flying and collapses in the wet sand like a jellyfish.

Hurry up, my little Nicolas. My great idiot of a brother is taking an age, pulling off his shirt and then folding it up at his feet. Unless his studied slowness is also part of the dance.

I'll never be able to . . . the guy, I'd just go straight over and eat him up!

"Seconda possibilità?"

And by the same stroke of magic, another tiny piece of transparent lace is dangling from Maria-Chjara's fingertips. She stands there for a moment, up to her belly in water displaying her trophy, then she takes a couple of steps forward until her parted thighs form a bridge just above the water, licked gently by the waves and the foam.

Nicolas has abandoned all patience. His underpants are hauled off with his trousers. As soon as I catch a glimpse of my brother's bum, forgive me for dumping you here, my nocturnal reader, but I've got to close my eyes.

By the time I open them again, Nicolas and Maria-Chjara are invisible, and I can just hear laughter in the water, playing, advancing and retreating. As soon as the laughter stops, I promise myself that I will block my ears, sew up my eyelids or, since it might be easier, just leave.

And that's what I should do, I know.

Too late! Maria-Chjara comes out first. Naked. Impossibly beautiful, as I will never be, as hardly any other girl will ever be. So beautiful as to be cursed by all the other girls in the galaxy.

She goes on laughing, slightly hysterically; it sounds as false as the notes from Nico's guitar, and makes her a bit less sexy, I think, but having said that she's still got the edge on the rest of the field.

She picks up her bikini top, her bottom, her white linen shirt two meters further away.

Hurry up, my Nico, she's going to slip through your fingers!

Little by little I'm starting to understand the game. Thank you, Chjara.

She's already dressed as Nicolas leaves the water, his nakedness slightly shameful. Time for him to put a foot, a thigh, into his jeans, like a heron standing on one leg. Maria-Chjara kisses him for a long time, then runs away.

For Nicolas to catch up with her, he'd have to be the world hopping champion.

"A domain, amore mio," giggles the beautiful Italian girl. *"Domani, t'offrirò la mia chiave."*

And the filthy girl, while running, casts off one of her shoes.

A few seconds later, when the darkness has swallowed her, Nicolas picks it up. My brother finds himself standing there like an idiot holding her flip-flop, a campsite Prince Charming in a kingdom of bikini-clad Cinderellas.

I creep away.

"See you tomorrow . . . "

It will be August 23.

In fact, no, it's five o'clock in the morning. The day when it's all going to happen is already here.

* * *

"Forever Young," he murmured.

The yearning in that song, the desire to die young or go on forever.

They weren't even given that choice.

46

August 22, 2016, 8:00 P.M.

H idden by a hedge a short way off Oscelluccia beach, you might have thought that the guard posted outside the caravan had been joined by three friends, as solid and muscle-bound as he was, but more eccentrically dressed. The bodyguard whose task it was to keep an eye on the Italian singer was wearing an immaculate charcoal suit, while the three men surrounding him wore hunting gear (the first two) and a dark tracksuit (the third). If anyone had come closer—although the beach was almost deserted, and the caravan isolated from the beach—they would quickly have learned their mistake.

Four dark faces, certainly. One black man and three men wearing balaclavas.

Maria-Chjara studied them for a moment through the Velux of her dressing room, then turned towards her guest, who was standing by a raspberry-coloured leather armchair.

"You didn't need to call your gorillas down from the *maquis*," the singer said. "I would have opened the door without them."

Clotilde stepped forward and peered through the window at the four men who were sharing a thermos of coffee, and almost seemed to have struck up a friendship. Their rifles rested modestly against two rubbish containers.

Papé had been efficient. During their slow descent from Capu di a Veta, he had used Clotilde's phone to call a few friends who would be capable of discreetly neutralising Maria-Chjara's bodyguard.

After the two-hour walk down to Arcanu Farm, Cassanu had been exhausted. He had collapsed on a chair in the middle of the yard, under the shade of the holm oak. Mamy Lisabetta had listened to his hoarse breathing and, ignoring his protests, had summoned Dr Pinheiro, whom he normally refused to see for anything other than his anti-flu vaccine. Pinherio had immediately called an ambulance and ordered that the patriarch should undergo a period of extended observation, then a rest cure, at the Balagne medical centre. Clotilde had felt sorry in advance for the unfortunate nurse who would be given the task of telling Cassanu that he would have to spend a few more days in bed after the initial observation. At the age of almost ninety, the Corsican still walked several kilometers a day, or swam a few hundred meters.

Clotilde turned away from the window.

"I came to see you, Maria, the other day after the concert, without my escort, and you wouldn't open the door to me then."

"But that evening you weren't accompanied by Brad Pitt."

The Italian woman stared directly into the eyes of Natale, who was sitting on the second armchair, which was apple green.

Ill-shaven and his fair hair tousled, in his haste to join Clotilde, Natale had pulled on a pair of jeans with holes in them and a white polo shirt with a loose neck. Calm and handsome, he emanated a feline strength that contrasted with the brute force of the big bears planted outside the door. Clotilde tried to extinguish the embers of jealousy that were burning in her belly, but Maria-Chjara was taking it upon herself to stir them. She sat down on the little stool in front of her dressing table: a large mirror, a basin and dozens of coloured glass bottles, cotton buds, amber phials, tweezers, and sticks of make-up in every shade of red, purple and ochre.

"What a pleasure," the singer continued, "old friends

dropping in unexpectedly for tea. But you'll forgive me, I must get ready. My concert begins in two hours. My audience awaits me!"

She winked with amusement at her mirror, clearly in no doubt about the motivation of the pre-pubescent teenagers who came to see her diving into the pool in a transparent white bikini. Clotilde took one last look outside at the hooded men, then pushed back the curtain.

"I'm sorry," she said. "I had to use force to get a meeting, but . . . " The singer had slipped the leopard-skin dressing gown from her shoulders. It hung on the chair like an abandoned hunting trophy while Maria-Chjara, wearing only a pair of red panties and a red bra, offered them an unrestricted view of her back, and the rose tattooed from the curve of her neck down to her bottom. The dressing-room mirror brazenly exposed her other side.

Natale sat as impassive as the fake marble of the furniture around them. A table, a chest of drawers, a statue of Venus and Cupid. As kitsch as it comes. A flat belonging to a high-class hooker for moneyed old men must look something like this, Clotilde thought mischievously. The fake leather, plywood and drapes concealing the wretchedness beneath.

"You know," Maria-Chjara joked, "after twenty years spent playing starlets on Canale 5, I've seen every kind of soldier . . . "

Tweezers, cotton buds, foundation flowed through her expert fingers. Two hours to mask her wrinkles.

"Since it's so urgent," the singer continued, "go on, don't waste your time."

Clotilde began. She told her the whole story, and Maria-Chjara didn't interrupt even once. She combined the details recalled by Cervone Spinello with her own memories of the twenty-third of August, 1989; Nicolas's planned trip to the Camargue, his borrowing of the Fuego, which he had tried to drive with Maria-Chjara sitting in the passenger seat, the apparently benign accident. There was no damage to the car . . . apart from the steering column, the bolt, the connecting rod.

When Clotilde had finished her story, the Italian elegantly swung round on her stool. While she was talking, Clotilde hadn't watched Maria-Chjara putting on her make-up, but the result was astonishing. She had painted on the face of a thirty-year-old diva: full, velvety red lips, big black-framed eyes, high, luminous cheekbones, a smooth, rounded brow. Miraculously rejuvenated, as if she were about to dive into the Trevi Fountain for a Fellini film, rather than into a plastic pool immortalised by dozens of iPhones switched to video.

She rolled her stool across the jasmine carpet and she took Clotilde's hand.

"Of course, my darling, I do remember your brother. Nicolas was touching, he was different, he was handsome. Even more than that, there was a kindness about him that was disarming. A desire to seduce without ever really doing it, playing the guitar so badly, showily taking his clothes off when in fact you knew he was as modest as a child. He was so charming, the day before the accident. Right here, on Oscelluccia beach, by the campfire."

Clotilde cut in abruptly.

"So why did Nicolas, that charming, touching boy, not say anything? Why didn't he speak to my father? Why did he choose to get into that car a few hours later rather than admit to the accident?"

"Nicolas couldn't have done that."

Clotilde's hand twitched but Maria-Chjara held it firmly in place.

"Nicolas couldn't have done that," the starlet repeated. "And you know that very well . . . "

Tears were beginning to well up in the corners of Clotilde's eyes. Her left hand sought Natale's on the armchair next to her.

Her right hand was clutched tightly between the Italian woman's fingers, the crimson-painted grip of an eagle.

"Cervone Spinello is right about one thing. I did want to be sure that Nicolas knew how to drive before agreeing to go off on that trip in the Fuego. Your brother really did steal the keys to your father's car, and he suggested that we take a short test drive over to the Galéria. But what happened next is slightly different from the account you've been given by the campsite manager. Nicolas drove cautiously and confidently." Her fingers gently closed around Clotilde's, like the retractable claws of a cat. "And I can assure you that I pushed the test to the max, kissing him on the neck, hands under his shorts, or in mine. He got us back safe and sound to the Euproctes campsite. Without once going off the road."

Clotilde remembered Cervone's words. Nicolas bending to look under the engine of the car. "It's nothing, it's nothing," bringing his black hands towards Maria's white lace dress, and Maria recoiling, cursing, fleeing.

Who was lying?

Her voice trembled. "But Cervone heard you talking in the car park."

"That's true. I don't remember the precise words, once we got out of the car, but I told Nicolas that since he had passed the test, I would agree to get into the car with him that night. But on one condition . . . "

Maria-Chjara's fingers tightened again on Clotilde's, and as if an electric current had passed through them, Clotilde's returned their grip.

"On the condition," she continued, "that we went on our own, just the two of us, without those other fools from the campsite."

Maria-Chjara's words had a miraculous power, like some super-strength painkiller that could eradicate a migraine in an instant.

Cervone Spinello had invented it all!

Nicolas wasn't guilty of anything, he wasn't responsible for anything. That story about an accident was nothing but a monstrous defamation.

Clotilde had managed to hold back her tears, and now she was filled with a sweet euphoria. Maria-Chjara, on the other hand, was openly weeping, tears spilling down her cheeks and leaving thin, pale rivulets in the ochre powder she had so patiently applied.

"I waited for your brother, Clotilde. I waited for him the next day. I had put on my very best dress, a shower of stars around my eyes, roses in my hair. I waited for him all night. I wanted him to be my first. Your brother, and no one else. So I waited beneath the stars until they went out one by one When the last one had faded, I thought he was an utter bastard and I went to bed feeling nothing but contempt for the male of the species. The next morning, at dawn, I found out. The accident . . . The unthinkable . . . " The crimson nails sank into her hand, but Clotilde didn't draw back. "I swear, Clotilde, I swear, every time I make love, and God knows it happens often enough with all kinds of men, I never forget to think of your brother. If I was a writer, I think it would be a dedication, or something like that. Yes, Clotilde, I never forget to dedicate to him that 'little death' that he never knew. Which I had refused him, out of defiance, out of stupidity. And perhaps even today, if I seldom say no, even to the most awful jerks, if I rarely wake up next to my conquest of the night before, it's so that Nicolas will forgive me."

Maria-Chjara went on sobbing as she spoke, but Clotilde had stopped listening. Her brain was concentrating only on certain truths.

Maria-Chjara wasn't lying, that much was obvious.

So Cervone had made it all up.

But why?

Out of jealousy? Out of spite?

Or was Cervone's game simpler than that? She had only to connect two facts: Cervone had made up the story of an accident to explain the damage to the Fuego's steering. But Sergeant Cesareu Garcia was unequivocal: the bolt had been tampered with, the steering rod had snapped, and the policeman hadn't mentioned a twisted steering column. He had talked about sabotage. Who could have an interest in lying about the cause of her parents' accident but the saboteur himself?

Maria-Chjara got to her feet and smiled as she looked at the disaster in the mirror.

"With only a few minutes to go before the concert, it's going to be difficult to paint a new masterpiece." She stuck out her tongue at her reflection. "They don't care anyway, they don't come to see me for my beautiful eyes."

With the skill of one accustomed to performing the gesture on a daily basis, her fingers deftly removed her bra while her other hand plucked her white bikini from the clothes-rail.

"According to clause 1 of my contract, I am to dive into the pool precisely at the end of the second verse of "Boys Boys Boys," wearing a bikini. According to paragraph a of clause 1: a bikini size 36C."

She turned her breasts to face Natale, but this time Clotilde felt no jealousy. Maria-Chjara's revelations had completely won her over.

"So, Brad, treat yourself, have a good look. A private session. They're not mine, so enjoy. Or not mine yet—at 3500 euros a boob, I've had to take out a ten-year loan. Paying for your youth on credit is one hell of an invention, isn't it?"

Contorting herself to put on the tiny white bikini top, Maria-Chjara addressed Clotilde.

"Don't be cross with me, darling. You must be nearly the same age as me, you're pretty as a picture, your lover is bewitching, so don't be cross with me. Men love you for your smile, your energy, your elegance, while with me it's only my tits they've ever looked at, ever since I was fourteen. They are, you might say, my identity. My double identity! It was either that, or follow my father into the broccoli business and I don't have much time for vegetables!"

She burst out laughing.

This time it was Clotilde who took her hand.

"You sing well, Maria. I heard you singing 'Sempre giovanu' recently. You've always had a beautiful voice. That was what attracted men, your singing, not your body."

Clotilde immediately reproached herself for having used the past tense, but Maria-Chjara didn't notice, or didn't seem annoyed by it.

"Thank you, my darling. That's kind. Excuse me now, I have to go for a dip."

She exploded with laughter again and stared for one last time at Natale, adjusting her bikini top, which was already slipping down to reveal two dark nipples, studiedly symmetrical. Then she turned round, gently whistling the tune to "Boys Boys Boys," this time without glancing in the mirror.

⌒

As soon as they left the caravan, the hooded guards disappeared into the night. Natale took Clotilde's hand to help her through the crowd that was beginning to swarm onto the beach. They were walking in the opposite direction to the groups of excited young dancers approaching the stage, a bit like suddenly turning around in a corridor of the Métro. Clotilde, lost in thought, allowed him to guide her.

The teenagers and young adults, noisy, glittery, fluorescent, formed a kind of carnival around her which, rather than making her feel intimidated or distracted, prolonged the feeling of serenity that lifted her heart above the seething tide of spectators.

Nicolas hadn't killed her parents.

The steering of the Fuego had been sabotaged.

Cervone Spinello was more than a suspect. He was starting to look like the guilty party. The death of her father, her mother and her brother would be avenged. Light had been cast on the areas in shadow. Why had her wallet been stolen from their bungalow? Why had that breakfast table been laid? The letters signed with a P? To conceal the murder of her family twenty-seven years ago? Clotilde, in the end, would know, would understand, would start her life afresh.

The crowd on the beach continued to thin out the further they went from the neon signs of the Tropi-Kalliste. Clotilde took advantage of the fact to take out her phone.

She would deal with Cervone later on.

Tomorrow morning, at dawn.

Before that, she wanted to make the most of this night.

She let go of Natale's hand and moved a little further away. He stood slightly off to one side, studying the groups of teenagers, viewing with apparent envy the bottles of alcohol that were being passed from lip to lip.

Where are you?

Clotilde had just pressed the "resend" button on her phone: she had already sent the message to Franck and Valentine ten times that day, but had received no answer from her daughter or he husband. She waited for a few moments. Still nothing.

Perhaps they didn't have much network coverage on the high seas, but Franck and Valou wouldn't be sailing at night. Valentine's indifference was nothing new, she rarely replied to her mother before she'd received ten texts from her, and even more rarely on the same day.

Franck, on the other hand . . .

Clotilde examined the blank screen one last time, then looked up towards the black and deserted part of the beach, closed off by jagged rocks that looked like hairy monsters. As they strode over the first few rocks, tufts of samphire crunched under her feet. A few meters from the shore, at the foot of the sleeping reefs, the shadow of a little moored fishing boat danced. The *Aryon* was waiting, rocked by the peaceful waves, attached to its rusty ring by a threadbare rope.

The music behind them was like a powerful wind, driving them out towards the sea.

Clotilde gripped Natale's hand.

"Take me to the boat."

Natale stared at her and smiled. Without a word, he rolled his trousers up above the knee. Then he led her through the darkness, as if he knew by heart each undulation in the sand, each rock that they climbed, and suddenly, before plunging into the water, he lifted her in his arms, trying to keep her dry for those last few meters that separated them from the boat.

By the time he set Clotilde down in the *Aryon*, like a cargo of dynamite that must not, under any circumstances, be allowed to get wet, the water had reached his chest, and even though he had held his cargo tightly in his arms, they were both as soaked as each other as they dropped into the hull. Lying there, the boat's sides shielded them completely from the dancers on the beach.

The sea wind chilled them.

Clotilde felt intoxicated. She had a sense that she was living out the final moments of a long nightmare and that, in a few hours, the truth would finally emerge. Perhaps, however stupid it might seem, that idiot Cervone might finally confess that her mother was still alive, that she had been waiting for her all these years.

One last time, Clotilde glanced at her mute mobile phone, before sliding her wet shorts down her legs like a snake sloughing its skin. She was much worse at striptease than Maria-Chjara, she realised. She made up for it with self-mockery.

"So, did you find our beautiful Italian arousing at all?"

With the same reptilian wriggle, Natale removed his shorts. His polo shirt, which he had already pulled over his head, had been used to sponge his body before being draped carefully over the rail.

"Hm . . . *molto molto*," said Natale. "And if you could go on calling me Brad . . . "

"No way! For me, you are and will remain Jean-Marc. More than that, my Jean-Marc in his unique role as the dolphin man."

They lay down side by side without another word, silently shedding their underwear. Clotilde, pressing her cold, wet body against Natale's, understood that they would have to make love like that, side by side. She imagined that if they ever made love again they would always have to do it like that, as sardines (the image made her smile), and find even more unlikely places—in a grassy field beside a busy road; on the top bunk, right under the ceiling, of a sleeper train on the way to Venice; under the stage of a theatre with the performance going on above them . . .

The boat rocked gently.

So did her life.

⌒

"What if we loosened the moorings?"

Clotilde and Natale were lying in the bottom of the *Aryon*, naked, on their backs; swaying in a cradle beneath the stars.

Clotilde could no longer recognise Betelgeuse among the myriad points of light.

"What if we loosened the moorings?" Clotilde repeated.

The *Aryon* was held only by a single rope. A pen-knife, teeth, a sharp fingernail would have been enough to sever their bond with the land.

In the distance, the cathedral-like silence was broken by an unaccompanied Maria-Chjara singing *"Sempre giovanu."* Clotilde had tried to wait for that song before uniting her body with Natale's, imagining that their pleasure would be all the more intense; summoning all her patience while she waited for that moment, the fantasy of her adolescence, the fantasy of a lifetime for over thirty years. She hadn't succeeded. She hadn't been able to hold out for more than a few minutes, and had come during the chorus of *"Joe le taxi."*

All that for that.

What if they loosened the moorings? Clotilde repeated again and again, this time in her head.

Natale hadn't answered her question.

Clotilde wasn't going to ask again.

They lay there in silence, waiting for a shooting star, losing all track of time.

Or at least Clotilde did.

"I've got to go, Clo."

The stars danced as if some mischievous god was trying to mix them up.

"Home?"

"My wife gets off duty at midnight. I've got to be back before Aurélia comes home."

Find Betelgeuse among the jumbled stars, the Little Prince's asteroid, any star that might have inspired love since the dawn of time.

"Why, Natale?"

The boat rocked again, but this time it was because Natale

was looking for his boxers and his belt, like a lover who was still drunk in the early morning.

"Why have you stayed with her all these years? With a woman like her?"

He smiled at her, a smile that meant "You really want to know?"; a smile that she did not refuse.

"Even if you find it hard to acknowledge, Clo, Aurélia has made a huge effort to be with me. To accompany me on my life, to arrange it, to bring some order to it. Aurélia is organised, she's attentive, honest, straight, reliable, reassuring, present, loving . . . "

Clotilde tried to burn out her retinas by staring at the most dazzling of the stars. She didn't try to control her tone of voice, which was shrill, like the harsh scrape of metal on metal.

"Fine, I see, I believe you."

She forced herself to relax slightly, to sound more serious, before she went on.

"But that doesn't change my question, Natale. Nothing you can tell me about Aurélia changes a thing, because I know you don't love her."

"So what, Clo? So what?"

Go . . . Go and see, my love . . .

Natale had left. Clotilde had been dressed for several minutes when a message arrived on her phone.

Franck.

All fine.

We'll be back in a few days as planned.

You mean a lot to me.

The words she had exchanged with Natale still clashed, mirroring her own life.

I know you don't love her.

So what?

Wednesday, August 23, 1989, seventeenth day of the holiday.
Seaweed-blue sky.

I t's the big day!
I've been talking to you about August 23, for quite some time, my reader of yesterday and tomorrow, and now here we are.

Saint Rose: the morning of tenderness, the evening of promise, the night of caresses.

Day P for Popped Cherry for my twit of a brother Nicolas, I don't need to remind you. Day W, Wednesday, for White Lies for Maman and Papa, who will exchange them on their anniversary, who will swear they still love each other, that love exists, yes, of course it does, isn't love what puts the presents beside the fireplace, among the cold and crumpled sheets, when the lovers have gone to sleep? Love is the grown-ups' version of Father Christmas.

But I don't care. I still believe in it!

When I was little and my friends swore in the playground that Father Christmas didn't exist, I refused to listen.

One day, perhaps a lover who leaves me will swear that love doesn't exist, and I will put my fingers in my ears.

I swear that I believe in Father Christmas, in people who live in the stars, in unicorns, mermaids and dolphins that can talk to humans.

Natale believes in that too.

I'm running towards him.

I'm meeting him in the Port of Stareso to tell him that I have cajoled, charmed, and flattered Papé Cassanu, the big oak of

Arcanu, the bear of the Balagne, the hawk of Capu di a Veta, the guardian of Revellata, and that he's going to say yes to the plan for a dolphin sanctuary at Oscelluccia beach. Then Natale will owe me more than a kiss, he'll owe me a kiss every day, and trips on the *Aryon*, endless swimming with Idril and Orophin, and a whole series of other promises for when I'm older and have stopped believing in Father Christmas but still believe in love.

I'm following the path along the crest of the Revellata Peninsula, then I'll climb down to the Port of Stareso in the north-east, towards Punta Rossa, with the Revellata lighthouse straight in front of me. It's the highest and narrowest part of the peninsula, you look out over the sea on all sides. If I were to pee here, just by my feet, I wouldn't be able to guess which side of the sea my little jet would flow down into. To the west, over the top of the cliff like a waterfall, or to the east, towards the beach, as a stream?

Just thinking about it slows me down. As it does every time, the sight of this amazing view. Wondering what giant palette could have produced all the shades of red on the peninsula and the turquoise in the water. Is God a bearded painter who created the world with three brushes and an easel? I like that thought. I stare at the houses peeping out between the rocks in the Port of Stareso; they're built into the cliff like caves, but a cubed version. Down at the doll-sized jetty, there's no sign of the *Aryon*.

This time I stop, I concentrate on the sea, empty but for a ferry as yellow as a scrap of sun. I hesitate. I tell myself that the best thing to do would be to stay here, up on La Revellata, in the blazing sun, in the battering wind, and look out towards the horizon. Natale's boat will have to come back to port. I just have to pull my Bon Jovi cap over my ears, put on my dark glasses and sit on a rock.

"Waiting for your boyfriend?"

The voice behind me made me start.

"Who's that?"

"Your boyfriend! The old man."

The voice belongs to Cervone Spinello, and I realise that the bastard has been spying on me, that he knows all about Natale. Unless his father, Basile, has been shooting his mouth off. I'd be surprised.

"My boyfriend? That's rubbish! It's strictly business beween me and Natale Angeli."

"I hope so for your sake. Because Angeli likes them old."

I can't even be bothered to defend myself in front of this fool. His eye is fixed on Recisa cove, the bay to the south of La Revellata that is colonised by windsurfers. It's the best spot in the Balagne according to the guys in wetsuits who sometimes crowd into the shower block at the Euproctes.

"Listen," Cervone goes on. "I understand Angeli. The older women are the ones with the money. You see that inlet down there, the one that the sailing boats leave from? That's where I'm going to set up shop as soon as I can."

He's right, the bastard. Out at sea, the dance of the wind-surfers is crazy, a mad ballet of coloured wings. On the other hand, I don't see where that dimwit Cervone could set up shop, Recisa Bay is all rocks and stones, more soil than sand, battered by the wind and the shifting dunes.

I continue to gaze out from the peninsula, from one sea to the other, still waiting for the return of the *Aryon*.

"There's nothing on Recisa beach."

"Exactly. I'm going to open a beach bar there. With para-sols so that you can read in the shade and games for children."

I must have looked at him oddly. I didn't think reading and kids were really Cervone's thing.

"You think you can make money like that?"

"Who's talking about money? It's just a mega-way of chat-ting up girls."

And off he goes with his ideas. I'm afraid I'm going to bang on a bit, and I can't guarantee that these are exactly Cervone's words, but it's just to give you an idea of what he's like, a kind of genius in his own way, a genius with twisted ideas that might actually work, ideas that could bring in the money, to him.

The opposite of Papé. The opposite of Natale as well.

"You see, Clotilde, I've spent hours, years, studying that cove. The people who come and windsurf in Recisa Bay for the first time are young, they're unattached, they have no kids. They're muscular guys, tanned, adventurous types, and hot athletic girls, who look Californian, Australian or Hawaiian, even if they come from Lyon, Strasbourg or Brussels. They meet up here, they share the same passion, they each think of the other as gorgeous and cool, they fall in love, they have sex like crazy, they become a couple, have one kid, then another one, buy a van to put their surfboards on and the kids inside, and of course they come back to the same beach, the same spot every year to do their surfing. Except— and this is true, I've seen it every summer—the guy won't give up his passion. Never! So it's the wife who's left sitting on the beach with the kid. And where's Papa? Down there, you see, that big red sail going very fast, that's Papa! She sits waiting, with a bucket and spade, a bottle of water, a book, in the shade of the beach bar if there is one; she gets bored, she has time to chat to a guy if there is one, a nice waiter, a local boy, particularly since her kid is busy with the two or three children's games set up there. And anyway, her little blond-haired two-year-old is already starting to climb over the turn-stiles, and she already knows that she's only going to able to hug her little prince out there on the sand until he's six or eight at the most, before he goes and joins his hero dad on the waves; and when he comes out of the water he'll say, 'You should have seen us, Maman. Papa and I had a brilliant time,' and then she will smile and feel happy, happy for them at least, when she hasn't been out windsurfing for ten years, and she waits the whole year for those three weeks of holiday and sits there alone on the beach, just waiting for her son and her husband; and in the evenings she will hang up their wet suits and tend to their bruises. I could go into even more detail, Clotilde, but I think you understand my plan of attack. Can you tell me of another place on the planet where the most beautiful girls in the world are sitting all on their own, getting bored? No! When the big muscly men men are out at sea, your only chance is the waiting room. That's the place for men whose only true advantage is to be in the right place at the right time."

My eyes swivel from one side of the peninsula to the other, and then they come to rest on Cervone. I stare at him, with his two-bit sociology, incredulous. Still no trace of the *Aryon*.

And he's got me.

"Don't believe me then, Clotilde. Don't believe me. Find yourself a surfer, an explorer or a spaceman who promises you the stars and then we'll talk again. But Recisa Bay is where I'm going to find a girl who's better looking than me, who's kinder, and hard-working, and affectionate."

"You really are hopeless!"

I shouldn't have said that, I know, but it just came out like that. I immediately felt a bit like the representative of all the surfers' wives, and before them the wives of the sailors, the lorry drivers, the soldiers, all those women who spent their lives waiting for their lovers to come home.

Cervone is clearly annoyed.

"Bitch! What do you expect from that old man of yours? Stop scanning the horizon, he's not coming back any time soon. You want me to tell you where the *Aryon* is? Where your Natale Angeli has gone? He's taken a trip with your mother! Oh yes, my girl, the only thing those dolphins are going to get to eat is your mum's bra and panties when your angel throws them in."

I want him to shut up. I stare like an idiot at the white sails gliding gently on the horizon. Sailing boats, just sailing boats, no fishing boats. But Cervone is off again.

"Don't be sad, my darling. Don't be cross with your mother. She's pretty. She's sexy. It would be wrong for her to deprive herself. And also she's been delicate enough to go out and have Angeli screw her on the high seas. Not like your father . . .

"What about my father?"

And here that bastard Cervone has scored a point. He doesn't add a word, he just stares at the Port of Stareso on his right, from where the *Aryon* set off, and gazes along the customs path, until his eye comes to rest on the Revellata lighthouse.

Then he says:

"The lighthouse, like everything else around here, belongs to the Idrissis. I think your father must have the key."

I left him.

I walked along the path, towards the lighthouse a hundred meters in front of me.

I pushed open the door, which wasn't bolted.

I stepped forward, I heard muffled laughter

I looked up.

I slowly climbed the spiral staircase, until I was seized by vertigo, not because of the spinning stairs, the heat, the height, the sheer drop you were aware of each time you passed a slit in the wall, but because, in my naivety, I expected that there would be two of them, dad and his mistress.

Only two.

* * *

It's the big day, he said to himself again, closing the note-book.

The day when the witnesses must confess . . . or be silent for ever.

48

August 23, 2016, 8:00 A.M.

C ervone Spinello liked to get up early, walk around the campsite before the tourists woke up, stroll along the deserted alleys, listen to the snores from the tents, sometimes the sighs, count the empty wine bottles under the cold barbecues, pass silently by the campers wrapped in their sleeping bags. He imagined himself as a landowner surveying his domain, greeting people, his peasants, assessing the harvest that was about to come; ensuring order and harmony simply by his presence.

Cervone liked to get up early, but not too early.

The alarm at 7:30; jumping out of bed at 7:45.

Anika, his wife, went to work a good hour before he did every morning, and stood at reception settling the accounts, managing supplies, recording arrivals and departures; a ritual which meant that from daybreak she was entirely at the disposal of the first campers who came to claim their breakfast, their morning paper, or to ask for ideas for that day's outing.

Perfect

Anika didn't look up from her Excel spreadsheet when Cervone passed in front of her with his coffee. Cervone was aware that behind his back people were asking questions. Anika had just turned forty, and she had the energy of a twenty-year-old summer camp instructor—bossy and hardheaded with the suppliers, tender and patient with the children, laughing and flirtatious with the men, affable and chatty with the women, and fluent in six European languages including Corsican and Catalan. Anika was a former windsurfer, who had come from Montenegro one summer and settled in Recisa Bay. Cervone had stolen her from her boyfriend, a nouveau-riche Kosovan who had disappeared again all by himself in his 4x4 Chevrolet. Quite reasonably people wondered, what was such a charming, competent, intelligent woman doing with such an idiot?

I.e., him.

To be honest, Cervone asked himself the same question every morning. That he might have seduced her twenty years ago, when she was on a beach far from home, fair enough. But that she stayed? Over time, it must have dawned on her that he was a liar, that he was calculating, a bit of a smooth talker. And you had to admit that even the most perfect women could only love damaged, tormented, broken men. A bit like billionaires doing charity work. Perhaps Anika stayed with him out of pity.

"My God," Anika suddenly said without taking her eyes off the screen.

Amongst her other morning tasks, she had developed the habit of reading through all the local news.

"What?"

"They've identified that man who drowned in Crovani Bay. It's as everyone feared. It's Jakob Schreiber."

Cervone pulled a face.

"Shit . . . Do they know what happened?"

"No idea, it's just a three-line story on the *Corse-Matin* website."

Cervone plunged his right hand into his pocket, gripping the key ring that formed a bulge there. He needed to say something, quickly, something that would seem natural in the eyes of his wife.

"I'll go to the police station in Calvi this morning. I'll ask Captain Cadenat, he'll tell me more."

He was in a hurry to leave reception, knowing that Anika

was fond of the old German, as she was of all their loyal customers. He didn't want to put on an act for her, at least not this morning.

He set off down the nearest alley, trying to gather his thoughts. He had managed to win himself some time with the disappearance of the German, along with all that nonsense he had told Clotilde about her brother. But now the noose was tightening, and too many people were getting closer to the truth. Now was not the time for everything to go up in smoke. His Roc e Mare palace was under way, old Cassanu had been taken to hospital in an ambulance—in short, the future looked rosy, he just had to hold on a little longer.

He continued his inspection, stopping by the dustbins: the cats had torn open the bags, scattering greasy bits of paper everywhere, crumbs of polystyrene, crushed milk cartons. The filth! Those beasts were at it every night.

He raised his eyes. Another member of the Euproctes staff was up too, earlier than him: Orsu. The ogre limped along, dragging an endless hosepipe; his task was to water the whole of the campsite grounds between 9 in the evening and 9 in the morning, before the sun could dry up the water poured on to the cracked soil in a split second.

The campsite manager waited for Orsu to come over to him.

"Damn it, I told you about the cats!"

Orsu looked at his boss without responding, without reacting.

"Christ, it's the same every morning."

Cervone couldn't shout at the cats, and he had to find someone to blame. He kicked at the debris.

"Disgusting!"

If he just went on about it, if he got annoyed, he wouldn't even need to ask, that big fool Orsu was quite capable of setting up his camp bed by the bins and watching them all night.

At least it would keep him busy. Orsu loved making himself useful, he loved to obey, he loved being shouted at.

"We need to get rid of those beasts!"

Don't ask, merely suggest. Orsu, backwards though he was, had grown up on a farm; he must know what to do with those vermin, catch them, strangle them, slit their throats.

"It's your job, damn it."

Orsu stared at him. Cervone thought he could see the hint of a smile, as if the big lump was already thinking up a plan to trap the moggies, a cruel way of making them suffer. Orsu had the face of a killer. He had always scared Cervone, ever since he was a child. One day he would kill somebody, if he hadn't done so already, if Cassanu hadn't already told him to.

In the end, Cervone reassured himself as he walked away, by exploiting this monster, by keeping him busy, by suggesting that he unleash his violent impulses on the cats, he was doing society a favour. He turned for a moment towards the grove of pine trees that sloped down towards the Cave of the Sea-Calves and, as he did every morning, he closed his eyes and pictured the skeletal trees being replaced by a six-hundred-square-meter infinity pool overlooking the Mediterranean, for which he had already had an architect in Ajaccio draw up plans. All he needed was a bank loan . . . and planning permission. Yes, the future looked rosy indeed.

However, when the boss of the Euproctes passed in front of the building where all the sports and leisure equipment was stored, a fresh alarm went off. The door wasn't closed. Something else that Orsu hadn't checked. Anyone could have got in and helped themselves. There was tens of thousands of euros' worth of equipment in there, with all the diving, canyoning and kayaking gear.

He cursed. He went in. He picked up an abseiling rope that had been badly rolled up. For a moment he thought again of the carabiner on the harness, the one that had failed in the

Zoïcu gorge after Valentine had put it on. He had fewer doubts today than he'd had when he loosened that bit of metal and twisted the clip just as much as he needed to; in the end everything had gone as planned, everything had turned out well. Little Valentine had had a big fright, just enough, he hoped, to keep that little snooper Clotilde at bay. But no! The girl had departed with the husband, leaving that meddling woman behind.

A meddling woman who was going to work everything out . . .

So what choice did he have now? The theft of the wallet from the safe of their bungalow hadn't given him anything either, apart from letting him find out a bit more about Cassanu's granddaughter. What choice did he have apart from getting rid of her too? Except that while his brain was quite capable of dropping a teenage girl in the water, ordering the murder of some cats, or even whacking a senile old German in the temple with a pétanque ball almost by accident, becoming a cold-blooded murderer was another thing entirely. All that nonsense that was said about Corsicans, about vendettas and murders, *omertà* enforced by bullets from a Beretta, that propensity for violence that was supposed to flow in the islanders' veins—what bullshit! For each Cassanu Idrissi, cold and determined, there were ninety-nine people between Calvi and Ajaccio incapable of shooting anything other than a wild boar or a woodcock. Still, he had to find a way to deal with this nosy lawyer.

He turned to look outside the building. Orsu appeared to have vanished. Had he already gone off cat-hunting? Cervone Spinello bent over the diving suits; that dickhead of an instructor hadn't put anything away properly, not the neoprene suits, nor the masks, nor the snorkels. Even the harpoon guns were all over the place. Anyone could have grabbed one.

The campsite manager methodically put all the equipment

back in the boxes or on the pegs, sorted it, counted it. He had a complete set of underwater fishing equipment for eight adult divers.

But something was missing . . .

Eight suits, eight compressors, eight lead belts, but seven harpoon guns. He bent down again, searched under the table, under the cupboard.

Nothing.

"What are you looking for?"

Of course. Cervone recognised the voice. A moment later, he also recognised the missing harpoon gun.

Aimed at his heart.

"You should tidy up your things, Cervone. You should also treat your staff better. And share your secrets a little more. It's risky to keep a treasure like that all to yourself."

It lasted three minutes. One for Cervone to decide to talk, almost two for him to admit the unthinkable, then less than a second of silence after his confession while he hoped for a pardon.

Yet the moment he finished, he understood that his honesty wasn't going to save him. The last image that passed through his mind was that of Anika, the first time he had seen her in Recisa Bay, she was twenty-three, reading *Letter from an Unknown Woman* by Stefan Zweig; she was as beautiful as a flower that you didn't dare pluck. But he had dared to do just that. Everything else, everything he had done since then, everything he had tried and failed to do, had been to impress her.

The finger pulled the trigger.

Would Anika miss him, at least?

The harpoon pierced Cervone's heart.

49

So, killing, was that all there was to it?
Trembling.
Coming in silence, firing an arrow, leaving.
Considering a problem solved.
Forgetting.
He sat down calmly and opened the diary again.

* * *

Wednesday, August 23, 1989, seventeenth day of the holiday.
Death-blue sky.

I went on up the stairs of the lighthouse, a few spiral steps
to get a better view, like a cameraman filming a pair of movie
stars. Now I've got a three-quarter view of them. I stop, I'm
standing perhaps twenty steps below them; from my position I
can only make out the top of the lighthouse, the iron
balustrade, and their two shapes silhouetted against the sky.

Two huge shadows.

From where I stand, Papa seems almost as tall as the lighthouse itself. He is wearing a windcheater, and its fluorescent
blue hood flaps like a bag that's about to fly away. I can't help
it, I climb another three steps, like a quiet little mouse. I'm
used to doing that—when I want, I can be the most discreet of
spies, even when what I'm spying destroys me.

She stands facing my father. She runs a hand up his back, a hand that rises towards the back of his neck, that toys with the hairs on the nape, then settles on his shoulder. Or rather grips it, as if he too were about to fly away, leap over the balustrade, escape. From my position—a low-angle shot, as they say in the films—she also looks tall, perhaps as tall as my father, even though it's hard to judge from this perspective.

They kiss. On the lips.

Just in case I had any doubts.

I can hear them laughing still, all those huntsmen at Basile's. I hope there's a tunnel under the lighthouse that leads nowhere. But afterwards. I'm not going to run this time, not straight away. I go on climbing. Another two steps. If they look down they won't be able to miss me. No danger of that, though. They're too busy hugging each other, pressing against each other, like two coastal trees mingling their roots together the better to resist the wind from the sea.

Her back is half-turned to me, but I still see her for the first time. She is dark, very beautiful, and is wearing a long, light-coloured dress that is both sober and sexy. Mysterious, alluring, loving. Just as you imagine a mistress to be, desperate with sensuality; exactly the way you must hate them to be, I suppose . . .

Except that Maman is no less beautiful than she is.

A draw, I would say.

I would almost admire my father, if I didn't want to strangle him so much. My turf-selling Papa, Corsican when he feels like it, bowling over the prettiest girls.

One last step.

One last step, I promise . . .

First I see one wheel, then another, then two more, then the whole pram. Then, of course, I see the baby. I didn't tell you before, but I'd spotted it the moment I arrived.

How could you miss it?

I'm not very good at guessing the ages of babies, but seen like that, from not very far away, I would say it was a few months old, less than six, anyway. But to tell you the truth, once the first moment of shock has passed, what surprises me isn't the child.

What surprises me is that the sexy brunette, the brunette who is kissing my father, isn't holding her baby.

Do you get it this time? If she isn't the one carrying the baby?

My Papa is.

50

At dawn, once the party-goers of Oscelluccia beach had gone to bed, once the lights of the Tropi-Kalliste had been turned off, once Maria-Chjara had put on her dressing gown and the last echoes of the techno music had faded, been drowned, been washed away by the reassuring toing-and-froing of the waves, Clotilde had fallen asleep in the hull of the *Aryon*. Huddled against a dirty old blanket that lay in a corner of the hull and smelled of a mixture of salt and tar. After hours spent half-asleep, gazing at the stars. Being strafed by the green and purple strobes from the beach bar. Wondering whether her mother had come back to life on an asteroid, and if sometimes she came back down here again. Dreaming of comet-men who left her. Exploring the black holes of her memories, then ones hidden behind the big bang at the Petra Coda precipice. After hours of this, Clotilde had finally drifted off.

The sound of her telephone woke her.
Natale!
The bastard who had dumped her here and gone back to his wife, his tail between his legs. Or his fin, rather. Who had left her, abandoned her dreams, at the bottom of the *Aryon*; she had slept on them, and they smelled of tar and seagull droppings. That bastard who had relinquished his life for the ghost of an architect. She had been willing to poke her nose into his abandoned files, to put her mouth to them, her tongue, everything

she had in her heart, in her belly and between her legs, to become an advocate for his aborted destiny. But she was too late, far too late, more than three decades too late.

At least Natale had the decency to phone her to apologise.

"Clotilde? It's Natale. My father-in-law wants to see you."

Funny way to apologise . . .

"Sergeant Garcia? Where is he? In his Jacuzzi?"

Clotilde sat up, the water lapping around her. She felt light, free, prepared to loosen the *Aryon*'s moorings.

"No, at my house. At Punta Rossa."

"So you've told him you're getting rid of his daughter and asking for my hand in marriage?"

"Clo, I'm serious. There was a murder this morning. At the campsite, at the Euproctes."

Clotilde's hand gripped the dirty blanket. Immediately, without knowing why, she thought of Valentine.

"Cervone Spinello," Natale went on. "Cervone has been murdered."

She pressed the stinking fabric to her face.

Cervone Spinello had lied to her about her brother Nicolas, Cervone was probably the one who had sabotaged the steering of her parents' car. If he had been murdered, he would take his secrets with him.

She held back an acid retch. Her fingers, her arms, her body smelled of petrol, salt and shit. Each roll of the *Aryon* amplified her desire to vomit.

"A harpoon through the heart," Natale explained. "Spinello died on the spot. My father-in-law Cesareu wants to talk to you one-on-one. He has some things to tell you, some important things about your family. He would rather tell you himself before you're summoned to the police station."

"I was asleep on your boat when he was murdered. On my own. I don't see how I can help the police find the one who did it."

"That's not it, Clotilde. The police don't need your help."

"Why not?"

"They've already caught the murderer."

Clotilde threw the blanket aside. She staggered to her feet, staring at the sea, like a castaway lost on a raft thousands of kilometers away from the nearest land.

"Who . . . who killed Spinello?"

"The campsite handyman. You must have bumped into him, you're bound to have noticed—he's the bearded giant. One arm, one leg and half of his face are paralysed. The murderer is Orsu Romani. The police have already taken him in."

Aurélia was holding Natale's hand, standing in front of their house by the sea, perched on Punta Rossa. Cesareu Garcia was standing a little to her left. Parking the Passat a few meters away, Clotilde reflected that the scene looked like a postcard, or a setting from a magazine, a picture specially composed for a photograph on shiny paper. The dream home, the handsome fair-haired man in front of it, the blue frame, the authenticity of the old stones combined with the modernity of wood and glass. Even Aurélia didn't spoil the scene: while she was still a charmless woman, her slender figure might have given the impression that she had once been beautiful; a luminous face, fine eyebrows, a slim waist, long legs. An attractiveness that might have been maintained through sacrifices both physical and financial, judging by her severely elegant dress, her stockings like a second tanned skin, the high heels that she wore with a slight arrogance. It was difficult, for anyone who had not known Aurélia at fifteen, to guess the awkwardess of her youth.

Clotilde was aware that the contrast between them must have been striking. She had come straight from Oscelluccia beach

after a night spent in the hull of the *Aryon*. She hadn't showered, she wore no make-up, no perfume, and she still carried
on her body the taste of Natale's kisses, the marks of his
caresses, and inside her the warmth of his sperm.

Aurélia carefully looked her up and down.

Could a woman smell that on a rival? The scent of forbidden love?

It didn't matter, even if Clotilde wasn't showing herself to
her best advantage, she still enjoyed playing the role of the
panther, the alley cat breaking into the territory of her Angora
rival, letting all hell break loose

They didn't greet each other, Cesareu Garcia didn't give
them the time. He walked in front of his daughter and his son-
in-law, crushing the picture postcard with the great mass of his
body.

"Come on, Clotilde. We haven't much time. Give me the
keys, Aurélia."

He took the bunch from his daughter's hand and pulled
Clotilde towards a shed a few meters away from the house. The
building looked like a dark garage, with no windows or adorn-
ment. Four stone walls and a bare bulb hanging from the ceiling. A chair. A table. And stacked on iron shelves fastened to
the walls, dozens of cardboard boxes which seemed to be as
well organised as the old wines in a sommelier's cellar.

"They're very useful, these shacks," the retired policeman
observed, closing the door behind them. "You can find them
all over the coast, they were used as shelters for the shepherds when they moved their flocks down towards the sea.
Walls half a meter thick, flat clay roof, no need for air con-
ditioning inside, as safe as a bunker. I keep all my archives
here, my equipment, my memories, all the things I wasn't
able to leave at the station when I retired. I come back and
work here from time to time. I have more room here than I
do at home, and it's nice and cool. In my own stupid house

the sun gets in on all sides." He looked around at the blank walls lit only by artificial light. "Yes, I know what you're thinking, that it's stupid to come to Punta Rossa, with the sea all around, and lock yourself up in a cellar. So I'll tell you, Clotilde, and strictly between ourselves—having the sea right in front of me all the time makes me sick of it! Like having a woman, even a very beautiful one, in front of you every single morning."

We haven't much time, Clotilde heard the words inside her head. But the retired policeman seemed determined to talk about everything but the case. She decided to cut straight to the chase.

"Orsu is innocent," she blurted suddenly. "I don't know who killed Cervone Spinello, but it wasn't Orsu."

Cesareu merely smiled.

"What do you know about that? You weren't even there."

That was true. What did she know?

"Call it what you like, an intuition, a conviction . . . "

She saw Orsu's face in front of her, his physical condition, his disability; he was the ideal victim, fodder for the hangman.

Cesareu Garcia held out a file to Clotilde.

"His prints were on the murder weapon. A harpoon gun. The one used to kill Cervone Spinello."

Clotilde's reflexes as a lawyer took over, even though for years her skills had been focused primarily on dull divorce cases. She had quite a good reputation, particularly with men, and she almost always recommended an amicable separation. Logically, no man who wanted to enter into negotiations for custody or child support would have dared choose a woman to defend him.

"Orsu's prints?" she queried. "They must be all over the campsite, he's the one who puts everything away. The diving equipment, and everything else."

"He was one of the only people who was up and about at

the time of the crime," Cesareu Garcia insisted. "He was told off by Cervone Spinello a few minutes before the murder. Humiliated might be a better word."

"If all workmen who were humiliated by their bosses stabbed them in the heart with the first sharp object they came across, my colleagues in the union would be out of a job."

Sergeant Garcia smiled again, before opening the file in front of him. The room was cool, but his tight white shirt was already drenched in sweat.

"There's something else, Clotilde. The police have searched Orsu's house. They found some pétanque balls."

"Pétanque balls? Are one-armed men not allowed to own them? Is that a crime in Corsica? No wrist action, no jack?"

"These are rare, Clotilde. Prestige Carbone 125. It wasn't difficult to identify them. Only one resident in the campsite owned this make."

A silence.

"Jakob Schreiber. The German who disappeared three days ago. And on those pétanque balls," the policeman wiped the drops of sweat from his temples with a corner of his shirt, immodestly revealing a fat belly that almost rested on the table, "the investigators identified traces of blood. Blood and grey hair. Without a doubt they belonged to the old German."

"I . . . I don't believe it . . . "

"Orsu isn't an angel, Clotilde. He isn't some poor, tortured little cripple. He does stupid things, he has plenty of convictions—for violence, for hitting people—even though, I acknowledge, it's not impossible that someone asked him to deal those blows. Orsu is easily manipulated. A mother who committed suicide before he had time to remember her, a father he never knew, his grandmother Speranza who did her best to bring him up . . . "

The vague image of Orsu as a baby in his pram, under the holm oak at Arcanu Farm came back to her. A calm and quiet baby. Clotilde had been fifteen at the time, and hadn't paid the baby any more attention than if he'd been a doll.

The question burned Clotilde's throat, it gnawed like acid.

"Does anyone . . . does anyone know who Orsu's father was?"

A question to which she already knew the answer.

"It's an open secret," the policeman replied.

He forced a laugh. With each movement of his neck or his arms, the damp fabric under his armpits stuck to his skin then came away again.

"But an open secret that no one likes to talk about. That's why I wanted to talk to you here. Because of his various imprisonments for actual bodily harm, Orsu's details have been held on the national DNA database. It wasn't hard for me to check the rumour that had been circulating since he was born."

Get it over with. Was the old policeman finally ready to drop his bomb?

"I think you've already guessed, Clotilde, unless you remember. There is no doubt about it—you and Orsu share a father. Your father had this child with Salomé Romani, Speranza's daughter. The child was conceived in August 1988 and was born on May 5, 1989. He would only have known his father for two weeks, sixteen days to be precise. Although 'known' is a generous word—Paul was married, married and the father of two older children, Nicolas and you. I'm not even sure that Paul ever met him, or acknowledged him, or was even aware of the child."

Distant images whirled through Clotilde's mind: a spiral staircase, a lighthouse, a baby in her father's arms. Images she had repressed so often, but never forgotten, filtered out, perhaps. Like a story with some pages missing. The last in particular, the ones that would explain everything.

"He . . . Was Orsu born disabled?"

"Yes. Salomé didn't want to keep him, but the Romani family

don't have abortions, they're as Catholic as they come. So she tried to tolerate him, as they used to say in different times. You know, like in *Manon des sources*, when Papet asks at the end of the book, 'Was he born alive?' 'Alive, yes, but hunchbacked.' One of Orsu's arms was paralysed, and one of his legs, and part of his face too, and probably part of his brain, the part that governs language."

Orsu? Her half-brother? Clotilde couldn't grasp it. She felt as if her brain was on automatic pilot, appealing to her pre-conditioned professional reflexes: she had to concentrate solely on the murder of Cervone Spinello, she would deal with everything else later, only then would she wonder about the implications of having a half-brother in her life.

"OK, OK," she said to Garcia. "Orsu was an unwanted child. But that doesn't make him a murderer."

The retired policeman seemed relieved. For him, the hardest part was over.

"Is it the blood ties that make you say that?" A brief hiccup of laughter made his shirt slap against his fat belly. "It's true that the Idrissi family don't tend to inform on one another."

Clotilde suddenly raised her voice.

"Baron! My surname is Baron! Maître Baron. And for now, Orsu just needs a lawyer."

Garcia searched for a dry flap of shirt to wipe his face with but didn't find one. If the conversation continued, the old policeman would shrivel up right there, dehydrated like a beached sperm whale.

"Well, now I need your help," Clotilde added.

She suddenly rose to her feet and paced round the room, examining the walls, the files, the lined-up boxes. After a few minutes, she asked Sergeant Garcia's permission to borrow one of the smallest cases, a box containing everything she needed to take fingerprints: a brush and some magnetic aluminium and copper oxide powder.

"I assure you, Clotilde, those are Orsu's prints on the harpoon, but if it amuses you . . . "

"I want his file as well, Cesareu. Or at the very least a copy of his fingerprints."

"Just that?"

"Just that."

Garcia got up and slowly went to look for the file stored under the letter R.

"I keep copies of everything," he added. "Of course you're not strictly supposed to, but in Corsica, for an officer who's spent his whole career here, it's a kind of life insurance."

He opened a file and took out a simple black-and-white photograph.

A thumb and three fingers.

"Your brother's signature. A hand that would be easily recognised among a thousand others. The hand of an ogre, with more strength in it than the hands of two able-bodied men."

"Thank you."

She stepped towards the door, hesitated for a moment and then turned round.

After all, Sergeant Garcia was the one who had started opening the box of secrets.

"While we're at it, how did your daughter manage to get her claws into Natale Angeli?"

The attack was brutal and unexpected, but Sergeant Garcia didn't flinch. He calmly put the file back on the shelf, then slowly sat down, as if the effort of moving a few meters had been enough for the day. Sweat streamed down his neck.

"Aurélia loved him. Really loved him. My daughter is a reasonable woman, very reasonable, on almost every level. But strangely, as far as her emotional life is concerned, she has always been attracted to men who are unusual, the jesters, the tightrope walkers, the troubadours, like a grey moth drawn by the light. It might have something to do with her being a nurse. Or perhaps the only way my poor Aurélia could have introduced a bit of fantasy into her life was by letting a Pierrot into her bed?"

"That wasn't my question, Cesareu," Clotilde answered crisply. "I was asking you why Natale said yes. Why he married a woman like her? No offence to Aurélia, but he could have had any other girl he wanted—the most beautiful, the funniest, the youngest."

The policeman's eyes wandered over towards the files. His life insurance, he had just joked. He seemed to hesitate before replying, then went ahead.

"To protect himself, Clotilde. It's as simple as that. In these parts, marrying the daughter of a policeman means putting yourself under the protection of the law, meaning the army, the state, France."

"To protect himself against whom?"

"Don't be so naïve, Clotilde. Against your grandfather, of course. To protect himself against Cassanu. After your parents' fatal accident, Natale was gripped by an irrational, oppressive, paralysing fear."

Clotilde thought about the almost incoherent words Natale had uttered to her.

The same second when your parents' car crashed onto the rocks of Petra Coda, the second when your brother, your father and your mother lost their lives, I saw her appear here through my window, I saw your mother, as clearly as I can see you now. She stared at me as though she wanted to see me one last time before she flew away.

Was her mother's disappearance and then that crazy apparition what had driven him mad?

Even if Palma, by the most incredible of miracles, had survived the accident at Petra Coda, had been taken alive to Calvi in an ambulance, she couldn't have somehow pulled out her drip on the way, to reappear smiling outside the house at Punta Rossa.

"Was he worried about his project?" Clotilde suggested, not really believing her own words. "About his dolphin sanctuary? That after my parents' death Cassanu wouldn't want to have anything to do with it?"

Garcia swept the argument away with a wave of his hand.

"Cassanu didn't give a damn about the dolphins. It was about the accident. I shouldn't be calling it an accident, by the way, it was an act of sabotage. A steering rod doesn't disconnect itself. For Cassanu, and for me, it was murder pure and simple. And what he was looking for was a murderer."

Clotilde suddenly felt dizzy.

Natale? A murderer? Sabotaging the steering of a car to eliminate his rival? To get rid of my father because he loved my mother? That didn't make sense for a second.

"And Cassanu never suspected Cervone Spinello?"

"His best friend's son? Cervone was less than eighteen at the time. No, Clotilde, not to my knowledge. And in any case, why would the kid have done that?"

"No reason . . . no reason . . . "

She opened the door. She didn't want to give away any more. She needed to get to Calvi as quickly as possible. She needed to question Orsu. But before that, she needed to check out a hunch, a simple test that would take her only a few seconds.

She was about to step outside when Sergeant Garcia's loud voice called her back.

"One last thing, Clotilde. I think it's better for you to know, if you're going to go rummaging about in the past. Aurélia has been asking Natale this for years, and she was so insistent that he finally gave her an answer; he swore, absolutely, and I believe him, that nothing happened between him and your mother. Your mother was faithful, your mother just wanted to make your father jealous, but she didn't love Natale." He was silent for a moment. "And Natale didn't love her either."

Contradictory images flooded into her mind. Old images that raised doubts. The policeman's voice suddenly sounded almost forceful.

"Please, Clotilde, another second before you leave. Natale confessed to Aurélia years ago, so I'd rather warn you than see you caught off guard."

"Confessed to what?"

"He confessed to her, because he thought he would never see you again, because years had passed and he thought it was ancient history." His face lit up with a regretful smile. "He confessed that in 1989 you were the one he loved."

The sun exploded as soon as Clotilde left the darkened room. It bounced off each wave around the peninsula, like a bank of spotlights dazzling the actors onstage. It took a few seconds for the shapes facing her to become clear.

Aurélia clung to Natale's arm as if he were some precious object that belonged to her, some exotic treasure that she had brought back from the ends of the earth and jealously preserved. In a flash, Clotilde saw Aurélia twenty-seven years before, on Oscelluccia beach, clinging to her brother's arm. Exactly the same gesture. Natale, motionless, stared out at the horizon as if the sea around him were nothing but a curse.

At that moment Clotilde was sure that Aurélia knew.

About last night, in the *Aryon*, with her husband.

Too bad.

Or so much the better.

She no longer knew.

She had to leave Punta Rossa, she had to concentrate on Orsu, on the murder of Cervone Spinello, on the killing of Jakob Schreiber, on the sabotaging of her parents' car. Everything was connected, everything *had* to be connected.

She needed to call Franck too, and Valentine, she hadn't heard from them since that short text the previous night.

All fine.
We'll be back in a few days, as planned.
You mean a lot to me.

She walked to the Passat in silence, unable to avoid wondering if that was the last time she would see Natale.

In films, men in love tear themselves away from the arms of the woman they don't love, and rush into the arms of the other woman, and that's what everyone expects, everyone forgives them, no one has the slightest consideration for the woman who has been abandoned. In films, everyone errs on the side of the heart, no one cares about reason.

But Natale didn't move. He made no attempt to free himself from Aurélia's grip.

Clotilde got into the car.

Maybe he would send her a text?

Perhaps once in his life, once at least, Natale might show a bit of courage?

Perhaps he would dare to loosen the moorings?

That was the last question Clotilde asked herself.

Then she started the engine.

⌒

After taking a dozen bends she reached the edge of Calvi, and parked the Passat by the edge of the road, a few hundred meters down from the police station. Feverishly, she undid her seatbelt and bent over her handbag, which was on the passenger seat. She cursed herself inwardly for the incredible mess she had accumulated—mostly papers, old receipts, scribbled and forgotten Post-its, old flyers which had been handed out in the street, everything she didn't want to throw on the ground, or hadn't yet summoned the time to take to a bin. She emptied everything onto the seat and spread out the contents before picking up what she was looking for between her fingertips.

A letter, of which she reread the first few words

My Clo,
I don't know if you're as stubborn now as you were when you were little, but there's something I'd like to ask of you.

Calm down. Be methodical for once. She set the letter down on the dashboard and took out the brush and the powder. She had seen the police do this once or twice on the instructions of a family court judge, reducing wonderful love letters to sordid pieces of evidence proving a forbidden relationship.

She had to wait for a few seconds, and took advantage of the fact to search her pockets again. She pursed her lips and blew on the letter so that only a few grains of the powder stuck to the paper, then took the corner between her right thumb and index finger. In her left hand she held the piece of black-and-white card given to her by Cesareu Garcia.

She brought them together so that her eyes could compare them, rather than superimposing the two.

It took a second, a second to be sure; after that her fingers were trembling too hard.

The words danced frantically.

My whole life is a dark room.
Kisses,
P.

Among the different smudged prints there appeared those of an ogre's hand.

Orsu.

It was illiterate Orsu who had written that letter.

Or at least carried it.

51

Wednesday, August 23, 1989, seventeenth day
of the holiday. Crumpled-paper sky.

8 o'clock in the evening . . .
Order has been restored.
The *Aryon* has returned to the harbour.
Papa has come back from the lighthouse.

And everyone is gathered, as planned, around the big family table beneath the oak tree at Arcanu Farm, with Papé Cassanu at one end, as the head of the family, and Mamy Lisabetta standing there like a conductor.

The food is being passed around, sweet and savoury *canistrelli, saliti au figatellu*, slices of *panzetta, prisuttu* and coppa, *maquis* terrines, all carried in and out by Lisabetta and her old servant whose name I don't know. There are also some distant cousins I've never met before, of all ages, the older ones drinking wine, the famous Clos Columbu produced by a great uncle, and the younger ones drinking Coke. No choice about that, even though Papé clearly isn't too happy about it—there's Corsican wine, but no local fizzy drink.

I've counted about fifteen Idrissis around the table. It's long and narrow, essentially a large plank resting on four trestles, its dimensions calculated precisely so that the groups can't mingle. At one end, the men are talking about politics, the environment, heritage, things I would love to hear about but can't, only scattered words such as taxation, speculation, pre-empt. At the other end, the teenagers and the kids. And in the middle the women, almost hidden by the large bunches of yellow roses brought by Papa; they're talking among themselves, but

I'm sure they're discussing other subjects, and most of them are speaking Corsican. Deliberately, so that Maman doesn't understand?

Maman yawns, in her black dress with the red roses, the one that Papa bought for her in Calvi. She's bored. You would never guess that in less than an hour, after the aperitif, she'll leave the Idrissi tribe with him, and climb up to share a loving tête-à-tête at Casa di Stella, while the rest of the *familia*, apart from the outsiders like me and Nicolas, will drive over to the church of Santa Lucia and the inevitable concert by A Filetta.

Quite honestly, it feels as if Maman would like to get going as soon as possible, while Papa would like to stay a bit longer. Seen like that, their night together looks like a bit of a compromise, something that won't satisfy either one.

Is that, my trusted companion, what married life is like? Is that what adulthood is about: compromises? Settling for a freedom that is half-baked?

Once they're up there, what will my secretive parents talk about? The Liguro-Provencal current and the dolphins you can see from the *Aryon*? The Revellata lighthouse and its rotating lens? Or perhaps they'll talk about nothing, everything, us. They will make white flags from the tablecloth they eat on, the sheets between which they will make love, a yearly truce, like peace on earth on Christmas Eve.

I don't know. I don't really care either. To tell you the truth, I've already moved away, I'm sitting on my bench, hidden, headphones on, Mano Negra in the background, so that I can write to you in peace. The drinks, given the time, must be coming to an end; it will soon be nightfall. Even I'm starting to doze off after my almost sleepless night.

I reread my words.
Perhaps I even fell asleep between two of them.

Everything was calm, my phrases neatly laid out, I was lulled by music, when all of a sudden I heard shouting.

It's like a fight in the yard; I think I can hear conflict, tears.

I wonder if I should go and see what's happening. But not for long. I don't care much about the settling of scores among the Idrissi family. I put my headphones back on and turn up the volume, way up.

Perhaps I even fall asleep again.

* * *

He turned over.

He discovered one more handwritten page.

The last one.

After that, all the others were blank.

.

52

W hen Clotilde stepped inside Calvi police station on the Route de Porto, the atmosphere seemed fairly relaxed. Not really the HQ of a team of investigators working at full steam; clearly the experts in Calvi kept a cooler head than the ones in Miami. Captain Cadenat was reading *L'Equipe* over a bottle of Corsica Cola. He looked up and seemed genuinely delighted to see her.

"Madame Baron?" he said with the over-attentive politeness of a shopkeeper greeting the first customer of the day.

The beautiful lawyer didn't seem to be in the mood for pleasantries, however. The policeman folded his newspaper, set down his cola, and seemed to feel obliged to justify his idleness.

"Have you come about Orsu Romani? He's in the next room. He has company. The DPP in Ajaccio sent over two inspectors this morning, they're taking charge of the case. Clearly Cervone Spinello had some influence, and his murder has caused a stir. So the local brigade here is left twiddling our thumbs—although we're also on fire duty, since people seem to think the whole place is about to go up in flames."

The policeman appeared to think his duty was done, and that he could unfold his newspaper again, but Clotilde had already stepped forward and put her hand on the door handle of the room in which Orsu was being questioned. Cadenat suddenly panicked.

"Madame Baron, no . . . "

He cursed and crumpled his newspaper into a ball, knocking over his Corsica Cola.

"You can't go in there! The big bosses are grilling him!"

Clotilde stared straight into his eyes.

"I am his lawyer."

That didn't seem to impress the rugby player.

"Oh? Since when?"

"Since right now! And by the way, my client hasn't been fully briefed."

Cadenat hesitated. Clotilde Baron wasn't bluffing, he had known about her profession since she gave her statement ten days before. And after all, the idea that, by bursting into the interrogation room, this lawyer might mess up the plans of the bigwigs from Ajaccio didn't bother him at all.

"Sort things out with them," he said at last. "And if the special units of Southern Corsica don't throw you out, well, good luck . . . Your client isn't the chattiest witness we've ever had on the island. You might even say that he takes the notion of *omertà* to a level that's almost sublime: according to our preliminary investigation, he's never uttered more than three words in a row since he was born."

Clotilde stepped into the room. Orsu was facing her. The two policemen, wearing grey suits and ties, had their backs to her. They turned round in unison, like poker players in a saloon when the door swings open. She wouldn't have been surprised if they'd knocked over the table to use it as a shield while drawing their revolvers.

Fast . . . But not fast enough!

Clotilde was the first to draw.

"Maître Idrissi."

She held her card up under their noses, a card that gave her name as Maître Clotilde Baron, but they didn't read it; the title—informing them she was a lawyer—and the name had the desired effect.

The older of the two, who wore a pair of thin rectangular glasses, was the first to compose himself.

"To my knowledge, Monsieur Romani did not mention having a lawyer of any kind."

Shall we see about that? Let's up the stakes.

Orsu was still frozen in his usual inexpressive state, but Clotilde took advantage of a vague movement of his hand to claim her victory.

"Well, I am. Two points, gentlemen, two important points. The first is that Monsieur Orsu Romani, henceforth my client, also happens to be my half-brother. The second, which is quite obvious, is that my client is innocent."

The two points left a silence.

It was a lot to take in all at once.

The name of Idrissi, for one thing. The two inspectors had the ideal suspect—a mentally disabled person with a criminal record, overwhelming circumstantial evidence, no one was going to defend an almost mute outsider—and now, from up his sleeve, he produced a lawyer, a lawyer whose name announced her status: a lawyer who was also a blood relative!

Clotilde mightn't have won the game, but she did know the law. For any infringement of the criminal law the lawyer was not obliged to be present at the first interrogation: the preliminary hearing had only to keep her informed about the case. The lawyer could speak to the accused only after questioning, for a maximum period of thirty minutes. In the face of these two poker players she had no option but to bluff.

"I expect you've had time for an initial interrogation of my client? I would like to be able to talk to him on his own."

"We hadn't finished," said the younger of the two men, the one with a small goatee.

Translation: the dumbass hasn't said a word in an hour of grilling.

"My client will talk to you. My client will talk to you after I have had a conversation with him."

Apart from the way his eyes were fixed on Clotilde, Orsu showed no sign of compliance.

The two policemen glanced at one another.

The name of Idrissi forced them to play a cautious game, they were aware of treading on dangerous ground. The suspect seemed perfectly capable of withstanding forty-eight hours in custody, even seventy-two, without opening his mouth, even if he needed to pee. What did they have to lose by letting this lawyer, who had just fallen from the sky, try to help out?

"Thirty minutes, no more," said the policeman with the spectacles.

They left.

They left Clotilde and her half-brother along together.

Or not entirely. Orsu had another friend, an ant that was strolling along the table in front of him. His sole fixation seemed to be to put his finger in the right place so that the insect would agree to climb it. Clotilde was expecting to deliver a monologue, although she wasn't used to it. Normally, in divorce cases, her female clients tended to be loquacious about the wrongs committed by the partners from whom they wanted to separate.

"I'm going to put my cards on the table, Orsu. We'll talk about our father later, if you like. But first of all, I'd like to sort out the matter at hand."

The only thing that moved was his left index finger, cutting off the ant's retreat.

"First of all, I know you didn't kill that bastard, so I'm going to get you out of here, trust me."

The ant attempted to get away in a series of desperate zig-zags. A thumb and a middle finger closed the circle.

"Secondly, I know you understand very well what's being said to you, but you don't want to let it show. You also know much more than you want to admit. Like Bernardo in *Zorro*. So if you want me to help you, I'll need a bit of give and take, my little brother."

The ant went round and round in a circle. For the first time, Orsu raised the same eyes towards Clotilde as he had when she'd yelled at the stupid teenagers in the shower block at the Euproctes. Shy and embarrassed eyes that begged her to leave things as they were, that seemed to murmur "let it go," "I don't deserve this," "thank you, but you didn't need to." Expressing all that in a single look was proof that Clotilde had gained his trust, even if Orsu still wasn't ready to speak to a stranger.

She rummaged in her bag and placed two pieces of paper on the table, then ran her finger along the final lines of the first.

My whole life is a dark room.
Kisses,
P.

Then the second.

Wait there. He will come and guide you.
Wrap yourself up, it's bound to be a bit cold.
He will lead you to my dark room.

"I just want an answer, Orsu. Just a name. Who wrote that?"
She could go on talking; he was only interested in the ant.
"Was it my mother? Was it Palma who wrote those letters?"
Ask the question again, communicating via antennae . . .
"Do you know her? Have you seen her? Do you know where she is?"
The ant panicked, imprisoned, trapped. Clotilde thought of

crushing it with her thumb, just to get a reaction from this mollusc.

"Damn it, Orsu, it's her handwriting, they're your fingerprints, you brought me these letters, you guided me to the cabin in the *maquis* that night. But . . . but I saw my mother die in that car accident, I saw her crash against the rocks. So please, if you know the truth, tell me before I go mad."

Suddenly, after hesitating for one last time, the ant climbed on to Orsu's hairy finger.

"Campa sempre."

Clotilde didn't understand.

"Campa sempre," her half-brother repeated.

"I don't speak Corsican, little brother, what does that mean?" She passed him one of the sheets of paper and picked up a pen from the desk. "Can you write it down for me?"

Slowly, and with hesitant, childish handwriting, Orsu wrote, taking care not to disturb the ant that was now running about on his forearm.

Campa sempre.

Clotilde ran from the room and held the sheet of paper up beneath the noses of the two policemen from Ajaccio.

"What does that mean?"

The two men looked at the words, studied them, then shook their heads as if it were written in Sumerian. Clotilde cursed, she didn't want to hear their excuses, hear them say that they were only civil servants who had been transferred there from the mainland and didn't speak a word of Corsican . . . English, yes, Italian, at a stretch, but the bloody language of the island itself . . . She strode past the rugby player from Béziers without even stopping. He wasn't going to be any use either.

Campa sempre.

Damn it, this was all she needed, to find herself in a police station in Calvi without anyone who could translate two words of Corsican for her. She thought of running out into the street, standing in the middle of it and stopping the first person who came past.

Campa sempre.

A sound from the next room made her start.

The toilet door opened. The cleaning woman came out. She wore a headscarf and a blue tunic edged in gold: Moroccan, like a tenth of the local inhabitants. With her bucket and mop she inevitably reminded Clotilde of Orsu. Clotilde stepped forward and held the scribbled piece of paper level with the woman's eyes.

"Campa sempre," the Moroccan woman read with an impeccable Corsican accent.

Clotilde's hopes soared.

"Please. What does it mean?"

The woman looked at her as if it were obvious.

"Alive. Still alive."

53

Wednesday, August 23, 1989.
Bruise-blue sky.

C lo?"
I sulkily take off my headphones. I prefer Manu's voice
to my brother's.

"Yeah."

"We're off."

Off where?

I sigh. I wake up. I'm still a bit zonked. The stones of the wall cut into my back and the splinters from the bench scratch my thighs. There's silence at Arcanu Farm, you'd almost think everyone else had gone.

But gone where?

I close my eyes, I see the faces of the Idrissi clan around the table, the yellow roses, the Clos Columbu wine, their noisy conversation. I open my eyes. Nico is standing there in front of me, looking like a union representative, or a negotiator with the special forces, the kind of person who bargains with robbers holed up in a bank to get the hostages out one by one.

That's not going to work with me!

Manu Chao in my ears, singing about a heart that's been consumed. I turn the volume up again. I don't want to leave my weird dream. I sit down, pick up my notebook and my pen.

I'm still drowsy, I don't know how long I've been asleep for, or really where I am. It's nearly dark, it was broad daylight when I dozed off.

I emerge slowly . . .

So about that dream, shall I tell you about it before it evaporates? Before I go back to sleep? You'll be amazed!

You know what?

You were there, my visitor from the future. You were in my dream!

Yes, honest truth, or rather, not you exactly, but that weird dream happened in *your* time, a long time from now. Not ten years, or thirty, even longer than that. I'd say at least fifty years from now.

Nicolas is still standing in front of me. He looks annoyed.

"Clo, everyone's waiting for you. Papa isn't going to . . . "

Papa?

Did I miss an episode? Has Papa changed his plans?

My eyes slide, for a moment, to the moon in the sky, the reflection of its twin in the sea, and I start writing even faster. My beloved reader mustn't get cross with me if I haven't time to finish one of my sentences, if one of my words is left hanging, if I leave you waiting for more. It'll be because Papa has grabbed me, gripped my arm and forced me to follow him, leaving behind my notebook and my pen. So I'll send you a kiss right now and say see you soon just in case we don't have time for a hug later.

I'll continue.

In front of me, Nicolas is pulling a strange face, it looks as if during my dream a kind of apocalypse has befallen the island, a meteorite has crashed right in the middle of the yard, a tsunami uprooted the big oak.

Quick . . . I mustn't go or my dream will fly away.

My dream takes place close by, but a long time from now, on Oscelluccia beach—I recognized the rocks, the sand, the shape of the bay. They are still the same. But not me, I've grown old. A grandmother. The rest isn't the same either. Strange buildings have sprouted among the red rocks, built with weird materials, almost transparent, like in science fiction—a bit like the ones Maman designs. Only the pool looks the same as today, a big pool and I'm dipping my wrinkled old feet into it.

I'll speed up, OK, I'll speed up. I can hear footsteps, Papa's footsteps.

In my dream of the future Natale is there too. In the pool there are children, perhaps they're mine, my children or my grandchildren, I'm not sure. All I know is that I'm happy, that no one around me is missing, everyone is there, as if nothing has changed in fifty years, as if no one has died; as if, in the end, the passage of time is innocent, and we're wrong to accuse it, to call it a murderer . . .

* * *

He stared into space.
The diary ended with that word.
Murderer.
He read it again one last time and then closed the notebook.

54

Clotilde had been here before, but at night.

At night, guided by Orsu.

By day, she had no idea how to find the shepherd's cabin. The landmarks were vague: cross a river, then climb a steep slope and pass through endless scrubland.

She had been wandering around the *maquis* for an eternity after parking her car at the foot of the path that led to Casa di Stella, the very place where she had waited for Orsu at midnight—doors left open, keys in the engine, she didn't care. She had left the police behind at Calvi station.

Campa sempre.

She hadn't been able to get anything more out of Orsu, but it didn't matter; she had learned the most important thing. That her mother was alive.

Even though she had seen her die, right in front of her own eyes, even if Orsu hadn't explained anything. Her half-brother had merely confirmed something she had been certain of ever since she set foot back in Corsica; that secret that she had carried deep within herself, for so long.

She's alive.

She was waiting for her.

In the shepherd's cabin.

Clotilde climbed onto a small hillock from which Arcanu Farm was visible about a hundred meters below.

Go and stand for a few minutes beneath the holm oak, before night falls, so that I can see you.

I will recognise you, I hope.

Of course—her mother had hidden somewhere on the mountain so that she could see her, she was still hiding there; from any point on the mountain, in the *maquis*, with the broom and heather up to your waist, you could see without being seen, you could hear without being heard, you could spy without being detected. Stupidly, Clotilde had imagined that once she was in the area, in broad daylight, she would remember; she would recognise the shadows of the night, she would find the landmarks, the shape of a rock, the curve of a tree trunk, the thorns of a wild rose. Impossible. Impossible to find your bearings in this maze of chestnut trees and oaks surrounded by broom, arbutus and heather. *Maquis* as far as the eye could see, the scent making her head spin.

She was about to give up, to go back down, head back to Calvi, barely five minutes with her foot to the floor, and persuade the men from Ajaccio to grant her a second interview, to make them agree to let Orsu leave the station with her, and guide her as he had the other night. Even if it was the most ludicrous of ideas. Her half-brother was in custody for murder. It would take weeks before she could obtain a letter from the examining magistrate, allowing her to stage a reconstruction.

She was about to give up when she saw it.

A stain, a purple stain lost among the arbutus berries.

A drop of blood.

And then another, a meter further off, this time on dry earth. A third, on the trunk of a cedar tree. As if Hop o' my Thumb, having run out of breadcrumbs or white pebbles, had opened his veins.

To show her the way?

Instinctively, she followed the bloody path. Once more, she felt stupid. It could have been left by any wounded animal, a fox, a boar, a deer. She ran her finger over the scarlet traces. The blood was still fresh.

What other possibilities could she come up with? That a stranger, a few minutes ahead of her, had tried to reach the shepherd's cabin? A stranger who was losing blood and wanted to get there before she did? It didn't make any sense. As she followed the trail through the *maquis*, she got the impression that the heather seemed to have been parted, that some branches were broken.

Unless it was the other way around, she thought all of a sudden. Unless this injured stranger hadn't climbed up to the cabin, but had come down from it. It didn't matter, the more she followed the trail of blood, the more convinced she became that it would lead her to that clearing where she had found herself three days earlier. The place where Orsu had left her, and Franck had joined her; her husband knew the way too, although she didn't understand why or how. She hadn't managed to contact him at all that morning, in spite of her constant calls.

Interminable ringing.

Voicemail.

Please, Franck, call me back.

Call me back.

Call me back.

Later, ask those questions later.

Campa sempre.

It was all that mattered. She had to keep going. She remembered some details now, a gentler slope, a thinning *maquis*, a big cork oak. She walked another few meters, and the traces of blood that guided her came closer and closer together. Suddenly the *maquis* opened up and the shepherd's cabin appeared.

Clotilde's heart nearly exploded.

My God!

Her stomach lurched, she gulped, and she resisted the desire to turn around, to run away. Hop o' my Thumb was there, lying on the ground, and he hadn't cut his wrists to guide her.

He had been stabbed. A huge brown stain covered his right flank.

He was dead, and probably had been for a while, lying among the faded petals of mauve and white cistus. If Clotilde hadn't followed his bloody trail, she might have thought he was asleep.

She walked over. She hesitated to bend down. Hesitated to speak.

"Pacha?"

There was a harpoon sticking out of the labrador's neck. The dog who had the same name as another one, the dog of her childhood. As if someone had wanted to deprive her of him for a second time.

The cabin door was open.

Wasps buzzed around the corpse, already inviting themselves to the carrion picnic. Clotilde walked towards the stone building. At night, she hadn't had time to notice the thick bolt that barred the wooden door, the metal lock of the medieval dungeon, as impregnable as the bars on the only window, flanked also by a massive and imposing oak shutter.

The stone prison was inhabited. There was someone inside. Someone weeping.

Was it her mother hiding in there? Walled in? Alive?

Trembling, Clotilde went inside.

This whole scene, everything she had been experiencing for the last five days, defied the imagination. She discovered a bed. A wooden table. Some dried flowers. A radio. Books, dozens of books, piled up on the wooden shelves, lying on the floor, reducing the size of the room almost by half.

And in a corner, with her back to her, an old woman crouching on a stool.

Long grey hair fell to her waist, like a wise old grandmother who'd taken the ribbon from her hair to reveal how beautiful she once was; unveiling it to her mirror, her grandchildren, a former lover.

There was nothing of the sort in this small room.

The old woman, almost kneeling, was conferring with a corner of the cold stone walls. Like a child who was being punished, that was the image that came to Clotilde. A child forgotten for a lifetime, who would never be rescued, but who would stay there, who would grow old there, because she was obedient and had been ordered not to move.

"Maman?"

Slowly the old woman got up.

Her hands, her arms, her neck were stained with blood.

"Maman?"

Clotilde's heart was almost bursting in her chest. Was it even possible? Another image appeared before her eyes, the one that had obsessed her for all these years—of her mother's body, twenty-seven years earlier, also drenched in blood. Being crushed by a rock. And yet her mother was standing here in front of her, alive, in spite of appearances and despite all the evidence.

At last the old woman turned round.

Clotilde knew, she felt, that it was her.

Maman?

But this time the words stuck in her throat.

The old woman looking at her with pleading eyes, begging her forgiveness, was over eighty years old, but still beautiful, dignified and proud. How she had suffered for all those years.

But this old woman was not her mother.

III
SEMPRE GIOVANU

55

They were like twin brothers who had aged at different speeds. The first wore a polo neck, and the second had a tattoo of a snake on his shoulder blade. The first had the thick glasses of a short-sighted person on his nose, and the second a silver piercing in his nostril. The first wore a thread-bare bottle-green corduroy suit, the second a red and white tracksuit, the colours of Ajaccio, a little too tight.

Castani Brothers, second-hand and parts, it said in the adver-tisement.

The one in the polo neck had come in the truck, the one with the tattoo in the red car.

The one in the polo neck counted the banknotes, the one with the tattoo lifted the dented bonnet.

"1,500 euros," he said, wiping his hands on his immaculate tracksuit, "but don't expect to drive across the continent in it."

The customer wasn't chatty, but he paid cash. He had asked for a discreet meeting, in the car park of the reservoir on the edge of the Bocca Serria forest. In the end, his intention hadn't been to put the Castani brothers out: no technical checks, no registration document, just a few banknotes in exchange for an antique that was barely roadworthy.

The one in the polo neck slipped the banknotes into his pocket.

"Be careful . . . That car's been asleep in a shed for years, and I don't want you to come a cropper."

The man with the tattoo closed the bonnet.

"I've checked what I can, the steering, the wheel alignment, the brakes, they should hold out for a while. But try not to get stopped!"

He held out the keys.

"Have fun."

Tattoo winked at polo neck and the two brothers got back into the truck without asking any more questions. Usually, when they sold old collectors' items it was to do-it-yourself car mechanics, amateurs hooked on restoration. But clearly this customer wasn't into mechanics. Tattoo put his foot down as polo neck watched the man disappear in the rear-view mirror. In the end, the Castani brothers didn't care what he did with that antique.

⌒

He waited for the Castani brothers' truck to disappear behind Cap Cavallo, then looked at the car for a moment, almost in disbelief. In just a few hours on the Internet, you could unearth what even the genie of the lamp couldn't bring you. He walked to the 4x4 parked behind the Corsican pines in the forest. He hadn't chosen this meeting place by chance: it was isolated, and you could park off the road. He opened the door of the 4x4 and picked up the notebook from the passenger seat, then put it on the front seat of the car he had just bought.

A matter of training.

The hardest part was yet to come.

He opened the boot of the all-terrain vehicle parked under the pines and parted some branches, ignoring the sting of the needles.

"Shall we change cars?"

She opened her eyes wide, stretched her arms and legs, stiff after spending hours in there. She smelled the scent of pine.

"Shall we change cars?" he had said.

Why?

She was bent double, almost paralysed from lying curled up in the boot. He helped her out, helped her walk a few steps. She didn't understand, walked blindly on. Her eyes blinked in the light, struggling under the glare of the sun.

Gradually they got used to it.

It was then that she saw the car; right in front of her.

A red Fuego. A GTS.

He felt the woman's legs giving way, and held her up. He had anticipated her surprise.

"Does that bring back memories, Madame Idrissi?"

56

T he old woman wasn't her mother.

She stared at Clotilde, her face covered with blood that was still flowing; unless those were red-tinted tears that were leaving tracks down her swollen bruises. She wiped them away with her long grey hair, like Mary Magdalene, the sinner.

No, Clotilde thought, delving into her memories, the weeping woman in front of her couldn't be her mother.

The woman in front of her was older. A generation older.

The woman in front of her was Lisabetta, her grandmother.

One more mystery, one more trap, one more misfortune.

Clotilde didn't have time to wonder about this any longer. The shepherd's cabin was suddenly plunged into shadow, as if a black curtain had been pulled over the door. Clotilde turned round; she wasn't mistaken, the room had been darkened not by a curtain but by a black dress. Speranza's dress, the witch whose shadow turned the room into a cave so that the rats, spiders and beetles could leave each crack between the stones and greet her arrival.

Speranza spoke to Lisabetta, paying no attention to Clotilde.

"They've taken Orsu. There's no one left."

Who are "they"? a voice shouted inside Clotilde's head.

"She's killed Pacha," Speranza went on.

Who's "she"?

The words collided in her skull. Perhaps witches communicate by telepathy, perhaps if she thought very hard about her question the witches would reply.

"The door was open when I got here," Lisabetta said.

"Who?" Clotilde asked softly. "Who are you talking about?"

No reply.

Perhaps the witches were deaf. Perhaps ghosts didn't have hearing aids.

"Where is my mother?" Clotilde yelled this time. "Orsu told me she's still alive! *Campa sempre*. Where is my mother?"

Lisabetta slowly got to her feet. Clotilde thought she was going to give her an answer, but it was Speranza's voice that echoed around the shepherd's cabin.

"Not here, Lisa. Not here. If you want to talk to her, talk to her down below."

Lisabetta hesitated, but the witch persisted.

"Cassanu is coming home. The ambulance is going to drop him off at Arcanu before midday. Nothing is ready, Lisa. Nothing."

Nothing is ready.

Clotilde hadn't understood at first.

All three of them had gone back down to the farm in silence, without exchanging as much as a word. The old women walked quickly, almost faster than Clotilde. They seemed to know every branch to grip with their wrinkled hands, every rock to step on. Their legs were accustomed to the journey, and their thin bodies had never been so light to bear.

Nothing is ready.

It was almost as if they were in a panic. They kept consulting their watches and as soon as they arrived, the two women seemed to forget about Clotilde. The lawyer merely followed them, feeling useless, like a guest who had arrived too early, and was now being ignored while preparations were under way. The two women went straight into the kitchen.

Lisabetta opened the fridge.

"*Figatellu* with lentils."

They were the first words that she had said in almost thirty minutes. Speranza didn't reply, she just stooped down to the vegetable baskets and took out tomatoes and onions. Clotilde's grandmother had already put on an apron, taken out a chopping board and placed the *panzetta* and *figatelli* on it.

At last, as if reassured, she turned towards her granddaughter.

"Sit down, Clotilde. Cassanu has spent more than twenty-four hours in Calvi hospital. He won't have eaten anything, just think, their vacuum-packed ham, their yoghurts and purées . . . ," she looked at the clock. "Not once in seventy years, Clotilde, not once, has Cassanu sat down at the table without a meal being ready for him."

She smiled as she washed her hands.

"Is that hard for you to understand, my darling? It's not how things work in Paris. But it's how it is here, and it's not even the men's fault, we're the ones who bring them up like that, from when they are little."

"Where is my mother, Mamy? Where is Palma?"

Lisabetta looked at the clock again, then picked up a huge knife.

"You sit where you are, my darling, and I'll tell you everything. Before your grandfather arrives. Corsican women know how to do that, I assure you, take care of the house and talk at the same time."

Perhaps Lisa could do that, but not Speranza. Head down, the housekeeper was resolutely cutting the *panzetta* into cubes.

"It's a long story, Clotilde. It's your story too, even if it started long before you were born." She took her eyes off her knife to look over at the witch, who was neatly separating meat from fat, before going on. "Fifty years ago, Speranza was already working at Arcanu, although perhaps working isn't the right word. She lived here and, as she does today, she helped me take care of everything—the household, the food, the garden, the animals. Speranza's daughter, little Salomé, was born at Arcanu in 1948. Three years after your father. Salomé and Paul grew up together, they were inseparable." She stared again at Speranza, who seemed to be concentrating on the size of the cubes of smoked meat that she was chopping. "Everyone here knew that they would end up getting married. That was how it was, it was written . . . As each year passed, Salomé became more beautiful. Tall, dark, with hair down to her waist. Eyes like the does in the forest of Aïtone, the grace of a kid and a laugh that would have cracked Calvi Citadel. A fairy story, my darling, Paul the prince, the heir to eighty hectares of *maquis*, and Salomé the lovely Cinderella, penniless, but we don't care about that here, all that matters is the clan, rank isn't so important. From the age of fifteen we'd married them off to each other. Yes, my darling, a fairy tale: once upon a time in La Revellata, Paul and Salomé would get married and have many children."

She stopped. Her firm fist cut the *figatellu* into four exactly equal parts.

Another glance at the clock.

11:27 A.M.

"Everything came crashing down in the summer of '68," Lisabetta went on softly, apparently having calculated the duration of her story with the same precision as that of her cooking. "And none of us suspected a thing. To tell the truth, when your father started flirting with that young Franco-Hungarian tourist camping in the field that was about to become the Euproctes campsite, we weren't particularly worried. The Corsicans here hunt the Corsican swallow in the winter and the continental swallow in the summer. Palma would leave at the end of the season like all the other girls. Paul would shed some tears by the ferry, but then get over it a week later. What I believed was the same as everyone believed. But they wrote to each other. If you knew, my darling, how much I wanted to take those letters with the Paris postmarks that the postman brought up here to Arcanu and throw them in the fire . . . If I had done that, my love, you wouldn't be here listening to me, of course. It's odd, saying all this to you, but so many tragedies and so many deaths would have been avoided. If you only knew, my poor darling, how many times I have cursed myself for not burning them." She abandoned the lentils she was sorting for a moment and gently took her granddaughter's hand. "Paul joined Palma in Paris for the first time at Christmas in 1969, and then again at Easter, then for Ascension, then he stayed up there and we didn't see him all summer. He spent that summer in the Cyclades, he sent us cards from Naxos, from Sifnos and Santorini, as if he wanted to make our island jealous, perhaps he thought we weren't jealous enough already. And it was all over, we understood that. Everyone but Salomé. Poor thing, we were all aware that she would never forget Paul. And even if she tried, her childhood sweetheart came back every summer; first with his wife, then with his wife and son, from the summer of '71, then with his wife, your brother and you from the summer of '74, and all the summers after that. We welcomed you in Arcanu, we kept up appearances, I even taught your mother to make *figatelli*, *fiadone*, and boar stew. Speranza went with her to pick herbs: oregano, mint and angelica. We welcomed her because she was family, even if she had stolen our son, even if we were angry with her, even if basically, just for that reason, we never loved her."

She was worried about the time, 11:32 A.M., and let go of Clotilde's hand, then added the lentils to a pot of boiling water. Speranza peeled the onions, not betraying the least emotion.

"Every summer," Lisabetta went on, avoiding Speranza's eyes, "Salomé went off to cry. She was a proud girl, so she chose to hide rather than see Paul kissing his wife on Alga beach. Or see him playing with his children. So she wouldn't feel like poking her own eyes out at the sight of the happiness that should have been hers. That, my darling, is why you hardly ever saw her." She slid the cubes of *panzetta* and the onions into a frying pan and added olive oil. "But time was Salomé's ally. Between the Penelopes and the whores, the Penelopes always win out in the end."

The word "whore" coming from old Lisabetta's mouth made Clotilde jump. What hatred must a grandmother feel to use such a coarse term? Speranza punctuated her words with the sound of plates being stacked.

"After ten years or so," Lisabetta continued, "all of Palma's trump cards began to fade. Everything that had charmed your father. The unfamiliar, her difference, her exoticism, call it what you will. Paff! It's always like that here. The Corsicans become sailors, teachers, businessmen, so they can leave, because they're young, they feel as if they're suffocating on the island. They think they'll be able to breathe better elsewhere, somewhere that smells different, but in the end all that remains are the scents of childhood. You see, my darling? His Austro-Hungarian princess had sentenced him to live not in a palace, but in a detached house in the Normandy suburbs. With a garden twenty meters by twenty, when eighty hectares awaited him here. The view of cornfields rather than the Mediterranean, not to mention the lack of sun, his childhood friends, or his job as a turf salesman. So, yes, he missed Corsica, but he was trapped and inevitably, unconsciously, he blamed Palma."

She checked the heat of the stove, stirred the chopped tomatoes, and then gently took Clotilde's hand again.

"I don't know anything more than that, my darling. Was

it your father who beckoned to Salomé? Or did she come to him? I can't tell you which summer it was when they started talking to each other again, which summer when they kissed, which summer they fell in love once more, whether it was all on the same day or took years." She glanced briefly at Speranza. "I can't even tell you if your father was sincere, whether or not he still loved your mother, whether he really loved Salomé again, I don't know anything about that, no one knew, not me or Speranza, when Salomé jumped from the Revellata lighthouse at Christmas in 1988. Dr Pinheiro took us aside and told us that Salomé would survive, that there was nothing wrong with her, that the broom bushes had broken her fall . . . but now she had to have additional tests, not for her but for the baby. It was the baby he was worried about."

Speranza wiped the corners of her eyes with her apron, then threw away the onion and tomato peelings.

"Salomé was pregnant. It was too late for her to have an abortion, she was too far gone. The baby was born on May 5, 1989. He came into the world without a cry, with one arm, one leg and half of his face already paralysed. So Salomé adopted another strategy, that of the young mother who has nothing left to lose, let alone her honour, but who will risk everything to save that of her son. That summer, for the first time, Salomé stopped hiding. She started showing herself at the beach, she set down her towel a meter from your mother's, she undid her top on the pretext of breastfeeding her son; she strolled around the market in Port de Stareso in a flimsy dress, she even rolled her pram over Palma's feet. Of course your mother knew it was Salomé. Of course she knew who the baby's father was. Yes, that summer, even though you couldn't have known at the age of fifteen, Salomé took your mother to the brink. And it worked—probably beyond all her dreams."

11:36 A.M.

Lisabetta added the *figatelli* to the frying pan, scattered it with thyme and dropped in half a bay leaf.

"Your mother took a lover . . . "

Clotilde was about to protest, no, Mamy, that's not what happened, nothing happened between Natale Angeli and my mother, but her grandmother knocked the stewpot against the gas with a sound like a gong, and Clotilde imagined it was to make her stay quiet.

"Salomé confronted your father, reminded him of his responsibilities. She carried little Orsu around in a scarf, wrapped against her breasts. Now it was child versus child, woman versus woman, Corsica versus Continent. Your mother's name was Idrissi, seven letters at the bottom of a register in the town hall, but everything else, everything that the name Idrissi represented, belonged to Salomé."

A thought darted into Clotilde's mind. That her father, in that summer of '89, might have thought about abandoning them, letting them go back home with Maman while he stayed there, in Arcanu, to bring up another child, to establish another family.

Lisabetta uncorked a bottle of wine, Clos Columbu, 2007.

"Everything came crashing down on August 23, 1968—the day when Palma put up her tent on La Revellata. That day would be played out over and over again."

She tasted the wine and pulled a face before going on.

"Your mother still had the advantage, I can assure you. Your father was a dutiful man. He would never have abandoned you. He would never have let your mother take the ferry back alone, without him. Palma was going to win, as she did every year. On that particular day, August 23, 1989, he had decorated the table with yellow roses, while every other year they were red, for passion. In the language of roses, yellow means a plea for forgiveness, for a mistake, an infidelity. On St Rose's day she and your father would go and have the gourmet menu at Casa di Stella, they would spend the evening there, they would spend the night, make up for a year, until the following summer. Salomé had no choice, she had to bet everything she had on that evening. I suppose you remember that last evening, my darling, there were about fifteen of us around the table, friends, cousins, having a drink before going to the concert at the church of Santa Lucia in Prezzuna. But you can't have known what happened next, you had left the table and gone to sleep on a bench with your music in your ears."

Clotilde remembered those last moments. Her notebook, the crazy rhythm of Mano Negra, the shouting in the yard that she had ignored.

"When Salomé came into the yard, holding the baby in her arms, we were all thunderstruck."

There was a silence. Lisabetta seemed reluctant to continue. Slowly, Speranza got to her feet and walked towards the next room. When she came back, she merely swept aside the scraps of meat with her sleeve and set down a frame on the table. Without a word. It was a portrait. A very beautiful woman. Slightly luminous skin. Black almond-shaped eyes, a straight, slightly prominent nose, like the crest of a ridge cascading down towards her parted lips.

Definitely Salomé. Clotilde was disturbed by this stranger whose face and form seemed surprisingly familiar. Lisabetta raised her knife and pointed it at the photograph.

"Yes, your mother and Salomé looked similar. That's probably why your father first noticed her. Same eyes, same waist, same smile, same grace, but with added mystery."

Clotilde stared at the portrait. Images rose to the surface, images that she had almost erased, of the first time she had seen Salomé, the day before the accident, at the Revellata lighthouse. From behind, never quite face-on.

11:42 A.M.

Lisabetta firmly mixed the cubes of *panzetta*, the chopped

figatelli, the onions, the thyme and the tomatoes, holding the wooden spoon in one hand and adding more oil with the other. For a moment she seemed to concentrate on her cooking, before turning down the gas under the frying pan and looking back at Clotilde.

"Yes, my darling. We were all thunderstruck. Your mother must have interpreted our silence as support for Salomé, but I think that most of all it was just surprise. Salomé had decided to go for broke, to make your mother understand that Arcanu wasn't her place, that it never had been. However beautiful she might have been, Palma could be rejected and replaced by another. So far, in order to win your father back, Salomé had fought dress against dress, bikini against bikini, skin against skin, to prove that she could be just as pretty. But that evening she had taken it a step further. When she walked into the yard that night, Salomé was wearing her hair exactly the way your mother wore it, in a chignon fastened at the back by a black ribbon, the same make-up, the same dark line on her lips, the same bracelet, the same ruby necklace, the same perfume, Imiza, with its immortal scent. Your mother must have spent over an hour in front of the mirror to be the fairest of them all that evening at Casa di Stella, wanting to please your father . . . and Salomé had done exactly the same. Tendril for tendril. Brushstroke for brushstroke. Salomé had even taken her insolence a stage further. You must remember, Clotilde, that evening your mother was wearing a Benoa dress, the one that your father had bought for her in Calvi. Salomé was wearing the same dress! She had spent almost 300 francs on it, I found out later, on an outfit identical to her rival's, to show Paul that in the same short, low-cut dress she could be just as seductive. Arousing, even. As soon as she arrived she handed the baby to his Speranza, his grandmother, without saying a word. The conversations all came to a sudden halt, and it takes a lot to shut up fifteen Corsicans who have already drained five bottles of Clos Columbu. Only Cassanu dared to say anything. 'Sit down, Salomé. Sit down.' He got to his feet and drew up a chair, right between himself and me."

Clotilde looked out of the kitchen window at the empty courtyard of the farm, the pergola, the big holm oak. She couldn't believe it had all happened here, on August 23, 1989, over the course of a few minutes, while she was asleep, because she'd spent the whole of the previous night spying on her brother, because she liked to isolate herself, because she hated endless family reunions. Behind her, Speranza got up to throw the debris into the bin and then came and sat down again, apron around her neck and knife in her hand, silently listening to the rest of Lisabetta's story.

"It was so provocative, my darling. Such a humiliation for Palma. None of it was premeditated on our part, but we did nothing to stop her. I even joined in, to tell you the truth, and poured Salomé a glass of wine. How could your mother respond to this girl who was taking her place as if she had never existed? This girl who was attacking her without saying a single word? What could your mother say, my darling? Nothing, like the rest of us? You remember her, Clotilde, saying nothing wasn't really her style. Your mother got up, I remember it as if it were yesterday, I remember each word, each breath, each sound. We've weighed up every one since then, believe me. Not a day has gone by when I haven't thought about it again, when I haven't wondered if it wasn't the greatest folly of our lives."

Clotilde was shivering with cold. Even though she was sitting down, her head was spinning. She rested her frozen fingers on the immaculate tiles of the nearest wall.

"Your mother pushed back her chair," Lisabetta went on, "turned towards your father and simply said, 'Tell her to leave.'" Your father didn't say anything, so your mother repeated, in a louder voice, 'Tell her to leave.'

"All the cousins, the whole family, all the friends were look-ing at him. All hostile to your mother. All against him if he took her side. 'Don't ask me to do that, Palma. I'm here, in my home. With my family. You tell her to leave.'

"I still remember the silence, my poor Clotilde. Even the birds, even the wind in the branches of the oak tree had fallen silent. Your father took such a long time to answer, as if his whole life depended on it. Which it did, of course. Finally he said, 'Please, Palma. This isn't easy for anyone. We've all got to make an effort.' When I think of your mother's face, I can still see her fury. We all saw it, that look. Of anger. Of hatred. And that clinched it. Only your father didn't notice, I think. Losing his wife didn't matter in that moment, he wasn't afraid of los-ing Palma. At that moment the only thing he was afraid of was losing his honour in front of his family. Then he added, 'We all have to make an effort. Me. You. Tonight I'm leaving my fam-ily behind in order to spend the evening with you.' And she said, 'An effort? Today?'

"Then Palma pushed over the chair in front of her, the nearest vase of yellow roses and a bottle of Clos Columbu. Maybe you heard some of the noise at that moment, some shouting? Maybe you woke up?"

Clotilde saw herself shrugging, turning up the volume of her Walkman, sinking back into her dreams.

Lisabetta turned off the gas under the frying pan, checked to see how the lentils were doing and started laying the table. 11:57 A.M. Perfect.

"Not many words were exchanged after that. Four sen-tences, no more, all shrieked by Palma. Four sentences that sounded normal at the time, four sentences that we expected, perhaps that we'd even hoped for. It was after-wards, after the accident, when we recalled them again, like an endless tape . . . it was afterwards that they assumed such weight."

"What did my mother say, Mamy?"

"She said four things, and with each phrase she took one step further into the darkness that was falling over the mountain."

"*Go to your concert, go with her!*'

"A step.

"*I'll make way for her, because that's what you want, what you all want.*'

"A step, and this time she turned round.

"*But I warn you, don't take the children with you.*'

"One last step, before leaving the yard.

"*You hear me, off you go with her. But don't take the children in the car. Leave them out of all this.*'

"My poor darling, I have thought so often about those last words. I've often told myself that here, in the yard, faced with us, faced with the clan, you were all your mother could cling to, that if Corsica took back her husband, she would never agree to it taking her children. Her only battle would be to keep you by her side. Even if that girl took her place, stole everything from her, she would never touch her children. That's what I thought, probably because I'm a mother and that's how I would have reacted myself. I think that's why Palma was so insistent that your father and Salomé didn't take you to the polyphonic concert."

Behind her, Speranza banged a pile of plates down violently on the table. Clotilde didn't turn around. Lisabetta went on.

"But neither Cassanu nor Speranza nor anyone else to my knowledge thought as I did. Your mother ran off down the path, straight down the hill to where the car was parked. As soon as she was out of sight, Salomé pushed her chair back, went over to Paul to kiss him and slide her hand down his back, as if nothing had happened during the last fifteen years, only a simple parenthesis that she was closing again. She stayed like that for a long time, and then, at a leisurely pace, she went down towards the Fuego and sat down in the passenger seat. She had won!"

Speranza banged down every glass, every fork, every knife at her disposal.

"You know what happened next, my darling. Your father was probably reluctant to run after your mother, but he probably would have done so if he hadn't had fifteen pairs of eyes fixed on him, including his father's. He had just lost all of his dignity. He had been a mere toy in Palma's and Salomé's hands. And so he tried to regain the little authority he had left, and did what all men do when they are humiliated—they raise their voice to their children, sometimes their hands, although your father never did the latter, as you know. They issue orders, even unfair ones, to prove that they too can command obedience. The whole clan waited, as if watching a play, to see what your father, the heir to Arcanu, would do. His mistress was waiting for him in the car. Your father got to his feet and raised his voice to Nicolas, ordering him to go and find his sister, to get into the back of the Fuego and not to say a word."

Lisabetta stopped for a moment and stared right into her granddaughter's eyes.

"I don't know what your brother had planned to do that evening, perhaps an outing with some friends or his girlfriend. Oh, how disappointed he was. My God, when I picture his face, he looked as if he had been struck by lightning, as if his mother's departure had been nothing in comparison. But he didn't flinch. I didn't know your poor brother well enough to be sure who he got his pride from, that sense of duty—your father or your mother, both, perhaps—but however great his disappointment, his rancour, his sense of injustice, he didn't say a word, he didn't try to negotiate and he went in search of you."

Clotilde heard her brother's last words as she sat motionless on her bench, she saw her father's hand closing around her wrist, dragging her, hurting her, as he had never done before.

Now she understood.

"You emerged, my darling, still in your dream world. No one said anything. How could you have suspected that the woman sitting in the car in your mother's place, that woman whose hair was done like your mother's, who was dressed like your mother, whose make-up emphasised feature for feature the striking resemblance with your mother; that woman who was holding your father's hand; how could you have suspected that that woman wasn't your mother?"

The images passed again before Clotilde's eyes.

The silence in the car, barely troubled by the few words uttered by her father or Nicolas. What she saw of the woman in front of her, a chignon, the back of a neck, an earring, a dress, a thigh. The rest, her mother's face, her smile, she had invented over the years, she had added it all to the woman sitting in the car who could only have been her mother. That woman whose hand her father had taken just before the Fuego crashed onto the rocks.

Nicolas knew. Nicolas had seen, heard and understood the tragedy that was being played out.

But how could she have suspected it for a moment?

12 noon.

Lisabetta got up and walked towards the courtyard.

"The ambulance will be punctual. Giovanni, the driver, is an old friend. He knows that Cassanu doesn't like to be kept waiting."

Clotilde couldn't take her eyes off the portrait of Salomé. Lisabetta's voice softened as she anxiously looked at the clock.

"You have understood, my darling, it isn't your mother's grave that Speranza goes and waters every day in the mausoleum of the Idrissi family. It's her daughter's."

Clotilde saw Speranza carrying her watering can in the graveyard, digging her secateurs into the marble of the mausoleum, scratching out the name of Palma Idrissi; heard once more the old witch's insults.

She shouldn't be here. Her name doesn't belong here, engraved with the rest of the Idrissi family.

Behind her, Speranza spoke for the first time, her voice like an echo.

"I didn't hesitate, Clotilde. I didn't hesitate for one second to bury my daughter under the name of another so that she could rest side by side with your father, in the Idrissi mausoleum. To claim that Salomé had died, that she had committed suicide after the accident, and bury an empty coffin in the Marcone cemetery. Because that was what she would have wanted. She had always dreamed of being a part of your family." Speranza stuck the knife she was holding in the loaf of bread on the table. "She only achieved her dream by losing her life. Leaving me with her child. Because . . . " She was choked with emotion, and her eyes stabbed into Clotilde's with the same ferocity with which she had plunged the knife into the loaf. "Because your mother killed her!"

One minute past midday.

The ambulance slowly entered the courtyard and, for the two women, nothing else seemed to matter all of a sudden. They glanced around to check that everything in the kitchen was in place, hung their aprons on hooks and went outside.

Clotilde was left on her own, Speranza's words still echoing in her ears.

Because your mother killed her . . .

Instinctively, she reached for the phone in her pocket. She had received a text. Franck, at last. Her husband had been trying to contact her.

We heard about the murder of Spinello.
We're on our way back.

We're nearly at the Euproctes, where are you?
See you very soon
Franck

The text had been sent almost three quarters of an hour ago. In the yard, Lisabetta held out her hand and a cane to Cassanu. Speranza had already come back inside, as if to check whether the food was cooked or anticipate a request from the patriarch.

Because your mother killed her.

Clotilde went and stood in front of her, blocking her passage, not caring whether the *figatellu* was burning on the stove.

"You didn't answer my question. You've told me your story, but neither you nor Mamy have given me an answer. Where is my mother? Where is she?"

"She ran away, my little darling," Speranza croaked. "She cut Pacha's throat and she ran away."

57

August 23, 2016

For the campers, passing through the gate in the fence surrounding the Euproctes, simply in order to go to the beach, had become more complicated than a Mexican in Tijuana trying to get into the United States. Two young, smiling but inflexible policemen made each camper open every beach bag, unroll every towel, and present ID; they also noted entry and exit times, and stopped just short of running metal detectors over the tanned and bikini-clad girls. What was the point, the ones in a hurry grumbled. They'd found the murder weapon, they'd banged up the guilty man, what else were they looking for? In the end, the only real question for the tourists, who had spent 1,200 euros a week renting their bungalows, was who was going to clean the toilet blocks that day, since the keeper of the brooms was in prison in Calvi, and who was going to hire his replacement, since the boss was in the morgue in Ajaccio.

At the heart of this shipwreck, behind the reception desk, her face ravaged with tears, Anika Spinello was reassuring everyone, in every language in the world, explaining that yes, all the campers would be questioned, that no, the tents wouldn't be searched, that yes, the campsite was still open, that nothing was going to change, that they could go on enjoying the sand and the sun, no, there would be no activities today, no diving, no pétanque, that no, she hadn't slept, that yes, thank you, Marco, she would like a cigarette, a tissue, a whole box, no, she didn't want to rest, or go to bed, take sleeping pills, yes she did want to stay there, like a captain at the wheel of a ghost ship, because this campsite was Cervone's life, his work, his kingdom, and now that he was dead, she was the quartermaster, no, the Euproctes wouldn't close, that would mean killing Cervone a second time, yes, my little one, that's kind, I'm touched.

Valentine placed on the counter the bunch of wild thyme she had picked, and the condolence card she had written.

"I liked your husband," she said. "Even though not everyone in my family shared that opinion. We came back as soon as we heard."

Anika smiled.

"Was your sailing trip good?"

"Yeah . . . "

The answer wasn't too convincing.

"Isn't your dad around?"

"I don't know."

Anika didn't have the strength to continue, she was lost in her thoughts, far away, years earlier, when she had given up windsurfing and washed up on these shores like a lost mermaid, only to be gathered up by Cervone.

"You wanted to see me, Anika?"

The woman seemed already to have forgotten. She tried to concentrate.

"Oh, yes, sorry. I had a message for you. You're to go up to Arcanu. It's urgent, your mum's waiting for you there."

Three police vans were parked outside the campsite, but just around the corner there was nobody about. The contrast was striking. As if the cicadas, the crickets, and the grasshoppers were ignoring all the excitement and just getting on with their lives. Valentine understood why it was so easy to get lost in the *maquis*: you only had to run a few meters into the scrubland and, hey presto, job done, nobody would ever come looking for you again. Not even a police dog, with all those scented flowers around to cover your trail.

Now she was climbing straight up towards Arcanu along the path. After the turning where the path crossed the road, she saw the parked car. At first she didn't make the connection, even though she was intrigued by the vehicle, it seemed to bring back a vague memory. More of an image. Its shape, its colour. Perhaps it was like the vintage car that belonged to some television detective. She went on walking towards the road, wondering what her mother might want. "Urgent," Anika Spinello had said. Valentine sighed. She'd had it with all these stories, Arcanu, her grandparents, her great-grandparents, her mother, ghosts, the dead . . .

That's it!

Now she remembered. The car. She had seen it in old photographs, Maman sometimes got them out at home. A . . . Valentine got annoyed with herself, the name was on the tip of her tongue. What was that stupid red and black car called? It had a weird name, something slightly Latino . . .

She walked over. An old woman was sitting in the car on her own, in the passenger seat. Valentine had never seen her before, but when her eye came to rest on the figure, a shiver ran down her spine.

She had just encountered a ghost.

She tried to chase the impossible idea from her mind—this old woman looked just like her! For a moment, Valentine thought she was looking at herself in a mirror, a mirror that aged her; recognising herself, but in sixty years' time.

Stupid.

Come on, keep on climbing. There were two hundred meters of slope to go before she could rest her bum under the Arcanu oak tree. Yet she kept looking back at the red car and met the old woman's eyes once more. They seemed to be imploring her, pleading with her, trying to express a message that her lips could not utter. There was no one else around them. Only the buzzing of the evening insects. The silence suddenly disturbed her.

"Shit," Valentine whispered to reassure herself, "what was the name of that car? The one from the accident that Maman's always going on about."

"A Fuego," said the voice behind her.

58

August 23, 2016, midday

Cassanu Idrissi refused the hand that the woman extended to help him down from the ambulance, handed a 20 euro note to Giovanni the driver before he set off again, and rejected with still greater irritation the cane that was proffered.

"It's fine, Lisa, I've still got two legs."

He climbed the step into the farm and observed the laid table, the cutlery, the plates, the glasses. Set for four.

It was only at that moment that he turned and noticed Clotilde.

"We have a guest," Lisabetta said quietly.

Speranza had returned to the stove. Nothing seemed more important than the cooking of the meal. Had she already forgotten everything else? Saint Rose's night, her daughter's death, the last words that the old witch had spat at Clotilde?

She ran away, my little darling. She slit Pacha's throat, and she ran away.

No!

Clotilde couldn't bring herself to accept it. That her mother would have waited twenty-seven years, all alone in the middle of the *maquis*, only to make her escape on the very day when her daughter came looking for her, at the exact time when her daughter was climbing towards the refuge. After sending letters with an explicit invitation.

It didn't add up.

"A guest," Cassanu mused. "When the children were here,

with all the friends and cousins passing through or staying, when family still meant something, I never knew this table to have less than ten people sitting around it."

Lisa was twisting her fingers.

"She . . . she got away . . . "

Cassanu gave her a strange look but didn't say anything.

"She ran away," Speranza repeated. "She killed Pacha and then she ran away. And . . . Orsu . . . "

"Orsu is in jail," the old Corsican cut in, "I'm aware of that. Giovanni told me everything on the way here. The police say he murdered Cervone."

He drained the glass of Clos Columbu, and placed his knife on the table between his plate and his napkin. Just as Cassanu was about to pull out his chair, giving the impression that this information had nothing to do with him, or that his orders had already been given, Clotilde grabbed her grandfather's sleeve and erupted at him.

"Orsu will be fine. I'm defending him. I'm his lawyer. Orsu is innocent!"

Cassanu set down his glass.

"Innocent?" he said with a hint of a smile that disappeard as he wiped the napkin over his lips.

That's right, treat me like a little girl! Well, apologies to your poor heart, Papé, and apologies to your stove, Mamy, but I'm about to put my foot right in it!

"Innocent," Clotilde repeated, raising her voice. "Orsu couldn't hurt an ant. I know, and not just because he's my brother." She paused to assess the effect of the bomb she had just dropped. "I know because he was the only one who loved my mother. He was the only one who helped her all these years."

A petrifying bomb, Clotilde thought to herself. Six hands froze. Bodies mummified. Only the lentils, the thyme and the bay simmered away in the pot, abandoned by the witch who seemed turned to stone.

"I want the truth, Papé, I beg you. Tell me what happened."

Cassanu Idrissi hesitated for a long time. He looked over at Speranza, Lisabetta, the pot, the wine bottle, the bread, the four plates, the knife, then finally pushed his chair back.

"Come on, then. Follow me."

This time Cassanu was careful to bring his walking stick with him. They left the yard and headed towards a path lined with black elders that rose up behind the farm. Passing in front of the kitchen window, they heard the carillon of plates being washed. He turned towards his granddaughter.

"Four plates . . . that's only the beginning of the end. Those two mad old women will have to get used to eating on their own, I won't be around for much longer. That's how it is, it's the fate of women, to look after men who leave, to accompany them, wait for them, visit them. Choose a house near a school when they are young, near a cemetery when they are old."

Clotilde merely smiled. For a moment she thought of taking her grandfather's hand, but Cassanu pointed at the path ahead of them.

"Don't worry, we're not going to climb Capu di a Veta, even if Dr Pinheiro is a dunce. My legs will go on walking even after my heart has stopped. I'll explain everything, Clotilde, and show you Corsica as we go, its history will help you understand ours. Come now, and tell me what those two old crazies have told you."

They proceeded along the narrow path. Clotilde told him what she had just learned, about her father's mistress and the secret child, what had happened on the evening of August 23, Salomé taking her mother's place, the accident, Lisabetta's fears over the last words Palma had uttered.

Cassanu nodded.

"Lisabetta never agreed with me. She had, let's say, different ideas. But she never said anything. Lisa is a loyal wife. She respected our choice."

"The men's choice?"

"If you like, Clotilde. But Speranza was on our side too."

"What happened, Papé? What happened after the accident?"

The old Corsican's cane struck the ground as if testing its solidity.

"Everything happened very quickly that evening. We heard about the accident shortly after 9 P.M., it was Cesareu Garcia who called me, he was at the scene of the accident and described what he saw. The car in the Petra Coda ravine. The absence of any survivors apart from you. Otherwise, no one knew anything. Was it an accident? Murder? Revenge? I had a few enemies in those days." An enigmatic smile flitted across his face. "At the time I imagined all kinds of possibilities, but my first decision was to find your mother. She had fled Arcanu farm, but the last words she had cried out under the tree still echoed in my head: 'off you go with her, but don't take the children in the car'.

It was like a threat, as if she knew what was going to happen."

Clotilde said nothing. She turned round and looked towards La Revellata several hundred meters below them. From that distance, the wooded peninsula, edged with tiny beaches, a few scattered villas and small white paths could have been paradise. What an illusion. A peninsula is also a cul-de-sac.

Cassanu followed her gaze.

"It wasn't hard to guess where your mother would go. I sent two men, Miguel and Simeone, who caught her near the Revellata lighthouse, just above Natale Angeli's home, just before she could reach her lover."

The ghost, Clotilde thought, the ghost that Natale had seen

that evening. The spectre that had haunted him all his life. The truth seemed so simple now. So obvious. Natale hadn't been dreaming. It was Palma who had smiled at him on the hill by Punta Rossa, before Cassanu's men caught up with her. It was Palma who had come to see him, probably to give herself to him that evening, or merely to weep in his arms. Who could know? No one, not even him.

They continued along a track that smelled of lavender. On their right, they passed a rock filled with bullet holes. Cassanu had chosen his route carefully; Clotilde remembered that this was called the Federate Rock, because Corsican resistance fighters had been executed there in September 1943, a few weeks before the liberation of the island. Cassanu merely ran his fingers along the bullet holes as he continued his story.

"Your mother went to join her lover. You understand, Clotilde, this shed a whole other light on the events leading up to the accident. In front of us all, in the Arcanu yard, in front of Salomé, your mother had played the victim, she had recited the soliloquy of the humiliated wife. For the entire holiday, she had been obsessed with Saint Rose's day and her famous anniversary meal with your father at Casa di Stella, but it was nothing but theatre. Your mother desired only one thing: Natale Angeli! At the time, my darling, I almost listened to you. You had me convinced, up there, and I could easily have agreed to let him have a scrap of land for his dolphins. My poor dear, you too were nothing but a pawn. Those two were accomplices, even if I never had any proof regarding Angeli. Was he in on his mistress's plan? Was he involved in my son's murder? Could he have prevented it? If he was involved then yes, of course, I could have had him executed. I started threatening him, trying to extract a confession from him, to know for sure. Perhaps I frightened him too much. The coward went and married Aurélia, Cesareu's daughter. Sergeant Garcia turned a blind eye to many things in this corner of the island, but he would never have ignored the murder of his son-in-law. Over time, I'm not going to tell you that I forgave Natale Angeli, oh no, but I did reach the conclusion that he had been manipulated as well. That the drunkard, behind that handsome face of his, didn't have the balls to be a murderer. Or even an accomplice."

Clotilde took her grandfather's arm.

"An accomplice in what?"

Cassanu didn't reply but continued walking. With every meter they climbed, the path opened up to the east, on the boundary between the *maquis* and the villas of Calvi, flanked by their pools and their balconies overlooking the Mediterranean.

"Forensic tests were done on the Fuego the very next day, and the official verdict was delivered: an accident. Case closed. Bodies delivered to the family. They could bury them and forget, and the authorities could breathe again. It it had been a murder, a settling of scores, there would have been a battle of the clans in the Balagne, no question, the Idrissis against the Pinellis, the Casasopranas, the Poggiolis. The official line— that the car had accidentally left the road, because of tiredness, speed, alcohol, fate—suited everyone. But Aldo Navarri, Calvi's expert mechanic, is an old friend of mine. My father and his father liberated Corsica together. Even before talking to the police, he told me his conclusions: my son's car had been sabotaged, the bolt on the steering mechanism had been unscrewed. For Aldo it wasn't a theory, it was a certainty. The tie rod was intact, it hadn't been twisted, proof that it had failed before the car came off the road, all of a sudden, and not after the impact. I asked him to keep his views quiet, to tell the police what everyone wanted to hear, that nothing untoward had taken place. Aldo had no qualms about giving the police a false report, he was called on as an expert witness less than three times a year, and he agreed with me that some family stories were none of their business."

Cassanu looked out across the villages that clung to the Balagne. Montemaggiore. Moncale. Calenzan.

"It took Cesareu Garcia a few months to reach the same conclusion I had. He asked one of his friends to carry out alternative forensic tests . . . Too late, far too late."

Clotilde stared at him, horrified, hoping that she hadn't guessed what her grandfather was about to tell her.

"You employed your own police? You carried out your own form of justice?"

"My own form of justice? What other kind of justice would you expect? The one conjured up by bureaucrats from the mainland? Juries chosen by a lottery who aren't even involved, and who are constantly being reminded of the presumption of innocence? In the face of the evidence? Acquittal because of a lack of proof? You're a lawyer, my darling, you know what we're talking about. I've taken part in that Punch and Judy show enough times to know. No, Clotilde, I've never had any faith in that form of justice. I've never trusted that version of the law, not that one, nor the laws of urban planning, nor the laws of commerce, least of all the penal law."

Clotilde staggered slightly. The almost perfect curve of the Bay of Calvi was laid out in front of her.

"So you delivered justice yourself?"

"Your mother had the right to a trial. As equitable as if it had been organized by the French justice system."

"Did my mother have a lawyer to defend her then?" Clotilde said sarcastically.

Cassanu looked her up and down. There wasn't the merest hint of cynicism in his voice.

"I'm sorry, Clotilde, but I've never understood the point of lawyers. I don't mean you, don't worry. You deal with divorces, child custody and maintenance payments. That's fine, it's all part of the times we live in, no one is good or bad, people just need a referee to sort such matters out. But this is a crime I'm talking about. What's the point of a lawyer in such a case? There's an inquiry, evidence, a file, you assess where the truth lies; and on the basis of the facts you punish, or you don't. What's the point of a lawyer except to push the evidence towards the wrong side? Why would a guilty party need a lawyer?"

"And the innocent?"

This time Cassanu laughed heartily.

"The innocent? I know justice in this country, my darling. An innocent man is just a guilty man with a good lawyer."

Clotilde clenched her fists as her thoughts boiled in her skull. You are lucky, Papé, you're lucky that I want to know how far you took your madness, because I have some things to say about your concept of justice, and I would also like to talk about your grandson, who is rotting away in prison at this very moment. You'll be willing to pay the best lawyer on the island to get him out of there, if you don't have any confidence in me.

"Go on, Papé, tell me about this equitable process."

Cassanu stared at the tree in front of them and stopped. Clotilde remembered the old legend. It was here that the condottiere Sampiero Corso was said to have hanged the members of his family by marriage, who had betrayed him and sold him to the Genoese; he had shown the greatest mercy to his wife Vanina, and had merely strangled her with his own hands.

"I assembled some friends, local people, to be the Arcanu jury. Reliable people, with a sense of honour, of family. People to whom the clan was important. About ten in all."

"Was Basile Spinello one of them?"

"Yes."

"Who else? Cousins? People who had witnessed Salomé's entrance on St Rose's evening?"

"I know what you're thinking, Clotilde. You're sure that your mother was already condemned from the start. But you're wrong. I wanted a proper trial. I wanted the jury to be presented with the evidence, I wanted them to rule on the case in full knowledge of everything that was involved. To deliver their sentence on the basis of the facts and the facts alone. It was the trial for the murder of my son and my grandson. I wasn't just looking for someone to blame, Clotilde. I was looking for a murderer."

"And you found Palma? My mother? Lying under our car and unscrewing a tight bolt? You found ten jurors who'd believe that?"

"Your mother was an architect, Clotilde, that's a man's job, she knew her way around a car, and in any case I'd followed up other lines of enquiry. The Casasopranas, the Pinellis and the other clans assured me that that they had nothing to do with it, on their honour, and I believed them. In Corsica, you don't sort out family quarrels by sabotaging a car and killing the children; you kill your enemy directly, point blank. Think about it, only one thing in that file is certain: someone sabotaged the steering of your father's car. Someone who knew that the Fuego wouldn't survive a sharp bend in the road. Then, since it was a premeditated crime, everything comes down to two questions: who had a motive to kill your father; and who could know that he would get into that car? The answer, my darling, was obvious, even if you don't like it. Only one person. Your mother. It was your mother who had refused to get into the Fuego that night. Your mother who had encouraged her rival to sit there, beside the man who no longer loved her, the man who was going to leave her, the man who was going to take away her children, because he would never have stayed in Corsica, with Salomé and Orsu, without you and Nicolas. The man who, if he asked for a divorce, would make her give up everything, including the Idrissi fortune which he would one day inherit. While if he died in an accident, and they were still married . . . "

Cassanu looked up at the high branches of the tree where Sampiero Corso had hanged all those people.

"That night, your mother ordered your father not to take you with him in the car. Not you, or Nicolas. She insisted, twice, and then she left."

They carried on walking, allowing a few seconds of silence as they climbed over some rocks. Another thirty meters in direct sunlight, then they plunged into the shade of the *maquis* again. Cassanu rested for a moment, cautiously placing his hand on the flat, hot stones. What if he was right? Clotilde thought. Cassanu had expressed his arguments so sincerely. And what if the only point of lawyers really was the dishonest destruction of evidence? Making the obvious look circumstantial? Undermining convictions with emotion?

"I never had any doubt," Cassanu went on as if reading her thoughts. "Your mother was the only one who decided who would get into the car that evening and who wouldn't. Your mother had a motive, several motives, in fact—love, money, her children. Your mother went to see her lover that evening. Your mother accused herself by trying to protect you, but she had no other choice."

He turned around and, for the first time, he took his granddaughter's hand. Cassanu's hand was light and wrinkled, as if emptied of flesh and blood. A piece of cork bark.

"I assure you, Clotilde, I did look. I looked for other possible culprits, other explanations, but none of them was credible."

At last, Clotilde spoke her mind.

"My mother's guilt isn't credible either."

Cassanu sighed. They were walking past a cleared field where some goats were browsing untethered.

"And there you have it, Clotilde. That's exactly why I didn't want a lawyer. That was why I wanted real justice. The justice system of this country would have shared your reasoning. No tangible proof, so no culprit, no sentence. The justice of this country would have left the case there, unsolved and unpunished. The murderer of my son and my grandson would have carried on with her life peacefully and with impunity. How could I have accepted that? The Arcanu jury had to condemn the person against whom there was the most evidence. And the Arcanu jury had no hesitation. They voted unanimously, no one ever had any doubt."

My God . . . Clotilde felt her whole body shivering. Cubes of ice seemed to flood through her veins, while the sun at its zenith, through the thin branches of broom and arbutus, scorched her skin. They came to a meadow and Cassanu sat down on a granite cairn. Clotilde remembered coming here often as a child, to the plain of Paoli; it was said that the independence fighters had buried a trove of gold coins here, coins struck at Corte just before the Revolution, when Corsica was no longer Italian and not yet French. A treasure trove that would come in useful when the island became truly independent.

No one had ever found a chest or a single coin.

A legend, a rumour, but no proof . . .

"The Arcanu jury," Papé went on, "recognised your mother's guilt. In other times, those described by Mérimée, the days of Colomba or Mateo Falcone, Palma would have been executed." His hand, like a dried-out sponge, tensed in Clotilde's. "Twenty-seven years ago I would have sentenced her to death without hesitation, but others were opposed to that. Lisabetta first of all, Basile too. In spite of everything Palma remained a member of our family, an Idrissi, the mother of our grandchildren. Also, Lisabetta argued, your mother hadn't actually confessed. What if we were to learn a different truth one day? Basile put forward another argument to save her; he claimed that we couldn't be less civilized than the justice system of the French, who no longer had the death penalty even for the worst crimes. And so the sentence was decided: life imprisonment. There was no shortage of places above Arcanu, in the *maquis*, to lock someone up for a lifetime. Besides, your mother didn't protest. Even though she never confessed, she never defended herself either. She never tried to get away."

Until today, Clotilde thought. At the time of that mockery of a trial, her mother had just lost her husband, and her son, in a car in which she should have been a passenger. Alone, traumatized, accused, cornered, racked with guilt, how could she have found the strength to defend herself?

She had lost everything that evening.

Everything but her daughter.

Clotilde was going to speak, but Cassanu rested his hand on her shoulder.

"I am not a monster, Clotilde. Your mother lost only her freedom. That was all she could pay, the same price as any thief, any rapist or murderer. But otherwise, she hasn't been badly treated. On the contrary, she has been treated better than any of the prisoners crammed into the jail at Borgo. I can assure you that the meals made for her by Lisabetta were better. That her guard, Orsu, was more respectful than the screws you get in jail. That his dog, Pacha, was more affectionate than Alsatians that are trained to kill. We aren't monsters, Clotilde, we only wanted some justice."

Clotilde took a step back.

"And now? Now that she's fled? What will you have achieved? She'll run to the police and report you."

Cassanu smiled, shaking his head.

"If she had done that, the police would already be there. No, my darling, your mother hasn't run to the station to tell them her outlandish story. Locked up for years in a shepherd's cabin? She hasn't gone to report us, and yet that's what any hostage would have done, don't you agree? Yet more evidence,

Clotilde, yet more evidence of her guilt." His eyes darted around. "We'll look for her, and we'll find her. You'll be able to talk to her. A Corsican can disappear into the *maquis* for an age, but not a foreigner, not a foreigner who hasn't set foot outdoors for twenty-seven years."

For a moment, as their eyes met, Clotilde imagined that they were thinking the same thing. Perhaps Palma had simply set off again, as she had on August 23, 1989, to the place she had never reached, in the same direction, towards the same house, to find the man who lived there.

Natale Angeli.

After all, he still lived in Punta Rossa.

"Come on," Cassanu said, "let's get back to Arcanu."

They walked back in silence, past the hanging tree, the Federate Rock, respecting a moment of silence that Cassanu probably calculated would give her time to admit the inadmissible, to believe the unimaginable. Images paraded through Clotilde's head. Her mother imprisoned, the friendship that grew little by little between her and Orsu, the silent boy assigned the task of delivering her food. The puppy that was born, and which she had named. Scraps of conversations that she must have caught, a few words exchanged with Lisabetta, perhaps, and after all those years of life in her dark room, lit only by Betelgeuse on certain evenings, she suddenly learned that her daughter was coming back to Corsica; she used Orsu as her messenger, she entrusted him with some scribbled words, enough to give her daughter proof that she was alive, then told him to lay a breakfast table identical to the one from twenty-seven years ago, then to lead her, at midnight, to her prison. To see her, just to see her, not to put her in any danger.

What danger?

What secret was her mother hiding?

Her mother would never have slit Pacha's throat. She

would never have run away just as she was about to be found. She would never have touched the steering of that car. She could never have put the lives of her children in danger, or killed them, even by accident. Only one piece of information counted among all the others, each crazier than the last, that had been thrown at her today.

Her mother was alive!

Campa sempre.

Now it was Clotilde's turn to gamble. It was her job.

To prove her mother's innocence.

Cassanu slowed down, perhaps because the path was sloping gently towards Arcanu, or because he had eased his conscience and was now contemplating the *figatellu* that awaited him.

Not so fast, Papé, Clotilde thought. Not so fast. There's a risk your granddaughter might take your appetite away.

She rested a hand on her grandfather's, the one holding the walking stick.

"Papé . . . What if there was another trail? Another possible culprit?"

Cassanu didn't stop, in fact he now speeded up slightly.

"I was right," he said simply. "It was better to sort the whole business out without a lawyer."

Clotilde tried to add a touch of irony to her voice.

"And whose fault is it? You're the reason I chose this vocation! You remember, twenty-seven years ago, at the top of Capu di a Veta. Perhaps it was all predestined, perhaps you gave me the idea of becoming a lawyer just so that, years later, I could prove to you that you've committed the biggest error of judgement in your life."

That didn't even make Papé smile.

"We've followed up on every other lead and suspect, Clotilde, believe me."

"Even Cervone Spinello?"

This time, the rhythm of Cassanu's footsteps fell out of synch.

"Cervone Spinello? What has he got to do with anything? He was fourteen at the time."

"Seventeen."

"Seventeen, if you like. But he was only a kid! How could he possibly have sabotaged the Fuego? Is that the way continental lawyers work? Choosing someone who's been dead for a few hours and blaming him?"

Clotilde didn't react. They went on walking until they could see the top of the Arcanu oak tree. With her grandfather, as with all men, you had to do some bluffing.

"Cervone knew about my mother, didn't he, Papé? About her trial, and her life sentence? Did Cervone blackmail you?"

Cassanu raised his eyes to the sky.

"It has nothing to do with the sabotage of the car, but yes, years later, Cervone heard Basile, his father, talking about it with another juror. That weasel Cervone was always listening in on everything. After his father's death, in 2003, when he inherited the campsite, he didn't blackmail me, as you call it, we don't use words like that here—those are words that would leave you bullet-ridden on the terrace of a café. He just let me know that he was aware of what had happened. We didn't even need to discuss it, we both knew the terms of the pact. If he spoke, to the police, a journalist, anyone, I risked going to jail, and my whole family with me, and that would have meant abandoning Arcanu. Cervone simply asked me if he could build on a few hectares, renovate the Euproctes by enlarging the restaurant, providing additional shower blocks, Finnish chalets, and bungalows, and put a bar on Oscelluccia beach, some land that still belonged to me but which he wanted to exploit. As to the land for the Roc e Mare marina, he bought it but he asked for my protection, as you might say. When it came to protecting the family's honour at the cost of some concreted hectares, he knew which choice I would opt for."

"If that isn't blackmail, then what would you call it?"

"A negotiation. Cervone knew he wasn't risking anything with me. He was my best friend's son."

"So it wasn't you who had him murdered?"

Cassanu's eyes bulged from their sockets. They had reached the Arcanu courtyard, and the oak tree cast its shadow over them.

"No. Why would I have ordered his murder? Cervone Spinello was ambitious, he was unscrupulous, with a keener sense of business than of the land, but he loved Corsica in his own way. A different way, the way of a different generation. Perhaps he was even right about all the concrete."

Clotilde didn't pursue it. Her Papé was basically like everyone else. A man who had somehow abandoned his dreams, because the world was turning too quickly, a huge machine that swept away any chance of utopia. She hesitated, and for the time being she decided against telling him her version of events: Cervone Spinello unscrewing the bolt from the steering of the Fuego because he was sure that, that evening, Paul and Palma Idrissi wouldn't be taking it, that they would climb along the path as planned and sleep at Casa di Stella. Because the one who was supposed to be driving the car that evening, even though none of the adults was aware of it, was Nicolas. Nicolas, with Maria-Chjara. They were the ones the murderer wanted to get rid of. Out of envy, jealousy, out of spite. Cassanu couldn't have come up with that hypothesis—nor could anyone over the age of eighteen. The secrets of a group of teenagers are more difficult to penetrate than those of a Corsican village under the rule of *omertà*.

They crossed the courtyard of the farm, passing by the beds of orchids planted by Lisabetta. Contrary to Clotilde's expectations, Cassanu didn't hurry towards the kitchen. He sat down on the bench, the one on which she had fallen asleep before the accident twenty-seven years ago.

No, she reflected, no one could have guessed what was going on amongst that group of teenagers that summer. No one.

Unless . . .

Clotilde watched Cassanu catching his breath on the bench. He looked like a cat. A big, dozing cat that you think is tired, listless, incapable of making the slightest effort, but which leaps at the slightest hint of danger. Swift, accurate, ruthless.

Lisabetta had emerged from the house and was approaching them anxiously. Speranza stayed in the doorway, ever vigilant.

"Are you all right, Cassanu?"

The old Corsican didn't reply. He gently closed his eyes, allowing the sun to soothe him, but yes, he nodded, he was fine. A walking stick, a hat, his farm, his oak, his tribe.

Unless . . .

Clotilde's thoughts were in a spin.

She was sitting there, where Cassanu now sat, a few minutes before the accident. She had gone to sleep, listening to Mano Negra, and had scribbled down a few last words before her father forced her to get into the Fuego.

Unless . . .

No adult could have guessed at the dramas being played out among the teenagers in the summer of '89.

Unless one of them had read her diary.

Mamy Lisabetta came over and rested a hand on her shoulder, reassured that her husband's health seemed to be fine. She leaned towards her granddaughter's ear, as if she had a secret to tell her. As if she had read her thoughts.

"On the evening of the accident, my darling, you left your notebook behind, on that bench. Well . . . "

Before she could continue, Clotilde's phone rang in her pocket.

Franck!

At last.

Clotilde walked a meter away.

"Franck. Are you back?"

Her husband's voice was halting, and out of breath. It sounded as if he had been running, or the wind was blowing around him. They hadn't spoken for two days, but he didn't even say hello.

"Is Valentine with you?"

"No, why?"

"I'm at the campsite, at reception, with Anika. You left a message, you asked Valentine to go up to Arcanu, you said it was urgent."

The ground fell away beneath her feet. She clung on to the bench to keep her balance.

"That wasn't me, Franck! I never left any message."

"Maybe your grandfather did, then? Someone else at Arcanu?"

"I don't know, it's strange. Wait, I'll ask."

Clotilde went and stood in front of Lisabetta, but even before she could question her, her grandmother managed to finish her sentence.

"The evening of the accident, your notebook. I was the one who picked it up."

59

August 23, 2016, 7:48 P.M.

The Fuego drove carefully along the narrow, stony track. Almost every meter, a low-hanging branch scraped against its paintwork, leaving long iron scratch marks scented with resin. The Castani brothers wouldn't have appreciated the way he was treating the collector's piece he'd just bought.

More likely, they wouldn't have cared.

Nor did he.

In a few hours' time, what would be left of the paintwork . . .

In one hour and fourteen minutes, to be precise.

The same car.

Same time, to the minute.

Same place.

Same passengers.

Same corpses, when the police found them. Disfigured.

Since he had to put an end to it, he might as well go out with a bang. He might as well finish as he had started, taking his revenge on fate, defying it, closing the trunk with a double lock and dropping it to the very bottom of the Mediterranean.

He reassured himself, checking in the rear-view mirror, that the car couldn't be seen, either from the D81 or from the hiking path a few meters further up; the track was used only by bulldozers from the quarry and it was closed today. No tourist would venture all the way out here. Still less a local. He had time to check out the area. He'd had twenty-seven years to do that.

8:30 P.M.

He was going to wait here until zero hour; peacefully, calmly, serenely. And if the girls got bored, he had brought along some reading.

For Valentine in particular.

He chose the shade of a large Corsican pine, switched off the engine, put on the handbrake and then turned to his right.

"Second-to-last stage, Madame Idrissi. I hope you're going to like it. I've organised everything, really, so you won't be disappointed."

Of course, Palma Idrissi didn't reply. He leaned towards the passenger sitting on the seat next to him.

"Excuse me, Palma."

He undid his seatbelt, opened the glove compartment, took out a plastic bag and turned round. Valentine was in the back seat, hands bound, body covered with blood, mouth gagged with a flesh-coloured foam bandage, and eyes rolling furiously as she struggled to contain her panic.

"I didn't have time to gift-wrap it, but you can open it, Valentine."

Clumsily, with her bound hands, the girl pulled from the plastic bag a washed-out notebook with warped and yellowed pages.

"Youth before beauty? Don't you agree, Palma? Besides, you're already familiar with the contents of this diary, aren't you?"

Palma Idrissi didn't answer.

"You can move your wrists, Valentine. Your eyes too. I'm sure you're going to love this book. We all dream of that, don't we? Being able to see inside our mother's mind."

Your mother when she was your age, he added to himself.

Valentine hesitated, her fingers gripped the notebook, but it was clear that as soon as she lowered her eyes, as soon as she recognised her mother's handwriting on the cover, she wouldn't be able to resist the urge to open it. From the first lines she read, she would know that the notebook was Clotilde's, even though it had been written years before she was born.

After all, she too had the right to know.

To know who her mother was. To know who her grand-mother was.

Before plunging.

Before plummeting.

Like everything else—like this car, like this notebook.

Like its three passengers.

60

F ranck? Franck? Are you still there?"
Clotilde raised her voice. Everything sounded far away,
as if her husband were still out on the waves on a sailing
boat, answering his phone as he emerged from a diving session;
unless it was here, in Arcanu, in the middle of the *maquis*, that
the network coverage was patchy.

"Franck! No one sent a message to Valou. Not me, Papé, or
Mamy. None of us asked her to come up to Arcanu."

"Good God!"

"What does this mean, Franck? Is Valou not with you
then?"

"I went to have a shower, it was barely fifteen minutes.
Valentine was upset about the murder of the campsite manager. She wanted to talk to Anika, tell her that she liked
Spinello, present her condolences, and so on . . . She was quite
unsettled. By the time I came back she had disappeared. Anika
told me about the message so I called you."

The bench, the oak, the yard and the whole farm seemed to
spin. The island drifted from its moorings. The whole mountain slid into the Mediterranean.

"How long ago was this? Could she be on her way up?
Somewhere on the path? Dawdling?"

Her husband's voice grew quieter. With the constant buf-
feting of the wind, she could hardly hear him. She had to press
the phone to her ear.

"She isn't on the path, Clotilde."

"How do you know?"

"I know where she is."

Did I hear that right? Is he pulling my leg?

Clotilde screamed. Perhaps a message bouncing off the mountains would reach her husband quicker than a voice from phone to phone.

"What? What the hell are you talking about?"

Lisabetta was standing beside her, listening to half of the conversation. Cassanu, still dozing, hadn't heard his grand-daughter's cry. Speranza had gone back inside the farm.

"Valou is ten kilometers away from here. Somewhere in the forest of Bocca Serria, above Galéria."

For a moment Clotilde thought her husband had kid-napped Valentine. That he was holding her prisoner in the middle of the *maquis*, as her mother had once been held. That he was threatening her, that she would never see her daughter again. She let her rage explode, and the mountains trembled.

"Tell me what you mean, damn it!"

At the other end of the line she heard Franck stammering, as if reluctant to confess something painful. In front of her, Lisabetta looked at her uneasily. She had vaguely grasped the fact that Valentine had disappeared.

"What's she doing there?" Clotilde said. "How do you know she's in that forest?"

"I . . . I put a bug in her phone . . . A Spytic . . . It's a track-ing device that allows us to follow her, it means we can know her geographical coordinates at all times." His voice faded, like the voice of a child caught in the act. Only some scraps of words reached Clotilde. "Just in case . . . something happened to her . . . I'm . . . You know me . . . I'm always anxious about Valou . . . I didn't mention it to you, you wouldn't have agreed . . . But that's what's happened, Clo . . . Something has happened to her."

Like a sun appearing suddenly from behind a cloud,

Clotilde's head was filled with clarity. A revelation. At first she felt a violent discharge of hatred, but it was swept away almost immediately by a huge wave of relief.

"Did you put this Spytic in my phone too?"

"Well . . . "

"I don't care, Franck, there's no time to waste on this. I just want to know: did you put a bug in my phone as well, and is that how you found me three nights ago, in the *maquis*?"

"Yes."

She closed her eyes and clenched her teeth to prevent a flood of insults from spewing out of her mouth.

"Call the police, Franck! Call the police and give them the coordinates from your damned tracking device. Make them close off the whole area, make them close off the forest of Bocca Serria. At least then your nasty trick will have achieved something. I'm on my way, I'm going back to the campsite. Where are you?"

But her husband had already hung up.

Lisabetta was still standing there, not saying a word and asking no questions. Just waiting to be needed, like an object tucked neatly on a shelf, useful and in the right place if you wanted it. Solid, barely worn, just a little bent.

In contrast with her grandmother's calm, Clotilde was panicking. Her hands flapped about, and she hesitated between running towards the Passat and taking a few seconds to sort out her head. It was all going too quickly, everything was a jumble. She didn't have time to order all the information she was being given—her mother, her daughter, vanished but alive; at least she hoped so. She had to collect as many clues as possible, facts, facts, facts, perhaps everything would fall into place all of a sudden, at the right moment.

Cassanu had woken up. He was putting his hat back on his head, dazzled by the sun, with no clue as to what was going on all around him.

Clotilde took her grandmother's hands.

"Mamy, that notebook, my diary. After you picked it up, who kept it? You have to tell me, Mamy, it's important. Who else did you show it to? Who else read it?"

Lisabetta's hands tried to get away like a pair of captive butterflies.

"I . . . I don't know, my love."

"You didn't show it to anyone?"

"No."

"So . . . you . . . you're the only one who's read it?"

Tears welled in the corners of the old woman's dark eyes. Her eye-liner ran, making her tragically beautiful.

"What kind of a person do you think I am, my girl? I picked up your diary, of course I did. But I didn't open it. It was yours. It was all yours. So I took it to the campsite, to your bungalow, with the rest of your belongings that we had at Arcanu, some clothes, some books, a bag. You were in hospital. We couldn't have taken everything there."

"When I got out of hospital, Mamy, I was taken straight to the mainland. I never went back to the campsite."

"I know, my love, I know . . . Basile Spinello was supposed to collect all your belongings from the bungalow."

Now Clotilde's hands were trembling, while Lisabetta's were calm, tame.

"And that's what he did, Mamy." She paused. "Basile brought me everything. Except the notebook."

61

August 23, 2016

He crushed the mobile phone against a long flat rock with the heel of his shoe. Even though he didn't understand the technology, he had seen enough police dramas to suspect that a mobile phone, even one that was switched off, would be enough to betray their location. More or less precisely. Although that would require a certain amount of time.

So he wasn't in a rush. While Valentine was reading her mother's diary, her hands tied, mouth gagged, eyes wet with tears, he had studied the contents of the girl's phone.

What a disappointment. He had discovered nothing at all.

He had opened the box of sent and received messages, read the texts, opened up the stored photographs, listened to a few scraps of downloaded music. For a few minutes he had immersed himself in the universe of this fifteen-year-old girl without finding anything interesting at all. Not a word out of turn against her parents. Not an inch too much skin revealed in the photographs. No bottle in the background, no boyfriend to arouse, no girlfriend to infuriate.

She was simply a good girl.

Comfortable in her skin. Well behaved.

Free of hatred, free of problems, as if life was nothing but a gift from a nameless benefactor, something to unwrap and appreciate, then smile and say thank you, blow out the candles without a hint of sadness, believing that Father Christmas would always be there, along with Maman and Papa, the Lord

God or Buddha. A flawless adolescence. The contrast with her mother's diary, written at the same age, was startling.

Was it just a matter of the technology? he wondered. After all, a phone connects you to the world, a diary protects you from it.

Or was it just this new generation?

He picked up a rock and smashed it against what remained of the Samsung. He was sure that if anyone was trying to find them using this phone, the last signal transmitted would be from this forest.

So no more hanging around. It was time to get going.

He glanced at the rusted doors of the Fuego then looked through the window at the faces of the two women, Palma and Valentine. The resemblance was striking. Tall, slender, straight-backed. They both had that classical beauty, that way of carrying their head, that proud expression, that regal assurance unaltered by the years, wrinkles, or a little extra weight. Elegant, attractive, comforting.

On that level, the contrast with Clotilde was remarkable. Clotilde Idrissi was pretty too, but her charm was based on very different qualities: she was small, energetic, non-conformist.

Perhaps, he considered, as he hurled the stone into the distance, the wizard who mixes together the genes at birth has only one supply per family, and he has to distribute the same ingredients as best he can, among parents and children, brothers and sisters, until he cooks up another batch. That way the genes could skip a generation.

He walked towards the Fuego, still thinking about the daughter, the mother and the grandmother. Clotilde had never been able to communicate with her mother, it said as much in her diary. She couldn't communicate with her daughter either, he had observed her enough to be able to tell that.

The irony of it . . .

Because the grandmother and the granddaughter would

have loved, appreciated, and understood each other. That much was blindingly obvious.

A pity.

A pity that their first meeting should consist of two hours in a scratched and dented Fuego, their mouths gagged so they couldn't kiss each other on the cheek, their hands tied too tightly to be able to embrace one another.

But his thoughts had wandered off again. He had to get out of this place.

He opened the door of the Fuego.

8:30 P.M.

Perfect, he would be in exactly the right place at the right time.

He glanced once more at Valentine, sitting on the back seat. She was still turning the pages of her mother's diary, but didn't seem to be reading them. She could no longer make out the words because of the tears flowing down her face. Would that notebook help her to love her mother at last? Or hate her?

It didn't matter.

Valentine would never have the opportunity to tell her.

He opened the door.

No one moved.

"It's time, Madame Idrissi. We have an appointment on the road at Petra Coda."

62

August 23, 2016, 8:40 P.M.

Clotilde was standing beside the Passat, feeling manic, desperately searching through her handbag for her keys. Everything was jostling in her mind, she didn't even know in which direction she should head when she turned on the ignition. Towards the police station? The campsite? Follow the road and hope to spot Valentine? Or her mother? She couldn't put all the pieces of the puzzle together, although she had a vague intuition that the tragedy of the summer of '89 had been played out as much between the adults as it had between the teenagers—two separate circles—and that her old notebook was the only connection between the two.

Written by a teenager, herself, and containing all that she had observed, recorded and since forgotten.

Read by an adult. Stolen by an adult who had discovered in those pages a truth, her truth. Who had found a key in the muddle of her diary. And she couldn't even find one in the mess of her handbag! She cursed like an idiot by the closed door of her car, almost in tears. What a fool! Where had she put that stupid key ring?

Her phone vibrated.

At least she knew where to find that.

"Clotilde? It's Anika. What terrible news, what a tragedy . . . "

Anika sniffed then managed to say a few words between her tears.

"Cervone, murdered this morning. And now your daughter . . . disappearing . . . "

Her sobs drowned out her words once more. The ex-windsurfer was breaking down; the boss who had kept the Euproctes campsite going single-handedly, because of her faith in hospitality, was sinking.

"Are you at the Euproctes, with Franck?"

"No . . . I'm on my own, at the gate of the campsite."

"Where's Franck?"

"I don't know."

"Has he gone to get the police?"

"I don't know . . . maybe he's talking to them, the police are . . . here already. They've been here since this morning . . . Because of Cervone . . . " Her sobs got louder. "I know you didn't like him, Clotilde, that you never liked him . . . but Cervone deserved better than . . . "

"Are you calling me right now to talk about your husband?" Clotilde cut in.

She had finally found her keys and was desperate to hang up and leave the line free.

Anika's reply was without animosity. Maintaining that spirit of hospitality, in spite of everything, to the end.

"No, Clotilde. No, I'm calling you because I remembered something."

Clotilde's heart thumped in her ears as the key got stuck in the door of the Passat.

"The message we got at reception telling Valentine to go up to Arcanu was a simple note scribbled on a piece of paper and signed with your name. I should have been more suspicious and checked . . . but my God I'm so exhausted . . . "

"What was the thing you remembered, Anika?"

"Just before or just after that note was dropped off, a car was parked in front of the campsite. It slowed down, it stopped, then it waited for a few minutes. At the time I didn't think about it. I've only just made the connection."

Clotilde opened the car door and put the key in the

ignition, ready to speed off as soon as Anika had finished talking.

"Cervone told me everything," she went on. "So many times . . . But it was such a long time ago. I was just curious, it was like an association of ideas that weren't quite slotting together . . . then I found the message, and Valou turned up and I forgot."

"What was it about the car, Anika?"

"It was a Fuego. A red one. Like the one that Cervone told me about so many times. Like the one in which your parents and your brother lost their lives."

☙

Clotilde turned the key and the engine of the Passat rumbled into life, but she didn't put it into reverse, she didn't put her foot on the accelerator. Three alerts were going off in her head, three sirens wailing, a triangle of fire.

First of all, a red Fuego.

Then some map coordinates, the ones revealed by the spyware in Valou's phone. Franck had mentioned the forest of Bocca Serria, which wasn't far from Petra Coda.

Last of all, her mother and her daughter missing.

Everything converged on the same obvious fact: someone had deliberately borrowed a car identical to her parents' car, had put her mother and her daughter in it, and was bound for the corniche at Petra Coda.

Clotilde didn't know who, how, or why, but she was sure that something was going to happen there. She stared anxiously at the clock on the dashboard.

8:44 P.M.

Someone—a lunatic, a psychopath—was heading towards the Petra Coda ravine so that everything would happen exactly as it had twenty-seven years ago. On the twenty-third of

464 · MICHEL BUSSI

August. Without her, but with another fifteen-year-old girl sitting in the back seat. Her daughter.

She thought again of the coastal road, ten days previously. The bunches of wild thyme. Franck and Valou who hadn't cared, the cars brushing past them on the narrow road. Now she was sure of it—this mad person would be there at exactly 9:02 P.M. And send the Fuego flying over the parapet.

Go back into the house. Drive straight there. Alert everyone she could contact.

She needed people down there. Before he got there. Before she did.

In exactly eighteen minutes from now.

She barely had time.

The car started to move and she automatically looked in the rear-view mirror. And slammed on the brakes.

Cassanu was standing behind her, white and wrinkled, his stick in the air, his hat pushed back, like a disoriented Gandalf. She had a sense that he had heard everything. Understood everything too.

"Please move, Papé . . . "

"I want to come with you."

"Get out of the way. You've caused enough trouble already."

The tyres of the Passat sent the gravel flying. Cassanu barely had time to jump aside as the car reversed. A second later, it disappeared in a cloud of dust. Clotilde took one last glimpse in the mirror. Cassanu was still standing there, as if rooted to the spot, as if he were never going to move again, as if his only hope now was to return to nature, to become a tree, a pebble; to be nothing but a harmless object, as his wife Lisabetta had always been.

The road down to La Revellata, then another few kilometers further on, the corniche of Petra Coda, was just an endless sequence of tight bends. Clotilde cursed the long detour she was going to have to take along the tarmacked road to get away from Arcanu and back down to the main road by the campsite, when as the crow flies, by the path, the distance was only a few hundred meters.

8:46 P.M.

She accelerated along the very short length of straight road then braked too hard as she took the bend.

"Shit!" she exclaimed, her eyes fogged with tears. "Calm down, calm down. You'll go faster if you stay calm."

Except that her head was threatening to implode. Who could this lunatic be? It didn't matter, she had to get to Petra Coda before he did, before they did. And she wouldn't be able to do this on her own. Without slowing down, she held the wheel with her right hand and, with her left, took out her phone. Her eyes flicked between the snaking road and the number she was trying to dial. Why in God's name hadn't she dared to save his number, even under a false entry? Why hadn't she just memorised it?

06

A turning, she turned.

25

Down to second, then speed up again.

96

No one coming, no one down below, three bends lower down, drift to the left, eat up the white line and gain a few seconds.

59

Accelerate again.

13

Hear it ringing.

Answer, damn it, answer!

Brake, lose time, down to first.

"Shit, shit, shit. Pick up!"

Accelerate again.

Yell a message.

Natale! Natale, listen to me. They've taken my daughter. I don't know who. I don't know why. They've taken Palma too. I just know they're heading towards Petra Coda. In a red Fuego. To kill them, Natale. To plunge into the Mediterranean. You're near there, Natale. You're nearby, you can get there first.

Taking advantage of the last straight before reaching the main road, she hung up and lost concentration for a moment.

She slammed her foot on the brake just in time.

"Shiiiiit!"

Cassanu was standing right in the middle of the road. The crazy old man had taken a shortcut down the path. He was shaking, bent over, leaning on his cane, like a marathon runner who has used up all his remaining strength. She made her decision in a flash: it would take her longer to avoid running over this old man in the middle of the road than it would to let him get in.

She leaned over and opened the door.

"Damn it! Don't you think you've done enough already? Come on, get in!"

8:50 P.M.

She had lost thirty seconds. Cassanu climbed in but didn't say anything. He was getting his breath back, panting, coughing, as if his heart was about to explode. That was all she needed—her grandfather dying in the passenger seat! Papé must have started running as soon as the Passat drove away, he must have sprinted, ignoring Lisabetta's cries, dashing down the path whose every secret he knew, every stone, every place to skid.

The bends in the road sped by. Gradually, the old Corsican's breathing returned to normal, unlike the car engine, which seemed to be getting very hot. A smell of burnt toffee spread through the open windows.

The brakes?

It didn't matter, the car would last another eight kilometers.

"Clotilde, I don't think your mother escaped."

A bit too late to be sorry now, Papé . . .

She turned the wheel sharply as the Passat got too close to the edge, brushing for several meters against the stone parapet that separated them from the precipice.

"I think . . . I think she was taken."

The phone rang. The tyres squealed.

Natale?

Franck?

Clotilde picked up as the car headed straight towards the void.

"Bend to the right," Cassanu said gently. "Two hundred meters, a hundred and twenty degrees."

She turned hard. At last the old man might be useful to her. He knew every inch of this road by heart, a more effective co-pilot than the most experienced rally-driver on the Tour de Corse.

"Clotilde? It's Maria-Chjara!"

She was so surprised that she nearly drove the Passat straight into the stone wall in front of her. She just missed a little floral shrine, a Virgin with a cross and three plastic flowers; the memory of another car, another life that had been extinguished here one day, one night?

"Bend to your left, a hundred and fifty meters, hairpin."

"Maria?"

"I was thinking about our conversation again. Cervone Spinello's lies. That story about the sabotaged steering column."

"Yes?"

"Bend to the right, very tight, one hundred meters, one hundred and sixty degrees."

"Cervone didn't really invent that story."

Lightning flashed through Clotilde's brain. Maria-Chjara

was going back on her statement. Cervone, the ideal culprit, was first murdered then cleared. Lightning followed by a thunderclap. If Cervone had been cleared, did that mean her brother Nicolas was now the guilty one?"

"You assured me that . . . "

"I've been thinking about it ever since we talked. Trying to remember every minute of that day, every word, every gesture . . . "

"A slight chicane to the left, a hundred and fifty meters. Eighty degrees."

"Every gesture, Maria? So long after it all happened?"

"Listen to me, Clotilde, listen. For all these years, I've been sure that the death of Nicolas and your parents was an accident. But if you need to look for a murderer, if someone did sabotage the car that your brother and I were supposed to borrow that evening, if someone wanted to kill us both, it couldn't have been Cervone. He wasn't the one who was dying of jealousy."

"Chicane to the left!" Cassanu yelled.

Clotilde turned at the last moment without letting go of the telephone, the car clinging to the edge of the road, throwing up gravel and a rain of yellow sparks as it skidded through the sea of giant fennel that grew in the hollows by the roadside. Sweat pearled on her forehead.

"I have no doubt," Maria-Chjara went on. "I will never forget those eyes that followed me and Nicolas on the day of the accident, at Oscelluccia beach in the early evening, when everyone had left except him. Then that same look the day after the tragedy, resting only on me. Today I understood. It was . . . it was because he wanted to kill us . . . Because he had killed Nicolas."

"Straight ahead, four hundred and fifty meters, go on . . . You can speed up now."

"Who, Maria? Whose eyes?"

Clotilde heard laughter on the telephone. The forced laughter of an actress. Maria-Chjara was also ridding herself of all the years she had spent carrying a vague sense of guilt.

She had made someone jealous, jealous enough to turn him into a murderer.

"You might remember too, Clotilde, you must remember him. His eyes. Even if more often than not you only saw one of them."

63

8 *:52.*
  The tight bends were coming almost in slow motion now. The Fuego scrupulously stuck to the speed limit, its driver felt the need neither to accelerate nor to slow down, he had programmed the Satnav and he knew that as long as he didn't exceed the limit, if he followed to the letter the instructions of the robotic voice that was guiding him, the Fuego would reach the first bend at Petra Coda at exactly 9:02 P.M.

In nine minutes, it would all be over.

A little sooner than predicted, as far as he was concerned.

His doctor had given him something closer to nine months.

The Passat was approaching the D81. The road was straighter now, a little further from the coast, and Clotilde managed to shift into fifth gear, getting close to a hundred kilometers an hour for a few hundred meters, before she had to slow down again.

She had wedged the mobile phone between her thighs.

"It's Hermann!" Clotilde shouted. "That bastard the cyclops!"

Cassanu turned towards her.

"Hermann Schreiber?"

Clotilde didn't take her eyes off the road.

"Yes, he's the one who killed them. And he'll do it all over again in less than ten minutes if we don't get there in time. He's kidnapped Valou and Maman."

"Impossible."

8:53 P.M.

"Oh, no, Papé, it's not impossible at all. I was talking to that bastard Hermann Schreiber on the phone the other day and . . . "

Her grandfather rested a hand on her thigh.

"That's impossible, Clo, I can assure you. You couldn't have talked to the German." He look a deep breath. "Hermann Schreiber died in 1991, eighteen months after your parents' accident. When he was less than twenty years old."

⌒

8:54 P.M.

The Fuego passed by the rock of Capo Cavallo, six kilometers south of La Revellata.

Arrival time 9:02 P.M., said the display on the Satnav stuck to the windscreen.

The screen showed a miniature, stylized version of the landscape opening up before them. An electric-blue sea, a khaki mountain, a café-au-lait sky.

A depiction that was both drab and gaudy, as ugly, Jakob Schreiber thought, as the reality was sublime. In front of him was the Revellata Peninsula, the lighthouse, the Calvi citadel, blushing in the setting sun, like a girl whose shyness made her all the more pretty. He slowed down a little to enjoy the view for a few seconds. So much for his precise adherence to the Satnav; he would catch up on lost time by accelerating after Punta di Cantatelli. The landscape would surely be the only thing in this world that he would miss.

The road turned towards the mountain again, past a dry patch of *maquis* and some thin cows. He speeded up. Basically, thinking about regrets over the next few minutes, before the great leap, was stupid. Even if Clotilde Idrissi hadn't turned up at his bungalow five days ago, reopening old wounds that had barely closed over, this summer would have been his last. In any case, the oldest resident of the Euproctes campsite would always have preferred to bid farewell to the world here, in Corsica, rather than fade away slowly in the clinic back home in Germany. You might as well crash in a setting that looked like paradise, since no one could be sure that there was one after death.

Nine months maximum, his doctor had told him.

The first alert, the first tumour, had slipped in just above his liver eight years before. They had cleaned out his oesophagus the way you unblock a gutter with a high-pressure hose, but the acid rain had continued to fall—on his pancreas, his lungs, his stomach. The tumour had won. He even thought it would triumph sooner; he had always thought he wouldn't survive retirement for more than five years, when the accountant from the company for which he worked had told him he'd be getting a bonus of 300 marks a month as soon as he left, for the fact that, throughout his whole career, he'd been exposed to hazardous products, solvents and pollutants. He had stuck with them for over fifteen years, he'd been an executive, he'd kept an eye on the production lines through the screen of a computer. Luckily for the company, the workers employed to handle the products and clean the vats were less expensive to the company, when they retired, than he was.

He glanced in the mirror, wondering whether his passengers had any idea of what awaited them. Palma would have understood, inevitably: the red Fuego, the destination that appeared on the Satnav, her granddaughter in the back seat, all the clues were plain to see. Valentine must have realized too; she knew everything now, she had read her mother's notebook. Yet they both remained calm. Although what else could they do, trussed up like a pair of Christmas trees in a net? Perhaps they were hoping that this little drive was nothing but a charade, a bad joke, a piece of theatre . . . or that the parapet at Petra Coda had been reinforced since 1989.

Coming within sight of the Bay of Nichiareto, Jakob Schreiber maintained a cruising speed. The last few days, rereading Clotilde's diary, page after page, had revived the burning embers of a hatred that had never truly gone out.

His son, Hermann, wasn't responsible for any of this.

It was all the fault of Maria-Chjara, Nicolas, Cervone, Aurélia—of all the other teenagers in that group during the summer of '89, with their contempt, their selfishness. He hadn't invented anything, Clotilde had described the situation perfectly in her notebook. They were the ones who had fed that fury, that jealousy, that madness. Without it, nothing would have happened. His son was a nice, serious, hard-working, well-mannered boy. At the Catholic primary school and then at the local grammar school; a Cub Scout from the age of six, a Pioneer at less than fifteen, always with a sculptor's chisel in his hand, a bright pebble in his pocket, a blade of grass between his teeth.

Hermann was a gentler person than the average.

He loved music. He loved beauty. He learned how to sing, to play the violin, he painted seascapes, skies, pale with washed-out colours, in a studio run by a retired watercolourist. Hermann was an only son. He liked to make a world that was all his own, build a universe from treasures assembled at random; he hadn't hung posters of tennis players, singers or Formula 1 drivers on the walls of his room, but dozens of pages from an herbarium that he constantly enriched, month after month. At the age of ten, he'd had the idea to create a magnificent collection: a collection of stars, all the ones he could find, starfish, gilded Christmas-tree decorations, sheriffs' badges, stars photographed at night, in the depths of the forest, stars printed on flags, posters, and novels. Hermann had been a brilliant student, he had been accepted into the Polytechnische Schule in Munich, to study applied arts. Hermann was both an artist and a craftsman. He was interested in the way things worked, in physics and mechanics, but above all he was attracted by beauty, by the material existence of beauty, convinced that nature was the greatest creative genius the earth had ever known, and that it alone attained the ultimate harmony and perfection; that men should merely admire it, and draw inspiration and nourishment from it.

Hermann was a simple, straightforward creature.

Often alone. Shy, secretive, misunderstood, but a stranger to lies. Unaware of evil. It was the others who had taught him that. The ones his own age. Hermann didn't understand their codes. Hermann was too fragile. Hermann wanted only to be like them, to be accepted for a summer. He didn't know about their cruelty. Without all that, Hermann would never have sabotaged the steering of that car, the car that Maria-Chjara and Nicolas were going to get into. Hermann had never planned to kill them, he just wanted to take his revenge; he only wanted their attempt to run off together to fail, he wanted to make the car impossible to drive in the middle of the night so that they would end up on foot, and Nicolas would have to shed his arrogance and Maria wouldn't give herself to him. He just wanted to frighten them, to teach them a lesson. He had never known a girl in the true sense. He didn't want Nicolas's hands to sully all that beauty, the grace, the perfection of that face, that body with which he was obsessed, the body of that little whore Maria-Chjara.

Jakob Schreiber stared at the rocks that tumbled into the Mediterranean, and slowed down once more.

No, of course, Hermann didn't intend to kill Maria and Nicolas. Nicolas was supposed to borrow his parents' car that evening to go to the Camargue, that damned nightclub, with

Aurélia and Cervone; Nicolas had promised them all. But during that day, Hermann had followed them. And a few hours later, after they had parked at the campsite, he had heard Maria-Chjara agreeing to go with Nicolas, but without anyone else, all those idiots from the campsite . . . A trip for the two of them. Which would be cut short, Hermann had imagined as he lay down under the car. How could he have anticipated the change of plan? That it would be Paul Idrissi who found himself at the wheel, with his wife and children? That he would cause the deaths of an entire family? That he would find himself wearing the skin of a murderer, when he wasn't even eighteen years old?

8:56 P.M.
Arrival time 9:02 P.M.

These days, Jakob Schreiber thought, you could plan your death to the minute.

Hermann had said nothing. The police had concluded that it was an accident.

But Hermann had never got over it. He was responsible for the deaths of three innocent people.

Hermann had spent a term being unable to set foot inside the Polytechnische Schule, cloistered away in his room, with his herbarium and his stars. It had taken almost thirty therapy sessions before Hermann confessed to them, before he told them everything—everything that Anke and he had already understood since that day in August 1989.

Hermann continued to see the therapist. He took up the violin again. He went back to collecting plants and observing the stars. Jakob had found a new college for him, less prestigious than the Polytechnische Schule, but a private school that specialized in marketing, where you could take year-long courses; he got him a job at the company, less to make him work than to keep him busy.

Hermann was better, Jakob believed, wanted to believe, tried to convince himself.

On February 23, 1991, exactly eighteen months after the accident at Petra Coda, Hermann got too close to a vat of lye on the production line he was supervising. His body was devoured by the substance, like some horrific scene from a science fiction film in which a body is reduced to a smoking broth before disappearing. Jakob wanted to believe that it was an accident, just an accident. But ten workers, in studio B3 of line 07 in the factory, had seen Hermann deliberately toppling the vat and pouring it over himself.

Hermann was gentle and talented. Hermann had had a brilliant future ahead of him, he could have enjoyed an important role in a large company, could have seduced a beautiful woman, lived a life in harmony with his ideals, the life he deserved; identical to the one that Jakob had described to Clotilde Idrissi two days earlier on the phone, when she had called and he had passed himself off as his son. He hadn't made it all up. He had simply described the life that had been stolen from his son.

Anke had died a few years later, of grief. In August 1993, his wife had insisted that they should holiday in Croatia, on Pag, an island vaguely reminiscent of Corsica, with its cliffs and its villages. One morning, as she went to fetch some bread in their Mercedes, she had come to a bend in the road with a sheer drop underneath. She hadn't turned the wheel. There was one word on a note in the wallet that she hadn't taken with her. *Entschuldigung.* Sorry.

There was an investigation.

The Mercedes had been kept in immaculate condition. The steering worked perfectly.

Since then, Jakob had had time to reflect. Hermann and Anke had paid for a crime that they hadn't committed.

He had had time to weigh up the responsibilities.

Yes, the Schreiber family's tragedy was a match for that of the Idrissi family.

After August 23, 1989, after the accident, when he had found Hermann sitting helplessy on the steps of their mobile home, Jakob had guessed that his son bore part of the responsibility. They were supposed to have another eight days of holiday, but they decided to return to Germany the following day. That morning, Jakob went to bungalow C29, where the Idrissis had been staying. It was empty. But the notebook belonging to Clotilde, the little survivor, the one she always carried around with her, was on the kitchen table, along with the other things Basile Spinello was supposed to bring to her in the hospital. Jakob had simply taken it. So that he might understand. So that he alone could read it, in case there were any clues, in case there was any kind of evidence against his son concealed among its lines.

He had read and reread that notebook; and once more that summer. There was nothing to indicate that Hermann was the murderer, unless you were the most perceptive reader of detective novels. Clotilde Idrissi certainly wasn't aware of anything.

But there was one witness, a direct witness. Cervone Spinello. On August 23, 1989, working at reception in the campsite, he hadn't taken his eyes of Nicolas and Maria-Chjara; he had seen Hermann sliding under the Fuego, then he had heard rumours about the damaged steering column. Cervone had been careful to let Jakob know that he knew who had murdered the Idrissis, but he never publicly accused Hermann, he never talked about him to the police or to Cassanu Idrissi. Jakob had wondered why, at first, until the first bricks of the Roc e Mare marina began to grow, until the breeze on Oscelluccia beach blew on the Tropi-Kalliste beach bar and it didn't fly away. The explanation was obvious. Cervone Spinello was blackmailing Cassanu Idrissi. He had a hold on him, even if Jakob didn't quite understand, didn't know which version, which false truth he had invented. He knew only that Cervone held a trump card in his hand: he knew who the real murderer of Paul and Nicolas Idrissi was. Cassanu would never have suspected Hermann Schreiber, the young German tourist whose existence he was unaware of.

Jakob glanced back. Valentine wasn't reading the notebook any more, he had heard her putting it carefully back in the plastic bag. Palma Idrissi and her granddaughter were motionless, only their hair was moving, stirred by the wind that passed through the slightly open rear windows. The two women were staring at him, at the back of his neck, his shoulder, his arm. And his eyes, which met those of Valentine in the rear-view mirror.

He had waited patiently for this August to come around, he had waited to see the Mediterranean one last time, to share one last beer, play one last game of pétanque. According to the doctors, the cancer would at least allow him that, one last summer, just one. And all of a sudden here was Clotilde Idrissi, getting off the boat, searching, investigating, claiming the impossible. That her mother was alive! A hobbyhorse, a folly, but she was stirring up the past, interrogating Maria-Chjara, Natale Angeli, Sergeant Cesareu Garcia and his daughter Aurélia, she was bringing back memories, stripping the shrouds from the ghosts. As he had foreseen, she had come and asked him if she could see all the pictures from the summer of '89. Who knows whether one of them mightn't have helped her guess the truth? He had feigned his surprise perfectly in front of Clotilde Idrissi, when he had opened the empty file. And if he had wanted to retrieve the photographs held in the cloud, it was so that he could destroy them for ever.

He didn't think the danger would come from Cervone Spinello. He didn't suspect that the campsite manager had even more to lose than he did. Before he pulled the trigger and the harpoon pierced his heart, Spinello had confessed everything to him. Spinello had been frightened, the evening when Jakob had come to ask him for a Wi-Fi connection so he could recover his photographs. Cervone had panicked. Since Clotilde Idrissi had come back to the Euproctes, he had done everything he could think of to make her go away again, but Clotilde was stubborn, she was perceptive. Moving, too. Cervone was worried that she might persuade Jakob to admit the truth, that the two survivors of those two families destroyed by the tragedy might fall into each other's arms, so that he might finally ease his conscience.

Jakob Schrieber clenched his fingers on the wheel. In front of him, the sun formed a long line of fire that set the sea ablaze. Yes, Cervone Spinello had been afraid of losing everything. If Clotilde discovered the truth, if she brought it out into the daylight, his whole business would collapse. Even worse, if that old Corsican up at Arcanu learned that twenty-seven years ago Cervone had witnessed the sabotage of his son's car, and had kept his mouth shut for so many years, then he would probably have had no qualms about having him executed, whether or not he was his best friend's son. Then Cervone had knocked out Jakob, without premeditation, in haste, by smashing a pétanque ball against his temple. He would probably have managed to do more than that if some campers leaving the poker game hadn't called out to him as they walked along the path. It was impossible to hide the corpse, there was no time to clean up the scene of the crime, and Cervone had had to leave the mobile home. He probably planned to come back a little later, at night, to finish off the job. Except that Jakob had somehow found the strength to flee. To drag himself away from the campsite, taking something with him to sterilise the wound. After roaming the area for fifty years, he too knew the *maquis*.

What else could Cervone do except affect bewilderment,

the following morning, before the pétanque players who were waiting for the old German? Except pretend to be surprised in front of Clotilde, when he found the mobile home empty. What choice did he have but to wait, tremble, hope that the German had gone off to die in a corner like a wounded, frightened animal?

Jakob had waited calmly, letting him ripen, so he could kill him at the right moment.

He'd simply needed some time.

That unidentified body dragged from the Bay of Crovani had been the opportunity he had dreamed of; probably some reckless swimmer, the kind they fished out of the sea almost every summer. Jakob had only had to throw some clothes, a watch and his papers off the top of the Mursetta headland, where the current in the Mediterranean was the strongest. The police wouldn't fall for it for long, it would only take them a few hours, perhaps a day, to find out the real identity of the corpse, or at least to work out that the decomposed body did not match his own. But a few hours was all he needed to lull Cervone into a false sense of security.

The campsite manager couldn't have known that Jakob was already a condemned man, and that he didn't care how he ended it all. That his hatred wasn't reserved only for the Idrissis; that he planned to make everyone here feel it, everyone who had taken away his paradise. Cervone couldn't have suspected that grief and loneliness had driven him mad, that he too was giving half of his pension to a therapist; that he too, in studio B3 of line 07 in the factory, had come to a stop by the vat of lye; that he had made himself dizzy leaning over the white rocks on the island of Pag, the red rocks of Petra Coda, at the foot of the Revellata Peninsula.

It was only this morning that Jakob had learned Cervone Spinello's secret, the one that had meant he could enjoy Cassanu Idrissi's protection.

Palma Idrissi. Alive.

Sentenced by a people's jury in place of Hermann; imprisoned ever since the summer of 1989 in a shepherd's cabin.

Over the years, Cervone had staked his lot on both versions, letting each party believe his own truth: Cassanu was unaware of the real culprit, Jakob Schreiber was unaware of the accused. Cervone hadn't even needed to lie—his silence had been enough to make him master of the situation. Until the return of Clotilde Idrissi.

Cervone Spinello hadn't deserved to die, but firing an arrow into his heart was merely a patient form of self-defence. The Idrissis, they deserved it. And they deserved to suffer before they died. If it wasn't for all their lies, over three generations, none of this would have happened.

9:01 P.M.

The sun had not yet disappeared behind the Bay of Calvi. It was floating above the citadel like a dazzling spotlight, transforming the world into a theatre of shadows. Jakob's eyes became blurred. Ever since this morning, since this summer, for twenty-seven years, he had been replaying the same words in his head:

We were just an ordinary family, we liked simple things, we came here to spend our holidays in the sun.

On the Island of Beauty.

We didn't know that such beauty burns anyone who approaches it, that such beauty lies, that it escapes anyone who wants to touch it.

We hadn't taught Hermann. That you could damn yourself by coveting it.

Hermann was too pure, too different.

They couldn't bear it.

They killed him.

I am going to join Anke. Join Hermann.

On August 23, at 9:02 P.M.
In a red Fuego.
At Petra Coda, on the Revellata Peninsula.
A man, a woman, a fifteen-year-old girl.
Three corpses.
And all will be concluded.
In beauty.

64

August 23, 2016, 9:01 P.M.

J ust over a minute.

Her eyes filled with tears, Clotilde continued to accelerate. She had thrown her mobile onto the dashboard, it was only making her lose precious seconds. The Revellata Peninsula stretched in front of them, but she had to drive around the edge of it, climb to the middle and then back down again, about fifty meters of descent, twenty short bends.

She wouldn't make it.

Unless Jakob Schreiber was late. Unless his watch, the clock in his car, his telephone weren't all synchronised to the same universal clock, even a few seconds might be enough.

On the passenger seat, Papé Cassanu said nothing.

The landscape closed in on them for the duration of a few turnings that snaked along the foot of the peninsula, with the campsite to the south and the lighthouse to the north. Clotilde took them at speed, driving in the middle of the road, not worrying that a car might suddenly appear in front of her. The white line was now nothing more than a ribbon, preventing the Passat from taking off, like an adhesive strip to which the car was glued.

The car now climbed again, sending up a cloud of dust as they passed some vehicles parked in the car park. Tourists taking pictures of the view cursed the girl racer as she sped by without noticing them. The road was clear for almost a kilometer. After the ten bends leading down the hill they could make out the corniche of Petra Coda.

*

Clotilde spotted him.

She felt Cassanu's wrinkled hand gripping his seatbelt as she recklessly pressed down on the accelerator.

The red Fuego had only just appeared a kilometer further down, emerging from the Port'Agro cove, driving smoothly towards them. It was now only a few hundred meters away from Petra Coda.

Taking the first turning in fourth, at over eighty kilometers per hour, Clotilde felt as if the two wheels on the left were about to lift off, as if the Passat was going to flip over; she counter-steered at the last minute, too much, losing more seconds, but fewer than if she'd slowed down. Her foot came down again on the pedal. She had to concentrate on the road, not stare at the red dot coming towards them in the distance.

It was impossible, however. Her daughter and her mother were inside that dot.

At first she thought it was slowing down. She was seized for a moment by a flicker of hope that went out as quickly as a match in a gale. The Fuego suddenly accelerated again, along the long straight line that finished with the deadly bend above Petra Coda.

Clotilde did the same, barely braking now. There were only four bends to take and she clung to the hope that she could still make it, that she could confront the red car, cut it off, crash into it, catapulting her own car into the ravine that she had survived long ago. It wouldn't matter, if the crash saved her mother. Her daughter.

The Fuego was continually gaining speed like a rocket on a ramp.

The parapet had been raised, Clotilde remembered, she had noticed that when they left the bunches of wild thyme by the roadside. The wooden fence had been replaced by a small stone wall half a meter high. A vehicle, even going at speed, would bounce off the parapet, go into a spin, it might even flip, or carry on along the road, bouncing between the wall and the mountain like a mad ball in a gulley, but without toppling over the edge.

Two last bends, barely three hundred meters.

Too late.

In a second the Fuego would crash at full speed into the wall that separated it from a twenty-meter drop, bristling with thousands of rocks, red with blood, and anxious to quench a twenty-seven-year thirst.

Clotilde closed her eyes.

The Fuego was still there, behind her eyelids. In the sky, her father took a hand that she had thought was her mother's, Nicolas chose to smile, to die smiling.

Cassanu cried out, gripped the wheel of the Passat and wrenched it to the left. The car bumped against the slope, beheading some branches of giant fennel that smashed in drops of gold against the windscreen, but it didn't stop, it barely slowed down.

9:02 P.M.

The Passat was jumping about too much, still going at full speed, as the tyres struck the hollows and pebbles of the hillside. Despite herself, Clotilde opened her eyes.

She saw the Fuego deviate slightly from its trajectory, as if to avoid crashing straight into the stone wall above the precipice. For a moment, she thought the vehicle was merely going to skid along the wall, scraping against the stone, to lose a wing, or a door, but then slow down, brake, stop.

But no. She hadn't understood. Jakob Schreiber must have

photographed that turning a hundred times, studying it, taking a survey for his final moment.

The German didn't crash against the parapet as her father once had; he threw the Fuego at an area just beside it, wooden logs that overlooked not the rocky slope, but an even steeper inlet.

The tree trunks exploded. For one unreal moment the Fuego hung weightless in the sky.

Clotilde knew that her mother was inside.
That her daughter was inside.

The Fuego fell. A vertiginous plunge down to where, twenty meters below, the sea smashed against the rocks.
It was over.

65

The Passat reached Petra Coda less than ten seconds later. Clotilde put her foot down hard on the brake. The car swerved and slid a few meters along the road, stopping in the middle, and preventing any other car from getting by.

Clotilde left it there, without even bothering to turn on the hazard lights, turn off the engine or put on the handbrake. She tore open the door and rushed over to the wooden barricade shattered a few moments earlier by the Fuego.

The red car was floating on the water, twenty meters below, bobbing on the waves like a cork among the reefs. It was impossible to tell what state the bodywork was in, but Clotilde imagined that it must have bounced against the rocks, twice, ten times; in spite of its speed, there was little chance that it had plunged straight into the deep, narrow inlet. Second by second, it began to sink.

Two thirds of the Fuego was already covered by the sea.

Another few seconds and it would sink once and for all into the turquoise water. She surprised herself by hoping that Valentine and her mother had been killed outright, on impact, that they would be spared the slow agony of drowning.

Her eyes smarted as she stared at the metal carcass barely protruding above the water.

My God.

Only the rear window was still above the waterline now, washed by the waves. Clotilde thought she could make out two silhouettes, two frantically moving shadows.

Was it an illusion?

She would never know. A moment later there was nothing above the surface but a joyful foam taking possession of its playground, enjoying itself once more by throwing a thousand fleeting bubbles at the bare rocks.

"Get out of the way!"
Clotilde didn't even think. She got out of the way.
Cassanu went right up to the edge, then he dived.
In a flash, Clotilde remembered a conversation she had had with her Papé a long time ago: "All the young Corsicans used to dive into the sea there . . . your grandfather was the most daring of them all." She bit her lip hard.

Could a body, after all these years, preserve the memory of that perfect balance you had to attain in order to dive twenty meters without it shattering against the surface of the water? Maintain that ability to concentrate that was indispensable if you wanted to control your fall; aim for exactly the right point, reach the sea without crashing into the jaws of the cliff which parted only for a few meters? Remain sufficiently clear-sighted, to the very last moment, in order to judge the depth of the basin and avoid the submerged red icebergs planted like stakes in a moat?

Yes.

Yes, Cassanu's body had not forgotten a thing.

Was it mere chance, or had Papé always been an exceptionally good diver? His leap described the perfect trajectory, a straight line, deftly avoiding the granite spikes so that he disappeared into the eddying water at the precise spot where the Fuego had plunged.

Nothing.
Clotilde saw nothing for endless moments. Cassanu hadn't survived his fall, he had sacrificed himself, he hadn't jumped in to save them, he had committed suicide to avoid facing his guilt.

Sirens wailed behind her. Doors slammed. Rushing footsteps, making the tarmacked road surface vibrate. Clotilde turned her head reluctantly for a moment, just a moment, before turning back to the water again.

All that mattered was the surface of that turquoise pool.

Pray pray pray.

Pray to see a body, a head, a hand splitting the surface.

Behind her, the new arrivals were moving about. Clotilde had had time to recognise, among the four or five uniformed officers, Captain Cadenat, Sergeant Cesareu Garcia, his daughter Aurélia, and Franck.

Franck had done what needed to be done. He had alerted the police, and they had come quickly; but what did the swiftness of their reaction matter now? One minute too late might as well have been an eternity.

Franck took her hand. Clotilde didn't resist.

An eternity.

The Mediterranean never gave anything back, never.

Clotilde's heart exploded.

"There!"

Papé's head and shoulders had just emerged; he was holding a body in his arms. Clotilde could see how desperately he was trying to lift it from the water. At last its head, its neck, its shoulders appeared.

Valou!

Alive.

Her daughter's long brown hair floated like tentacles around her face. Franck gripped Clotilde's hand even tighter. Valou didn't cough, she didn't spit salt water from her lungs, her mouth was covered with a bandage.

"Shit!" her husband shouted. "She's bound and gagged, she won't be able to make it!"

The rocks at the bottom of the inlet were too sheer, almost vertical and smooth-sided. There was no chance of Cassanu, let alone Valou, being able to hold on to them.

Cassanu had already dived again. Valou was floating as best she could, opening crazed eyes, probably using her legs—Clotilde didn't know if they were tied or not—trying to keep herself on the surface.

"She won't make it," Franck said again. "Throw her a rope, damn it, a lifebelt, anything!"

The policemen looked at each other, perplexed. They had leapt into their vans as soon as Franck had called them, but had prepared for a kidnap situation, not a sea rescue. They could never have imagined . . . They were waiting for the fire service, who were on the way.

Valou was trying desperately to keep herself horizontal on the surface of the water, but the waves were too powerful, rocking her back and forth before exploding against the rocks. Each one seemed as if it might drag her under, each one covered her as it swept past, but Valentine reappeared as soon as the wave subsided.

She was clinging on.

How can you cling to a void? To liquid?

Clotilde shouted, since her daughter had no voice.

"Damn it all, is no one else going to jump in?"

The men hesitated.

The opening in the rock was narrow, the drop vertiginous, there were so many boulders sticking out of the water that you would have had to be a professional diver even to think about risking it. Even a good amateur hadn't a chance in ten of making it, without missing and hitting the rocks.

Franck was the first to climb over the parapet.

"We must be able to get down. Find a way, jump from lower down."

He slid a few meters on his bottom, holding on to the

branches of the few clumps of broom that grew among the rocks. The four policemen followed him.

"Quick!" Clotilde cried again.

Papé had just resurfaced. He looked exhausted, his body racked by coughing, spitting water, blood, his guts, but he was holding another body. With the last of his strength, he lifted it up to the surface.

Maman!

Eyes closed. Unconscious.

But she was breathing, she was definitely breathing. Because if Papé was trying to keep her alive, to save the woman he had hated so much, the one he had sentenced to life imprisonment, it was because she was alive!

This time, Cassanu didn't dive again. He passed an elbow under Palma's arms, the way you might support a floating package, a deflated mattress, a sagging life-jacket. With his other arm, he tried to reach Valentine.

They would only be able to survive like that for a few moments.

Franck and the policemen were stuck half-way down. Trying to climb down had been a very poor idea. Without equipment, there was no way of doing it—there were no further bushes to cling to, the walls of the inlet were almost vertical, and there were other rocks below so it was impossible to jump. The one narrow fissure that also led down to the the inlet was back up level with the road. They only noticed it now. Too late. They had to climb back up.

Still no sign of the firemen.

It's hopeless, Clotilde thought.

Well, as there was nothing else for it . . . After all, Cassanu had given it a go.

Clotilde stepped forward and prepared herself. Never in her life had she dived from a board higher than three meters.

Too bad.

A firm hand held her back, gripping her wrist.

The hand of a giant, the kind you don't resist. Sergeant Cesareu Garcia didn't let go, didn't speak, he merely gave her a look that said: no, that's enough, enough people have died, one more sacrifice wouldn't help anyone.

There were only three of them now, standing beside the broken barrier.

Cesareu, Aurélia and her.

"Let go of me."

She tried to pull away, but the sergeant didn't budge. Clotilde felt a wave of hysteria welling up inside her, she had to act, she couldn't let her daughter and her mother perish like this.

"Listen," said Aurélia.

Listen to what?

The wind was blowing from the sea. Perhaps it would carry the sound of a fire engine's siren coming towards the mountains? She listened intently but could hear nothing. Nothing but the wind blowing stronger and stronger, at least that was how it seemed to her, creating waves that were getting higher and higher, and ever more deadly.

She lowered her eyes.

Cassanu had managed to get hold of Valou's shoulder, he was still clutching Palma, and they all pressed tight together, like bales fallen from a cargo ship. Floating desperately, being dragged under, rising again, shaken, soaking, exhausted. With no other hope but to hold on, hold on, hold on.

Why? Until when? Who could reach out a hand to help them?

"Listen," Aurélia repeated.

For years Clotilde would reproach herself. She never really got over the fact that Aurélia had recognised the sound before she did, even if she had almost never heard it. That engine noise.

In the moment, Clotilde merely poured all of her emotion into her voice, shouting as loud as she could:

"There! There!"

She called out to Papé:

"Hang on there! Please God, hang on, you'll be rescued!"

A hundred meters away, behind the last rocky cape that concealed the rest of the Revellata Peninsula, the Cave of the Sea-Calves, the lighthouse, and Punta Rossa, a small boat had just appeared.

Bigger than a rowboat, smaller than a trawler.

The *Aryon*.

Engine down, splitting the waves, slaloming easily among the reefs that it seemed to know by heart. Natale, at the wheel, wore a red windcheater and his fair hair was whipping about in the wind.

Never had Clotilde's heart beaten so hard.

Within a few moments, Natale had closed in on the three bodies floating in the water. He turned off the engine and leaned down to grab Valentine first.

It wasn't easy, the powerful waves made the boat roll as soon as the engine was turned off; Valou, her arms trapped, was unable to help him. Only Cassanu was able to help, pushing the girl's body up, while trying not to let go of Palma. Natale leaned so far over the railing it looked as if he might fall in.

At last he managed to haul Valentine into the bottom of the boat.

Palma's turn.

She was moving. She was moving now. Enough so that her body wasn't a dead weight. She did her best to help them, and curled up so that Cassanu Idrissi could pass one arm under her waist, another under her thighs, and raise her up towards Natale as a groom carries his bride across the threshold of their new shared home.

Clotilde had a sense that their eyes met in that moment. That some words were exchanged in that look.

In Papé's eyes, she read, "Sorry."

In her mother's, "Thank you."

Palma joined her granddaughter lying on the floor of the *Aryon*.

Saved.

Finally Natale held out his hand to Cassanu.

Papé had fought for almost seven minutes against the sea, the waves, the current, the rocks.

The battle was not equal, yet he had succeeded. He had held his ground.

The old man was exhausted.

At least that was what the police concluded, it was what the Corsican journalists put on their front pages, the story the hunters told, with great pride, at the Euproctes bar. It was even what Clotilde would say to Valou, and Palma, every time either of them asked her how it had ended.

That Papé had fought to his very last breath.

None of the witnesses ever said what they thought they had seen.

Natale Angeli held out his hand. It was barely a few centimeters from Cassanu's.

He didn't take it. He let himself sink.

66

There had seldom been so many people on the coastal road at Petra Coda.

Not for at least twenty-seven years, at any rate.

Parked in the midst of this complete chaos were three fire engines, two ambulances, four police vans, and an impressive number of tourist vehicles stuck on the only road connecting Ajaccio and Calvi; only a few motorbikes and the evening athletes—joggers and cyclists—managed to get past, turning their heads towards the precipice as they did so.

Firemen had thrown down a rope ladder and were securing it to the rocks with steel grips, a coast guard Zodiac searched the inlet where Cassanu had disappeared, but in vain. The *Aryon* was firmly moored using steel chains that complemented the polyester ropes. Once it had been stabilised in this way, Palma and Valou were helped up the rope ladder, using a winch, and framed on either side by battle-scarred rescuers who were more used to saving hikers from the mountain tracks.

Thus escorted, they reached the road, and were almost obliged to force their way through a row of rubberneckers, policemen and locals: *Keep back, keep back.* The granddaughter and her grandmother were wrapped in a gilded foil blanket. *It's all fine, it's all fine*, an emergency doctor who looked like a young Harrison Ford had quickly pronounced, but he still insisted on them being transported to the medical centre in Ajaccio. The ambulance door was wide open, the stretchers

prepared, the engine was running, the driver drew on his cigarette, ready to get going. Palma raised a weary hand: *Gently,
gently.* Clotilde barely had time to hug her daughter and her
mother before the first-aid workers separated them: *Later,
madam, later.*

Natale was the last to climb up to the road using the rope
ladder, without the aid of a winch or an escort. Cesareu Garcia
helped him off the final rung, with a firm hand to hoist him up,
a sound clap on the back, a physical, manly, almost silent way
of saying: *Well played, my boy*, the kind that is enough for an
exhausted man returning from heroic deeds, leaving the fiery
pit or exiting the pitch victorious.

Franck had walked a short way towards the cars to fetch
Valentine some dry clothes, a pullover, a pair of trousers, some
trainers.

Aurélia was chatting to Harrison Ford, adopting the professional persona of a nurse who managed such situations with
competence and compassion.

Clotilde, without even thinking about it, found herself face
to face with Natale once more. She still found him incredibly
attractive, with his blue eyes swept by his salty hair, his untrou-
bled, heroic smile. She was filled with an irresistible desire to
throw her arms around him, a spontaneous impulse, a natural
and obvious need to shout *Thank you, thank you, thank you*
into his ear, and to tell him that she had always known he
would untie the moorings, that the *Aryon* would sail again, that
they only had to go back down the rope ladder, set sail and run
away. Her daughter, her mother had been saved; they had been
found again. Everything had been sorted out. It was time to go.

She took one step.
She felt an animal desire to press her body against Natale's,
as if he alone had the mixture of strength and serenity that
could soothe everything.

Aurélia left Harrison Ford behind and took two steps.

Franck entrusted his daughter's dry clothes to the first ambulance man he came to, and took three steps.

Cesareu Garcia took a step back, like a wrestling referee leaving the ring to the fighters.

"Natale!" Aurélia cried.

He didn't move.

"Clo!" Franck cried out behind her. "Clo!"

She didn't move.

"Clo. Valou wants to see you."

She hesitated.

"She has something important to give you."

The driver of the ambulance had spat out the stub of his cigarette. A stretcher-bearer came forward. The coast guard Zodiac was moving in ever increasing circles, taking the search further out to sea.

Clotilde's heart felt veiled.

What else could she do? Abandon her daughter?

She turned around.

Valou and Palma were sitting side by side, the same golden blanket over their thighs, the same white towel wrapped around their hair, the same bent position. They looked startlingly similar.

"Yes, Valou?"

"Maman, I . . . I've got something for you."

Valentine got to her feet, staggering slightly, then took out a plastic bag that had been wedged between her legs under the blanket. She hesitated for a moment, then leaned towards her grandmother.

"No . . . you should give it to her."

Palma's voice trembled, she was struggling to articulate even a few syllables.

"Please . . . call . . . me . . . Mamy . . . "

She found the strength to smile, to hold on her knees that

mysterious plastic bag, without letting go of her granddaughter's hands.

Clotilde walked over to them.

Their six hands mingled, holding the parcel together, making the plastic crinkle. Palma forced herself to speak again.

"It's . . . for . . . you . . . "

Palma and Valou opened their hands. They were crying, both of them.

Clotilde unwrapped her present gently, not understanding at first what could have provoked such strong emotions. At first she glimpsed something blue, faded blue through the plastic; then she felt a shape, rectangular, a book, no, not a book, more like a notebook, judging by its thickness.

The plastic bag flew off towards La Revellata and it didn't occur to anyone to catch it.

Holiday diary. Summer '89.

The writing, on the cover of her teenage diary, was still legible.

She opened it extremely carefully, like an explorer unfolding sheets of papyrus found in a pharaoh's tomb.

Monday, August 7, 1989. The first day of the holidays. Sky summer-blue.

Hi, I'm Clotilde.

I'm introducing myself just to be polite, even if you can't be polite back because I don't know who you are, whoever it is reading this.

That will be in a few years' time, if I manage to hang on. Everything I write is Top Secret. Totally embargoed. Whoever you are, you've been warned! Besides, o my reader, in spite of all my precautions, I don't know who you might be.

My lover, the one I have chosen for the rest of my life, the one to whom—quivering on the morning after my first time—I will entrust the diary of my teenage years?

Some idiot who has just found it, because, being the total disaster I am, that was bound to happen?

Tears welled up in Clotilde's eyes. The letters, the words, the lines were intact. The pages were sometimes warped at the edges, yellow in the corners, making her private diary look more like a witch's old book of spells. For a moment Clotilde felt as if she were meeting herself, herself seventeen years ago, like two heroines in a book with two parallel stories who finally come across one another in the final chapter.

Valou looked at her proudly.

"I saved it, Maman. I saved it!"

They were crying, all three of them.

One arm gripped her waist, another rested just above her chest.

Franck.

She turned around, brushed against her husband's body and rested her head against him; Franck might have taken it as a gesture of tenderness, but she was merely looked over his shoulder.

Aurélia was huddled against Natale in his windcheater, sheltered.

Clotilde slowly pressed the notebook against her heart.

67

August 27, 2016, 12:00 midday

L isabetta, amused, studied the crowd in the yard of
Arcanu Farm. The sun at its zenith beat down on the
gathering dressed in their Sunday best, each one seek-
ing a corner of shade to protect themselves, and not finding it.
They were all trapped. Cassanu would have loved it.

He had always hated the kind of gloomy scene some
Corsicans still went wild for, the black-clad women singing
lamenti and *voceri*, all those ritual gestures to evoke death,
closing the curtains of the house of the deceased, putting
sheets over the mirrors. Cassanu wanted none of that on the
day of his funeral, and Lisabetta had promised him.

She had kept her word.

Still, they hadn't been able to prevent the crowd from coming.

Numerous, curious, silent. Lisabetta watched them per-
spiring litres of sweat, puddles forming under their feet, she
imagined, rivulates that would flow all the way to the
Mediterranean.

There wasn't an inch of shade in the courtyard of Arcanu
Farm.

And so the crowd waited, crushed by the leaden weight of
the sun.

All prisoners in this courtyard, more like an oven. As if
Corsica were taking its revenge.

Slowly, very slowly, the crowd came forward.

The coffin set off first, carried by Osru, Miguel, Simeone

and Tonio, the most closely related cousins. One by one, like grains of sand in an hourglass, the members of the gathering followed, emerging from the farm in a dense procession and turning down the path that led to the coastal road, all the way to the Marcone cemetery. The endless black caterpillar crawled slowly along. The path was too narrow for the mourners to walk more than two abreast, or to space themselves out and breathe. It wasn't until they reached the coastal path that a gentle breeze made the walk more bearable—the last kilometer of the three from the farm to the mausoleum. The procession stretched out along the entire distance, and by the time the coffin reached the Marcone cemetery, the last of the visitors still hadn't left Arcanu Farm.

Among the crowd of anonymous faces, it might have been amusing to pick out a prefect, four councillors, seven members of the Corsican Assembly, a president of the Upper Corsican Hunting Federation, a director of the Regional Natural Park . . . Yes, Cassanu's Corsica was having its revenge. The higher the rank of the dignitaries, the more they were dressed up in tight shirts, buttoned-up waistcoats, and polished shoes, and so the more they suffered in the intense heat, envying the children in their shorts, the girls in their miniskirts, the local guys wearing T-shirts to the cemetery as if this were a game of boules.

Like one last wink from Cassanu against the established order.

Most of the crowd were still at Arcanu.

The oak tree had been stripped bare.

Lisabetta had thought about it for years; every day, for hours, from her kitchen window, when she observed the huge holm oak in the middle of the courtyard, she imagined that the ceremony couldn't be otherwise. She had asked Cassanu to write it into his will.

No flowers, no wreaths.

For everyone, for her, the Arcanu oak, the Revellata oak, that was Cassanu. And so, as Lisabetta had promised herself, every friend, every guest, every visitor who came to pay their final respects to her husband had been offered a branch from the holm oak to set down on his grave. There were more than a thousand stacked up around the trunk, which no longer offered the shade everyone dreamed of.

All of the branches of the three-hundred-year-old tree had been cut off.

The oak was bare, as if it were the depths of winter. A skeleton. A huge corpse stripped of its flesh.

That was what Lisabetta wanted. She didn't care about how it affected these people, this great crowd. In the end, this tree alone would be dressed in mourning.

For a summer.

And then, in a few months, it would blossom again. And Arcanu could come back to life. For hundreds of years, since Cassanu and that oak were one and the same. It wasn't blood that flowed in his veins, but sap. The sap of the Idrissis, since the dawn of time.

Lisabetta was impressed by the ballet of branches as they were carried along by thousands of black ants. The last members of the procession were now leaving the courtyard. She would bring up the rear, she had decided. Before setting off, she glanced one last time at her flower bed, on which no one had dared to trample, her little garden, the flowers that she watered every morning.

She thought that when she died, on her grave she would settle for an orchid.

⌒

Lisabetta slowly walked past the crowd, which was no longer moving; the first arrivals were already crammed into the pocket-sized cemetery, and the rest of the procession was unable to progress; as she came upon them, the crowd parted or moved aside, like spectators at a very fine but incredibly slow Corsican rally. It was almost as if the crowd was inches away from waving the oak branches while chanting Halleluia, although thankfully no one dared.

It took the widow almost an hour to reach the end of the queue.

The crypt was open, with a view over Revellata Bay. And yet, however beautiful the scenery, Lisabetta didn't like crypts, particularly the monumental ones belonging to the important families. In spite of their splendour, with their Greek columns and Ottoman domes, they were little more than huge cupboards in which the generations are stacked in drawers. One day she would share with Cassanu, for all enternity, the fifth drawer up on the right. Tidied away neatly with their parents, grandparents, great-grandparents, great-great-grandparents in the storeys below. With their son waiting for them another floor up.

She slowly advanced towards the crypt. Of course, she would be the first to throw an oak branch on the coffin, but she had decided to share that honour. She struggled over the last few meters, or at least that was what the impatient crowd thought. Lisabetta turned her head to the right and Speranza understood without a word; she stepped forward and took Lisabetta's arm. She too would be the first to approach the mausoleum.

Salomé, her daughter, rested there.

Lisabetta's head now turned to the left, and with a look that brooked no opposition she invited Palma to join them, taking her other arm.

Paul, her husband, rested there.

The three women, supporting one another, approached the coffin.

Lisabetta had taken it upon herself. She'd had the idea the previous day, and reflected on it during the night. To reconcile Palma and Speranza if only for the duration of a ceremony. To make peace. In Corsica, women have that gift.

Together, with a single movement, they threw their three branches. The green leaves settled gently on the varnished planks, as if, by magic, the oak coffin had come to life, blossomed, and turned green; and if it were left there, on the ground, without the marble cupboard being closed, then by next spring the planks would have turned into a tree trunk, roots would sprout, acorns would grow, and ospreys would nest there. Behind them, Clotilde and Orsu now came forward hand in hand. Brother and sister reunited by the fate that perhaps regretted having left them as orphans. They held just a single branch between them, supported by the only hand that Orsu could use, the right one, as if they were a pair of lovers joining their fingers around a single flower.

After them, everyone followed.

A mountain of cut branches piled up; the bare old oak had offered every shade of green, from moss to jade, from lichen to opal, as if, indifferent to the black of the mourners' clothes and the white of the crypt, it wished only to challenge the blues of the Mediterranean and the reds of La Revellata's rocks.

Among the anonymous crowd and the officials whose faces and ranks she often didn't know, Lisabetta recognised certain faces that were dear to her, or whose stories she had learned, stories that were linked to her own.

Anika stood by the grave for a long time, inconsolable. In that same cemetery, accompanied by a crowd a tenth of the size, she had buried her husband. Lisabetta had discussed the situation with her at length, advising her to stay as the head of the Euproctes campsite. She would see, she would see . . .

Maria-Chjara Giordano was beautiful and dignified, dressed all in black, from her sun-glasses to her shoes, from the lace covering her sober cleavage to the two bodyguards on either side of her.

Franck threw his branch modestly, quickly, discreetly, then stood aside, leaving Valentine there on her own. She stood motionless, for an eternity, her eyes blank, not crying, as if she were trying to see right through the planks of the coffin. To see her past. Her father had to tug slightly on her sleeve before she would move away

At last Aurélia arrived, on the arm of Cesareu Garcia. The sergeant was the only guest who hadn't been made to wait at Arcanu, walk along the path, and climb to the mausoleum, but even so the retired policeman's dark shirt was covered with dry, white patches of sweat.

Aurélia walked back on her father's arm, smiled at Lisabetta, then stared out to sea.

Everyone was there.

Only Natale had refused to come.

Finally the crowd dispersed. Clotilde, after hugging Lisabetta for a long time, walked over towards a bench that overlooked the Mediterranean. Palma remained seated and silent. In spite of the heat, she had put a fine silk shawl around her shoulders: black with a pattern of wild roses. Valentine sat beside her, tapping on her mobile phone. Had her grandmother known, in her prison, that they'd invented a contraption that all teenage girls were addicted to?

There were so many things Clotilde's mother didn't know. There were so many things she didn't know about her mother. Now they had all the time in the world to catch up. It wouldn't be easy. Since regaining her freedom, Palma hadn't talked much, hadn't told many stories, most of the time she had remained silent. Listening.

She was sixty-eight years old, too much light made her tired, as did noise, agitation, questions, everything went too quickly for her, there was too much information to take in. Too many surnames, too many first names.

She got confused. When she saw Valentine, her grand-daughter, she sometimes called her Clotilde, as if time had stopped during her captivity, and her fifteen-year-old daughter had been transformed.

Transformed into what she had hoped for. A daughter who looked like her.

Clotilde didn't care. Today, she was at peace.

She stood beside the bench where her mother and her daughter were sitting, her eyes turned towards the sea.

"He . . . he's gone," said Palma.

Clotilde thought at first that her mother was talking about Cassanu, then she realised that she had been looking out beyond the Revellata lighthouse.

A boat was heading out to sea, and they both recognised it as the *Aryon*, Natale's form bent over the wheel.

"He's gone," Palma repeated.

For the first time since her release, her mother tried to put a few more words together.

"I've thought . . . of him a lot . . . I was about forty years old . . . when I went into . . . my dark room . . . I was still . . . a beautiful woman . . . I think . . . I had a mirror . . . I forced myself to forget Natale . . . My greatest fear . . . was that he would see me again . . . Time is cruel . . . unfair to women . . . a man in his fifties . . . doesn't love a woman . . . of seventy . . . "

Clotilde didn't reply.

What could she say?

She merely allowed herself to be swallowed up by the view, since she loved it so much, allowed her eyes to roam from the

Austrian cross at the top of Capu di a Veta, to Calvi citadel, then further down to the Euproctes campsite, to Alga Beach, to Oscelluccia, the ruins of the Roc e Mare marina, the Revellata lighthouse.

"Look, Maman," said Valentine, who had finally unglued her eyes from her mobile phone.

"What?"

"Down there, out at sea, just past the lighthouse."

She couldn't see anything.

"Towards the *Aryon*. Four black dots."

Clotilde and Palma narrowed their eyes but couldn't see anything.

"It's them, Maman! Orophin and Idril and Galdor and Tatië. Your dolphins!"

Clotilde was startled, and wondered for a moment how her daughter knew those names from her childhood, before she understood. Her notebook, of course, the notebook from the summer of '89 that her daughter had read when she was bound and gagged in the Fuego.

"I'm almost sure of it, Maman! It's obvious. They've recognized the *Aryon*."

Was her daughter, normally so serious, really capable of imagining something like that? Would the dolphins really recognize the noise of the engine of the same boat, twenty-seven years on?

"A dolphin lives for over fifty years," Valentine insisted, "and they have an incredible memory, you remember, you told me, Maman. You once said they're capable of recognising a partner more than twenty years later."

Clotilde studied the horizon, but she couldn't see any fins.

"Too late," Valou said after a moment, "I can't see them any more."

Had her daughter, through the miracle of reading her notebook, learned how to bluff? Valou continued, as if she hadn't put everything on the table. She lowered her eyes towards the rocks overlooking Oscelluccia beach.

"Now that Cervone is dead, what will become of the Roc e Mare marina?"

"I don't know, Valou. It'll probably stay like that for years."

"That's a shame."

"Why is it a shame?"

Valentine turned towards her grandmother, then back towards the crypt, examining every name engraved on the marble, not only those of her uncle and her grandfather, but those of all her ancestors for the last three hundred years.

"It's a shame that my name isn't Idrissi."

A silence. This time it was Palma who filled it.

"What would you do . . . with the name . . . Idrissi?"

Valentine stared at her. She seemed to be looking behind her grandmother's wrinkled features, trying to find the seductive woman described in her mother's notebook.

"Were you an architect, Grandma?"

"Yes."

Silence again. Clotilde picked up the baton and repeated her mother's question.

"What good would it do you, Valou, to have the Idrissi name?"

Valou stared at the crypt again, then at the spot in the sea where she had claimed to see the dolphins, and then at the Roc e Mare marina.

"Not to let all of that go to ruin!"

Twenty-seven years later

68

"Mamy, can we play in the swimming pool?"

Mamy said yes, with a complicit smile at her grandchildren. She, not their mother, was still the one they went to if they wanted permission to do something. Their mother wouldn't let them. Their mother always said no, about swimming and everything else.

Too cold, too hot, too wet, too dangerous.

Their mother was a bit of a bore.

"Thanks, Mamy Clo!"

Félix and Inès jumped in, knees brought level with their faces, clasping their legs with their arms as they burst through the surface of the water. Clotilde observed them for a moment, then looked up to cast her eyes further away, towards Alga beach and the Revellata Peninsula. The pool looked out over the peninsula. Tursiops, the dolphin sanctuary, had opened its doors almost fifteen years ago now. The main building, the reception area, the museum, the laboratories and the conference rooms had been built entirely in Corsican pine, according to Palma's original plans. A minor masterpiece of integration with the natural environment, of energy self-sufficiency, using the wind and the sea, an educational success. Nothing remained of the ruins of the original Roc e Mare marina, apart from the Brando stones that had been used on the path and the stairs leading to the pool and on the observation deck for the dolphin pool.

"Aren't you coming swimming too, Mamy Clo?"

"Leave your grandmother in peace!" Valentine called out to her children before immersing herself once more in the columns of figures that marched up and down her tablet.

Clotilde hesitated. She still swam almost every day of the year, often with Cirdan and Eöl, the dolphins from the reserve, or Aranel, the porpoise they had saved from the fishermen's nets in Centuri. And in the summer with Félix and Inès . . . At last she got up from her chair, deciding to make the most of the time she had left with her grandchildren. In two days' time they would be returning with Valentine to their apartment in the heart of Bercy Village, with a direct view of Papa's big office, and Clotilde would be left alone. At the end of August the crowds of tourists began to thin out, but the laughter of other children still echoed in the corridors of the sanctuary; from the start of September, Turiops was filled with groups from the schools of Corsica. It was her seventh "back to school;" Clotilde hadn't left the island since she retired.

Her eyes wandered over to the universal clock that hung over the pool, the meter that measured the quality of the water, the built-in weather station, and paused on the wooden plaque, a tribute to the architect, that was placed below the high-tech equipment. Her mother's name was framed by two wild roses, identical to the ones planted around the park, blooming in every shade of pink and mauve between April and July.

Her mother was buried next to her father, in the Idrissi family crypt. After being freed, Palma had lived on her own, in a dark little flat in Vernon, barely ever leaving it, and Clotilde had been terrified that her mother might not wake up one morning and that no one would know. She had understood that Palma would allow herself to die once the work was completed, so she called her on the phone every day, placing no confidence in her reassuring words, and insisted that Valentine take up the baton during the holidays. Clotilde couldn't disentangle her feelings, somewhere between sadness and relief, when one evening on her way back from court she found her mother at home on her bed, serene and peaceful, as if she had fallen asleep; she had died only a few hours before, the doctor told her.

Palma had wanted to be buried in Corsica, next to her husband. Room was made. In the crypt there was already another woman sleeping in her bed. So the decision was made to move the body of Salomé Romani a few layers down, so she could rest beside her mother. Speranza had died one evening in May 2020, in the yard at Arcanu, under the shadow of the holm oak, with a basket of freshly picked mastic, angelica and marjoram resting by her side; Lisabetta had followed three months later, her heart giving in one morning without warning, as she pulled up the nettles that surrounded her orchids.

Clotilde set down her towel and walked towards the pool in her swimming costume, confidently displaying the figure of a young seventy-year-old. She still felt comfortable in her skin, and admired without envy the perfect bodies of the young tourists who were reading, sleeping or kissing on the deck chairs. A life, she reflected, came down to that: enjoying the beauty of the world. Its harmony. Its poetry. Contemplating it before it all disappeared. Basically, you don't die, you go blind. You understand that it's over when all the wonders around us fade away.

But today, they still shone! In the pool below them, the one directly overlooking the Mediterranean, Eöl, the younger dolphin, was undulating gracefully in front of Matteo, the fair-haired, muscular angel who fed him; the young man's calm, precise gestures seemed to meld with the dolphin's choreography. Matteo had the crystal laugh of a Little Prince, she had first heard it about ten years ago when she had encountered him on Alga beach, immersed in *Harry Potter*, and had confessed to him that in the old days his father was nicknamed Hagrid! No one today would have dared use that name for

Orsu, the serious, authoritarian manager of the Euproctes campsite.

Clotilde dipped a foot in the water. Under a sunshade, under his hat, under a book sitting open across his nose, Natale was asleep. She checked a sudden desire to go over and splash him. To ask Félix and Inès to help her to lift the deck chair all of a sudden and throw it into the water, or to suggest that they bomb into the pool beside him so violently that they would shower him with water.

Clotilde had separated from Franck a few months after Valentine had turned eighteen. They had signed the divorce papers in January 2020, by mutual consent, saving on lawyers' fees. And then, for the rest of that winter, all though spring and all through July, Clotilde had had only one obsession: to go back to Corsica and see Natale. She was free. The *Aryon*, the sanctuary, the dolphins, it could all become a reality now, with Lisabetta's money, Palma's plans and the marketing done by Valentine, who was taking a preparatory class at business school.

The news had gone round, and Clotilde had received a long letter from Aurélia, telling her that if she came back to Corsica and Natale wanted to join her, if it was his choice, she wouldn't stand in their way. (There were a lot of "ifs" in Aurélia's letter.) Even if Aurélia went on loving Natale, even if she sincerely thought she was the woman he needed, even if she had been able to protect him from his ghosts for all those years, even if she'd had to tiptoe around him since he came back to life. Even if Natale had never loved her, he wouldn't have been happier with anyone else.

And it was true, Clotilde knew. It was Aurélia who had coordinated the Turiops project that Natale had always dreamed of. She had built the dolphin sanctuary almost despite him; Natale had had the will, but not the energy. Natale was indecisive. An extraordinary lover, Clotilde remembered, but a man she probably wouldn't have been able to bear in the end. She had cursed his impassioned letters followed by months of silence; his magnificent promises, so quickly forgotten. The love had passed. Natale would remain an accomplice, a boy for whom she would always have an infinite tenderness, but Aurélia loved him more than she did. After her divorce, Clotilde had taken several lovers, travelling companions, handsome, intelligent, brilliant. Sometimes married, sometimes foreign. When she had one that she'd kept until August 23, she took him to the Casa di Stella to make love all night. Under the stars.

"Watch out, Mamy!"

Clotilde gave a start and looked up at the big diving board outlined against the perfect blue sky. Slightly apprehensively. These days she couldn't see anyone jump into the void without thinking of Cassanu.

Around the pool, the tourists in flip-flops were mesmerised.

The body flashed into the water like an arrow, almost without making a splash.

A perfect dive.

The dive of a professional.

Of a mermaid.

Maria-Chjara re-emerged a few seconds later. A pair of firm, pointed breasts swelled her transparent white bikini, a seventy-year-old water nymph.

Félix and Inès applauded. They loved Aunty Maria.

Clotilde burst out laughing. She and Maria-Chjara had become friends. Maria liked to joke about how she had her breasts reinflated each year, just before the summer. The day she died they would lay her in her coffin, but wouldn't be able to close the lid!

And no Corsican polyphony, *lamenti* or *voceri* at her funeral.

She adjusted her transparent bikini in front of men with V-shaped and hairless torsos, startled by this particular grandmother. In front of their scandalised wives, consenting victims in the dictatorship of beauty.

Time is a killer.

But sometimes there are extenuating circumstances.

"Are you coming in, Mamy?" Félix and Inès called.

Clotilde smiled and was rocked by gentle melancholy at the sight of Natale lost in his dreams, Valentine concentrating on her accounts, and then Maria-Chjara winking at handsome Matteo who was just about to finish feeding his baby dolphin.

Sempre giovanu.

ACKNOWLEDGEMENTS

To Luc Besson and Gaumont.

ABOUT THE AUTHOR

Michel Bussi is among France's bestselling authors. His novels have been published in thirty-five different countries. He is also the author of *After the Crash* (Hachette, 2016) and *Black Water Lilies* (Hachette, 2017).